OB-LA-DI
OB-LA-DA

A NOVEL BY
DIANA CURRAN

ISBN #9781729042632
Library of Congress Control Number

Cover Design & Interior Formatting: Lisa Neuberger

TO JOHN, PAUL, GEORGE, AND RINGO

SHE'S LEAVING HOME

CHAPTER 1

Life goes on. And on and on. Susan's days stretch out in front of her like an infinity mirror. Each one a reflection of the last, or the next. She rises at dawn to brew yet another pot of coffee that too often smells better than it tastes. After breakfast she sweeps up scattered toast crumbs, tufts of dog hair, and shriveling opportunities into the dust pan. Then it's upstairs to make the bed she shares with her husband of forty odd years, pulling the white cotton sheet over the cold, isolated depressions in the mattress. Her dying love life waits for last rites, toe tag at the ready.

At least this time of year gives her purpose. Baking her traditional repertoire of Christmas cookies to share with family, friends, and church members. Decorating her home for holiday gatherings with handmade crafts and heirloom ornaments. And finding the perfect gifts for loved ones, both nice and naughty, though the job has become harder as twenty-first century wishes outpace her limited budget.

She tucks her shopping list inside her purse, sets her iPod loaded with Beatles songs on random play, and eases the white Ford Taurus onto the entrance ramp to I-70. Rural Sullivan, Colorado fades in her rearview mirror; the suburbs of Denver loom ahead. The concrete furrow cuts a swath through fallow fields and past forsaken clapboard homesteads, their sagging wire fences no longer a barrier against the future. It grieves her that these open spaces of her country childhood are being drawn and quartered, so gentleman farmers can erect mini manors and play at husbandry. Change appears to be inevitable. Her life is still waiting for the memo.

As she pulls into the parking lot of the Walmart, her retail refuge, a last line from "She's Leaving Home" sticks in her head. "Something inside that was always denied..."

"Merry Christmas," she says to the bell ringing volunteer, stuffing a couple of dollars into the red Salvation Army kettle. She exchanges holiday cheer and a quick laugh with the elderly greeter, takes the proffered cart, and aims for the music section.

"Excuse me," she asks a twenty-something in a blue vest, "I'm looking for CD's by Taylor Swift and Lady Gaga."

Without raising her head, the sales clerk continues stocking inventory, waves her hand more or less to the right, and drones, "Over there."

"Thank you so much. And Happy Holidays," Susan says with a smile, disheartened though not surprised when there is no reply to even the politically correct greeting.

Before dropping them in the wheeled container, she examines the pictures lining the plastic cases. Taylor looks like a nice country girl. Lady Gaga? Hmm. One-hit wonders no doubt, but her granddaughters adore them. She scans the large display of rock and roll music, the five by five albums organized alphabetically, and rifles through the B's. Beach Boys, Beastie Boys. Beatles.

Mini versions of her comprehensive timeworn LP collection, plus remastered mixes and new compilations. She has them all, of course. Now those were the days.

They called the four of them the Beatle Girls in high school, for they had fallen under the spell of Beatlemania. They combed through the pages of *16 Magazine*, devouring every detail of the group's lives; they memorized lyrics and picked out melodies on the piano at school; they slept with a picture of their favorite guy under their pillows. Real boyfriends had yet to materialize, so the lads from Liverpool served as introductory surrogates. Even now, Susan's belly flip-flops as she remembers buying the latest 45 from the Fab Four, then rushing home to play it with her friends, giggling and gushing all the while.

And that's when it hits her. In two weeks it will be 2010. Ringo will turn seventy in July. And she will be sixty in September. Six-zero. The same age as her Mom when she passed on, her dreams shoveled along with the dirt into her grave. Is she destined for that same fate?

Suddenly her heart flutters like a moth trapped in a window and the garish lights of the store begin to dim. She closes her eyes and bends over the cold steel handle of the cart until a reflexive tightness in her throat signals that her breakfast is making a comeback. She abandons her buggy and races to the ladies room. She smacks open the nearest stall door and leans over the toilet. Several slow deep breaths eventually secure the barricades outside her stomach, and her galloping bosom slows to a canter.

And then, a faint sweet scent threatens to undo her valiant efforts. She gags. Is it soap? Or disinfectant? She sniffs gingerly. More like cologne. Yes, that's it. Oh, my God. She takes in another whiff, triggering a memory of comfort and happy times. It's Evening in Paris. Mom's perfume.

3

"Mom, are you in there?" she asks the porcelain bowl.

"Can I help you?" a voice responds.

Her knees buckle at the unexpected reply, and she slinks down to the floor, the metal walls containing her fall and sudden fear. When she spies two sneakered feet in the neighboring cubicle, she breathes a sigh of relief that her brief ride off the rails is at an end.

"No, sorry. Thought she might have come in here," she fibs as she struggles to rise and then make an exit.

She splashes water on her clammy face, patting it dry with a paper towel, and stares in the mirror. Not her usual ruddy complexion, but not like she's just seen a ghost either. Geez, Susan, get a grip. Feeling better, she leaves the restroom to find her cart, and her way back to reality and the meaning of what just happened.

Distracted by the experience, she wanders around the racks of the clothing area, grabbing and dropping graphic T-shirts, multi-colored scarves, and fuzzy slippers into the metal basket until her eyes are drawn to a wall partition in the women's section. Hanging there like a beacon is a deep-teal George faux wrap sweater, a far cry from her usual bulky polyester tunic in a neutral palette. She finds her size among the double digits and X's and slips it on in the dressing room. It's soft, feminine, even sensual as she runs her hands up the three-quarter length sleeves and down her torso. It nips in at the waist and skims over her hips, complementing her ample curves. It puts Thelma and Louise front and center. She turns her back to the mirror and twists from side to side to check every angle. And at only $17.99, it seems too good to be true. She opens the curtain, hoping the store monitor is nearby. She needs a second opinion.

"Hello. Would you mind? I mean, how does this look on me?"

4

The woman is one of her kind. Over fifty, over-weight, and overlooked. She gives Susan a once over and replies, "Wow, that looks amazing on you. Change is good, right?"

"So they say. I guess it's a keeper then. Thanks."

Though appreciative of the praise, Susan suspects the clerk flatters everyone to increase sales. As she lifts the top over her head, the earlier fragrance from the bath-room engulfs her. Seriously, is her mother really visiting her from the beyond? But instead of a shimmering vison or a whispered word, she's showing up as a spritzer from the perfume counter. So does that mean she's here to col-lect her because the end is nigh? After all, she did nearly faint. Or maybe it's to direct her at the crossroads of Sixty. Either way she now has something nice to wear.

She strolls over to the book section to finish her task of tying up the loose ends with bows. She chooses an historical novel, a sports biography, and a cookbook for daughter, husband, and sister. She slashes through those items with her pen and makes a U-turn toward the check-out counter. A nagging feeling pokes at her though. Has she forgotten someone? With her face scrunched in thought, her eyes shift from list to cart, matching up peo-ple with presents. She startles when an employee taps her on the shoulder

"Sorry, but thought maybe I could help you," the salesgirl says.

"Having a senior moment," Susan laughs. "Trying to make sure everyone's accounted for, but it feels like I'm missing somebody."

"Maybe it's you. What's on *your* list for Santa?"

"Oh, a million dollars to start," Susan blurts since, of course, money is always a good answer. But she doubts elves print money. OK, how about something to spark her lackluster marriage? She blushes at the thought of Jolly St. Nick and the Mrs. stocking aphrodisiacs at the

5

North Pole. Before she can give an answer, the woman crooks her finger and leads her to a row of romance novels, the naughty bits artfully concealed beneath tattered, windblown clothing. Who the heck is this lady, and how is she reading her thoughts? As if on cue, the sweet floral notes of violets and roses that infuse Evening in Paris envelope her once again. Yep, Momma has guided her to some soft porn. Eeeewww!

"Here's one you might like," the clerk says. "Not too steamy, you know, to start with."

The book is the first in a series about a plucky female journalist based in early 1900s Paris and the stories she puts to bed. So to speak. Brown paper bag in aisle three, please.

The aroma of the classic cologne seems to be following her everywhere now, enticing her to follow her heart. As she stands in line, she spots a French language course marked down to ten dollars. Her high school Spanish was useful with the seasonal farm workers her Dad hired, but she's always wanted to learn the language of love. Her novel takes place in France. Perfect timing.

Like a kid on Christmas morning, each new find sets Susan's heart racing, making her squeal with delight on the inside, impatient for the next surprise. What else does dear old Mom have under the tree? She spies the Victoria's Secret across the street. She's wanted to go in for ages but money and modesty always held her back. Well, not today.

She bounces on her sensible shoes into a blushing pink fantasy with classical music in the background. Bras in satin, lace, and sheers in every color, pattern, and size imaginable wait to push the Girls up, together, apart, and not quite over the edge. She'd love one but she can't justify spending that much money on an over shoulder boulder holder?

Instead she looks through the bins of panties. Bikinis, briefs, hipsters, boy cut. Thongs. Not going there. Some silky lace briefs are on sale at three for $18 so she chooses ravishing red, bawdy black, and passionate purple. OK, they're really just colored granny panties, but it still makes her feel hot to trot. Well, maybe warm to waddle.

"I've never been here before. I feel so girly," she confesses to the sales clerk, hoping her cheeks are less rosy than the tissue paper wrapping her delicate drawers.

"I know," the assistant says. "There's something about lingerie that brings out our inner and outer woman. And it's not all about showing them off to a man. Even on grubby home alone days, just knowing I have something sexy on underneath makes me feel attractive. Enjoy."

Susan grabs the handles of the pink striped bag. She wants to shout to the world that she has done something wild and crazy today, whirl about with her little packages and throw a hat in the air, but she settles for a grin that wraps around her face. She floats out of the store and into the sound of Christmas music ringing over the loud speakers. "Joy to the World." At least it's not "Gramma Got Run Over by A Reindeer."

Adventure has stoked many appetites this morning, and now her growling tummy is ready for lunch. She can't remember the last time she ate at a restaurant, unaccompanied, without a husband or a child. The hostess at the bistro seats her and Susan scans the food and drink menu. She downs a lite beer on occasion but nothing stronger. Today, however, is about bold choices and spirited endeavors. Belly up to the bar, Mrs. Anderson.

"Good afternoon, Ma'am," says the middle-aged waitress. "My name is Gerri and I'll be your server. What can I get you?"

"Hi. I think I'll have the fish and chips, an iced tea, and ..."

Susan rubs her moist hands on her slacks as her eyes drift back to the selection of adult beverages. A discrete sniff of the air reveals no maternal confirmation of her plan to wet her whistle. Maybe the food smells are too overwhelming.

"OK, I swear," she says, crossing her heart, "I don't usually do this, but today's been all about doing things I don't usually do." She clears her throat and continues. "And well, I've never had a martini ... and I'd like one of those."

"That's a pretty potent drink. A Cosmo is a less intense option. Vodka, Grand Marnier, and cranberry juice with a lime twist. Just the thing for the holidays."

"Sounds lovely, but, no, this day calls for the real thing. I promise," Susan says, "I'll sip it slowly. And tell me again, what is your name?"

"Gerri. Short for Geraldine."

A little chuckle escapes Susan's lips. Of course. There's the psychic high five. That's her mother's name.

It is noon. On a Tuesday. Beside her in the cushioned booth lay three multicolored sacks containing a change of underwear, a change of heart, and a change of attitude. She gazes around the room. Shop girls gossip over a quick lunch. Mothers, with their children off at school, corral only packages today. Gray-haired ladies hem and haw over the senior choices. Do these women have pent up passions and long-standing regrets like her?

When Susan and her friends graduated from Sullivan High, each was eager for the possibilities that awaited. Unlike her, Margaret, Kathy, and Linda created successful careers and fascinating lives. A little of their insight and inspiration could be just what she needs now. Time to get the band back together.

8

Susan toasts the Beatle Girls and the late Geraldine Bliss and sips her sophisticated cocktail.

The alcohol takes her breath away at first, burning her throat as it trickles down. She slides an olive from the toothpick and tries again, hoping the saltiness will temper the taste. Despite the lingering kick, she concedes that marriage, and maybe life in general, should be more like this martini. Strong and intoxicating so you only need the one, yet gently shaken with surprising twists. Oh, and just a little dirty. Bring it on.

A DAY IN THE LIFE

CHAPTER 2

Massive wrought iron gates safeguard the ivy-covered estate in northern Stamford, Connecticut that the Martinet family has called home since the late nineteenth century. Within the silk panel lined walls of her boudoir, its French windows draped with velvet curtains and a four poster canopied bed along one wall, Margaret sits at an ornate and sculpted cherrywood secretary. With pigeonholes and secret drawers, it's made for handwritten letters on vellum stationery in formal flowery language. Not half sentences dashed off in a rush, full of abbreviations, misspelled words, and emoticons. One hundred and forty characters will never be enough to express her thoughts. As a professor of English, she does her best to instill a love of classic prose and poetry in her students, but she knows Mark Zuckerberg holds much more sway. And so she relents to the twenty-first century and opens her laptop.

Susan, her dear friend from high school, has posted a message on Facebook about a proposed reunion of their small group known as the Beatle Girls.

She strokes the black cat curled in her lap and says, "Maya, seeing my old friends this summer may be just what I need. A welcomed distraction from my so-called life."

She types up an affirmative reply and steadies her hand over the mouse. An insistent pounding on the door startles her, and cursor and cat fly off in different directions.

"Are you coming to this party or not?" her husband yells from the other side. "That plug-ugly face of yours won't get any prettier. It's a lost cause."

Margaret clenches her fists, her nails digging into her palms. "I'm coming, Jeff," she replies in a clipped monotone. "It's only 8 o'clock. No one's going to be there yet."

Jeff has been drinking since five this afternoon, and there will be many more glasses to drain before the New Year arrives. Margaret would prefer to ring in 2010 with a good book and a mug of cocoa, but her husband seems unable to maintain his image at the law firm without her social prestige and financial assets.

"Well, I'm ready now. Get a move on."

Margaret exhales with a shudder. This reunion can't come soon enough. She clicks the send button with a firm jab and closes her computer. Susan's note was upbeat as always with the assumption that the life of a wealthy heiress must be wonderful. Well, Jimmy Stewart be damned. It is not. The final days of the year have long been the winter of her discontent, and if not for her beloved Maya and Denise, her colleague at Sacred Heart University, she would have found her "happy dagger," "her true apothecary" long ago.

She rises and plods over to the vanity. She picks up the two carat diamond earrings, a long-ago graduation gift from her father, and pokes the studs through her lobes. She adjusts the headband holding her gray shoulder length hair away from her face, a style she's worn since college. She swipes a coat of lip gloss across her thin lips, and drops it and her glasses into her black satin evening bag. Jeff is right. No silk purse from this sow's ear. Even Shakespeare agrees in *Henry V*. "Thy face is not worth sunburning." Her approaching sixtieth birthday ensures that the shadows will remain her refuge.

She stands to smooth the black Chanel sheath loosely draping her angular frame, its long sleeves covering the sagging skin and jagged scars on her arms. She peeks out the door, praying Jeff has crawled away to find a shot of Glenlivet. When he's nowhere in sight, she makes the sign of the cross and exits her room. While the cat scampers ahead of her, she descends the sweeping central staircase of her father's mansion with care, each footfall soft and precise. Still the aging steps creak and groan, as if criticizing her every move.

Maya is rubbing against the leg of a forest green leather club chair when she enters the wood lined study. It's a place where generations of men have pondered, pronounced, and partaken of spirits.

"Jeff," she announces her presence.

Her husband stands with his back to her, but she can see a Waterford cocktail glass filled with scotch at his lips, reflected in the mirror behind the bar. He turns at the sound of her voice and, stopping mid-gulp, plants the etched tumbler on the granite counter.

"Well, you've certainly outdone yourself tonight, haven't you," he sneers, shaking his head as he looks her up and down. "Margaret, you are an embarrassment. A total waste of space and flesh.

Margaret's shoulders round out of habit, her head sinking into her chest as his hateful words pummel her ego. The voices of her therapist and Denise ring in her head. 'Why do you let him do this to you? You know he'll never change. Why don't you leave him?' She dreads another evening of his boozing and schmoozing and verbal abusing, but dare she risk igniting Jeff's hair trigger temper in order to speak the words surging up her throat, clawing to get out?

"I won't be going to the party with you," she says, her voice barely audible, her eyes focused on the floor.

Jeff's fingers grip the glass. "You're springing this on me now? Then it's all on you if my promotion falls through. Maybe you're satisfied babysitting coddled twits, but I'm making a name for myself."

"Then make it on your own. I'm tired of being your dancing monkey." Her head lifts, and the door to the long captive fury stirring within inches open.

He gulps the remaining liquor and raises the empty glass over his head. "Don't try my patience, woman. If I say come with me, then by God, you come with me. And get that God damn hairball outta here."

Maya rests in the leather chair washing her cheek with a paw, oblivious to the heightening tension in the room. In an instant, Jeff hurls the crystal ware in her direction, barely missing her head before shattering against the door frame, the shards scattering across the parquet flooring. The cat hisses and bolts from the room.

Margaret glares at her inebriated husband, the rise and fall of each breath like a bellows, fanning her rage and fusing this last straw into a belated backbone for her fragile self-esteem.

"You bastard. Get out, get out of my house." She thrashes the air as she points toward the door. Her words snap from tight lips. "I'm done with this, and with you.

"You bitch! I'll fucking kill you!"

He lunges at her, shoving her up against the oak paneled wall, his bloodshot eyes searing into hers as his hands encircle her neck. She flails at his chest, scratches his face, tries to pry his hands away, but he is too strong. Like a Chinese finger trap, his grip only increases with her efforts.

"Don't," she says. The word is faint and powerless, escaping her lips before the pressure of his fingers restricts the oxygen flow to her lungs. Black dots dance in front of her eyes, and she resigns herself to her demise. How apropos that having lived constrained, afraid to speak out, she will die by strangulation. Her last word. "Don't." Just as she drifts into the calm of surrender, she hears a distant voice.

"Mr. King, what the hell are ya doin'? Let go of her, you arse!"

Sean, her long-time chauffeur and handyman, rushes over and launches his fist into Jeff's head. Jeff stumbles backwards and collapses on the floor from the one-two punch of brawn and booze. With the grip on Margaret's throat released, she coughs and slumps against the bar.

"Jayzus, Dr. King, are ya all right? Sit down here." Sean eases her into a chair and takes out his phone. "What the hell happened?"

Margaret tries to speak but only a rasping whisper comes out, and no sign of her short-lived bravado.

"I made him mad. Is he all right?"

"He's fine. But, Jesus, Mary, and Joseph, you got some nasty red marks around your neck. I'm callin' the cops," and he dials 911.

"No, no, hang up. I'm fine. It'll just make things worse," she begs, fearful of her husband's later retribution.

"Ma'am, he can't get away with this. This is assault. At least let me get the EMTs," he says.

"And say what? Say Jeff choked me, and they call the police. Say it was an accident, a door tried to strangle me or something. They won't believe you, and they call the police," she explains. "Either way, it only gets worse. See, my voice is better now. Give me some ice, and I'll be just fine. Just get him out of here. Please. And help me find Maya."

17

Sean hangs up the phone. "Ya know they'll call back to see if everything's OK. What should I say?"

"Uh, I was choking on food but now I'm fine. Really, I just want to go to bed. Did you see Maya?"

Sean wraps some ice cubes from the bar bucket in a towel. Margaret places it under her chin and heads for the stairs. Sean lifts up the passed-out perpetrator and drags him toward the door.

"Lock this door, Dr. King. He can sleep it off in the guest house with me. My cell phone's on so you call me for anything. The cat's in the house, hidin' somewhere. She'll come out now it's quiet. Don't worry."

"Oh God, Oh God, Oh God. How did this happen?" she cries as she reaches her bedroom, unable to contain her panic any longer. "What am I going to do? I can't do this anymore. Maya, where are you?"

It hurts to swallow now, but since she's able to breathe and speak, although not forcefully, she knows her trachea isn't crushed. She crumbles to the floor of her master bath as tears and snot run down her cheeks and nose. Her head throbs. Her body is limp. She lies there with the lights on, fully clothed, the image of her enraged husband's face swirling in her mind. Her sobs ring out, and then ease, until she falls asleep.

⌘⌘⌘⌘⌘

She awakes with a start, not quite sure of her surroundings. She rests on the bathroom tiles, her gown wrinkled, salty spatters down the front. She always hangs up her clothes at night. Dresses on padded hangers, shoes in their labeled plastic bins, jewelry in lined drawers. Instead she's sprawled on the floor. An eerie quiet permeates the air, broken only by the ticking of the clock. 11:30. Is it AM or PM? PM of course. It's dark outside. Maya is curled beside her. She draws the cat into her chest, comforted by the rhythmic purring until Maya grows restless.

Pushing herself up onto weak and shaky knees, she grabs the edge of the counter and pulls herself to standing. It takes a few seconds to recognize herself in the mirror. Her eyes are red and swollen, her pale lips and dull skin cast a ghostly reflection, and her throat ... Purplish-red speckled lines trace the circumference of her neck, each about a half inch apart. There is pain deep inside as well as on the surface.

Did she fall? Was she entangled in something? Had she ... Her heart and mind race until finally she remembers the hours before now. My God, he tried to kill her. He tried to kill her. Where is he, oh Jesus, where is he?

She grabs the phone in the bathroom and dials her friend Denise.

"Are you still up?" she asks, her courage hanging on by its fingertips.

"Margaret? Yes, I'm up, barely. Sitting here waiting for the ball to drop. Where are you? Thought you and Jeff had a big law firm party tonight."

"Denise, he ... he... oh, God, I don't know what to do?" and she bursts into tears.

"Margaret, take a breath. What happened? Is Jeff OK?"

"I ... I ... I don't know. And I don't care. I don't care." Her anger begins to resurface through her anguish and she blurts out the story.

"Oh, my God, are you hurt? Did you call the police? Please tell me you called the police."

"I'm OK. Sean wanted to call but what good would it do? I was so scared. Denise, please, can ... you ... come ... o ... o ... over?"

"Of course. But where is that asshole? Where are you?"

19

"I'm upstairs. I don't know where he is. I'm afraid to check."

"Stay right where you are and call Sean. I'm calling the police. This is past OK. You've put up with this crap for far too long, Margaret. Far too long."

CHAPTER 3

Kathy stands in front of her large living room window to greet the morning sun, the Pacific Ocean barely visible in the distance through the purple jacaranda tree. She moves through the poses of the Sun Salutation. She inhales and exhales as she dives into the floor, breaches the air as she arches her back, jackknives her hips before floating down, imagining the tide rushing through her spirit like the oxygen through her body. She finishes with palms to heart and a grateful namaste. Her soul is immersed in the sea. Her moon rises in Pisces. Whether summertime or the end of December, she needs to be near the water to feel its power, its serenity, its primordial connection.

"Come on, Murphy. Let's go walkies," Kathy calls to her Golden Retriever who responds with a flurry of tail wagging and eager barks.

A routine of early morning yoga and a hike along the sandy coastline of Venice Beach, combined with regular Pilates classes, helps Kathy maintain her slim and supple dancer's body even as she nears sixty. She pushes her arms into the sleeves of her cotton hoodie, laces up her Converse sneakers, and stuffs her wavy blonde ponytail under a ball cap, a reluctant acknowledgment that her "freckles" are really age spots and she needs to protect her skin. She grabs Murphy's tennis ball, his nylon leash, and a plastic poo bag along with a small thermos of water and stuffs them all into a small backpack.

"Ready? That's my good boy." She speaks to the dog in that high-pitched babyish voice reserved for those loved unconditionally. 'I like long walks on the beach with my dog' is not a cliché on her dating profile, but perhaps the best part of her day.

She and her best friend begin the three-block jaunt along San Juan Avenue, past the quiet mix of original craftsman and re-conceived modern single family homes, down to the Boardwalk and its parade of the buff and the bizarre. She spent her childhood on these beaches building sand castles, riding waves on belly and boogie board, and baking in the sun. A true California girl. Lock, stock, and bikini.

The crowds tend to lessen in the early hours of a winter's day. In the distance, a solitary figure meanders toward them. Max, an elderly gentleman with a white cap of hair, lives in the lower half of the duplex she owns. He sweeps the gritty carpet with his metal detector in search of money, jewelry, anything careless tourists might have left behind.

"Mornin', Max. Find anything interesting?" Kathy says as she catches up with him.

"Hey, Kath. Mr. Murphy." Max bends down to rub the dog's ears and give him several pats on his rump. "Nothing substantial. Not too many folks catchin' rays today," he laughs. "Still lookin' for a match to that first Rolex I found."

Max worked as an assistant or second location director during the Golden Age of Hollywood in the Forties and Fifties, and knew her father from Warner Brothers where her Dad had been a scenic painter. When Kathy purchased the building in the mid-Nineties, Max was her

22

first and only renter and has become a father figure, and a good friend.

"Hey, wanna ring in 2010 with me and my guy here? Watch *An Affair to Remember*. The one with Cary Grant and Deborah Kerr, of course. Maybe share a glass of bubbly?"

"Turn down booze with my beautiful blonde? No way, Jose."

"So, come on up around seven. I'll throw some food together and we can cry in our champagne. See ya, Max." They do their signature Hollywood air kisses before heading in different directions.

Kathy heads south with Murphy past the athletes pumping iron or spiking volleyballs. She romps with the dog in the squishy sand, tossing the ball and playing chase. It reminds her of father and daughter pas de deux when they danced the polka across the living room floor, Perry Como crooning "Papa, Won't You Dance with Me?" He was her faithful companion, watching her lessons and schlepping her costumes, ever ready to tie up her laces or corral a loose hair back into its topknot. And when she rose from her grande reverence at the end of each recital, she knew her father would always be there in the second row, clapping eagerly in a standing ovation. As the waves roll in and out, she's back on those long-ago beach strolls with her Dad. He could stop on a dime, whip out his sketch pad, and deftly capture the permanence of a changing scene with colored pencils, while she sketched with a stick in the wet earth, her work lost to the frothy sea.

He drifted out of Kathy's life gradually. As movie work dried up, the strain of mounting bills led to arguments and the slow erosion of the marriage, leaving Kathy and her sister in the ebb and flow of her parents' emotional tides. Her mother withdrew into a hard and bitter shell. Her father got caught in the undertow with his buddies and a bottle. Late into the night, she huddled under the covers with her sister, listening as harsh and spiteful words were tossed about, waiting for the storm to crash over them and reduce their world to flotsam.

Once back at her place, Kathy fills bowls with water and kibble for Murphy and fixes herself a cup of white peony tea and a slice of multigrain toast with almond butter. A quick cleanup should get the 1100 square feet she calls home ready to party. She takes the recyclables out to the bin and trades her Enya and Debussy CD's for some Ella and Duke. Max's favorites. Wayne Dyer's *The Power of Intention* and the latest issues of *Dance* and *Variety* go back to her bedroom along with a new linen jacket and her sandals. She brushes massive amounts of dog hair from the sofa and chairs and sweeps the floor. Suzy Homemaker has finished in fifteen minutes. A bowl of almonds to nibble and a veggie pizza from the freezer for dinner and the party is done. There's always a bottle of sparkling wine in the fridge for planned and unexpected celebrations.

She opens her laptop to her Facebook page and gives a rundown to Murphy, curled up on the couch beside her.

"No word from Disney. Too soon to hear about the new animation voice-overs."

She scrolls down through various inspirational posters and quotes and a link to a funny YouTube dog video. Murphy's not impressed. There's a picture of someone's lunch during a trip to Norway, and a message from her last date.

"Remember that pompous comb-over who wanted to take me to the steak house? He says, 'I'll learn to love tofu. Just give me a second chance.' Not in this lifetime, Sweet Cheeks," she laughs. "Really, are there no kind, intelligent, interesting men in this town willing to date women of a certain age?"

Murphy barks. "Yeah, you're probably right. This is LA. Anyway, you're the only guy I need," she coos as she ruffles his ears and kisses his nose.

There's a post from Susan Anderson about a reunion in August for their sixtieth birthdays.

"Faithful, Sweet Susan. Always keeps in touch. Not like some people we know, huh?"

Susan had been a godsend to her when she moved to Colorado, helping her navigate the new high school in the "Sticks." If not for her, she would have run off to a commune with a band of merry pranksters, but she stayed, and they bonded over the Beatles. The rest, they say, is history.

Kathy pulls up her calendar to check for upcoming commitments. Living in the moment keeps her open to the unexpected, like acting roles, and minimizes disappointments, like wayward fathers.

"Hey, I'm gonna go to this Beatle Girl reunion this summer. "It was forty-three years ago today," she sings as she types.

'How are you, luv? Sounds groovy to "come together" this summer. Be nice to see Linda, Margaret, and you. Count me in and call or write details as they develop. Happy New Year! KR (a.k.a. George)'

Kathy closes her laptop and flips through her CD collection until she finds her Beatles albums. *Meet the Beatles*. She slides it into the slot of the machine and pushes play. The chords of "I Want to Hold Your Hand" hurtle her back to December 1963, listening on her transistor radio as the song debuted on the airwaves of America. It still makes her shiver. She's lost in that magical musical memory until the phone jangles her back to the present.

"Hello," she says as she lowers the volume.

"Is this Kathleen O'Shea?"

"Yes. Who's this?"

"UC Health in San Diego. Do you know a Patrick O'Shea?"

"Yes, he's my father. Is he OK?" Panic catches in her throat.

"He's in the emergency department. Your name and number were in his wallet. We're having a difficult time getting a history from him."

"Not sure what I can tell you. Haven't been in touch for nearly fifteen years, but I'll do my best."

After relaying what little she remembers about her Dad's health, she tells them she'll be down as soon as she can. At last her wish to see him again has manifested. But Spirit, as always, is in charge of when and how.

CHAPTER 4

Linda arrives early at the Marriott Hotel in Denver's Cherry Creek neighborhood. She's expecting around seventy-five revelers including employees, colleagues, and important clients and benefactors for the 2009 New Year's Eve party for A Woman's Place. She co-owns the obstetrics and gynecology clinic with her ex-husband, Dr. Rob Charles, and since he invariably waltzes in fashionably late, it's always been up to her to oversee the festivities. The hotel's event planner waves her over.

"Linda, how are you this evening? We've got everything set up in the grand ballroom. I was just about to check with the catering staff. Would you like to accompany me?"

"Yes, I'm sure you and your people have done another wonderful job. That's why we keep coming back."

On the way to the kitchen area, she and the young woman sweep through the event room filled with a dozen or so large round tables covered with black cloths. Silver swag bags have been placed on each seat.

"We've put the beauty products and gifts cards in the bags like you asked, and hats and horns for later," the planner tells Linda. "I know they're silly, but everyone expects them."

Red chargers and silver cutlery are laid out at each place. A low, red rose floral arrangement graces the centers. Ribbon-tied balloons of red, black, and silver float from above. The band, a local combo with a diverse set list, are setting up on an elevated stage that has been brought in for the occasion, along with a ten by ten foot wooden dance floor.

Mouth-watering aromas greet the women as they enter the food prep area, swarming with sweaty, red-faced sous-chefs and scurrying waiters.

"We're going with a bit of this and that this year. We'll pass little bites as well as offer plated and communal tapas at the tables. We've got a salted caramel brownie bite that is to die for. Wanna try one?"

"Uh, yeah." She puts the morsel in her mouth. "Oh my God, that is delicious," she mumbles as her teeth sink into chocolate heaven. "Save me one if you can. Guess I'll go walk about, check out the bar before the crowd arrives."

The drink station is located in the far corner of the ballroom. No fly-by-night set up here, but a real expanse of wood with bottles of premium liquor on the glass shelves behind it.

"Hello there," she says to the gorgeous young man on the other side. "I'm in charge of this little soiree this evening." She rests against the bar and ogles him through her false lashes. "Why don't you show me what you can do with a martini. Grey Goose, shaken, three olives. So, tell me, are you a full-time barkeep or do you do something else on the side?" she asks, stroking her collarbone with her finger.

"I've worked at the hotel for a while, but I'm a student at DU. Law. Using the tips for books," he says as he shakes then pours the cocktail.

"Well, let's hope you won't need to represent any of my associates tonight." She takes a sip. "I'm impressed," she says with a slow wink and salts the tip jar with a twenty from her purse.

Linda makes her way to the entrance as her invitees begin arriving. The office personnel, the nurses, and the midwives not taking call have come out for a free first-class affair. The staff doctors mingle and discuss procedures and papers with their colleagues from other practices, while their significant others gossip about the doctors and whose eye has wandered the farthest. For the powers that be, it's just another function and a chance to promote a cause or their own egos.

"Genevieve, don't you look lovely tonight," she compliments her charge nurse.

"Nancy, I'm so glad you could make it. Your son is feeling better I take it?" she asks one of her midwives, cradling her hand in comfort.

"Mrs. Baxter, thank you so much for your support during our breast cancer fundraiser. You put us over the top, you know. Thank you," she praises the wife of an influential business man.   Linda stands tall as she works the receiving line. She shakes hands and gives a personal comment, tilts her head back in laughter, kisses cheeks or the air as she squeezes a shoulder.

All seems well until Rob walks in with his latest paramour, a bosomy blonde in her mid- twenties in a strapless, bedazzled, crimson tube. She clings as tightly to him as her dress does to her body, either afraid he might get away or to help her balance on her five-inch stilettos. Though Linda and Rob have maintained an amiable professional relationship since their divorce in the mid-nineties, she still feels a punch to her gut whenever she sees him with someone else. And that someone is ever younger and more beautiful. But seriously, couldn't he find someone older than their daughter Jackie? She swears she can smell Mennen Baby Magic lotion on her.

"Well, hello, Linda. You look gorgeous as always. Nice dress. Sapphire blue makes your eyes pop," he teases and lowers his gaze, "and the neckline pops a couple of other things."

"Hello, Rob." Linda rolls her eyes and turns to focus on the crowd. "Looks like everyone showed up. Great food, but we both know they're really here for the free booze."

"And what's your poison tonight, Linda?"

"My usual, but I'm sure they'll be a few flutes of Veuve Clicquot as well. It is New Year's. And who are you babysitting this evening? I don't think I've met this one."

"This, my dear, is Marlee. I met her at a club a week ago. Quite a dancer, so limber and sensual," he says, rubbing her smooth bare shoulder with his fingertips. "She's teaching me West Coast Swing, right, Babe?"

"Yeah, Robbie," Marlee says. "You know, Linda, he has amazing moves. I thought for sure he must have taken lessons like when you were married."

"Nah, Linda was always too busy for anything fun. That didn't fit in with the five-year plan. Or the ten-year plan, or any plan for that matter."

"Well, someone had to be the adult. So, you kids go party. Try to speak to a few people tonight before you get wasted ... *Robbie*," her voice thick with condescension.

Linda does not have high hopes that Robbie will stay sober. She only prays he does nothing scandalous or damaging to the clinic. She's invested considerable time and money earning her nursing degrees and building her practice. The alphabet soup of letters after her name impresses clients and colleagues, and gives her clout when the bottom line is on the line. She isn't about to let this playboy squander her life's work.

Linda floats her way through these high-class affairs with charm and composure. She chats with each guest just long enough to make them feel noticed, all the while able to see the whole room at a glance.

"Gentlemen, are you enjoying yourselves?" she says to a group of older physicians. "Looks like you all need another drink. Here, let me get a waiter."

She waves her hand in the air and a young woman appears in a gender-neutral uniform of white shirt with black tie, vest, and slacks.

"What can I get you, sir?" the server asks.

"Let's see, I had a Glenlivet straight. Bob, you had a bourbon on the rocks. Maker's Mark, right? And Jack, a Grey Goose martini with a twist. Got that, honey?"

The doctor slides his arm around the woman's waist, his hand dipping lower. Linda deftly reaches behind to take the old lecher's hand in hers, allowing the blushing server to sneak away.

Patting the naughty hand, she asks, "Have you *boys* tried our appetizers?" She corrals another staffer who offers a tray of nibbles. "The *stuffed* mushrooms are excellent, and the *tiny* shrimp bruschetta. So good. Oh, and these *mini* tacos come with a *little* margarita shot. Now, eat and drink up."

She has enough feminine wile and tact to emasculate her sexist colleagues without them feeling the tug. And looking decades younger than her true age certainly helps. Her skin is taut and her body toned, thanks to the diet du jour, personal trainers, and the judicious use of potions and lotions. Of course, the occasional nip and tuck hasn't hurt. She enjoys the rewards of her efforts. A vast network of rich and influential people stored on her Blackberry. The material goods she can buy, collect, wear, and consume. The prolonged stares of men and the envious glares of women. Linda Charles is a dynamo to be admired, and sometimes feared. Does she leave collateral damage in her wake? She rarely looks back to see.

But, tonight, her thoughts keep coming back to Rob's remark about fun not being in her plans. She's spent her life creating this successful image, but at what price?

What will it matter if she's all alone in the end. She turns sixty this summer, a milestone she is fully denying. Without the credentials, the bank account, the designer wardrobe, who is she? All sound and fury, signifying nothing?

⌘⌘⌘⌘⌘

"Ten - nine- eight- seven- six - five - four - three - two - ONE!! Happy New Year!"

The orchestra breaks into "Auld Lang Syne" as men in Armani and women in Dior lock lips with the nearest warm body, surprised or disappointed at who is on the other end.

"Happy New Year," Linda exclaims as she embraces one of the single gynecologists on staff, a muscular and tanned dark-haired man thirty years her junior.

"Whoa, and a Happy New Year to you too," she says to the silver-haired, handsy obstetrician from earlier, who kisses her with a little bit more tongue than she expected, or wanted.

But with her inhibitions loosened by the bubbly, she figures, what the hell. She circulates in her immediate area, twirling around to smooch with this man, running over to nibble another.

The mania of the midnight hour subsides with the guests returning to their tables, laughing and looking for the next drink. Linda has not seen Rob and Miley, or Mattie or whatever the hell her name is, for quite some time. Though she keeps telling herself she really doesn't care, a toxic need goads her into keeping tabs on the charming womanizer for whom she had once been the arm candy. And who broke her heart more times than she wants to remember.

"There you are, Linda. Still time for one more New Year's kiss?" a male voice murmurs, snuggling up behind her, wrapping his arms around her waist.

She leans into the firm, warm body for a brief moment before recognizing the voice.

"Oh, for God's sake, Rob, what are you doing? Where's Millie?"

"She's around, but I miss you, Lovely Linda. You feel so good in my arms. Just like old times, huh, Babe."

He kisses the top of her head, then her nose, and then, before she can say another word, he presses his lips to hers, and slips his tongue inside her mouth. Linda resists, pushing him back, but the alcohol and more than a decade without a man's touch dissolve any moral outrage, and she gives in to the moment.

"Come with me," Rob whispers as he slowly pulls away and grabs her arms.

Before she can object, she finds herself running out of the ballroom and down a corridor toward the nearest secluded room, hand in hand with her ex-husband like a hormone fueled teenager. Unfortunately, the nearest room happens to be the men's restroom, and she waits outside the door while he checks it for occupants.

"It's all ours, Babe," Rob says as he carries her into the spacious room with its golden faucets, fluffy towels, and bottles of men's cologne on the counter. He leans her against the cold black marble wall, pulling up her dress and unzipping his pants.

"Rob. No. What if someone comes in?"

"Who cares? I want you."

He forces her arms above her head and envelopes her lips with his mouth, probing and caressing ever deeper. His hands lower to explore the firm curves of her breasts, the contours of her waist, and down into the valley between her legs. He maneuvers his hand inside her lace panties and touches her. She gasps and quivers, and knows she won't stop him.

Just before she reaches that moment of long overdue ecstasy, the bathroom door bangs open and the attendant bursts in.

"Oh, my God," Linda cries out, whether out of pleasure or mortification she isn't sure.

The heavy breathing that had filled the room, in fact, all breathing, stops. Six widening eyes lock. And, as quickly as the young man entered, he hurries back out.

"What the fuck was I thinking? Rob, you are such an asshole."

"Oh, come on now, you enjoyed it. Hey, he's a nobody. I'll slip him a hundred and he'll easily forget. Here, get yourself back together and I'll guard the door."

Linda adjusts her panties and her dress, settles the Girls back into her push-up bra, and looks in the mirror. Her hair is a bit tousled, her cheeks with the rosy glow of sexual release. Well, sexual build-up, anyway. She actually looks pretty good. Little comfort for her mind however, reverberating with the possible consequences of her spontaneous indiscretion, both personal and professional.

"Christ," Linda sighs.

Rob peers in the door. "The coast is clear, Babe. Come out when you're ready."

"Call me Babe one more time and I swear ... Just go. And leave me alone."

Linda peeks out the door until Rob is out of sight and the coast is clear, then takes a deep breath and begins her walk of shame back toward the ballroom. As she turns the corner, the bathroom attendant faces her.

"Ma'am," he says politely, and nods his head.

"Shit!" she grumbles under her breath. "Shit, shit, shit!"

CHAPTER 5

Susan tip-toes down the stairs wrapped in a quilt of quiet. In the diffuse glow of a nightlight, the fuzzy familiarity of photos on the walls and the gray outlines of dated furniture comfort her as she edges her way into the moonlit world frequented by dairy-men, bakers, and sleepless menopausal women.

She shuffles into the kitchen of her tri-level home, greeted by the lingering smells of burnt brown sugar, spicy cloves, and crisp fat. The final remnants of the pink holiday ham. The chill of predawn settles on her exposed nose, cheeks, and hands before the furnace clicks, whirs, and blows the first warm wind through the metal heater grates. She hears the sound of tires crunching icy packed snow outside. But today, above all else, the amplified ticking of the grandfather clock near the front door, its pendulum swaying to and fro, captures her attention as it counts down the last hours of 2009. Before a sagging, liver spotted, crepey-skinned arm drags her into her sixtieth year.

The kettle whistles and she pours the steaming water into her World's Best Grandma mug, bobbing the mint green tea bag as she creeps back up the stairs to the small bedroom she's commandeered for her craft room. She settles into the cushioned oak rocker, the hand carved metronome that has dried tears and calmed fears as it moved to the rhythms of life in the Anderson home. With all the bustle of the holidays, there hasn't been much time to read her romance novel, so she takes advantage of her insomnia and escapes into her book.

She's faraway in Paris during La Belle Epoque when she hears her beloved black and white Springer Spaniel, Bungalow Bill, give a yelp as he struggles to rise from his overstuffed cushion in a corner of the breakfast nook. She marks her page and hurries back down the stairs. He moves stiffly now, his hearing all but gone, but his stumpy tail still wags with exuberance for his mistress.

"How's my good boy?" she says, ruffling his ears and kissing his rough black nose. "I know, gotta pee."

Susan lets him out into the mid-winter shadows of the backyard and waits while Bill sniffs out just the right spot to do his duty in the brown grass between the patches of snow. She leans against the cool glass and surveys the eight hundred square feet of land. She should have cut down that half-dead crab apple tree, but Steve likes the jelly she makes from the fruit and maybe there's one more crop in it. And that swing set should have been condemned ages ago. Just too many memories in those rusty chains and splintering seats. She'll buy a new one when her grandchildren marry and have babies, though there's no guarantee it will be in that order nowadays. She hears the distant roar of a jet heading east from DIA. Maybe it's headed to Paris.

She drifts back to the novel's setting, imagining herself sitting at a wrought iron table outside a sidewalk café, nibbling thin sugar-coated crepes filled with jam and drinking a glass of sparkling champagne. An accordion plays as her lover snuggles beside her. His hand cups her cheek and turns her face to his. He kisses her lips softly as fireworks explode above the Eiffel Tower.

'Bonne Annee, Ma Cherie,' he murmurs.

The dog barks, interrupting her fantasy, and returns her to Sullivan, Colorado, that blink of an eye on the way to Kansas. Bungalow Bill senses her husband's presence before Susan does, padding back inside to greet his master.

"Mornin', Hon," Steve says as he pats the dog's side. "Couldn't sleep again, eh? Coffee ready?"

Susan doesn't answer. She's chasing after the memory of Paris, and her imaginary paramour. As she closes the door, her face and her loins, wrapped in her newly purchased lingerie, feel warm despite the freezing temperature. She sashays to the kitchen island as sensuously as her fluffy white fleece robe will allow, whispering, "Just pretend ..."

"What'd you say?" asks Steve.

"I said how about something sweet to start your day?"

She sidles up to Steve and blows softly in his ear before brushing her lips on his balding head. She takes his unshaven, loose cheeks in her hands and leans in for a passionate kiss.

"What the hey?" he says, pulling away.

"Just givin' my husband some sugar."

"At seven in the morning? For God's sake. The only sugar I need is for my coffee."

Steve nearly trips backing away from her. He fumbles with the spoon, spilling the sweetener, and escapes to the kitchen table with his mug.

"So what's for breakfast?" he asks, avoiding Susan's eyes.

"Cold cereal," Susan huffs and turns away to pour her own cup.

"Could you fix oatmeal instead?"

"Your wish is my command." She bows with a flourish of her hand.

Susan bangs the pan on the metal stove burner and dumps in the oat flakes and water. As she stirs the thickening mixture, the porridge and her thoughts bubble up. Well, that was a disaster. Steve reacted like she was Great Aunt Ethyl, pinching his cheeks and remarking how much he'd grown. No doubt she looked like the Stay Puft marshmallow man lumbering toward him. Guess after 40 years, the fire's out. Not even enough heat for a s'more.

"I'll be getting things ready for tomorrow," she says, spooning out the oats. Seeing Steve's furrowed brow and narrowed eyes, she explains, "Remember, everyone is coming over for brunch. New Year's and all."

"Oh, yeah, right. Guess I was hoping for a quiet day of football. Seems like you always get stuck with these get-togethers. What's on tap?"

"Gramma's cinnamon rolls of course, but thought I'd make quiches instead of fried eggs. Something different, a little special."

"What's a quiche?"

"It's a bacon and egg pie, French style. Real men eat that."

His blank expression confirms he doesn't get the reference. She smiles. Her Parisian beau loves quiche. Steve sets the empty bowl in the sink as usual. Susan wonders why it is that men can fly to the moon and climb Mt. Everest but it is darn near impossible for them to get a bowl to the dishwasher.

"Off to putter," Steve announces on his way to the garage.

"Wait, could you put the extra leaves in the dining room table first? There'll be about twelve of us. Maureen's family and Shirley's, and ... Linda's."

"Oh, good Lord," he grimaces, "another day with Saint Linda. Just sit her as far from me as possible."

"Yes, I'll do my best to keep her icky cooties away from you."

She's well aware that her high school classmate can be a bit overbearing. And while the whims of life have altered their friendship over the years, there are deep bonds and even deeper secrets between them, and Susan will always be there for Linda.

"Hey, you didn't take your pills," Susan reminds him.

He rolls his eyes at her.

"I know, but the doctor says ..."

"These damn things are more trouble than they're worth. I'd be able to ... ah, what's it matter." He gathers the tablets from the counter and swallows them. "Down the hatch," he says, opening his mouth for inspection.

With Steve off on his mission, Susan gathers the ingredients to prepare the Bliss family cinnamon rolls. Flour, yeast, sugar, and spices along with the striped crockery bowl, used by her Mom and her Grandmother before that. As her strong hands toss and knead the dough, her mind works over her life.

Her muscles ripple under the flat brown age spots dotting the rough wrinkled flesh on her forearms. The sun and dirt from the farm, it would seem, is now permanently embedded in her skin. The rolls of flab that circle her middle push against the kitchen island. A lifetime of cholesterol and sugar now clog her arteries, adding inches to her waist, doubling her chin, and threatening to subtract years from her life. Yet here she is, spreading the rich raisin and nut filling across the flattened pastry.

She married Steve shortly after high school, an unexpected coup considering his prior girlfriends. Cootie covered Linda, for one. And despite the fact that Steve's teenage six pack has swollen into a middle-aged keg, she still finds him attractive. Maybe she's fooling herself thinking there can be fire after fifty, but she'd like to toss a match or two and see what happens.

Susan rolls her yeasty creation into a log and slices it into half inch portions. Her treats need to rise in the warm oven, so she pours another cup of coffee and wanders up the stairs toward the bedrooms, strolling past the gallery on the walls. The montages of her babies, and then their babies, in snapshots and school pictures chronicling their growth from infancy to adulthood. The family wedding portraits. The professional sitting done for their twenty-fifth. These are her reasons for being and her heart fills with love for them.

The timer dings and she returns to the kitchen. John Lennon said, "Life is what happens when you're busy making other plans." Perhaps she's been too busy tending other peoples' dreams while hers simmer and burn. No, it's time to find her *joie de vivre*. Word of the day, French lesson number six. And before it's too late. Right, Mom? As she slides the rolls into the oven, she remembers that poster from the Sixties. Tomorrow is the first day of the rest of *her* life. And she'll be wearing red underwear.

CHAPTER 6

Susan opens the door of her mid-seventies tri-level home with a smile as bright as the blue sky of a Colorado winter.

"Happy New Year, everyone. *Bonne Annee*," she says, greeting each of her family with a firm and welcoming hug. Sister Shirley with her husband Joe, and eldest daughter Maureen with her husband Dave and their children Jennifer, Amber, and Ryan. Unfortunately, her other children won't be joining them today. Daughter Caroline is working a shift at the hospital and son Josh is on assignment with the *Denver Post*.

"Mom, are you speaking French?" asks Maureen.

"*Oui*. I'm learning on my computer. A Christmas present to myself. *Entrez*," she says with a sweep of her arm.

"Grandma's rolls?" asks Shirley, taking in the smell of yeast and cinnamon.

"Ain't a Bliss get-together without 'em. Here, let me take your coats," she offers, hanging them in the closet of the small entryway. "There's cider in the crockpot downstairs to take the chill off. Help yourself."

She and Shirley continue their conversation while the rest of the family move on to the wood paneled family room seven steps down from the kitchen, the fireplace aglow in the center of a brick wall.

"Is Linda riding out with Jackie?" Shirley asks.

"No, they're coming separately," Susan says. "Linda's big New Year's Eve party was last night. I hope she shows up."

"I wouldn't hold your breath. Her little shindigs tend to run long, you know, and the morning after is usually not kind to her," Shirley says, raising an eyebrow.

"She works hard, Shirley. Shouldn't she be allowed to play hard as well? But, yeah, I wish she'd take it easier with the business, and the booze. Anyway, Jackie's bringing her boyfriend Matt. Have you met him?"

"A couple of times. He seems nice. Some kind of alternative doctor. I don't quite understand what that means, but I got the impression Linda thinks he's a quack. Apparently not enough of the right letters after his name," Shirley says, rolling her eyes.

The sisters busy themselves with last-minute preparations and chit chat before heading downstairs to join the others. The chime of the doorbell reverses Susan's course, and she hurries to greet the new arrivals.

"Jackie. You look great," Susan says as she ushers Linda's daughter and her boyfriend into her home. The two women share a rocking embrace while Matt gets a warm but less smothering squeeze from Susan. Not good to overwhelm the poor boy just yet.

"So good to see you," Jackie replies. "Matt, this is my Godmother, Auntie Suze. She and my Mom have been friends since they were kids. By the way, Mom called to say start without her. She's running late."

"No problem. Matt, welcome to our home. Brunch is almost ready so why don't you two go down and say hi. They're all checking out the new flat screen TV. Present from Santa."

Susan listens to the introductions and ensuing small talk as she takes the warming foods out of the oven and the chilling dishes out of the fridge, placing serving utensils in each. Her small kitchen has never had enough storage or counter space to suit her, and she'd love new appliances in any color but her present harvest gold. OK, not avocado green either. But she was taught that a good cook can make it happen with a hot plate and an ice chest. Maybe St. Nicholas will bless her with an update next year. It's ten thirty as she surveys her feast and deems it ready for consumption.

"OK, everyone, soup's on," Susan yells to one and all. *"Bon appetit!"*

The families circle the island counter laden with quiches Lorraine and Florentine, turkey sausages and bacon, hash browns, a bowl of winter fruit compote, and of course the Bliss family iced cinnamon rolls. One pan on the table, one waiting warm in the oven. When each has taken their fill, with Jackie and Matt passing on the sausages, the adults settle into their chairs at Susan's antique oak dining table, the children nearby at the smaller "kid's table."

Steve begins a quick prayer. "Lord, thank you for this food and this family. We welcome those we see every day, only on occasion, and for the first time. We hope 2010 is filled with the abundance of your blessings. In Jesus's name, Amen."

The group picks up forks and knives and digs into the blessed meal as compliments and conversation pass around the table.

"Jackie, how's the store?" Maureen asks.

"The boutique is doing well. We moved to a larger location about six months ago. There's three of us now selling our jewelry and handcrafted accessories."

"So Matt, tell us about yourself," Susan asks, steering the conversation to the new kid on the block.

"I'm a naturopathic physician. I use alternative and complementary treatments in a holistic approach to health. I studied at Naropa University in Boulder and have my practice there."

"So, what's Linda's take on this?" Maureen asks.

"She follows Western medicine for the most part," Matt replies, "but she recommends prenatal yoga, visual imagery during deliveries, and herbs for menopause. All complementary therapies."

As plates empty, Susan hops up to bring in and pass the remaining food from the island, including the second batch of rolls from the oven. No one will ever leave hungry from her table if she has a say in it. Susan overhears Jackie whispering to Matt as she stands behind them with the tray of pastries.

"I hope Mom doesn't blow this off." She catches Susan's eye and changes the subject. "So how's school going, Maureen?" Jackie asks, before explaining to Matt. "Maureen teaches middle school social studies in Sullivan. Medal of honor, by the way, for courage under fire."

"It's challenging, for sure, but if the politicians would just let us teach ..." she sighs. "Still, even with the late nights and weekends and continuing ed classes in the summer, I love it. Just glad my kids are finally old enough to take care of themselves. Jenny's a senior this year and we're waiting to hear back on her college applications. Got a pretty steady boyfriend, but I'm afraid young love is going to have to wait."

Susan notices her eldest granddaughter's head jerk toward the big table at the mention of her name. Maureen's way has always been the only way. She wonders how long that trend can continue as her daughter rambles on about the trials of living with her twenty-first century teenagers.

"My dear, you have outdone yourself today," Steve announces, and everyone chimes in with a raised glass or a word of gratitude to honor the chef and her efforts. "And, I believe I'll have me another one of those cinnamon rolls. You oughta sell these, Hon. We'd make a fortune."

"Thank you, Sweetie," Susan smiles. "Jackie, it's twelve thirty, do you think we should check on your Mom? I hope she hasn't had car trouble."

"Yeah, I'm surprised she's not here. We have something to share with her," Jackie says. "Let me try her cell." Jackie pulls up Linda's number on her Blackberry. "Mom, it's Jackie. Where are you? ... Are you still coming out to Susan's? ... It's only 12:30. Plenty of time to drive out for a visit. People haven't seen you in a while, and we, I have some news ... Well, don't take too long."

⌘⌘⌘⌘⌘

Linda's red Lexus pulls into the Anderson's driveway at 1:50pm. Susan opens the door to see Linda stamping snow off the red soles of her Louboutin heels. She's wearing a camel Burberry coat and carries two bottles of Veuve Clicquot champagne.

"Linda, you made it. You look absolutely beautiful. Come in, come in," Susan says as her friend steps into the entryway, a mutual hug made awkward by the bubbly. "Are you hungry?"

"No, I ate before I left so I'm good. Here's some leftover champagne. Thought you all might want some to celebrate."

"Thanks. I'll take them, and your gorgeous coat," Susan says, caressing the soft cashmere before hanging it in the closet. "Everyone's in the family room, more or less watching football."

Susan tries again for a warm embrace, but Linda offers only a Hollywood air kiss. While Linda has always been less demonstrative than her, it still catches her off guard. At least both cheeks were grazed.

"Hey, did you get my email about the Beatle Girl reunion?" Susan asks.

"When did you send it? Been kinda busy," Linda says.

"A day or so ago. Anyway, I'm thinking late August. Kathy and Margaret both said Yes."

"It sounds fun, but I'll need to check my schedule," she says before gliding down the stairs to join the others as Susan follows, feeling like she should straighten some invisible train trailing behind.

"Happy New Year everyone. Sorry I'm late. What's new?" Linda asks.

"Same old, same old here in the sticks, little Sis. Just us clodhoppers watchin' grass grow," her brother Joe drawls, embellishing with a head scratch. "Any liquor left in Denver or did you drink it all?"

"Oh, get off your high horse's ass, Joe. A little nip might put some life in you."

As the siblings wage a battle of evil eyes and snide retorts, everyone else in the now hushed room examines their nails, picks lint off trousers, anything to avoid the appearance of taking a side. Susan is about to referee when she notices Jackie elbow Matt.

"Dr. Charles," Matt interrupts, standing to offer his hand to her.

Susan sometimes forgets that this is Linda's official title. Her Doctorate of Nursing in clinical practice is a bright feather in her cap, and Matt is no doubt attempting to get into her good graces. Yet Linda's mouth barely curves as she acknowledges his greeting with a determined grip.

"Mom, Matt and I have something we want to tell you," Jackie says as she rises beside her man, her fingers interlaced with his.

46

Matt clears his throat and speaks. "Dr. Charles, Linda if I may, Jackie and I are planning to marry, and we'd like your blessing."

Linda neither replies nor moves, braced against the news washing over her. Susan and the others exchange furtive looks, unsure what to expect. Merriment or mayhem.

"Does your father know about this, Jacqueline?"

"Yes. Matt asked him first just because it's tradition, and he's cool with it. We haven't set an exact date, maybe late summer or early fall."

"And you expect to find a venue, get a dress made, arrange for caterers, a band, flowers, and everything in less than a year?" Linda asks, counting off the details on her fingers.

"Don't get ahead of yourself, Mom. We don't want a huge blowout, just something simple. You know, more meaning and less money."

"What, a barefoot wedding in a meadow?" Linda mocks, crossing her arms and looking down her nose.

"Don't worry, we won't invite the fairies and unicorns. And we'll be covering the costs. We do make our own money, you know," Jackie says.

After another uncomfortable silence, Susan's enthusiasm can no longer be contained.

"Oh, Jackie and Matt, this is so wonderful," she gushes, clapping her hands together. "I have a wedding cake recipe I've been saving for ages. And boxes full of magazines and catalogs."

A small reasonable voice in Susan's head cautions, 'Wait, nobody's asked for your help yet?' while a rambunctious little brat interrupts, shoving and shouting 'Let me do it.' Plans are already forming as she pulls the newly engaged couple into her bosom and beams at her friend.

"Isn't this great, Linda?"

"Well, of course, it is," Linda says, "I just want to know the plan, that's all." Her arms unfold in apparent acceptance. "Can someone open the champagne? I know I need a drink."

CHAPTER 7

Susan is down in the basement retrieving family wedding albums from the storage area. The rows of shelves resemble a library with photos, books, boxes of receipts and mementos, and other odds and ends, all arranged by subject matter, alphabetized, and/or in chronological order. Mr. Dewey would be proud.

She clambers up the stairs clutching several pastel and flowered scrapbooks and drops them in the middle of the kitchen table. Maureen, Jenny, Linda, and Jackie are gathered there nursing cups of coffee and nibbling on popcorn and Chex mix. The winter sun is giving way to dusk, and the flame shaped bulbs in the brass chandelier sparkle on the outstretched fourth finger of Jackie's left hand.

"Ooh, let's see your bling, Jackie," Susan says as she joins them.

"It belonged to Matt's grandmother. I'm designing wedding rings to complement it. Isn't it gorgeous?" she says, flaunting the finely etched antique treasure embedded with modest diamonds and pearls.

"I thought you were going to use *my* mother's ring. Vintage doesn't seem like your style," Linda says, fingering her own two carat rock. "Your choice, Dear, but there's no reason to go minimalist if you don't want.

Your father and I put aside money for you before the divorce. You're my only child and I want to make a fuss. I have lots of connections, you know."

"I appreciate that, Mom, but we want something laid back and simple. Just a celebration and a good time. No *People's* Wedding of the Year," Jackie informs her.

"Don't know if these qualify as laid-back," Susan says opening the wedding albums to buffer the rising tension, "but they were definitely simple."

The women flip through the books, the photographs now faded though the people had been in their prime. The bouffant flips of Susan's late Sixties nuptials and Maureen's big teased hair in the Nineties trigger laughter, especially from Jenny. Susan wed in a lace and crepe empire style, her chest and arms modestly covered, as appropriate for church. Maureen took her inspiration from Princess Diana, wearing a full satin skirt with puffy sleeves and a sweetheart neckline. By 2000 her daughter Caroline was strapless in a form-fitting column. Twenty-first century God can handle exposed skin. Though the faces and styles changed from one decade to the next, God hath joined them all in the same country sanctuary.

"We had a matrimonial emporium," Susan says, shifting back in her chair to straighten her posture. "I made all our gowns as well as the attendants' dresses for our family's ceremonies. Plus half the town has asked me to sew up something for them at one time or other. Mom would bake the cakes and Aunt Shirley sang and played the organ. We worked nearly every event at that church. Should have started a little business. *Four Weddings and a Funeral.* Course nowadays, there's more funerals."

"Gramma, I didn't know Linda was your maid of honor."

50

"Yes, and I was hers." she says giving Linda a smile. "Technically the matron of honor. I was already married to your Grampa by then."

"Can I help you, Gramma?" Jenny asks. "I've watched every episode of *Say Yes to the Dress* and *Bridezilla*. I think I'm gonna get married in that church."

All eyes gravitate to Jenny's way too girlish and innocent face. Maureen nearly chokes on her coffee. The panicked reaction is not lost on Jenny.

"Geez, not tomorrow, but someday. I'm almost eighteen, you know."

"Thanks, ladies, for the offers, but we're pretty much at square one," Jackie replies with diplomacy. "Give us some time to put our heads together."

"I remember your wedding was small," Susan says.

"Yeah, it was pretty low-key," Linda says. "I'd only been working a few years and Rob was just beginning his practice. I guess I was hoping I could get my bells and whistles through you, Jackie."

Linda gazes into the distance, rubbing the handle of her coffee mug. "Susan," she laughs, "remember making collages in junior high? Clipping out pictures of wedding gowns and heart throbs. I was going to marry *Dr. Kildare* and you were going to marry Buz from *Route 66*."

"Well, you did marry your doctor," Susan says, "and I guess I got my travelin' man. He just drove a tractor instead of a Corvette. Hey, anyone for more coffee? I can make another pot."

Without waiting for answers, Susan divvies up the remainder of the carafe and begins scooping fresh beans into the filter of her coffee maker. Leaving the machine to whir and grind, she returns to the group.

"Linda, you will come to the reunion, won't you? It's our sixtieth this year and ..."

"Please, don't remind me," Linda groans, "it's getting harder to face the mirror."

51

"Give me a break," Susan says, "you look forty. However, the rest of us are getting older and time's a wastin'. I've only seen the others, what, maybe once or twice since then, but, like I said, Kathy and Margaret are both in. Let's commiserate or commemorate together. Either or both."

"You said late August, right? Jackie, isn't that the same time you were planning the wedding? Maybe we need to space things out a bit," Linda says. "I've been known to multi-task but there's still only twenty-four hours in a day the last I checked."

"What if your friends also came to the wedding?" Jackie suggests. "I mean, I'm sure you guys will want to have lots of girl time, but I could add them to the guest list. Why haven't you ever talked about them, Mom?"

"It's just such a long time ago, you know. We all went our separate ways. People change. You move on."

Susan slides her chair back at the lull in conversation. "I'll get the coffee."

As she waits for the brewing to finish, her heart sinks thinking how Linda has distanced herself from her past. Her career is all that matters now. She can't be bothered with rural roots and the common folk stuck in Nowhere Land. Or an old friend she presumes does nothing but knit tea cozies for church bazaars and wipe endless snotty noses. And while this old friend will always be Linda's faithful companion and confidante, she is no longer her lady in waiting. Susan inhales and gets an olfactory nudge from her mother, the perfume lifting her mood and strengthening her resolve. No, Susan is ready to change, too. She straightens her spine and marches back to her family.

"Don't quote me," Linda says as if a sudden memory flashed before her, "but I think they both showed up second semester of eighth grade. Kathy saved us from interminable Bobby Vinton. She had Beatles records."

"Kathy, a.k.a. George," Susan adds, "was a California Girl who went on to become a dancer and actress. Kathy Rose."

"I'll look her up on IMDb," says Jackie. "What about the other one?"

"Margaret. Her ancestors founded the town at the turn of the century, and then struck oil on their ranch in the Thirties," Susan says. "She transferred in from a private school in Connecticut after her parents divorced. Eventually became a professor. So naturally her favorite was John."

"Wow, strong, successful women just like you, Mom," Jackie says. "So then, if Kathy is George and Margaret is John..."

"I'm Ringo and your Mom is Paul," Susan says. "Voila, the Beatle Girls."

MAGICAL MYSTERY TOUR

CHAPTER 8

Susan and Steve nestle in their side by side matching recliners as another twenty-two college athletes charge across the screen in high definition. The grass is greener, the players' numbers sharper, and each pass or run can be replayed frame by frame ad infinitum. Susan wants to spice up her marriage, but Steve, her, and a flat screen are not the ménage à trois she's imagining.

Taking advantage of halftime, she closes her magazine and turns to her husband, "Don't you think the brunch went well yesterday, Steve?"

"Sure, no one upchucked, no one fired a weapon, no one spilled on designer clothes."

"That was a bonus," Susan laughs, "but the big wedding announcement, my plans for our birthday reunion, Linda seemed OK with it all."

"So glad we pleased the 'Queen.' It always amazes me you guys are still friends. You're down to earth, and her feet haven't touched ground in forty years. Walking on water like she does."

"I know, I know, but cut her some slack. She is a good person and does good things. You always make her out to be such a monster. I seem to remember you two were pretty serious in high school. Of course, then you met me." Susan winks and blows him a kiss.

"Anyway, Jackie says she'll invite Kathy and Margaret to the wedding so I can coordinate the reunion with that ...You remember them, don't you ... I was thinking we could go to Red Rocks and see the Beatles tribute band since we didn't get to see the real thing back in '64 and, of course now we never will, so it may be our best chance to say we sort of saw them, and of course, Jackie wants me to help with the wedding, not sure just what, but that will be exciting ..."

Susan rambles on and on about her plans, her voice an octave higher and faster than usual. About how she can't wait to start planning. About how exhilarating it all will be. About how she hopes she won't feel overwhelmed. About how maybe she could be an event planner, or a caterer, or a pastry chef.

A referee's whistle halts her monologue, though Steve's attention has no doubt been on the first half highlights and talking heads. She returns to flipping through *Good Housekeeping* and its Super Bowl recipes to wait for the final play.

"Want another beer, Sweetie?" Susan asks, reaching for his hand, but the remote is firmly in his grasp, and not ready for hers.

"Sure, just let me get rid of the last one," Steve grunts as he pushes himself out of the chair, bending and flexing his right leg before heading to the bathroom.

Susan pours herself a cup of tea and grabs a Budweiser from the fridge. She thinks about fixing herself a martini, but that will raise more questions than she cares to answer so Earl Gray will have to do.

"So, how was your time with Matt?" she asks, handing Steve the bottle on his return to the kitchen. "What do you think of him?"

"Oh, he's a good guy," he says after a swig. "Seems pretty smart but I don't know about all that natural medicine stuff. Bottom line, he seems to love Jackie and would do anything for her. Nice to know there are still guys like that out there these days."

She looks into Steve's steel blue eyes. She had a guy like that once upon a time. Maybe she still does.

"There's so many little punks in the store and around town," Steve continues, "struttin' like roosters, disrespectful to everyone outside their little group. No interest in anything but their damn phones. That boy Jenny is seeing, Jackson or Jake ..."

"Justin, I think."

"He's one of them. Seems like she could do better."

"Speaking of Jenny, she offered to help with the wedding. Maureen was none too thrilled. Probably afraid she wants to marry instead of go to college. I should talk to Jenny, see what's ...."

"Suze," Steve interrupts, "as much as I hope she dumps that jackass, leave it be. You can't solve everyone's problems. Let Maureen and Jenny work it out, whatever it is."

"It's just you never know with teenagers today. Sex, drugs, cyberbullying." Susan shakes her head and sighs, "And I am now officially my parents. Speaking of the internet, I need to update Kathy and Margaret about the wedding, so I'm going upstairs for a bit."

"No problemo. Just hope I don't get lost in the shuffle with all this whoop-de-doo. I know your track record. Well, Florida and Cincinnati are coming up. Tim Tebow's last game."

"Honey, you're always number one on my list. Go Gators, right?"

She gives him a reassuring hug and a peck on his nose before losing him to surround sound and option plays. "Just wish I was your top priority," she whispers as she watches the former star athlete hobble back to armchair quarterback the game.

After her nest emptied, Steve helped Susan transform her son's bedroom into a sacred space of free-flowing creativity. He built shelves into the closet and along the walls, with nooks and crannies to store fabric, yarn, crafting books, tools, tubes of paint, tubs of glitter and gew gaws for whatever might leap from her imagination. Under the window sits a large table on which she can spread out patterns or projects, grateful she won't have to pack it all up at dinner time. And now, on an oversized desk, a computer sits next to her sewing machine allowing her to watch how-to videos online, or share ideas with like-minded crafters on social media.

She opens her Facebook account and taps out a follow up to both of her friends.

'So glad you're in guys. And so is Linda. Woo Hoo! And ... breaking news! Her daughter's getting married. No exact date yet, but maybe late summer, same as our reunion, so the bride says you're invited. I'm SO PSYCHED!!! Love you, Ringo'

Ever since her December to Remember with her Mom, she's been hearing about the Law of Attraction and how vision boards help manifest one's intentions. No better time for that than the first day of the rest of her life. She pulls out a blank poster from the closet along with a glue stick, scissors, and dog-eared magazines and lays them out on the rectangular table.

So what does she really want? Deep down inside. She wants to get out of her forty-year rut with Steve and shake things up. To feel alive again. Go on date nights, vacations, adventures, get a little wild and crazy. She searches for pictures of couples by candlelight, or walking along the beach, or sitting side by side in bathtubs and pastes them on her board.

And she wants to make her mark. Do something not as Mrs, Mom, or Gramma but as Susan. She'll leave the porch rocker and shawl for someone else.

They say all journeys begin with a single step. And the first one usually requires money. She takes the checkbooks from the center desk drawer and looks at the balances. A few thousand in checking, nearly fifty thousand in savings, Steve's growing IRA with work. Eventually she'll have her own small social security income, but that's several years down the road. The house and the car are both paid off, and they pay their bills on time and in full whenever possible. So, at least they're sitting comfortably if not pretty.

What she needs is a rich, doting, near death relative. All out of those unfortunately, but what about some mad money? Steve just said her cinnamon rolls could be a cash cow. Maybe she could sell them at the restaurant in town. She and the owner have been friends ever since they slung hash back in the day. And, if those were successful, she could expand to other heirloom recipes. All American favorites. She can already see the billboard along the highway as she pastes on photos of money and desserts.

She catches her reflection in the full-length mirror on the closet door. She definitely needs a makeover. Flapping arms and jiggly thighs are not what she wants shakin'. The unkempt graying curls and lack of makeup say 'I give up.' She pulls at her sweats. She has yet to wear her sexy little teal wrap top, and apparently Steve's not interested in taking a peek at her new undies. She'll do a Google search and bookmark some images of foxy plus-sized ladies plus some diet and exercise plans.

So it's a start. Her mission to desperately seek Susan should really have a name. Something that speaks to making changes and taking risks. And something Beatley. Something like ... Susan raises one fisted hand and shouts, "Revolution!"

CHAPTER 9

Linda wants to reach out and touch someone, anyone. Pick up her phone and lambast, admonish, or ream someone a new one to quench her anger and chagrin about the events of the last few days.

Rob is usually her first choice but she's not up for reliving the regret or dredging up the details of their ill-fated hook-up, knowing she'll have to see him soon enough on Monday. Though the engagement announcement caught her off guard, she really is happy for her daughter, just not ready to gush and gab about gowns and gardenias and a wedding she fears will be a pagan rite. Going back to the cow town of her youth, amidst country bumpkins who know nothing of the world, always leaves that unpleasant, earthy taste in her mouth. Family is important but, like salt, a little goes a long way.

And, then there's Susan. Though they have little in common now except family and the past with its long-buried secrets, the reunion does sound like fun, and isn't fun what's missing from her life? Still, better to resist her natural impulse and catch up on reading or end-of-year paperwork. Maybe even watch a movie over this first weekend of 2010. *The Big Chill* or *Michelle and Romy's High School Reunion?*

Linda sits in a buttery soft leather chair at her glass and chrome desk in her 7th floor Cherry Creek condo, the Denver skyline in the distance. Gazing at her surroundings, she knows her life is good. Her home is decorated in the stark neutral palette of black and white with pops of red that points to modern luxury. The high-end appliances in a kitchen rarely used imply affluence. The pricey abstract paintings and objets d'art suggest class and culture. But what and who is really reflected back through the smoke and mirrors? Linda or her interior designer?

Sipping her third cup of dark roast coffee, she scrolls through invoices and insurance papers. Work keeps her grounded and satisfies her need for power and purpose. Clients need care, she provides services, insurance companies pay her. Rinse and repeat. As she opens her calendar for January to check on upcoming meetings, the phone rings.

She checks caller ID. Christ. Really? What the hell does he want? She considers letting it go to voice mail, but perhaps it's something clinic related, or maybe he wants to talk about Jackie.

"Hello, Rob. What do you want?"

"Wasn't sure you'd take my call, Linda. I was hoping we could get together to talk about Jackie and the wedding. I hear they broke the news on New Year's Day. You OK with it?"

"And if I wasn't? No, I'm happy for her, just hope she knows what she's getting into. Do we really need to "get together?" Can't we just talk now or at work?"

"Sure, but thought I'd buy you dinner to apologize for the other night. You know."

"How gracious of you. And Missy is OK with that? Or maybe she's too stupid to be jealous."

"By the way, it's Marlee, Linda. And incredibly, she understands I have a daughter and that daughter has a

64

mother who I need to talk to on occasion. So what's your problem? I know I can be a jerk, but must you always be the bitch?"

"Christ, you really know how to make an evening with you sound enticing, don't you?"

"Linda, do you want to talk about Jackie over dinner or not?"

Linda hears Rob's exasperated exhale on the other end and realizes she needs to make a decision, if only to end the conversation.

"Let's see, I've already waterboarded myself, pulled out my fingernails, so this should be relatively painless. When and where?"

"How about the Club tonight at 7:30? Maybe we can talk some business and write it off. So see you there?"

"Sure. Shall I ask Jackie if she and Matt can make it?"

"Already done. This was her idea, anyway. Just wanted to see if I could get you to come with only my invitation, Babe."

"You ass." Why does she keep falling for his crap?

⌘⌘⌘⌘⌘

It's nearly six and she's still in her pajamas. It just felt like one of those days. She shuts down her computer and hops in the shower to get ready for the evening out. The plastic card on the nozzle reminds her it's time for a breast self-exam, first Saturday of the month, but she'll do it tomorrow. One day won't matter.

After browsing through her oversized closet, she finds the perfect outfit. The Diane von Furstenberg red jersey wrap dress. Classy yet approachable for her daughter, powerful and professional for Matt, and sexy enough to make Rob sorry he ever done her wrong.

She pulls up to the columned entryway of the Denver Country Club. After giving a twenty and the keys for her Lexus to a teen in a lime green Polo shirt and khaki chinos, she makes her way through the French doors and on to the Grill.

"Ah, Madam, lovely to see you. They're all waiting," says the maitre d'.

He escorts her to the table with heads turning and eyes watching as she passes, her breasts shown off to perfection, with more than one subtle wink from the male patrons.

"Hi, Mom. You look great tonight. So glad you could come."

"Dr. Charles, or may I call you Linda?" asks Matt, rising to greet his future mother-in-law.

"Linda is fine, Matt." She will never call him Dr. Stevens.

Rob smiles though says nothing as he assists with her chair and returns to his seat. Aren't we chivalrous, Sir Lancelot.

They order drinks, martinis for Rob and Linda, club sodas for Jackie and Matt. Her daughter struggled with alcohol during college, and it was the reason she dropped out. It's good to see her maintaining her sobriety, some five years now. Linda has always been in control of her own drinking, keeping it social only.

"So," Jackie begins, "let us tell you what we had in mind for the wedding. We want it small, simple, eco-friendly, preferably outdoors, probably in the Boulder area. I appreciate that you've set aside money for my wedding, but if you're still offering, we'd rather spend it on a house or our businesses. Even use it to pay back my loans. However, we don't want to waste it on a one-day event. We want to express our love, not impress society."

"You know," says Rob, "that makes a lot of sense. I could get behind that. How about you, Linda?"

Linda thinks carefully before she speaks. She wants a guest list of the rich and famous, the whole nine yards of tulle in the gown. She's attended plenty of weddings over the years, high-class affairs that people still rave about, and she wants to claim one of those for herself. But deep inside, she knows it's about her mother, the woman who shaped her destiny and its successes, and failures. The Momma giveth and she taketh away.

She looks into her daughter's deep blue eyes, the same eyes that reflect back in her mirror, and says, "Jackie, you're being so practical, so thoughtful, and I'm glad you want your special day to mean something. Of course, I'm disappointed you don't want to go all out, but ..."

Linda takes a sip of her martini, twirling the skewered olives around the glass, stalling until her throat relaxes.

"My Mom wasn't able to be at my wedding, and I know," she swallows, "I haven't been there for you ... more times than I want to admit. If you'll let me, maybe I can redeem myself by being the Mother of the Bride for you like I wished she could have been for me."

"Oh, Mom," Jackie says reaching over to take her mother's hand, "of course I want you there. And I'd love your input. You have great taste. I promise, we'll keep it classy. With just a little bit of quirk, OK?"

"OK."

They toast the evening with a bottle of champagne, even though Jackie and Matt only clink the glasses and do not imbibe. It's been a long time since her family shared a meal, and certainly one without drama, hateful words, and regrettable actions. She and Rob get acquainted with their future son-in-law and vice versa, scattering a few stepping stones in the gap between the medical philosophies of East and West. However, it is Rob, not Linda, who regales Matt with the heartwarming as well as comical and embarrassing stories of Jackie's childhood. Rob has been the first responder in their daughter's life; she but a bystander.

"This has been fun, Mom, Dad. Let's do this again. We gotta go but you guys stay and visit. It would make me happy if you did. Love you both. Night, night," and Jackie embraces her parents like she had as a child before heading off to bed.

As they watch their not-so-little girl walk out with the man who has claimed her heart, Rob says, "She's right, Linda, this was fun. I miss our family. Maybe this wedding will heal some wounds," and Rob lifts her hand to his lips.

Linda's heart and stomach meet somewhere in her throat, a reflux of nostalgia and bile. She was sure she left her feelings for Rob behind her. Too many last-minute phone calls full of excuses, too many strands of hair in the wrong color or length, and too many Marlees have whittled away at her trust. But this sexual longing he awakened in the hotel bathroom combined with the hope of a reunited family, blurs reality and bolsters her wish for a life do-over. Perhaps she can have her cake and eat it too, as long as she swallows her pride first.

CHAPTER 10

When Kathy returned to Venice Beach after college, forgiving her father came easy as they once again supported each other's creative dreams. He worked at odd jobs and sold his art at street fairs while she auditioned in between waiting on tables during the day and dancing on them at night. It took more effort when her star began to rise with roles as an extra, back-up, lead, or featured dancer, whereas his paint was drying up, his muse sinking back into the bottom of a bottle. But absolution was the hardest when his disappearances after benders grew from occasional nights to weeks and then months at a time. There were emotional reunions, a blend of bliss and blame, until once again he vanished like an early morning dream. After that, forgiveness, and trust, were tossed in the junk drawer along with tarnished pennies and overstretched rubber bands.

Kathy settles into one of the beige Naugahyde chairs down the hall from the ICU to use her phone.

"Max? It's Kathy. Sorry about bailing on you last night, but thanks for taking care of my boy. How's he doing?"

"Murph is fine. Glad to have the company. How's your Dad? Spoutin' poetry?" Max asks.

"No, not really," she sighs. "I expect I'll be here a while. Would you mind babysitting a bit longer? He's

69

got plenty of food in the pantry, but if you need something, keep the receipts and I'll pay you back. One less thing to worry about, you know, if you could."

"Of course, honey. So what's going on?"

"Dad's in liver failure. Probably has been for a while. He was in the Gaslamp District, acting confused, and someone called the police. Hepatic encephalopathy they're calling it. They say his liver is pretty much shot, and at 80, with his history, not much of a candidate for a liver transplant, so the plan is to just keep him comfortable."

"So sorry, Kath. I know how much you wanted to reconnect. Probably not the reunion you had in mind. Don't you worry about Murph. Us boys'll hold down the fort. You just spend time with your Dad. Keep me in the loop, OK?"

"Sure, Max. Thanks so much. Bye."

Her voice falters with those last words to Max, her tears barely holding on to the rims of her eyelids as she hangs up. She knows this is it. Nobody's going to say 'oops, sorry, we mixed up the lab results and he's got another twenty years.' Some compassionate insurance clerk won't be telling the doctors to go ahead with that transplant, there's a matching liver in a cooler en route to the OR. She's not going to awaken from this horrible dream with the two of them strolling down the beach. Cue music. Roll credits. No, that's not in the script this time.

Two days ago, she had traveled one hundred and fifty miles down the 405, arriving around four in the afternoon. Traffic was as light as it ever is in Southern California, but her mind had not been on driving. Not on the idiots weaving in and out of lanes, or pre-party revelers hurrying to pick up last-minute supplies, or families returning from Christmas gatherings and school break vacations. She had found her father. On New Year's Eve

70

she knew he was alive, confused, and in the care of medical professionals, but not much more. And now, she knows too much. There's only a limited amount of time, totally dependent on her father's mental status and physiological reserves, to share memories and forgive regrets.

She leaves the family waiting area with its rows of uncomfortable chairs and stale coffee, and shuffles back down the hall to the cacophony of bells and whistles serenading her father. He lies in the hospital bed, a patterned, pale blue cotton gown loosely draped over his ocher-colored body. A machine beeps out his blood pressure, pulse, respirations, and heart patterns in repetitive waves. One of his arms is attached to a bag of clear fluid and another IV by his collarbone pumps in some yellow mixture. A blood pressure cuff encircles the arm without an IV. A tube drains coffee-colored urine from his bladder. Green prongs near his nose blow oxygen inside, and a plastic clip on his finger measures how much. There could have been more equipment underneath his gown or his body, but that's all his primary care nurse explained. She's not looking further. Besides, her brain can't handle any more information. Maybe she should have auditioned for more medical roles.

He seems to be sleeping, so she sits down in the high-backed chair next to the bed, and lightly brushes the thin, reddish-purple skin on his hand, the discoloration evidence of his liver's inability to clot his blood. At the touch, he twitches and opens his eyes.

"There's my girl," he whispers.

"Hi, Daddy. How ya doin'?"

"Never better. Where am I? Have the aliens beamed me up? I definitely feel probed." Patrick's weak voice can't keep her father's humor and spirit from finding its way to the surface.

"Oh, have no doubt, you've been royally probed and more," Kathy laughs.

She bends over and leans gently against her father's frail body, fearful an unrestrained deluge of love might break his bones like it was breaking her heart. The bedding smells of antiseptic soap and stale sweat, but the flowery cinnamon scent of Old Spice aftershave slides up her nose just like it did when she gave her Dad one last hug before leaving with her mother for Colorado. She smooths back his greasy gray hair and kisses his wrinkled brow. Do her father's eyes still have that twinkle, or is it just the reflection from her moist eyes?

"Daddy, I've missed you." Her relief seeps out and spills onto the top of his gown. She dabs her eyes on her sleeve and sniffs, clutching both his hands as she rises.

"I know, sweetie, I know. I should have kept in touch. It was just too hard. But lots to catch up on, huh? So, tell me, what's new?"

What's new? It's been fifteen freakin' years. Where was she supposed to start? But no, there will be time for the hard questions, the harder answers. Just be happy.

"Well, hoping for a voice-over with Disney, my old high school friends want to reunite for our sixtieth, and my New Year's Eve date was my dog and eighty-year-old neighbor. Livin' large."

"My little girl will be sixty? God." Patrick looks away, a moment of silence rising between them. "Are you still dancing?"

"No, not so much. I lack swag, as they say," doing her best bad ass hip hop gesture. "Plus my feet are shot. My big toes scream if I even look at a pointe shoe. But, I'd love to open a studio. Teach budding ballerinas, you know. And, thanks to *Dancing with the Stars*, lots of interest in ballroom. I'd love to have a dance with you." She knows it's the wrong thing to say as soon as it leaves her mouth.

"Damn it, Kathy, I'm such a son of a bitch." His voice is raspy, altered by the years of drinking. "I

72

screwed my life and yours. I missed it all, and now I'm dying. Goddammit all!"

His arms thrash in the air, threatening to detach and disrupt the lines connecting him to the false hope of better health. The machines beep faster as her father's agitation increases.

"Daddy, Daddy, it's OK. You're here now. We're here together. It doesn't matter anymore," Kathy soothes as she eases his body back toward the bed.

Her father closes his eyes and turns his head away from Kathy. His breathing slows, the heart pattern becoming less erratic.

"Daddy, you rest now, OK? I'm gonna get a bite to eat but I'll bring it back here. I love you, Daddy." She kisses his temple and steps away from the bed.

"I love you, too." His voice is faint. "Two and a half and a peanut."

She turns back to respond but he is already sleeping. Her body wants to collapse into a ball on the floor, cry till there is no more. It has been so long since she heard her father say that term of endearment, that special phrase that belonged to no one but them. Was there too much time and distance between them now for a peanut to work its magic? She always put her fingers to her lips and whispered his name before her auditions and performances, evoking his spirit wherever he might have been. This time she does it because she knows where he is.

Before heading to the cafeteria, she stops at the nurse's station to let the oncoming shift know where she'll be.

"Hey, I'm Patrick O'Shea's daughter, Kathy, and I'm just going down for some supper. You have my cell number, right? I won't be long. He got a little upset for a bit but he's sleeping now. Please call me, for anything."

"Of course, Kathy,' says the older nurse at the desk. "Do you mind if I ask you something? I don't mean to be nosy, but are you Kathy Rose, the actress?"

"Uh, yes, I am." Kathy is taken aback. Not too many people recognize her.

"I spent time in England and I just loved *Two to Tango*. Loved you and all the characters who waltzed through your studio on the show. You haven't changed at all, so I thought it had to be you. Do you think they'll ever show that on PBS again?"

"It would be nice for a residual, but probably not. Glad you liked it," she says, her hand over her heart. "So did I."

"We'll keep a close eye on your Dad. I know it's hard."

"Thanks. You guys have a tough job. I appreciate all you do."

That was unexpected. If she still looks like her younger self after two days of sleeping in a hospital chair, maybe she needs to get out in front of the cameras again instead of hiding behind a microphone in a sound-proof studio. Always good to know your work made somebody's day. Had her father seen her work? Had it made his day? If it had, does he remember or are his memories lost in his alcohol-soaked brain, blacked out and irretrievable? Her phone rings.

"Is this Kathy O'Shea?"

"Yes, who's this?"

"I'm Lenore, Lenore Ingels. A friend of your Dad's. We live together ... um, in the same apartment building, and ... the other tenants and I were wondering how he's doing."

"Things could be better but he's stable for now."

"I'd like to visit but I don't want to intrude or any-thing. Perhaps I can bring some things for him."

"Well, clothing and toiletries are provided but I'll ask him."

Kathy brings the mixed salad back to her father's room and eats while he sleeps. Something secretive underscored this woman's responses making Kathy wonder about the relationship. Is she her father's girlfriend? Are they having one of those senior hook-ups? Hey, you go, Daddy.

She puts the disposable bowl and utensils in the trash and takes out her laptop to check for messages. Still nothing from Disney. Nothing on eharmony. The only relationship she wants now is with her father. Susan sent an update saying Linda's daughter is getting married around the same time as the reunion and she'll be invited. She wants to go but priorities have changed.

Patrick stirs and opens his eyes. "There's my girl. So, what's new?"

Kathy's heart drops. Has he really forgotten their conversation of no more than an hour ago? In the rush of reconnecting, Kathy lost sight of the reality of the disease with its progressive mental disorientation. The stroll down memory lane will be one step forward and two steps back. Kathy desperately wants to be the nine-year-old girl chatting with her doting father over Rocky Road ice cream, but that moment has passed. She pushes the anxiety away.

"Just checking emails, Daddy. Hey, do you know a Lenore Ingels? Lives in your building."

"Who? Who?" His eyes seem to search the room for clues but come up empty.

"Lenore Ingels. Like in the Poe poem. "Lies thy love, Lenore" or something. You used to recite it."

"Ah, of course," he says as if the poetry reference unlocked a hidden drawer. "She's my friend, Kathy. We share an apartment. Just companions now, but once we were more. Is she here?"

"No, but she wants to visit. Can she bring anything for you?"

"Yes, my book. She knows the one."

⌘⌘⌘⌘⌘

Lenore arrives within the hour, and as she peeks into the hospital room, her eyes travel first to Patrick and then to Kathy. Her small frame pitches forward. Her face is lined with wrinkles, her hair a yellowed white, not unlike the scratched and faded photo album she carries.

"Patrick, dear," she says as she walks to the bedside and adjusts the sheet across his chest before taking his hand. Kathy feels her stomach tighten as she watches this stranger attend to her father. 'Get away from him, you bitch' flashes across her mind.

"Guess news travels fast. I'm a little tied up here," he grins, presenting his collection of plastic tubes. "This is my daughter, Kathy. Kathy, Lenore."

"I've heard so much about you, Kathy. Your father loves you very much, you know."

"Yes, I know," Kathy replies and changes the subject. "What's this book you've brought?"

"My little peanut," Patrick says, "this is your life. I'm sorry I wasn't there in person, but I've watched your every move. I've been with you all the way. Look."

Her name is printed in bold letters on the cover, and inside are page after page of line drawings of her as a child; the letters and pictures she sent during her teen years; news clippings, movie ticket stubs, magazine articles from her career. He'd seen her work. He was there when she crossed her fingers and whispered his name. He never left her. And she would never leave him.

CHAPTER 11

Margaret slumps in the sea foam green couch in a mental health office on Bedford St. in downtown Stamford. Her coat is buttoned to the top with a black scarf encircling her neck. Red-rimmed eyes stare vacantly at the limp hands in her lap. Her regular psychiatrist is out of town for the holidays, but the office squeezed her in with one of the other therapists. Her friend Denise waits in the lobby.

"Margaret, I'm Sarah. What brings you here today?"

No response.

"Margaret. Margaret?"

She lifts her head slightly, vaguely acknowledging the doctor's words, but she does not speak. Her eyes shift momentarily to the center table with its Zen garden of sand and the ceramic bowl of smooth pebbles before she gazes out the window at the gray clouds. She pulls and twists the large diamond ring on her left hand.

"Margaret," the doctor repeats, "tell me, what brings you here today?"

She feels the trickle build in her eyes, slipping over the edge and meandering past her nose, the corner of her mouth, and dropping off her chin onto her coat.

"My ... my ... he ... choked me. Oh, God, oh God, oh God." The words stutter and hiccup into the air before her voice disappears into mournful sobs, her hands muffling the sound.

The therapist pulls a tissue from the box and passes it to her, saying nothing as the good cry irrigates the emotional wound. Five minutes go by, and then ten, and finally Margaret's muscles slacken, though her head remains bowed.

"That must have been truly frightening for you, Margaret. Were you seen by a doctor?"

"No, I was fine." Once again, she retreats into silence. After a few moments she continues, eyes closed. "It was my fault. I'm such an idiot."

"How was this your fault?"

"He was drinking. I irritate him then. I knew better. Should have kept my mouth shut." She opens her eyes and stares at her shoes. "But I was tired of his insults. Tired of ... him. And he tried to hurt my cat." With a touch of anger in her voice, Margaret lifts her head and looks at the counselor for the first time before her focus drifts back to her hands.

"You said he choked you. Was this new for him? Physical abuse?" the therapist asks.

"Yes. Always the words. Never the sticks and stones."

"How long have you been married?"

"My friend will say too damn long, but about 20 years."

"Tell me about your marriage, Margaret."

She shifts her view to the leafless tree outside the window before resting her head on the back of the sofa. Her eyes stare at the ceiling, scanning the tiles as if they are giant index cards listing the talking points of her relationship.

"We met ... after my father was killed. He was part of the team settling the estate. He was very good at explaining the details, easy to talk with. And he made me

78

laugh. I needed that. I never dated in school. No time and no offers. He was the first ... the only man to ... to treat me like a woman."

"So, there was love in the beginning?"

"I thought so. He took me out to dinner, movies. Even liked my French films. He did all the things I'd heard about from friends. When I took over the company, he proposed. Bended knee, champagne, violins, the works. My Prince had come. And then I resigned to go into teaching ..." Her mouth curves briefly. "I think Henry Kissinger said, 'Power is the ultimate aphrodisiac.' Without the trappings of CEO, I was merely a hag with a bag of money propping up his ladder to the top. So, I immersed myself in academia, and we drifted apart."

The words flow easily. Now that someone is listening. Her December slump had weighed her down. Perhaps the near-death experience is bringing her back to life. She unbuttons her coat though leaves it in place.

"Did you ever think about leaving?" the therapist continues.

"Off and on. Especially the last five years." Margaret looks away, rubbing her palms with her thumbs. "But I never followed through. Even when the affairs began. How could I blame him? I was no longer young and certainly not pretty. Besides, physical intimacy had never been our strong suit. It was just as easy to live our separate lives. He needed my money, and I guess I needed ..."

"What, Margaret? What do you need from him? Why do you stay?"

Margaret swallows hard, trying to keep her nausea at bay. This isn't the first time her judgement has been called out. Her father always berated her for her inability to make decisions. Procrastinating until someone else makes the call is her preferred strategy. Or else she waits

79

for the gods to swoop in with a deus ex machina. Like now?

"I don't know. Stupidity? Cowardice? Some distorted sense of commitment? My parents' divorce devastated me. I wasn't ready to go through that again. Guess I was comfortable with the Devil I knew."

"So are you still comfortable, Margaret?"

"He's moved out. I should feel safe. But even with my chauffeur standing guard ..." she shudders, "I'm afraid Jeff will sneak back to trash the house or burn it down. Most likely with me in it."

"Then why stay? What scares you about leaving?"

Margaret adjusts her position in the chair, pulling at her coat and dress, as if the answers to these questions will fall out of the folds of her clothes.

Her closed eyes squint tight as she shakes her head. "Change. And the cascade of change that inevitably follows." She lifts her head and pulls a memory from the ceiling. "I begged to go away on a special retreat when I was twelve. Father disapproved but Mother gave permission. When I returned home, suitcases lined the hallway. I was told my parents were separating, and I'd be moving to Colorado. After high school, I conceded to Father's plan to groom me for the boardroom, but I longed for the tweeds and suede elbow patches of the classroom, not a gray pinstriped suit. So when he died in the plane crash, I felt sadness of course but now I was free to do want I wanted. I married and began teaching. And now, that life is collapsing. Seems like with great change comes great failure."

"So better to be stuck in a rut, then teetering on the edge?" the therapist asks.

Margaret ponders the question before letting out a little chuckle. "No risk of falling if you're already in the hole."

Margaret fingers her ring again, rubbing the prongs that hold the diamond in place. She pulls it up and down, trying to move it past her first knuckle, but it doesn't budge. An obvious sign to stay with her Devil. Margaret closes her eyes. Her mind hurts from picking at these emotional scabs. If she could just sleep without dreaming, wake without remembering, this would all be over. No such luck, as the therapist goes on.

"Margaret, you need to be realistic about your situation. Regardless of whether or not your husband suffers consequences from his actions, he still assaulted you."

"We could get counseling, right?" Her voice cracks and she feels that damn ring tighten on her finger. Once again, her logical mind takes a back seat to the pleas of her sentimental heart.

"That's your call, but you have rights. Legal and human. I would encourage you to get a restraining order against Jeff, especially if you decide to divorce."

This is all becoming too real for Margaret. This talk of leaving, restraining orders, the D word. Why can't things just go back to the way they were? Jeff will calm down and she'll go back to walking on eggshells. But what if he blows up again? What if Sean isn't there to intervene? What if Jeff ends up hurting Maya? Her fingers dig into her temples as her private 3D Armageddon explodes across her mind. The scarf coiled around her throat reignites the suffocating terror of New Year's Eve. As her respiratory rate accelerates, she yanks at it to release its grip and rocks herself into a frenzy.

"Margaret, you're hyperventilating. Take some deep breaths. Here, in this paper bag."

Margaret leans over and blows into the sack, the hurried panting easing as the oxygen and carbon dioxide return to normal. Margaret relaxes into the cushions as the doctor continues.

"Do you handle your own finances?"

Margaret takes a breath and answers. "Jeff and I share a financial advisor. The vast majority of my money is in a trust that he can't touch. The prenup provides for him if we split, but I suspect attempted murder might negate that."

"I encourage you to contact a lawyer to represent your interests, especially considering your husband's occupation," the therapist says. "I can't make your decisions for you, but you need to consider your options. Talk things over with the people close to you. When Dr. Hall returns this Thursday, I'll recommend she see you once a week for a while. Are you having trouble sleeping, working, doing the normal activities of the day?"

"Sleeping, yes, especially at my house. I don't have much of an appetite."

"I see you're on Prozac, but I'll add an anti-anxiety medicine. And always, if you feel you might hurt yourself, call Dr. Hall or me, a friend, or 911. Have you considered a support group?"

"No, that's not for me. I just want things back to normal."

The therapist covers Margaret's hands with hers, a look of reassurance tinged with déjà vu in her eyes. "Margaret, you must realize that your life has not been normal for quite a while. I know change is hard, you fear the unknown, but maybe it's time for a new beginning, a new direction. To be and do what *you* really want."

HELTER SKELTER

CHAPTER 12

It's a bit early for chubby-cheeked rodents to venture out of their burrows with a Groundhog Day forecast, but Susan is ready for Spring, no shadows in sight. She shapes a ball of soft, yeasty dough into a foot-long log then slices it with a sharp, floured knife, each cut marking an inch of progress toward her goal. She snuggles the cinnamon and nut filled pinwheels in a pan and into the warm oven to rise, hoping her grand plans will expand as rapidly as her sweet bread.

It's been twenty-five years since Susan spent much time with Rick Jackson, owner and manager of The Homestead, where dining is as fine as it gets in Sullivan. Rick seemed intrigued by the business venture she shared with him last week, saying old family recipes were a perfect fit for his folksy eatery. The recession had created a need for reassurance, comfort, getting back to the simple things in life. And what promises 'it'll be all right' better than homemade sweets.

They worked together when the place was called Johnny's, and she was helping make ends meet after the family farms were sold off. They were in their thirties, the old guys among the mostly teenaged employees, and Rick flipped the burgers while she ferried them to the tables. Now they merely chit-chat when she and Steve stop in for a bite, or reminisce over barbecue and root beer floats during Hometown Days. But Susan wonders if he remembers the laughs, confidences, yearnings, and all the pie they shared back in the day. Or that hot summer night in 1985 that wove them together like a lattice pie crust.

"Do I smell cinnamon rolls?" Steve calls from the stairs.

"Yes, but sorry, they're for the Homestead. I'm auditioning them for Rick's breakfast menu. Meeting him at ten."

He trudges into the kitchen, his face drawn with dark circles under his eyes. Last night Steve had finally responded to one of her subtle but persistent romantic overtures. Unfortunately, it wasn't like riding a bike since the kickstand wouldn't stay up and the chains were quite rusty. Despite reassurances that it was no big deal for her, Steve's manhood was devastated, and she felt him tossing and turning into the wee hours. Best tread lightly today.

"You OK, Sweetie?"

"Couldn't sleep. So, you're really doing this?"

"Remember New Year's Day? From your lips to God's ears. Rick says if the rolls do well, I can bring in other goodies."

Steve braces his outstretched arms against the island counter and leans in toward Susan.

"How well do you know this guy you're getting into bed with? And what's in it for him?" he asks, his eyes as narrow as his apparent state of mind.

Susan steels herself against the unexpected interrogation, caught off guard by Steve's choice of words. What is he implying, for God's sake? She forces a smile and meets his gaze.

"Come on, it's Rick. You eat lunch at his place twice a week. He sees a good opportunity and wants to help a new entrepreneur."

"So that's what you are now? An entrepreneur?" He spits the word out with distaste, as if he meant to say manure and already had a mouthful. He clenches his jaw and pushes past her to get his coffee, avoiding eye contact.

She grabs onto the counter to steady the weakness she feels in her legs. She had expected him to be more supportive since it was his idea. But now her confidence and her knees are sinking like the middle of an overinflated cake. Are her plans destined to fall flat as well? Her lip quivers, the first stage of the slide into her usual meltdown after any slight. No, he's just upset about last night. Cut him some slack and move past it.

Steve continues his cross-examination as he faces her once again. "So where you doing all this baking? Can't wait to see our next electricity bill."

"Well, here for now until we're sure there's a market, but then I'll bake at the restaurant, I guess. I'll work that out with him. I promise I'll drop off a roll for you at the store every day on my way home. How's that?" she says, scooping out a bit of icing with her finger and offering it to Steve.

He scowls and brushes her hand away. "Just give me my breakfast."

Susan turns away and licks the icing herself. She cracks the eggs and slips them into the frying pan. Apparently things aren't going to be over easy today.

⌘⌘⌘⌘⌘

The two-story building south of Main Street that houses The Homestead has been around since the early 1900's when it was a general store. In the Fifties, the grandson of the original owner turned it into the quintessential greasy spoon, serving up variations on "fried." It became a country club for farmers during the slack winter months with humble coffee and cards instead of high-hat cocktails and golf clubs, and a canteen for the itinerant field hands on summer evenings after long, hot, dusty days harvesting wheat. Families came by after church on Sundays for chicken dinners in plastic waffle weave baskets, while teenagers hung out after school and on weekends slurping frosty shakes in a prelude to hot and heavy backseat make out sessions.

When Rick returned to town in the early Nineties, his Culinary Arts Certificate in hand, he updated the plumbing and electricity, converted the upstairs into additional eating space, put in a bar, and planted a garden in the back to supply fresh herbs and vegetables during the growing season. The backcountry bistro is decorated with distressed wooden tables and chairs, curtains and tablecloths in homespun fabrics, and an assortment of antiques from local families and garage sales. His wait staff wear overalls and gingham shirts and would chew on straw if it wasn't against the health code.

The bell chimes as she breezes through the front door of Rick's place, and Susan is back in her childhood and her own family's homestead. Her nose fills with the aromas of the same foods she helped her mother fix during harvest. Meats browning with their accompanying thick gravies, hickory smoked bacon sizzling in iron skillets, and fruity pie juices bubbling onto oven racks. The trip back to a time of comfort eases the stress of this morning's conversation with Steve, and her confidence springs back like a perfectly rounded loaf. She steps up to the cashier stand.

"Hi, Beverly. I'm here to see Rick. Got some sweet treats for him to try," Susan says to the hostess, displaying her 9 x 13 pan crowded with frosted solace.

"He's in the office. I'll go get ..."

"Hey, Suze, heard your voice. So where's these scrumptious rolls you keep braggin' on?" Rick says as he walks over to the front desk.

"Right here, waitin' for a cup of coffee."

"OK, then. Is there fresh in the pot, Bev? Bring a couple of mugs on back. Thanks."

"Bev, maybe a plate, knife and fork, if you could." Susan adds, "And a napkin."

Rick's office is in an attached building just off the kitchen that also serves as a storage area for paper products, non-perishable foods, and seasonal decorating items. His desk sits near the entrance, and he offers a wooden chair to Susan.

"I sure hope you like these. The entire family raves about them. Plus the church ladies think they're 'special'," she says, mimicking Dana Carvey's prim and proper character.

The hostess puts cups of coffee along with packets of sugar and creamer in an empty space amid the invoices and mail atop the oaken table that serves as Rick's desk. Susan carefully cuts out a single roll, places it on the serving dish, and waits for Rick's critique. She watches his mouth as his teeth sink into the icing, then disappear into the chewy dough. His jaw circles his tongue as the sweet and spicy flavors caress his taste buds. A bit of sugary frosting catches in his Magnum P. I. moustache, adding to the salt and pepper that now speckle the still full bristles. His eyes close as he concentrates on the taste and smell of the baked good as the little wrinkles beside his eyes deepen.

Susan feels a bit flushed, from nerves and the warm room she rationalizes, so she distracts herself by tearing open the little packets and doctoring her coffee. As she sips, she glances around the room, visualizing a bakery in the space. Little tables and chairs, a glass case full of pies, cakes, cookies, breads. The smell of yeast wafting out the door to the throng of hungry patrons. Whoa. Horse, then cart. Better see if he likes them before putting up the sign.

"Damn. Damn! These are good. Hell, they're heaven. What's the secret?"

"No secret. Just time, love, and tenderness." She impulsively puts her hand on his sleeve, and then withdraws it just as quickly. Tossing her head casually, she laughs, "Maybe the family name has something to do with it. Bliss, you know."

"Well, whatever, I'll take 'em. Let me get some staff input, but I can offer them as a special for a week or so, and then talk a permanent spot once I see how they sell. How many can you make a day?"

"Four dozen might be pushing it. I'm operating out of a 1970's kitchen. Could I use your equipment? I mean, if things go well."

"Of course. You can start coming in now if that would help. We open at 7 so we'll need some fresh baked for the sunrise crowd. Would that work for you? Are you an early riser?

"Rick, I'm a menopausal woman. Seven is late for me. What about ingredients? Do I provide or do you?"

"How about if I provide the flour and the flame, you the muse and the might, and then we split the profits? How does, maybe, three dollars per roll sound?"

"As long as you don't price them out of reach for the people who need comfort food the most."

Susan gathers the plate and utensils, brushing a few crumbs off the papers on the desk before rising from her chair in unison with Rick.

"So," she says, "I guess we have a deal, pardner. Do I need to sign something? Spit on my hand and shake?"

"I'll get my lawyer to draw up something ..."\

"Oh, my. Lawyers?"

90

"Nothing involved, just a simple contract of expectations. No worries. We can go over it together."

"Rick, thanks so much for even considering my venture. My first flight out of my empty nest. I'd like this to be a win-win for both of us. Wait, you've got icing in your moustache. Let me get it."

She picks up a napkin and wipes the frosting away from the hair. An innocent maternal instinct. Nothing more.

"Thanks," Rick says, licking his mouth. "I agree with you, this could benefit us both. How about that spit shake?"

"How about a hug instead?"

She embraces her old friend, closing the deal on a hopefully profitable endeavor. It feels good to be in those arms again. It feels right. And maybe just a little ... no, a whole lot wrong.

Susan hurries home, her mind racing with ideas, her heart racing with wistful memories. Was Rick really excited to see her, or just the cinnamon rolls? That easy familiarity, their good-natured banter. Just like old times. Did he feel the electricity when they touched? OK, when she touched him. Had she only imagined the approving whiff of her Mom's perfume among the medley of aromas at the restaurant? Seriously, Susan, you love Steve. Let it go.

CHAPTER 13

Susan hopes she can spend the rest of her day concentrating on someone else's happily ever after, not daydreaming about ill-advised pie-in-the-sky scenarios. Forget that damn pie and focus on cake.

The happy couple has set September fourth as the Big Day, and so far her only job is pastry chef. Today she's going to try her hand at one of the recipes she's picked out. Lemon curd and white chocolate mousse between layers of orange buttermilk cake covered with a piped and sculpted white chocolate and cream cheese frosting. And of course, artfully placed fresh flowers. Her mouth waters at the description. She butters and flours, beats and creams, sifts and stirs, and pours the sampler into the pan, then slides it into the 350-degree oven.

A quick trip to the mailbox while the cake bakes finds the usual ads and bills but also a letter from Margaret. She takes her correspondence upstairs to her computer and reads her friend's note. Bad news, good news. Mental and marital woes but Margaret says she *needs* to come for this reunion. She logs on to Facebook to reply and sees a private message from Kathy. Her Dad is ill, maybe dying, and it's a day by day situation, but don't count her out. She sends prayers and support to both and counts her blessings.

The oven timer dings, and she heads downstairs. The cake is perfect, nicely rounded and evenly browned. She sets it on the rack to cool. Susan glances at the clock. Already three. She still needs to assemble and frost the cake, plus fix a nice dinner for Steve. She may need a road map to locate her love life, but the way to her man's heart still runs through the kitchen. She was hoping to finish the romance series from her December day of awakening, but a final romp with her French lover will have to wait. There's been enough imaginary liaisons already today.

The doorbell pulls her away from her amorous thoughts. She rarely has afternoon visitors. Opening the door, she sees her granddaughter Jenny in tears.

Jenny is dressed in ratty jeans and a hooded sweatshirt, not nearly warm enough for a day in February but apparently teens do not feel the cold. Her ponytail exposes the full scope of her face, the clear supple skin of youth marred only by an isolated pimple and streaks of mascara running from her eyes. Her backpack pulls at her already slumping shoulders.

"Sweetie, what's wrong?" Susan says as she wraps her arms around Jenny and guides her into the house.

"I'm having a horrible day. Mom's busy. Dad's busy. And anyway, I can't talk to them. Can I just hang for a while?"

"Of course you can. Do you want something to eat or drink? I can make tea. That always works for the Brits."

They walk hand in hand into the kitchen. Jenny slides into a chair at the kitchen table while Susan fills the teapot and selects two floral china cups.

"I was working on a cake recipe for Jackie's wedding," Susan says. "I'm ready to fill and frost. You wanna help?"

Jenny lifts her head at the request and wipes her face with her hands. "Sure, Gramma."

"Go wash up then while I get things ready. I can't remember the last time we baked together. You were my best helper, you know." Susan kisses her eldest granddaughter on the forehead.

She takes the bowls of lemon curd, white chocolate mousse, and cream cheese frosting out of the refrigerator where they have been chilling since yesterday. The cake remains on the rack ready to be sliced in half, then filled and enveloped with fluffy sweetness.

"Shall we have a biscuit with our tea, Luv?" Susan declares in her best upper crust accent.

"Gramma, you are too funny. You always know how to make me feel better."

"And that makes me feel better."

They take turns spreading mousse and plopping lemon curd onto the bottom tier. After gently setting the top over the filling, they each pick up a spatula and begin covering it all with frosting. Susan wields her rubber utensil with the quick and precise strokes of an experienced baker, but her younger partner has talent as well. Susan observes her little Betty Crocker, waiting for the right time to help smooth over the problem that brought her distraught granddaughter to her door. With the last crumb hidden, they stand back to admire their work.

"I do believe it's turned out 'absolutely fabulous'! By the way, Miss Jenny, you've developed some mad skills. Have you been baking without me?"

"I watch the Food Network after school. I'm thinking about going to cooking school. Become a chef or something."

"Well, I think you'll be a good one. You're a natural. You know, I'm gonna sell my cinnamon rolls at The Homestead. Maybe we could start a bakery together."

95

Susan sees her window of opportunity and raises the sill. "So you decided not to go to college?"

"I don't know. Mom and Dad will have a cow if I don't, but ... the world won't end, right?"

"Of course not, but when do you hear back from the schools you applied to?"

"Not 'til the end of March. Gramma, do you regret not going to college? Just being a Mom?"

Ouch, that left a mark. "Sweetie, I would have loved to have gone. The chance to learn all about the world, dig into interesting subjects, go to parties. But, I'm happy with my life."

At least most of it, most of the time. No need to get into the details of her current post-menopausal moments of truth. Jenny turns and stares out the window, biting on her lower lip.

And Susan sees it coming. A little bubble forms in the corner of Jenny's eye and winds its way down her face and onto the table. Susan's shoulders tense as she waits for whatever worst-case scenario is about to be revealed. Without a word she covers Jenny's hand and gives it a squeeze.

"Gramma, I need to tell you something," she begins, her gaze traveling from window to table then ceiling. Everywhere but to her grandmother's eyes. "I'm ... um, I'm ..." her voice breaks, "I think I'm pregnant. Mom and Dad are gonna kill me. My life is ruined."

"Jenny, Jenny. Wait. Are you sure? Did you do a test, see a doctor?"

"I already missed a period. Isn't that pretty sure?"

"Well, I suppose, but before you start going down this road, let's get a test kit and ..."

"There's one in my backpack. I've been too scared to do it. Would you do it with me?"

"Of course. Can you work up a pee?"

Together they open the package from the dollar store. Susan waits outside the door while Jenny sits on the toilet in the upstairs bathroom.

"Gramma, I'm too nervous. My hand is shaking. What if I miss the strip?"

"Don't worry. You can do it."

Susan tries to distract her, and fill in some of the blanks for herself.

"Is Justin the father?"

"Yes."

"Does he know?"

"Yeah, but nobody else."

"Will he help? Marry you?"

"I don't know. I'm not sure I want to get married. Justin says we should just get rid of it. Don't tell Mom he said that. But ... how can I take care of a baby?"

Susan takes in a slow quiet breath. This is déjà vu all over again, only this time it's closer to home. Back then birth control pills didn't exist, abortion was expensive and disreputable, unwed mothers were shunned. Now, there are lots of Jennys raising babies, with or without Justins. But how to break the news to her parents without starting World War 3? Obviously she can't let her face Maureen alone.

Jenny opens the door. "Here, Gramma, you check it."

Susan holds the plastic wand and waits for this physiological Magic Eight Ball to reveal the future. Almost immediately the small oval window pinks. Past the first mark, then the second, and finally the whole area is in living color. The oracle has spoken. Jenny is pregnant.

CHAPTER 14

Kathy finds a parking spot near the gallery where her father has some of his art for sale. Lenore, her Dad's 'artist in residence,' wants her to see a couple of canvases in particular before the trip back to LA. Back to where Patrick O'Shea will spend his remaining days.

"Have you seen any of your Dad's paintings, Kathy?" Lenore asks.

"Some of the backdrops at Warner Brothers, a few things when we lived together but nothing for over a decade. I'm just glad he kept at it despite, you know, the interruptions."

The small studio is an eclectic mix of Southwestern, traditional, and kitschy creations done by local artists. Lenore has some of her pottery on display as well, and the occasional sale by either added to their modest social security incomes. Winding their way through the sculptures and *Dia de los Muertos* paintings, they finally come to the area where her father's paintings hang.

"Oh, Lenore, they're beautiful! Not dark and brooding like I imagined, but light and ethereal as if he mixed water colors with acrylics."

There are seascapes with waves crashing on rocks or sun reflecting off water. And landscapes of the Golden

Gate, Monterrey Bay, and San Diego. But this 18 x 24 canvas, Kathy knows, is the one she wants.

"That has to be me and my sister. After our first dance lesson we went to the beach and did pirouettes, our arms overhead, balancing on tiptoe in the sand, twirling our skirts. Daddy must have sketched us while we played. I'll get this one, and one of the seascapes. What will happen to the rest when ...?"

"I imagine any sales would go to the estate. Or maybe you'd inherit the lot."

Kathy suspects her father's estate will fit in a banker's box but the paintings, yes, she liked them. She's come to terms with her father's relationship with this woman, realizing how much she's done for him, knowing she wouldn't be having this opportunity to reconnect if she hadn't been there. Trying to be magnanimous, she makes an offer.

"I'd like something of yours as well. That turquoise vase will look great in my house."

"That's nice of you, dear."

⌘⌘⌘⌘⌘

Kathy and Lenore arrive at the hospital at nine the next morning. Her father will be transferred by ambulance to her home where he will receive palliative care. Kathy drove back a week ago to make the arrangements. She rented a hospital bed, commode, wheelchair, and other medical equipment and supplies, and rearranged her furniture in the living room so the bed looks out the window. And she sorted through pictures, movies, records, anything that might trigger memories, recall moments, and bridge the gaps in time for her Dad.

She spent the night at the small efficiency apartment Lenore shares with Patrick, sorting through his few clothes and personal possessions, his favorite paintings, some art supplies, and an anthology of poetry. A man in his eighties dying of liver failure won't need much, but it's in her car. The only thing to pack up now is her Dad for his ride in the ambo-cab with the EMTs.

"Hey, Daddy. Road Trip. Woo Hoo," she says upon entering her father's room with a smile on her face, pep in her voice, a firm grip on her emotions. "The guys said they'd play these CD's for you on the way up. Frank Sinatra, Tony Bennett."

"Yeah, that'll be great, Kathy."

Most of the tubes are gone except one for oxygen, a mini-IV port in his neck, and an opening in his stomach for liquid nourishment. His voice remains scratchy and weak. His eyes are dull, yellow, half open.

"Is Lenore here?" he asks.

"I'm here, Patrick." Lenore walks over to the bed and raises his purple hand to her lips.

"Hey, Kath, could you give us a minute?" her father requests.

"Sure, Daddy, take your time."

Kathy eases out of the room, leaving the door ajar, so the elderly couple can say their good-byes. She strains to hear their conversation but the voices are too soft, and she chastises herself for her intrusion into their privacy. Respecting her father's end-of-life wishes, Lenore will join them up north once he's settled, but she's torn between having someone who can fill in the gaps and having him all to herself.

⌘⌘⌘⌘⌘

Kathy leads the way off the freeway and into the narrow streets of Venice. Traffic is horrible as always, but the medics use their sirens sporadically to help the truck squeeze through. She worried about navigating the narrow flight of stairs with the gurney, but they assured her it's not a big deal. They'll carry him up in their arms if need be.

And so, in less than an hour, Patrick O'Shea is settled back into the duplex where he brought his bride and raised his daughters, though upstairs this time. Where he abandoned the same wife and children. And where father and this daughter will await the end. Come hell or high water.

"Daddy, welcome home. Why don't you rest for a bit. You want a shake or some water?"

"Not now, Kathy," he says, craning his neck to see around the trees. "Never made it to the top in my day. Just want to take in the view."

"Thanks guys, I appreciate you doing the heavy lifting for me," Kathy says to the medics, though one hundred pounds was all it had been. "I need to pick up my dog downstairs. Could you stay for just a minute?"

She hears Murphy's bark before she reaches the door and knocks. Max opens the door just an inch to keep Murphy from darting out, but once the dog sees her, his tail goes into hyperdrive, his body jumping in anticipation.

"Murphus, how's my boy! Momma missed you so much." Fur and drool fly in a frenzy of hugged necks and licked faces. "And hello to you too, Max. Everything OK?"

"Oh, we're fine and dandy. How's he doing?"

"Pretty tired from the trip. I left him looking out the window. Hospice is stopping by in a couple hours to give me my instruction manual. Murphy will be my nurse's aide. Once we're all settled and Dad's oriented and rested, come up for a visit. I'm sure he'd love to see you."

Kathy rises with the dog on his leash, and they head for the stairs. But first, she needs to talk with her boy about the changes coming to his life. They sit on the bottom step.

"Murphy, my Daddy's gonna stay with us for awhile," she says, holding his head in her hands with an occasional ear scratch. "You can't jump up on him, and he won't be taking walks with us 'cause he doesn't have a lot of energy. But he's a good talker and he's got some great stories. I know how much you like stories, Murph, so just listen and be there with him, OK?"

Kathy knows this conversation would seem crazy to many, but Murphy is a good dog, and a good friend, and she knows he will help them all get through this.

Not wanting to keep the EMTs from their work, she heads back up. She holds the dog outside as she peeks in the door. She catches their attention and thanks them profusely on the landing before they head back down to the ambulance with their equipment. And now, it's just her and Murphy. And her Dad.

Normally, Kathy takes off the leash before they walk through the door, but this time she holds it tight with less lead. Murphy stops and backs up when he sees the bed in the living room.

"Hey, it's OK, Murph. Let's go check it out." Kathy controls the dog as he sniffs the stainless-steel legs and rubber wheels on the hospital bed.

"Hey, who's there?" Patrick rasps, his eyes opening, searching for anything familiar.

"Dad, it's me. It's Kathy," she says, standing near his side as she takes his hand with her free one. "You're at the house in Venice. Remember, we drove up from the hospital this morning. You're staying here with me for a while. Wish I had a better view of the Pacific but maybe I can wheel you down to the beach sometime. I've got a friend here with me. Murphy, my dog. Do you want to say Hi?"

"Who? Where's Lenore? Get me the hell outta here," he shouts, pulling at the sheets, trying to move his legs to the edge of the bed. "Lenore! Lenore! Where are you?" Murphy's barking echoes Patrick's yells, both of them confused by this new situation.

"Murphy, quiet! Daddy, Daddy, it's all right. Lenore stepped away for a minute," she lies. "She'll be back. You're safe here with me. You're safe."

Reality makes its entrance. This is not going to be all looking through photos over coffee and late nights laughing and sharing memories. She realizes she is way underprepared for this role, a demanding physical and emotional marathon with more steps back than forward. This is unscripted improv, and she will need to dig deep.

CHAPTER 15

Linda peeks into her ex-husband's office, her high heels in her hand, her feet furious that she hadn't worn flats or sneakers today. Her usually well-groomed hair is in disarray and her makeup has faded, having had no time for her usual midday touch up.

"God, what a day! If I see one more head poppin' out some lady's hoo-ha, I'm gonna shoot myself. Wanna get a drink?" she asks.

"Glad my job is at the front end," Rob says. "I'll leave the grunt work to you and the ladies. But sure, just let me finish my charting and follow-ups. Meet you in your office in half an hour?"

Normally Linda only supervises her staff of mid-wives and nurse practitioners, consults in difficult situations, or serves as case manager. But on days like today when a full moon and an impending late winter snow storm bring pregnant clients out of the woodwork and into the hospital where they have privileges, she puts on her gloves and dives in up to her elbows to usher little ones into the world. It has always been the best part of her profession, but nowadays her body begs to differ.

Linda waits for Rob in her own private office, sitting in a stylish white microfiber chair behind her glass desk surrounded by white bookshelves and abstract portraits in a Madonna and child motif hanging from the walls. Ever since the family friendly dinner at the Club a month ago, she and her ex have been more cordial to each other, the sins of the past swept under a very lumpy rug. The possibility of a reconciliation with him no longer seems implausible or insane. And the wedding planning is already deepening her relationship with Jackie. Maybe she'll get her do-over, a mid-life mulligan.

She scans through her phone messages. Most of them can wait until tomorrow. There's one text from Jackie updating wedding info. And there's a call from a number she doesn't recognize. A 970 prefix. She plays the message.

"Hello, my name is Sandra Henry. I'm looking for a Linda Wilson who lived in Sullivan, Colorado in 1968. If this is you, please call me at your earliest convenience. Thank you."

She's trying to sort out who and what the hell that is all about when Rob knocks on her door.

"Ready?" he says.

"Too ready," she replies.

Too cold to walk, she and Rob drive their cars to the College Inn, a local bar they've frequented over the years during school at the Med Center, in the happier moments of their marriage, and even now for after-hours relaxation. The area around 9th Avenue and Colorado Boulevard, once full of students, staff, and patients scrambling to classes, clinical duties, or appointments, is in a state of flux as the new Anschutz campus in Aurora begins its tenure as a clinical teaching center.

"Docs," shouts the bartender in a *Cheers* greeting of honor. Their usual Grey Goose martinis, three olives each, arrive at their table in a matter of moments.

"Salut," they say in unison before guzzling half of adult beverage number one.

"You know, it's days like this that make me think about hanging it up," Linda says.

"What?" Rob nearly chokes on his drink. "You hang it up? You said they'd have to pry the afterbirth from your cold dead hand before you'd give it up. What else would you do?"

"I don't know. Teach? Do charity work?"

A belly laugh explodes from Rob. "No way in hell I see you in a third world country, sloggin' through mud and human waste to deliver some woman's twelfth baby. And ruin your Jimmy Choo's?"

"OK, that probably won't happen, but I could be a professor, right?"

"Not enough money. You need money."

"OK, I agree, but it's more about what you said at the New Year's party. About fun not being in my plans."

"Linda, it's no secret you could turn relaxing in a hammock with a froufrou drink into an ordeal," Rob smirks, poking at the olives in his now empty glass.

"Oh, come on, I'm not that bad. I admit it. I've been all work. So why don't you, Grand Master of Merriment, teach me to play?"

Rob bends down and peeks under the table before rising up with a grin. "Wait, where's that woman I came in with? And where has this one been for the last twenty years? Babe, your problem is you worry too much about what others think. You gotta let go every once in a while. You know, dance like no one's watching."

Linda sits up straight and, with double dog dare in her eyes, picks up her glass and chugs the rest of her cocktail. Slamming it down on the table like a gauntlet, she answers the challenge. "Then fix me another martini. I'm drinking like no one's counting!"

⌘⌘⌘⌘⌘

Obviously, someone should have been counting, and one too many martinis later, Rob is holding the tipsy ex-wife under her arms as she stumbles out of the bar.

"Come on, I'll take you home. We'll get your car tomorrow," Rob says as he pours Linda into the passenger seat of his little red Corvette.

"Why thank you, Robbie," Linda enunciates slowly. "I like your car." Linda caresses the leather seats and pokes at the electronic screens and gadgets on the console until Rob stops her from undoing all his carefully determined settings. "Turn on the music. I feel like dancing," she squeals and, even before the first note blares, she begins flailing her arms and rocking her body. Thank God nobody's watching.

It's a quick trip to her condo on 1st Street, and luckily no vomit has befouled the interior of the lean mean 'manopause' machine. Rob eases into a parking space and guides her out of the car and toward the elevator.

"Do you want me to help you to your door?"

"Sure, it's a long ride up," Linda giggles as they enter the car and push the 7th floor button.

Linda rummages through her purse as her feet zigzag down the corridor, Rob at the ready in case things go downhill. She finds her key and fumbles as she attempts to insert it into the lock. Rob steadies her hand with his and in that moment, all activity stops. There's a quick glance between them before they turn the tumbler together and fling the door open. No words fill the air, only gasps and groans and nervous titters as lips touch lightly at first. Then mouths open and tongues explore. Hands grasp belts, fingers fiddle with buttons; tasks performed with eyes closed using muscle memory from days gone by. Lust pulls and pushes them down the hallway and into the bedroom where they fall onto the bed with an ungraceful thud. They continue to remove pieces of clothing until enough skin is exposed to get at the naughty bits.

"Rob, slow down, slow down," Linda gasps as she grabs Rob's hands, her head starting to spin with all the activity, not to mention the alcohol. "It's been a while. I need time."

"Sorry, Babe, not used to that. Need some lube?"

"Eventually, but let's ease into this, OK?" Linda says trying to erase his last line from her head. While it may be essential to the job at hand, those three little words are not the ones to get her juices going.

With the urgency dropped down a notch, Rob channels his romantic, sensual side using the skills that made Linda ache for him back in the day, as did all the ladies he slept with before, during, and after her. He kisses her softly. Her eyes, her lips, her neck. He runs his fingers through her thick silky hair. He slides his hands down her neck to her breasts and cups them, caressing and suckling them gently.

"God, Linda, I love these girls. They're still perfect," and he continues to fondle them. He makes his way down, licking her belly and her inner thighs before grabbing her buttocks with both hands.

"Rob, stop," she pants. "I need a shower. I must be gross down there."

"Don't worry. Let go. No one's watching."

And he proceeds to take her to places she never thought she'd go again. There's something to be said about having a gynecologist as a lover. He knows his way around the nether regions.

"Now I believe it's my turn, Babe," Rob murmurs as he continues to nibble her here and there.

Still breathless, she reaches inside her bedside drawer for the damn lube, and unscrews the top. Rob's phone vibrates and rings on the tabletop.

"Are you on call? Shall I get that?" Linda asks.

"Just check the caller ID," he mumbles, his mouth otherwise occupied.

"It's Marlee," Linda says, throwing the phone at his head.

Whatever magic Rob had been performing vanishes and an uncomfortable silence settles into the rumpled sheets. Always on the other end of the phone in this situation, this turnabout makes her want to vomit. Apparently, it doesn't matter which side you're on in the game, cheater or cheated, it's all shit. These two sexual encounters have renewed her faith in her womanly passions, if not in her judgement, but whether Rob feels guilty or not, Linda has more than enough for both of them. Without looking at him, she gets out of bed, covering up with the nearest piece of tossed clothing.

"I can't do this. Be the other woman. Not with you."

"Come on, Linda. I'm not serious about Marlee. She's young. We have fun. I'm pretty sure that's what we just had, right?"

Her body shouts an enthusiastic affirmative but her brain shudders in her skull. "Oh, for God's sake, Rob. Just go. Go home to Marlee. I need a shower. See yourself out."

The hot water feels good on her skin, washing off the outer sleaze from her body if not her conscience, sobering her up, and bringing her back to reality. The thrill of the encounter lingers in her pelvic region, but any notions of romance have faded. She reaches for the body wash and spots the breast check reminder. Rob reminded her how exquisite her breasts are. She's put it off a couple of times and a clinical touch will remove any sense of the erotic from earlier.

Moving the pads of her fingers in concentric circles around her breasts and into her armpits, she checks for fixed, painless nodules. She feels her right breast. Nothing new. Then the left. She returns to the upper outer

110

quadrant of that breast again. And her throat tightens. Her fingers rest on the almost imperceptible lump that definitely wasn't there last month.

Shit! She's so good about doing the self-exams, getting mammograms. How could she have missed this? She does this for a living, for Christ's sake. It's probably fibrocystic tissue. Don't jump the gun.

She dries off and looks down at her breasts. They are real and they are spectacular. Still perky despite time and a failed attempt at breast feeding. The perfect French size. Just big enough to fit in a champagne glass, OK, a big margarita glass. No, don't panic. The Girls will be all right.

CHAPTER 16

Margaret stands before her freshman literature class, a motley mix of trust fund babies, hardworking scholarship recipients, and everything in between, most majoring in liberal arts under the auspices of Sacred Heart University's mission of intellectual rigor and social justice. In this last semester she is taking her students on a leisurely cruise down Stratford-on-Avon with a review of some of Shakespeare's lighter tales, doing her best to brand the Bard as the greatest rom-com screenplay writer of the 16th century.

"How do you know you're in love? What signs would someone see? How would you feel?" Margaret asks the group.

"Like, all nervous, waiting for him to text me. Imagining what I'll say or what we'll do. And I can't eat," offers Morgan whose waif-like body suggests she is in perpetual love.

"What about your physical appearance? Are you more concerned about your looks or less?" asks Margaret.

"Way more, Dr. King. Like I'm always taking showers, and messing with my hair," Austin says, his long unkempt locks indicating he's recently been dumped.

Margaret tries her best to relate to the vagaries of young love, but having never experienced them in her own youth, she finds the all-consuming tribulations of modern romance barely tolerable, and she moves on in the lesson.

"Let's read from Scene II in *As You Like It*, starting with line 339," she directs her students. "Austin, you read Orlando, and Morgan, you read Rosalind."

ORL. "I am he that is so love-shak'd; I pray tell me your remedy."

ROS. "There is none of my uncle's marks upon you; he taught me how to know a man in love; in which cage of rushes I am sure you are not prisoner..."

Margaret leans against the window sill while her students read, her book open to the lines but her eyes looking out the glass at the spring scene of flowering trees and green grass. The words, so familiar to her after multiple readings of the play, drift past her ears, some landing in her consciousness, others floating on by.

ROS. "But are you so much in love as your rhymes speak?"

ORL. "Neither rhyme nor reason can express how much."

ROS. "Love is merely a madness; and, I tell you, deserves as well a dark house and a whip as madmen do..."

The phrase, 'love is merely a madness,' jolts her back to the classroom and the lines her students are reciting.

ORL. "...Did you ever cure any so?"

ROS. "Yes, one; and in this manner...would now like him, now loathe him; then entertain him, then forswear him; now weep for him, then spit at him; that I drave my suitor from his mad humour of love to a living humour of madness..."

Margaret's pulse quickens at the passage about changeable behavior in curing a man of his love, seesawing from one extreme to the other, eventually causing him to go mad. Has she done this with Jeff? Or has Jeff done that to her?

In the early days of their relationship he'd been her champion in shining armor, full of chivalry and romantic gestures. But over time he'd morphed into the Black Knight, threatening to lock her away in the tower, take over her lands. A madman who drank, strayed, and tried to kill her.

Her head swirls with a kaleidoscope of Jeff's purplish face, bulging eyes and veins, mouth spitting out his venomous words, his fingers reaching out like snakes to wrap around her throat once again.

The scene is finished, the students waiting for instructions to continue. Margaret's hands tremble as the book falls to the floor, her breathing coming in rapid, shallow inhalations. Her ears ring, her fingers tingle, her whole body shakes as if she will seize. Eyes glazed over, she does not see the thirty students sitting at their desks, only Jeff standing before her.

"Dr. King, are you all right?" asks one brave soul.

"Get out of here you bastard! I hate you! I hate you! I hate you," she screams and lunges toward the student who scrambles to get out of her reach.

She can feel hands grabbing her arms and pushing her into a chair. A babel of cries shatters the air. "Call Security - She's gone bat shit crazy - Is this for realz?"

Even with her eyes closed and hands muffling her ears, images and sounds ebb and flow in her mind, a psychotic whack-a-mole of the alternating heads of a maniacal Jeff, a bug-eyed student, a stern guard, and the soothing visage of her colleague Denise.

"Dr. King, what happened? What's going on?" the guards are questioning but she remains non-responsive.

"Oh, my God, she totally had a melt down," one of the students replies.

"Margaret, Margaret, it's Denise. Dear, are you OK? What happened?"

Margaret rocks in the chair, still in self-induced sensory isolation. She's no longer spinning off into space, but the room is still a blur. Conversations stream in and out of her awareness.

"Guys, why don't I talk with her some place quiet. I'll let you figure out what happened here," Denise tells the officers.

Margaret offers no resistance when Denise walks her down the empty hall to their shared office and settles her into one of the upholstered arm chairs. Margaret sits, shoulders slumped, head down, hands twisting her wedding ring. She doesn't look up as Denise scoots next to her, nor when her friend picks up her hand and holds it in silence.

After five minutes, Margaret gives an acknowledging squeeze, wrinkles her nose and whispers, "The cat's out of the bag now, isn't it? Can I claim Lady Macbeth syndrome? 'Out, out damn spot.'"

"There's my girl," Denise says with a reciprocal clasp of her own. "I'd try another defense, but I really don't think you should worry. Sounds like you just frightened the poor lad. Seriously, I don't know how you've kept it together this long. Do you remember what triggered it all?"

"Turning love into madness. That's what he did, you know," Margaret states with a nod of revelation. "He's been trying to gaslight me. Drive me to kill myself so he could inherit the estate." Her attention shifts to her desk piled with books and papers, and she heaves a sigh. "Well, I suppose I best gather my fern, go to the Principal's office, and turn in my ruler."

"Margaret, your career is not in any danger. However, you do need time to deal and heal. Take a leave of absence, or even a sabbatical. Aren't you meeting up with your high school friends this summer? The divorce will be final by then. Go out there and let loose."

"Yes, I will, but in the meantime, what do I do? Wander the hallowed halls of my home quoting Shakespeare? Take up knitting?"

"Hey," Denise says, jumping up with a bolt of wide-eyed inspiration, "Why don't I come stay with you over break. Pretend I'm on holiday."

"I don't know, I've never had anyone over. Jeff's aura permeates the walls even when he isn't there."

"Then I'll bring air freshener. So anyway, picture this." Denise spreads her arms to open an imaginary scene. "Leisurely breakfasts overlooking the garden, museums and matinees during the day, and home for tea by four. Then it's off to wildly expensive restaurants for dinner. Or we could whip up something fabulous over wine and talk the night away. I can't think of a better way to spend a vacation." Denise rests her hands on the arms of Margaret's chair, bringing their faces nose to nose. "Or a better person with whom to share them."

"So you're not afraid of a crazy cat lady?" Margaret asks with a lopsided grin, leaning back to a more comfortable, less awkward distance for herself.

"Let the fur fly. We've been friends now, what fifteen years? Isn't it about time I got to know the real you?" Denise kisses the top of Margaret's head.

"And vice versa," Margaret says taking Denise's hands into her own.

"So then, we'll stop by the Dean's to give your statement, then go pick up some things at my apartment. Let's get this party started.

Margaret watches Denise pack up their briefcases, water the philodendron hanging near the window, adjusting the blinds to let in some light. Thank you, dear friend. What would she do without her?

WE CAN WORK IT OUT

CHAPTER 17

The wooden chairs in the waiting room of the North Denver Oncology group are upholstered in out of fashion mauve tweed and scratch against Linda's bare legs. She sits near the edge of the seat, back straight, clutching her Coach handbag against her buttoned Burberry coat. The spring issues of magazines on the occasional tables are all about losing those extra pounds before summer, Easter dinners and garden bulbs, and of course making your husband happy. Of no interest to her, fortunately, because she's already spritzed her hands several times with the Purell from her purse. She checks her cell phone for the umpteenth time before gingerly leaning back and doing some yoga breathing.

"Linda Charles. Linda Charles?"

Linda exhales and opens her eyes at the sound of her name.

"Yes, I'm Linda."

"Hello, I'm Nancy. Come on back. You're here today for a consultation, correct?"

Linda nods, and follows the nursing assistant down the hallway.

"Have a seat in here. He'll be with you shortly."

In her search for a competent but clandestine diagnosis and treatment, Dr. Ryan Chester was the best of those farthest away from the network of professionals she works with in the Southeast area of town. Linda scrutinizes the small room, beginning with the professionally mounted black frames hanging behind his desk. Graduated from Cornell, board certified in oncology, surgery, women's health. His bookcases are lined with medical tomes, everything from *Gray's Anatomy* to *Devita's Cancer: Principles and Practice of Oncology*. A neatly stacked pile of professional journals sits on his desk. The art work is nondescript, painted by no-name artists. She settles herself into the comfortable but conventional low backed chair, probably from American Furniture. Has she made the right choice by placing anonymity before quality of care? She startles slightly when a voice speaks from behind her.

"Hello, Dr. Charles. I'm Dr. Chester," he says in a deep register, moving around to face her with a smile and outstretched hand. He looks young, but hell, after you turn fifty everyone looks young. His clean-shaven face and dimples suggest jail bait, but he's probably in his early forties. "I see you practice at A Woman's Place in Cherry Creek. What brings you way up here for treatment?"

"Trying to keep things private," Linda says with a momentary smile. "Anyway, I've done some research, but cancer isn't my forte. I need you to fill in the blanks. Can you do that?"

"Certainly. Let's get down to it then."

Dr. Chester pulls up the images from her mammogram and MRI plus her medical records on his computer and turns the screen so Linda can see.

"First off, your tumor is roughly 9 millimeters. Not easy to find on self-exam, so kudos to your professional skills," he says with a thumbs up. "Your history states your mother died from breast cancer at age 52. How old was she at her diagnosis?"

"I'm not really sure. Back in the early seventies, nobody said anything until it was too late." She wonders if keeping secrets is hereditary.

Dr. Chester runs down a laundry list of questions about her history. Things already documented on her chart, but apparently needing further clarification. She feels like a suspect being grilled by a police detective. She crosses and uncrosses her legs, fiddles with the clasp on her purse, and waits for him to get to the fucking point. Are you going to slice off my boob like a chicken cutlet or not?

"Of course we'll need to check the lymph nodes before surgery for final staging, but the initial biopsy did reveal an elevation in hormonal receptors," the doctor says. "So that combined with a somewhat rapid growth of the tumor and your positive family history, I'm recommending we do breast conserving surgery, a lumpectomy if you will, followed by chemo and hormone therapy. Still a conservative approach but hopefully covering all our bases for the best prognosis."

Linda releases a slow exhale, her hand sliding to her chest to reassure her left breast that she is safe. Is that her heart shaking beneath her blouse, or her boob doing a happy dance?

"That's a relief. Thank you," she says, clearing her throat. "I would be interested in genetic testing as well. I have a daughter ... and I'd want her to know if she's at risk."

"Yes, I'll order a BRCA test. If there's no other questions, the gals at the desk will set up the surgery and lab-work and provide you with some educational pamphlets. Here's my card in case you think of something."

Dr. Chester has been professional and thorough in his information today. Not aloof or condescending. Not a god in human form. As Linda stands to shake his hand once again, she looks into his eyes. Deep, chocolate brown comforting eyes. Any other day that would have been all she needed.

But life as she knows it is about to change. Her surgery is scheduled for Friday, March 26th giving her the weekend to recuperate, but she'll need someone to drive her home and monitor her for the first few hours. The chemo and its inevitable side effects will result in time away from the clinic. Multiple absences, a haggard appearance, and repeated vomiting might fuel rumors that she's alcoholic, pregnant, or on death's door. None of them good for business. Well, a pregnancy might give Rob's infertility practice a boost.

No, she's going to have to come clean and spill the beans. But who can she turn to for support? Her staff? Of course they'll cover when she's out of the office, but it'll be all hands on deck then. She can't spare someone to play nursemaid. Rob? His bedside manner could use an upgrade, and she's not sure she wants him to see ... the damage. Jackie? Hadn't she just promised her daughter she'd be there for *her*? No, there's only one person she can count on to be there for her, who has always been there for her. Susan.

CHAPTER 18

Linda studies her breasts in the mirror for one last time. God's symbol of her womanhood. Still resting well above the crook in her elbow, the slightly elongated globes remain full with only a bit more give than they once had. The reddish-brown nipples stiffen as she lightly strokes them. Men have praised them as her best physical asset. And now, one of them faces the knife. While the disfigurement should be minimal, her left breast will no longer be pristine.

She finishes dressing. Loose-fitting sweats, a button front cotton top, Keds, and an alpaca wool shawl. A black felt fedora covers her new pixie cut, a wash and wear concession to restrictive post-op movements and the eventual shedding of her crowning glory. The whole head scarf thing smacks of Russian peasants, so a wig, matching her current style, awaits on its Styrofoam head mold. Sunglasses complete her incognito look.

Susan, her chauffeur and home health nurse for the day, will be here soon. She stares out her window at the sky, the rose and purple giving way to soft gold. It's been ages since she and the dawn have been face to face. They met frequently when she worked solely as a midwife, walking patients around the unit, coaxing labor to begin in earnest. Or after a long, exhausting slog through a difficult birth when she needed to step out for a bit of cool solitude. But the sunrise that colors her memory this morning is the one that crept in through the bedroom window as her mother slipped away from this earth.

Her doorbell rings and closes the curtain on her thoughts. Probably not a good idea to dwell on dying right before surgery.

"Susan. You must have made good time," Linda says, meeting her friend at the entrance to her apartment.

"Yes, I left early. I was awake at four as it was, thinking about you. Hope you slept well, though I guess you'll have plenty of time to catch up later today if you didn't."

"No doubt. Anyway, I'm ready. Let's do this."

⌘⌘⌘⌘⌘

Linda is encased within warm blankets in the pre-op area of the day surgery unit. Two nurses and the anesthesiologist reviewed her history, once again, as well as the last twenty-four hours of her life. Her heartbeats trace across the monitor and plops of fluid ooze into a vein in her right hand. Susan folds Linda's clothing and places it in the designated plastic bag, then adjusts the bedding, making sure there is plenty of room for her toes.

"It must feel weird being the patient instead of the nurse. I haven't been in the hospital since my kids. It's all so different now ..." Susan rambles on, her words drifting in and out of Linda's ears.

That kind-voiced, hand-holding, motherly care that Susan brings to every situation usually gets on Linda's nerves, but right now it's a welcomed distraction. The cancer diagnosis has been a wake-up call. Can she finally humble herself and return to the good graces of her family? Or will she keep hitting the snooze button, drifting half asleep until God rips off the covers like a new band-aid and yanks her ass out of bed?

"When I had my colonoscopy," Susan continues, "I didn't remember anything. Are you going to be completely out?"

"No," Linda answers, "they'll give me a sedative in my IV and a local, unless they run into complications. Technically I'll be awake, but I won't be aware of what's going on."

The curtain slides open and Dr. Chester enters wearing dark-blue scrubs and a cloth cap decorated with *Star Wars* images. Doogie Howser will apparently be fondling her boob today.

"Hello, Linda. Looks like you're all ready. Just need to dot the i's and cross the t's. I'm confirming that we're doing a lumpectomy on your left breast today with removal of lymph nodes as necessary, and I am marking your left breast with an X."

Linda wonders when every other medical or surgical procedure has some Latin or Greek root word, why hers sounds like they'll be picking through a bowl of poorly mashed potatoes. After asking Susan to step out temporarily, the doctor palpates Linda's breast, finds the small lesion, and labels it with a felt tip pen.

"Well, here I go." Linda gives a thumbs up as she's wheeled away, Susan squeezing the other hand in a death grip until the gurney slams through the double doors of the operating suite and leaves her behind.

⌘⌘⌘⌘⌘

Two hours later, Linda sits in a wheelchair in Recovery, waiting for Susan to return from filling the prescription for pain medication. The good news, per Dr. Chester, is that the entire tumor was excised. The bad news is the sentinel lymph node showed early evidence of cancer, and a total of three nodes needed to be removed. Her chest is now swaddled in an ace bandage to control bleeding and minimize swelling. The tiny 9 mm bullet of tissue is gone, but the full impact of its damage is yet to come.

"OK, here's your happy pills," Susan announces, striding into the room holding a paper sack like a kid's meal from McDonald's. She hands over the narcotics and a handful of discharge papers to Linda and slips behind the chair, whispering into her ear, "Let's blow this pop stand."

Linda scoots into the car, adjusting the seat backwards and flatter to make herself more comfortable. Susan tosses a bag of disposable supplies into the back seat, certain that the rubber- footed slippers and the matching plastic cup and pitcher are too useful to leave behind, and takes her place in the driver's seat.

"I tried to memorize how we came this morning," Susan says, accelerating onto the entrance ramp of I-25, "but I might need a reminder with left or right once we get closer to your place."

Linda is surprised at how easy Susan maneuvers in the traffic. She was sure she'd be driving with Miss Daisy, chugging along at fifty down the freeway, but it looks like she's in good hands and she relaxes into the seat.

It's a short ride up the elevator of her building, and despite Linda's assurances that it's unnecessary, Susan supports her like a wounded soldier leaving the battlefield. Her 'day nurse' eases her onto the leather sofa before rounding up pillows and throws to prop up and cover the patient.

"Linda, I'm putting some soup and individual servings of casseroles in your fridge," Susan calls from the kitchen. "You can just pop them in the microwave when you're hungry later. How about some tea or juice? Do you need a pain pill?"

"Maybe just some water. There should be some Perrier in there. And do bring me the Vicodin. Better to have something on board before the local wears off."

Linda pops the pill in her mouth and leans back, watching Susan scurry about gathering phone, laptop, TV remote, and enough magazines and books to while away the next six weeks.

"Susan, come sit down," she says to her. "If I need something, I'll ask. Besides, all this activity is making it hard to relax."

"Sorry," Susan says, falling into a chair next to the couch. "I hover. Did that with the kids, and my Mom, of course. After her stroke. Nearly wore me out. When she finally passed, I wasn't sure I was feeling grief or relief. Did you do that with your Mom?"

"Yeah. I was barely out of nursing school, so I was all clinical. Documenting intake and output. Monitoring vitals. Charting everything like it mattered. It was easier if I had something to do." She gazes toward the picture window. "Now I realize I missed out on just being with her."

"Regrets," Susan sings, "I've had a few.' I mean, don't get me wrong, I'm happy with my life, you know, Steve and the kids, but is it too late to make a few changes?"

"I hope not, or we're both screwed."

"But you have it all. Career, money, laurels to rest on. You're living the fantasy."

"But whose fantasy?" The pain pill is kicking in and Linda feels her eyes drooping, a heaviness settling into her body. And her guard coming down. "I've been chasing my mother's dream ever since high school. She'd pull and I'd pushed back, but then she'd pull even harder ... so I stopped resisting. I wanted to be the good wife,

129

only delivering other people's babies until my own came along." A wave of giddiness washes over her and she chuckles, "Believe it or not, I've envied your life at times."

She hasn't let it all hang out like this since bell bottoms were in vogue. And who better to listen to her truths than the friend who knows her lies. All of them.

"Seriously," Susan replies, an eyebrow raised in disbelief. "Guess we got caught in some *Freaky Friday* switcheroo."

"Think Rob, Jackie take me back?" Linda struggles to form the words as her lips lose their resolve.

"Hard to say, Sweetie, but you need to tell them about the cancer. No more secrets."

"I know. I will. Tomorrow, tom ..." And Linda sinks into opiate oblivion.

CHAPTER 19

White fingerprints are stamped on cupboard doors, forensic evidence of Susan's every move in her kitchen this morning. Flour clumps dot the pale golden Formica countertops while a fine dusting has sifted onto the linoleum floor surrounding the island like a chalk outline. Her hand brushes a wayward hair out of droopy red eyes, the refined powder kissing her nose and cheeks, before muscular forearms resume kneading the dough, turning it over to gather the loose bits back into the smooth, cohesive ball.

She wishes she could do the same to the scattered thoughts straggling inside her sleep deprived brain. Six weeks out from her initial foray into her part-time bakery career, rising doubts and falling energy threaten to lay waste to her revolutionary vision. She devotes her mornings to the culinary endeavor, rising at four to blend flour and yeast into breakfast bliss. However, the wifely duties of housekeeping, once her proud and primary purpose, have been shoved into the corners of the day like the clutter that threatens to overtake her home.

Mail lays unopened on the counter. House dust covers neglected furniture and floors; spring cleaning never stood a chance. Wrinkled shirts, left to fend for themselves, hang on hooks and door knobs. Hungry-Man TV dinners have become standard fare, much to the objections of the hungry man forced to eat them.

"Where's all my clean underwear?" Steve shouts from the master bedroom upstairs.

"In the white basket in the bathroom," Susan shouts back from the kitchen as she waits to pull out the last two batches of cinnamon rolls.

"Where? Oh, here. How come they're not in the drawer?"

"Because I haven't had time. Be glad they're clean."

Assembling and baking the required six dozen rolls at the café would be more efficient, but sharing eggs over easy before Steve starts his day has been a sacred part of their marriage for years. While laundry falls into that category as well, ironing has become negotiable along with folding and placing his tightie-whities in the chest of drawers.

"Hey, can you sew a button on this shirt for me?" Steve asks as he strolls into the kitchen, nearly tripping over the cans of sage-green paint that wait to transform the guest room into a welcoming retreat.

"You have others you can wear." Armed with pot holders, a wave of three hundred fifty degrees rushes into her face as she opens the oven door. She slides the top pan out, sets it on the cooling rack, and goes back to retrieve the bottom one.

"I know, but it'll just take a minute," he says, pointing to the gap just above his balloon of a belly. "What else do you have to do today?"

The rolls are halfway to their resting spot as Steve's words fill the air. She drops the baked goods, her hands hanging in midair as the bang of metal on metal reverberates in the room. She spins around to address his misguided question and sideswipes her finger on the scalding pan, adding injury to insult. She jams the reddening digit into her mouth to cool it, and glowers at him.

132

Steve's pushed her button now, and she's not about to sew it on anything.

"You wanna know what else I have to do? After I take these rolls to the café, I'm driving Jenny in to the doctor and running some wedding errands for Linda. And when I get back, I'm painting the guest room. And in my spare time, I guess I'm your freakin' valet."

"Geez, sorry I asked," he says, his chin hiding in his neck as his hands block Susan's tirade. "So remind me, who's holding the gun to your head and forcing you to do all this? It's not my fault you can't say no. Why can't Maureen take Jenny? If she spent less time with other people's kids and more time with her own, the girl wouldn't be in this mess."

"A bit late for that pearl of wisdom. Jenny just feels more comfortable with me, so I'll do whatever it takes."

"Well, you certainly don't have to redecorate this perfectly good house. Those women will only be here for a week."

"So? We haven't updated anything since Reagan was president. Why can't I have some new things? You got your damn TV," she says pointing an accusing finger at the flat screen. She knows that's a low blow since it was a gift, but Steve doesn't retaliate.

"What's Linda's excuse then?"

Susan has yet to tell him about Linda's diagnosis, waiting on her to make some sort of public disclosure. But with Steve questioning each of her tasks, mere friendship may not carry enough weight. Better to be vaguely truthful.

"She had surgery and can't drive for a few weeks," she says, hoping that will suffice. She glances at the clock. With only thirty minutes to get the rolls to The Homestead, she'll have to ice them there. She's defended her case as best she can and unless the prosecution rests,

133

Steve's breakfast will no longer be on the table. "I need to get going. These rolls won't get there on their own."

"Speaking of that, where's all that money you were going to make? Seems to me old Rick's getting the better end of this deal."

"It takes time, you know. Right now, I'm a loss leader so be grateful Rick's still willing to keep me on." Her voice quivers and she turns her head. "At least he isn't undermining my dreams."

"Honestly, is that what you think? Listen, I'm just tired of slapped together dinners, stepping over all this junk, and watching you fall asleep on the couch every night. But if being an entrepreneur," he says, miming air quotes, "means abandoning your commitment to me and running yourself ragged, then, sorry, I won't support that. So make a choice, Susan. I won't tolerate being last on your list," he says, wagging a finger in her face.

Susan's cheeks burn and sweat trickles down her temples as the heat from the oven and her husband's threat stokes her anger. Her head aches, her heart is bounding, and her blistering pinky throbs.

"You want a choice? OK, how's this? I choose me. First on the list. Me," she says jabbing her thumb into her chest. "And if you can't deal with that then get the hell out," and she flings the potholders at him.

Steve's eyes are mere slits, his clenched jaw grinding his teeth like mortar and pestle. He stomps to the garage, grabs his jacket hanging on the hook, and slams the door behind him. Only floured footprints in his wake. Not a kiss goodbye. Hell, no goodbye at all. Susan stands motionless, the proverbial deer in the headlights. What has she just done? The shit's hit the fan now. And no time to clean it up.

CHAPTER 20

Brian McDermott is the palliative care nurse caring for Kathy's father over the last six weeks. Older than she expected with a little paunch, his graying hair only serves to emphasize his pale blue eyes. He dresses neatly in jeans and a polo shirt, not the clinical white, *Ben Casey* style uniform she had imagined. Here for his biweekly visit, he carries a backpack full of odds and ends of equipment he says helps him manage whatever situation might get thrown at him.

"Come on in," Kathy greets with a sweep of her arm. "Dad's holding court in the luxury box in the living room. He's been a little confused today. It comes and goes, you know."

"Hey, Patrick. It's Brian. How's it going?" he asks, extending his hand.

"Hey, Brian." Her father raises a finger in recognition. "Have you met Murphy? My right-hand dog. Gets me whatever I want. Kibble, chew toys, all the finer things of life. And you know my girl here. Best legs in California. I got some pictures."

"Thanks, maybe later. I want to find out first how you're doing. Can I give you a once over?"

Kathy observes as Brian methodically examines her father. She follows his eyes as he scans the emaciated

135

body with its jaundiced skin and eyes. She winces as his hand palpates the protuberant abdomen full of fluid due to his damaged liver. His fingers slide along the spider veins on his torso, the scattered bruises on his extremities, and the red, excoriated palms and soles of his feet. He inspects the IV port near his collar bone and the feeding tube in his stomach, finally adjusting the oxygen tubing in his nose.

"So, Patrick, is anything bothering you today?"

"The damn itching," he says, rubbing his feet against the sheets. "Sometimes my skin just crawls. Can't sleep for shit."

"Yeah, that'll drive you crazy." He angles his body toward Kathy to relay the rest of his comments as he flips through the chart. "Since his compromised liver has to clear out anything we give him, I like to try non-pharmaceutical treatments when possible. A UV light might help."

"I'm a damn fool, you know," Patrick breaks in. "I got myself in this pickled state, so I deserve the consequences. But I don't want a long drawn out death scene. If God says 'that's a wrap' then let's cut, print, and put me in the can. Just hope I get some nice moments with my girls. My other daughter Mary's comin' for a visit."

"That sounds great. You and your girls are the ones in charge. I take my orders from you. Hey, do you mind if I have a chat with Kathy?" Brian asks.

"Nah, go ahead. Me and Murphy are waitin' for the sunset."

Kathy puts the kettle on and they chit-chat at her kitchen table, waiting for the water to boil and leaves to steep. With a full caseload of patients, Brian's visits are usually hurried but today he lingers. Much to Kathy's surprise, she looks forward to his visits, even if their conversation centers around her father's bodily fluids.

"How are you doing, Kathy? I know we threw a lot of nursing tasks at you at first, but you've turned into quite a pro since February."

She gives him a self-satisfied grin and tucks her thumbs under imaginary suspenders. "Yeah, I channel Nurse Ratchet and Nurse Jackie and ask what they would do. But really, I was expecting to dole out pills, fluff a pillow or two, or dab his brow while gazing with kind eyes. Not empty the commode. Is there an easier way to move him about? If my back gives out, you'll have two of us to care for."

"I'll show you how to use the sheets to maneuver him. Perhaps we can attach a trapeze to the bed, so he can help with the lifting."

"A trapeze, eh? Don't tell Lenore. Who knows what shenanigans those guys might get up to," she laughs. She takes a wary sip of the hot tea, staring at the pale green liquid for several seconds before turning her focus to Brian's cornflower blue eyes. "How long, I mean, things are going to get worse, right?"

"I'm sorry, Kathy, yes, a lot worse, but there's no timetable. Each case is different. He'll need his belly drained soon, and that means being transported to a clinic. And with any invasive procedure, there's risks. He'll continue to lose weight and his pain will increase. He's been pretty lucid, but that won't be the case in time. It's not a pretty picture I'm afraid. You can always take him back to the hospital if it gets too much."

Kathy gives her head a vigorous shake. "No, he doesn't want that I know."

"The best we can hope for is that he'll slip into a coma. But there are no guarantees."

Kathy covers her nose and mouth with her hand, keeping the lump in her throat at bay, but her eyes can't deny the reality of the frail, yellow man dozing in the bed in her living room. Her dance partner, her late-night

137

monster movie guardian, her two and a half and a peanut Daddy is fading like a Kodachrome photograph. Is she fooling herself to think she can pull this off? Be the emotional and physical rock this role demands? Hell, she nearly vomits emptying the bedpan. No, she must see this to the end. Her father will look out to the distant sea surrounded by whatever family he has. The show must go on and Kathy will find the strength.

"By the way, my sister may or may not come to visit," she tells Brian after a heavy sigh restores her resolve. "She's a violinist with an orchestra and has a concert in LA in a few months. Says she'll try to stop by, but she was always closer to our Mom. Not much sympathy for Daddy. I don't know what I'll tell him if she doesn't show."

"All you can do is encourage her to come. The end of life is fraught with drama. It brings up stuff you thought was long buried, and stuff that surprises the hell out of you. Has Lenore been staying with you?"

"Off and on. I think she feels like a third wheel. Probably my bad on that. I'm grateful she was there for him, but so was I and," she swallows hard to keep down the bitterness, "he's *my* Daddy."

Brian reaches over and covers her hand in that comforting way that nurses do. A lone tear runs down her cheek before she quickly wipes it away with her other hand.

"Don't be afraid to cry, Kathy. Even guitars gently weep," Brian says.

Kathy smiles back. He just referenced a Beatles song. Where has this guy been all her life?

CHAPTER 21

Margaret stares at the solid-red number one on her answering machine. The message has been there for months. She's not sure if she saves it as verbal self-flagellation or to rekindle her anger when it too often grows cold. There were others, less vile and abusive harangues that nevertheless shook her to her core, but she deleted those. Not this one. Denise tells her she's mad to listen to it; her lawyer advised her to keep it to make the case that her husband is a violent thug deserving of jail time. It's the only time she's ignored Denise's counsel.

Perched on the edge of the chair, her hand grips the cushion before pressing the play button, and she braces for the onslaught. The F-bombs and C-words; the degrading rants on her body, her intelligence, and her sanity; the promises to harm, burn, and destroy her cat, home, and life spoken by the guttural voice of a demon. Four months ago, she would have needed sedation afterwards. Today, though it still hits her hard, she will use it as legal and psychological ammunition as she meets with her nemesis and his lawyers.

Margaret times her entry into the revolving glass doors at the law office where she's meeting the attorney handling her divorce. She's never liked the claustrophobic feeling, worrying whether she'll be able to exit when the time comes. Much like her marriage to Jeff. She regards it as a good sign that she's not still circling and has been spit out into the lobby.

Margaret hasn't seen her husband since early January and is surprised he doesn't look different. Not baggy-eyed, sallow, haggard, unshaven at minimum with his jacket wrinkled, tie askew, his shirt with soiled cuffs. She wants some indication that he's been sleepless, feeling remorse for his actions, missing her company. But, no, he wears his power suit, the gray pinstripe Armani complete with vest, looking the picture of health and confidence. Like nothing happened. Just as she feared.

She wears her classic but dated navy blue Chanel suit with a single strand of pearls. Her hair is pulled back in a low ponytail that only accentuates her gaunt face. Her wedding ring remains on her finger. She notices that his is gone.

Margaret wanted to avoid a lengthy, adversarial court battle, preferring to dissolve the marriage with a diplomatic *tete-a-tete* between the two parties and their counsels leading to a mutually acceptable arrangement. Apparently Jeff did not get the memo and has brought his gun to her knife fight.

She and her lone attorney, an unassuming middle-aged man with kind eyes, sit across the expanse of mahogany table from Jeff and his representatives, two smartly dressed-to-kill men and one traitorous woman, brought along no doubt to counter any feminine defense. As if he reads her mind, her lawyer puts his arm around her chair and whispers reassuring comments about her strong case and the law being on her side to counter the show of strength and gamesmanship displayed by Jeff and his team.

Multiple copies of forms, papers, and evidentiary matter are removed from Italian leather briefcases and stacked in front of the litigants. A stenographer sits with fingers poised waiting to transcribe the conversations. Jeff leans back in his chair, his fingers tented, and gives her a steely glare. Margaret stares into her lap and picks at her cuticles.

Margaret's attorney fires the first volley in the settlement negotiations.

"I trust you've had a chance to review my client's latest offer. You can see she has been most generous with the terms, providing a fair division of assets that gives Mr. King a most comfortable life, post-divorce. Considering your client's behavior over the course of the marriage and specifically on New Year's Eve 2009, he should be counting his lucky stars."

Jeff's first chair is a beefy man with slicked back hair, the epitome of the term shyster. He pulls himself erect, dominating the chair and the room, and speaks in rounded tones belying his appearance.

"We agree that the estate in Stamford should remain with Mrs. King as it is a residence that has been in her family for generations. The apartment in Paris also falls under that category. However, we feel that since Mr. King has been forced from his domicile of some twenty years, an allocation of funds to provide for lodgings now and in the future needs to be addressed. Since he currently practices law in New York City, not inexpensive as you know, a sum in the area of twenty thousand dollars per month seems appropriate."

Margaret shakes her head imperceptibly, peering over her reading glasses at Jeff. How could he possibly need twenty thousand dollars a month? She scribbles a note to her lawyer. 'He has more than enough money.'

"Has there been a change in Mr. King's employment?" he asks. "We were under the impression that his income from retainers, billable hours, and other fees is in the upper six figures, which should certainly be enough for even a luxury apartment in the City."

"My client's income varies, as it does with all who practice law, depending on his caseload. And there are management fees, insurance and maintenance, and utilities that must be taken into account."

Jeff gives Margaret a crooked smile before turning to face his lawyer and whispering to him, his mouth covered with his hand. The lawyer listens attentively but pushes back as if disinclined to follow up with what he hears. He and his colleagues slide their chairs into a semicircle and confer.

When they return to their places, the female attorney takes the lead.

"I understand that Mrs. King has recently left her position with Sacred Heart University," she states, her words directed at Margaret. "We are concerned that the loss of this steady income from her teaching position might affect our client's promised payments. Perhaps there needs to be a greater amount allocated to Mr. King now to cover any future shortfalls, what with her needing to maintain both the Connecticut and Paris properties. Perhaps forty thousand would make him feel more comfortable."

As a smug little grin creeps across Jeff's face, Margaret fill her glass with water and takes several sips.

"Dr. King is on a temporary leave of absence, and has been assured she can return at her choosing. Mr. King is a well-qualified and well compensated attorney. I doubt he will come to ruin without support from Dr. King," her counsel chuckles. "Perhaps he might want to explore the idea of budgeting."

Margaret allows the corners of her mouth to inch up for the first time today.

"But isn't it also true that she left her position because of a mental breakdown wherein she assaulted a

student? Are you a danger to others, Dr. King?" the female attorney insinuates, her voice slithering across the
table. "Are you even competent to manage your affairs?"

Margaret can't believe Jeff is throwing this in her
face. Her *mentis* is quite *compos*, she longs to shout. Her
jaw clenches as she tightens her fists in her lap, imagining the remains of his repugnant, manipulative, socio-
pathic head oozing out from between her fingers.

She takes a deep breath, willing herself not to lose it,
and gives her husband a fierce stare.

"Your source is unreliable, Ma'am. There was no assault. She is quite sane, no thanks to Mr. King, and fully
able to attend to her finances. On the other hand, we have
grave concerns regarding Mr. King's ability to monitor
his accounts."

Jeff shifts in his chair, rubbing the back of his neck.
He swallows hard before taking his own large gulp of
water. Margaret can feel the tide shifting but, unaccus-
tomed to being on the crest of the wave, she moves her
fingers along her pearls, a rosary from the sea, to petition
to a higher power.

Her attorney slides copies of bank statements and
credit card bills across the table, items and lines high-
lighted in yellow, and continues his litany of Jeff's of-
fenses.

"He has lived off the largesse of his wife for most of
their marriage, racking up a number of debts due to his
alcoholism, adultery, and poor decisions. The prenup he
signed specifically provides for his welfare upon disso-
lution of marriage to my client, but ...," her attorney
pauses for effect, "is null and void if he is convicted of
any criminal actions. Dr. King would have been well
within her rights to file assault charges on December 31.
That option remains a possibility."

Boom. The shot lands hard. Jeff reaches up to loosen the constricting silk tie that encircles his neck. As Margaret watches his discomfort, she relishes the sweet taste of revenge. See how that feels, you bastard?

"Mr. King has no legal right to any of the monies in Dr. King's trust," her lawyer continues. "Since Connecticut is a community property state, he is entitled by law to half the income accrued while married, plus shares of stock in his name from the company previously owned by her father. Any personal belongings purchased with Mr. King have been catalogued. She has listed those items she wishes to retain, and he may do the same."

This is going way better than Margaret had ever expected. Perhaps justice will prevail today. She relaxes her shoulders and allows herself to settle into the chair.

"In lieu of this arrangement, Dr. King is willing to offer Mr. King a one-time ten-million-dollar payout provided he drops any further claims and actions against my client and refrains from any further contact. Mr. King, you have caused my client grievous physical and emotional harm. She owes you nothing while you owe her everything. Gentlemen, Ma'am, we await your response."

Jeff leans toward his team of legal advisors, waiting for them to jump in and fight for his cause. When no objections or rebuttals are forthcoming, he scowls and flings the pile of papers stacked in front of him to the floor. Margaret edges her chair back, knowing the pot has begun boiling and could overflow at any moment.

Margaret's attorney gathers his briefs except for the settlement papers, which he passes to opposing counsel. He eases out of his chair and helps Margaret to her feet, their hands lingering in an embrace of team solidarity.

Jeff shoves his chair backwards, upending it as he stands. He stomps over to Margaret, his face deep red, spittle on his jutting chin, and levels an upper cut toward

144

Margaret's head. Her advocate deftly shoves her out of the way, and the jab instead catches him square on his nose. Margaret's earnest attempts to defend him prove futile and Jeff pummels him wildly, blood spattering onto clothing and the shiny table.

After a seemingly undue amount of time, the female attorney calls security and the men rush to the aid of their colleague. As Margaret watches the guards sort out the shiver of sharks, it's obvious Mr. King, Esquire will now need counsel from a whole different legal specialty.

Margaret offers tissues and words of comfort to her champion while they wait for the EMT's. She can toss that recording of Jeff's aggressive threats. The live show has been so much more compelling. And his much-argued living expenses? She expects he'll be sharing a rent free cell for the foreseeable future.

HELP

CHAPTER 22

It's another crazy day for Susan. Up before the crack of dawn, and now that it's nearly summer, the dawn cracks even earlier. Their once hallowed morning meal is now hit or miss as she rarely sees Steve until nine now that she's baking at The Homestead. Still she stops at the John Deere store on her way home to deliver his promised roll, though his enthusiasm for his favorite treat is waning, and more often than not he declines it.

Susan has had little appetite herself for weeks now. A blessing in disguise. She was sure being around all the sweets would be her undoing, but since February she's dropped ten pounds and no longer has permanent elastic marks around her belly. She nibbles a piece of dry toast left over from the breakfast shift as she hurries home to tend to Bungalow Bill before picking up Jenny for her appointment this morning.

⌘⌘⌘⌘⌘

The soft-beige walls in the obstetrician's waiting room in the Medical Center of Aurora complex are lined with charts summarizing prenatal milestones, brightly colored paintings of parents and children, and photos of babies who have passed through the practice, in utero and out. Susan and her granddaughter check in at the reception desk and find seats amid the women sitting in the wood and fabric chairs, their bellies in varying degrees of protrusion. A few older mothers-to-be are flipping distractedly through the pages of magazines, checking their watches at regular intervals as their biological clocks tick down. Others sit at odd angles in their chairs, near-term abdomens denying a position of either comfort or support, as they fan themselves with anything that creates a breeze.

Jenny and Susan do not see any other teens today, so Jenny retreats inside her headphones. At twenty weeks, Jenny has developed her baby bump, though it's hidden beneath her oversized top and crossed arms. Susan basked in the glow of her pregnancies though she was not much older than Jenny at her first, but enlarging breasts, a heartbeat, and finally fetal movement has convinced Jenny that this baby thing is real. Maureen, on the other hand, prefers to ignore reality.

Susan and Jenny broke the news shortly after the official confirmation. Justin, the apparent sperm donor, has been slow to acknowledge his responsibility in the matter, and is showing little interest in marriage or fatherhood. Jenny's father asked the who, when, and why questions, and though disappointed, he seems ready to accept the facts. But Maureen just prattled on about Jenny losing out on college and being doomed to a life on the dole unless the child is whisked out of her life.

"Jennifer?"

"Here," Susan replies, tapping Jenny on her arm to extract her from the depths of rock and roll before they both rise from their chairs.

"Coming back with her today, Mrs. Anderson?" Susan nods and reaches for Jenny's hand. "I see we're doing an ultrasound today. Is your bladder full?"

"Oh, my God, yes," Jenny groans, extending a nearly empty plastic jug of water. "Two of these so far."

"Try to hold it just a bit longer. Let's get your weight and blood pressure."

There's a knock on the door of exam room #3, and Renee, the nurse practitioner who has been following Susan's granddaughter since mid-February, breezes in to them.

"Good morning, Jenny," she says. "How's it going today?"

"Gotta pee, but otherwise OK, I guess. Just chillin' now that I've graduated."

"Congratulations. You're halfway there with your pregnancy, but baby has lots of growing left to do. A few quick questions, and then we'll take a peek. Noticing baby moving around?"

"Yeah. That just started. I was expecting a real punch, but it was more like a little twitch. Justin felt it once but didn't think it was a big deal," Jenny sighs, caressing her belly as if to reassure her little one that he or she matters.

It's all Susan can do to not to shout, 'Justin, you little twit. It's a very big deal.'

"That must have been disappointing," Renee says, a practiced non-judgmental tone in her voice. She pulls up Jenny's medical information on the computer. "Your weight gain is adequate but get ready for an increase of about a pound a week. Blood pressure's normal but we'll check for protein and sugar in your urine after the sonogram. How about swelling in your hands or feet, bad headaches, spotting, contractions?"

Jenny shakes her head after each item and then asks, "That's normal, right?"

"Yes. Any decisions about keeping or adopting yet?"

Jenny meets Susan's eyes but doesn't answer. Susan rises from her chair beside the exam table to wrap an arm

151

around her granddaughter's shoulders. Trying to get the players in this drama on the same page has been like herding cats. Of course raising this child will be a burden on Jenny and the family, and dreams put on hold may never be fulfilled, but to let this child pass out of their life? That won't happen this time if she can help it.

"It's a tough choice but you need a plan," Renee urges. "Waiting until the delivery or afterwards is only harder. Talk it over but you need to make a decision."

"Thank you, Renee," Susan says, giving Jenny a squeeze. "We'll work on it."

"Now, let's lie you down and take some pictures. Do you want to know the sex?"

"Um, not yet," Jenny says.

Renee squirts the cold gel onto Jenny's abdomen inducing a little yelp from her. As she pushes down around her flattening belly button with the transducer, Susan and Jenny gape as black and white shadows appear on the screen. And while it's a little fuzzy, there is definitely a baby in there.

"Look, there," she points. "There's the head and the arms. And, see right there? Your baby's heart is beating. A nice rate of 150."

Jenny says nothing, only listening and gripping Susan's hand as the rhythmic swishing fills the room. Susan remembers hearing her own children's heartbeats. They used a stethoscope back then, but the confirmation that a living being was inside her, growing into a little person who would bring joy and sometimes heartbreak, always filled her with a love that almost hurt.

While Renee is busy clicking the mouse at spots on the monitor and typing on the keyboard, the two women squint to see the nose and the toes and all the other parts the nurse practitioner is pointing out. Like searching for the hidden objects in a *Highlights for Children* magazine.

"Everything looks great. Want me to print this out?"

"Yes, yes." The words tumble out of Susan's mouth before she realizes Jenny isn't clapping her hands with glee along with her. "I mean if you want it, Sweetie."

"Sure, Gramma," Jenny whispers. "That'd be cool."

Of course, if Jenny hadn't wanted the photo, Susan would have sneaked back and got one anyway. No way the miracle of life can be denied now. It's all there in grainy black and white. So why does Susan feel like the floor is dropping out from beneath her while her heart is racing upstairs? Just like back in December at Walmart. 'Mom' hasn't shown up in a while. Maybe she's here to check in on her great-great grandchild.

"I'm sure you need the bathroom, Jenny, so except for the urine sample we're done. Pick up the handouts at the front desk and when I see you next month, we'll talk about plans for the baby. Mrs. Anderson, are you all right?"

The nurse's voice is lost in the tinny roar that fills Susan's head. She sways on rubbery legs before collapsing in a pool of blackness with Jenny's panicked "Gramma, Gramma" following her down.

Her eyes open to Renee's concerned face as the nurse kneels beside her, two fingers on her wrist.

"You stepped out for a bit, Susan." Renee starts pressing on Susan's head like she's checking an avocado for ripeness before giving her arms and legs the same treatment. As she waves a light back and forth across her eyes, she asks, "Does anything hurt? Are you having chest pains?"

"What, no, I don't think so," she grunts trying to push herself up.

"No, no, just lay back. Ever faint before?"

"Almost. When the Beatles were on *Ed Sullivan*." Susan gives a listless grin, trying to put on a brave face. "I didn't eat much today. That's probably it."

153

"Let's get a wheelchair and send her over to the ED," Renee tells the nursing assistant who responded to Renee's call for help. Turning back to Susan, she says with a calm and assured voice, "They'll check you over, run some tests, figure out what happened."

"Where's my Jenny? Is she all right?" Susan asks, her voice anything but tranquil.

"Gramma, I'm here," Jenny says rushing to Susan's side. "I couldn't wait any longer. I had to pee so bad."

The nurse wheels Susan, with Jenny trailing behind, through doors, down halls, and into an elevator, until they arrive at the emergency room, otherwise known as Hurry up and Wait.

Feeling a bit like the little red pin cushion in her sewing box after two hours of prodding and poking, she now rests undisturbed except for the beeping of the heart monitor and the pull of the IV tubing taped to her arm. She hears the jangle of metal as a nurse pulls the curtain back and Jenny's head peeks in.

"All righty then, are we having fun yet?" Susan jokes hoping to lighten the mood. Apparently it's too soon.

"Oh, Gramma, I thought you were dead," Jenny wails, rushing to the gurney and falling across Susan's chest, her muffled sobs trapped in Susan's hospital gown. She rubs Jenny's back, her IV tubing swaying with each "there, there" motion until she relaxes. "So what happened?"

"Sweetie, I'm so sorry I scared you like that. And right after we saw the baby." Jenny sits up and Susan dabs her tear-stained cheeks with the hem of the sheet. "Apparently my heart got to beating so fast it made me faint," Susan explains, her hand patting the unruly organ. "Too much stress, they think. Need to take it easy. I'd hate to do that at the delivery and miss everything."

"For sure." Jenny reaches inside her jean jacket. "So hey, you up for looking at my baby?"

154

CHAPTER 23

Linda tucks her newly shorn locks into the netting of the wig, adjusting it with a pull down in front and a slide to the right before securing it with bobby pins. Except for the day of surgery, she's covered up her own thick tresses with the custom faux hair. They say chemo may change the texture or color after it grows back in. She wishes it wouldn't fall out in the first place.

She wants nothing to look out of the ordinary for one day longer, especially now as she readies to make the big reveal to her daughter. Susan, on her case for weeks to get things out in the open, will be her wing woman as they all meet up for lunch.

It feels liberating to drive once again, unencumbered by bandages and pain, as she weaves her Lexus through the weekend traffic on the short five-block jaunt from her Cherry Creek condo to NoRTH's. She follows her favorite hostess to her regular booth by the window and flips through the menu she knows by heart. Her friend is nothing if not punctual, and at 11:30 on the dot, Jackie and Susan amble into the upscale Italian bistro, chatting away in that easy manner that eludes Linda and her daughter. She waves them over to the table, easing herself out to share a hug and how are you. Thank God Susan remembers to reign in her legendary vigorous embrace. Susan scoots in on one side, while Linda and Jackie share the opposite space.

"Linda, I just came from Jackie's shop, what a great place, so many interesting things, and look what I bought." Susan turns her head to the side, pulling her hair back to reveal a dangling red crystal earring. "So not me, right, contemporary and all, but Jackie says they look great on me, brighten my face. They were forty-five bucks, and Steve will probably have a conniption but, hey," she says with her palms raised in a devil-may-care attitude, "besides my wedding ring, it's my only real piece of jewelry."

"Auntie Suze, I'll buy them for you if it's a problem," Jackie offers. "We can call it a gift,"

"No, I needed to do this for me. Anyway, I'll just sell a dozen cinnamon rolls and call it square."

"Yes, they're lovely. Shall we order? How does spinach tortellini and Caesar salads sound?" Linda asks, wanting to move things along. Hearing no objections, she hails the waiter and requests the food. "Plus two iced teas and a glass of Pinot Noir, please."

Susan gives Linda a raised eyebrow at her choice of beverage, no doubt worried it is detrimental to her health. But this will be the last alcohol to touch her lips until the chemo finishes, so raise two brows if you want, Susan. She's having a glass of vino. Maybe two.

"Haven't heard much from you since dinner at the club in January, Mom."

"I know, it's been too long, but life, you know," Linda says, fiddling with her silverware. "So catch me up on your plans. Before you get started though, any chance of moving the date to later in the fall? What about a Christmas wedding? This area is so pretty during the holidays."

"It's a little late for that," Jackie frowns, "since we're already booked for September at a venue in Boulder. I mean our flowers are blooming as we speak. We'll lose our deposit if we change."

"No, no, not to worry. You've made your plans, and I'm sure it will be lovely," Linda sighs and hurries a sip of wine.

"Anyway, Auntie Suze, loved the green ideas for the wedding. We're gonna do Evites, and since the ceremony's at a family farm, we'll get our locally produced vegetarian menu. Rhiannon, you met her today, is making my dress, I'm designing the rings, and we have friends who'll do the music. So if you do the cake, then everything's covered. We're only inviting about fifty people. That lemon curd and white chocolate one we sampled was A. Mazing. With your friends coming out and your bakery business taking off, you must be busy."

"Oh, thank goodness you said that," Susan says with a deep exhalation. "I had a health scare a week ago, fainted at Jenny's doctor, and I'm under orders to take it easy."

"Are you all right?" Linda asks, the nurse in her never far from the surface.

"Yeah, just stress they said, but I'm so glad you still want me to create your wedding cake, Jackie. That's what I had my heart set on anyway. It all works out, huh? Now I'll have more time to concentrate on our reunion. Linda, it's going to be such a hoot. Major girl time."

The waiter arrives with the food, and while Susan and Jackie dive into their entrees, Linda mostly stares at her salad, rearranging the lettuce with her fork in between multiple sips of her Pinot. The hodge podge of conversation ranges from high school then and now, current trends in matrimonial etiquette, and the latest celebrity couplings. Linda's mind is elsewhere.

Linda lays down her fork, lining it up with her other silverware, and wipes her mouth with her napkin before folding it under her plate. She shoots a laser stare at Susan and waits for their eyes to connect, giving her a sign, a psychic go ahead to rip this damn band-aid off. Susan finally catches Linda's drift and slides her arm across the table, her palm up and open. When Linda rests her own hand on top, she gives it a squeeze. A long shaky breath flows in and out of Linda's lungs, and she lays everything on the table.

"Jackie," she says turning toward her daughter, "I found a lump in my breast and had surgery a month ago. It was very small, early stage ..."

"Oh my god." Jackie's eyes widen on her pale face and she pushes against the table as if that will keep the news at bay. "Why didn't you tell me? Does Daddy know?"

"Yes, your father's been told, for what it's worth. And my staff and Susan, but I didn't want to worry you."

Linda reaches with her other hand to rub her daughter's shoulder, but Jackie jerks away, her arms crisscrossing her chest as if shielding her heart. With Jackie focused on the ceiling, Linda searches her lap for what to say. This wasn't how this was supposed to go.

As life goes on around them, time stands still in this little corner of the room. Jackie's eyes are closed, her hand covers her mouth, and she shakes her head whenever Linda tries to break through the silence. Even Susan has her index finger to her lips, encouraging quiet. At last Jackie opens up, apparently ready to continue the conversation.

"Did ... did you think I'd fall apart," her voice catching as she speaks. "That ... that ... I wouldn't be strong enough to handle this. I'm not fourteen anymore. Give me some credit."

"I know, I know ... but with the wedding and ..." Linda begins.

Jackie raises her hand and turns away, stopping her mother's explanation. After several slow breaths she angles back then leans in.

"Is this why you wanted to change the date? What else aren't you telling me?"

"Nothing, it's just that with the chemo, I'll probably be tired, maybe nauseated. I was hoping for a little cushion, just in case. I'll be done with treatment well before the wedding but it's just ... I promised I'd be there for you."

"Of course, you'll be there for her, Linda." Susan clasps Linda's hand in her right and then Jackie's in her left. "And Jackie will be there for you too. That's what mothers and daughters do." She draws the intertwined fingers to the center of the table and with an encouraging nod, signals for Linda and Jackie to join hands. "They say it takes a village. This is your village. If we can't count on each other, what's the point?"

CHAPTER 24

The layers of orange and crimson project onto the sky as Kathy and her father screen another Technicolor twilight nestled alongside each other in the best seats in the house, Patrick's tricked out hospital bed.

"Wow. If I have to ride off into the sunset, let it be into one of these." Patrick's voice is weak but full of admiration for one of Mother Nature's masterstrokes. "Wish I had the strength to paint. Just one more. One more."

Kathy squeezes his hand. "I have your paint and brushes, Daddy. It'll only take a minute to set it up. I'd love to watch you do your *thang*. Or we could do it together. See if I inherited any of your talent."

"Nah, better leave well enough alone. Always thought I could paint better with a few under my belt."

Tears tumble down the waterfall of jutting cheekbones, past the rocky cleft of his chin, meandering along the green oxygen tubing before pooling in the folds of his neck. Kathy wipes her father's face with her fingertips and presses his hand to her cheek.

It's been a rough day. Another visit to the hospital to drain his belly. Like tapping a keg, her Dad says. The fluid is building up more quickly, needing trips in the ambucab twice a week now. No sign of infection this time, but he got a little light-headed and needed an IV. Before the sea swallows the sun, her father is asleep.

Kathy heard from her sister Mary yesterday. She's here for the concert but says her time is limited. She'll try to call but won't be stopping by. Her father hasn't mentioned her visit in a while; either he's forgotten or figures she's blown him off. Kathy will leave it, let it be a surprise if and when she phones.

Lenore is back in San Diego for the time being, needing to check on the business and residence. In snippets of conversations, Kathy learned she met Patrick at an AA meeting ten years ago. She was sober for two years by then and offered to be his sponsor, but he refused, something about putting burdens on a woman. Instead they became friends and eventually more, sharing a love of art and a bed.

It no longer upsets her that her Dad found someone else. Her mother never did and the resentments and bitterness festered inside until cancer devoured her. That was her choice, and it is Mary's choice on how, when, or if she says her final good-bye. Forgiveness has less to do with the forgiven than with the forgiver. That lesson is slowly sinking in.

Kathy purees carrots, greens, and an apple in the blender, doubling the amounts in case her father wants to share her smoothie. She gives him Ensure and water through his stomach tube when he has no appetite or refuses to eat. Eventually, eating will become a moot point. The whir of grinding food wakes him and he cries out.

"Daddy, it's OK. It's OK," Kathy says rushing over to him.

"Where am I?" His eyes wander, searching the room for her face.

"You're here with me, Daddy." Kathy stands by the bed, rubbing his shoulder until his vision, and mind, come into focus. "How about a shake?" she asks, holding up the glass of green froth.

"Got anything stronger?" They say the hearing is the last to go. For her father, Kathy suspects it will be his humor.

His sober chip had been in his pocket on admission to the hospital and rests near his bedside even now, but Lenore says the craving for a little nip may never go away completely. Kathy wonders if it would really matter at this point if she added a little rum to his drink. Or at least an umbrella.

"We're teetotalers here, remember. How about a movie?"

"What's on the marquee?"

"A classic Sci-fi marathon. *The Day the Earth Stood Still, The Blob, Them.*" She plucks them off the shelf and stacks them in her arms. She holds up the last one with James Whitmore fending off enormous pincered insects. "I remember this one scared the bejeezus out of me. Whenever the giant ants came on, I'd hide my face in your shirt until you told me it was safe to look. You always kept the bad things away, Daddy."

"Except when I became one of those bad things, Baby Girl. I didn't want to hurt you. Jinx it for you by showing up at a premiere or play, acting like an idiot, ruining your chances. 'Who's that drunken old fool' they'd say when they snapped their pictures. So I stayed out of your life."

"But, I didn't care, Daddy. I needed you ..."\

Her voice squeezes through crumpling lips and Kathy tosses the DVD's on the bed. She retreats to her shelves, flipping mindlessly through the rest of her collection, trying to collect herself. But the dialogue for this unfinished script isn't in the rom-coms, the musicals, nor Shakespeare's tragedies. It's written on her heart, and she exhales and pivots to face him.

"But when you did show up, it was the best day of my life, even if you weren't always the Daddy I was hoping to see. Why didn't you keep in touch? I stayed here, at our home, so you'd always know where I was. I could have given you money, supported you."

Her father is silent, his head and shoulders collapsing into his bony chest as if Toto has pulled the curtain away, revealing the false god. The rose-colored glasses removed, Kathy sees arms that once lifted her to snatch oranges from trees only clutching half-empty bottles of cheap whiskey. Pictures legs that waltzed and jigged now staggering down alleys to topple onto trash heaps. And stares into eyes yellowed not with age but forty years of addiction.

Forced past the excuses, the truth that her father is a drunkard, a sot, a wino who deserted her, ignites a smoldering fire in her chest, a volcanic rumbling in her ears as years of buried resentment gets ready to spew. Her dying father lies helpless before her as she struggles to hold back the words she knows she'll regret, but knows must be said. Glaring at him, she swallows hard, but they explode from her mouth anyway.

"All I ever wanted was to have you back in my life. I turned down projects. Hell, I turned down men. Waiting for you. Waiting for you to walk with me on the red carpet. Walk me down the fucking aisle."

Suddenly Kathy can't bear looking at her father and escapes to the far corner of the window, her hands tingling, her breathing ragged, and focuses on the light from the full moon coming through the trees. What the hell is wrong with her? Screaming at her Daddy like that. Who's the fool now? What if those are the last words he hears from her?

She covers her mouth with her hands, shaking through several deep breaths, trying to regain her composure. She inches back around, praying that her father still breathes. Seeing his watery eyes blink, her face caves in on itself and she barrels to the bed, stubbing her toe on the roller.

"Daddy, Daddy, I'm so sorry. I'm so sorry. Say something, Daddy. Please."

"I take it you're mad?" he says with a nonchalant grin.

"Oh, you." She bends over to take his wrinkled face in her hands, alternating between laughter and tears as the pain in her little piggy now comes all the way home. "Can you forgive me?"

"In a heartbeat. Can *you* forgive *me*?"

"I love you, Daddy. Two and a half and a peanut."

"And I love you, three and a half and two peanuts."

Kathy wipes her nose and cheek on her shirt sleeve like she's five years old, once again giggling with the father who could do no wrong. "Hey, I know what we can watch. One of my favorites."

Kathy collects the movies scattered on the bed and shoves them on the book shelf. She sweeps through the remaining discs and pulls out one more.

"I think this one will be perfect. It makes me smile. *A Hard Day's Night.*"

CHAPTER 25

Margaret smooths the sand in the table top Zen garden with the miniature rake as she waits for Dr. Hall, her regular therapist, to return. She's been spending more time outdoors, reacquainting herself with the flora on her estate, trying her hand at horticulture. The late spring daffodils are in their prime and the roses are just budding, the peachy pink petals soon to unfold with abandon. As Anaïs Nin said, "And the day came when the risk to remain tight in the bud was more painful than the risk it took to bloom." Margaret smiles. She is ready to bloom.

"Sorry about the interruption," Dr. Hall says, settling back in her chair, notepad on her lap. "My time is all yours now. As I said before, you are looking well. How are things?"

"Quite good. My life seems to be finding a new equilibrium. My divorce is final end of July. Hallelujah," she says, her fist raised ever so slightly. "I'm working on moving forward, learning to enjoy being on my own. Can't believe I waited so long to leave."

"I assume the restraining order is still in place."

She covers her mouth with her fingers to contain a quick laugh. "You could say that. He's serving six months in jail for assaulting my lawyer. Finally, something stuck. He's been disbarred but I'm sure he'll petition to be reinstated somewhere. I offered a fair, take it or leave it compensation, and now he's totally off my books and my doorstep. And, I'm changing my name," Margaret says, pausing for a deep breath before announcing her new title. "Martinet-King. If 'King' wasn't attached to my professional life, it would be history."

So why is she still wearing his stupid ring? She glances at the nice but less than spectacular diamond. Most likely out of habit. Brush, floss, put on the ring. She hasn't decided whether to keep it, transform it, sell it, or dump it in Long Island Sound. What if it's some satanic talisman binding him to her? She shoves her hand under her skirt to block the bad juju until she realizes how irrational that looks and brings the bedeviled bauble back out.

"Stay vigilant, Margaret. How's work?"

"I'm leaving Sacred Heart, at least temporarily," she lowers her eyes and whispers, "after my little, um, dust-up. I decided against a sabbatical, tied to an agenda and time line and all. But, I want to travel, maybe do some writing."

Margaret shifts her eyes back to her wedding band, sliding it up and down between her knuckles, exposing the indentation in her flesh caused by years of wear. She shakes her head with a realization.

"You know that story about the elephant chained all his life to a stump, unaware of his strength, assuming he's trapped in place. That's me. Even now that I'm un-shackled," she says holding up her ringed finger, "the visible and invisible reminders of my imprisonment keep holding me back. I need to open up to my power, my options."

"Fifty points for Hufflepuff," Dr. Hall smiles. "As Boomer women empty their nests and head into retirement, many are rethinking lackluster marriages and pondering new purposes. The curtain is opening on their Third Act and they're ready to forget what was, reframe what is, explore the what ifs, and jolt everyone with a few what the hells. What about you?"

"I guess I'm hoping for a few what the hells." Margaret scoots her hips to the back of the couch, straightening her spine with her head held high. Never one for gesticulating as she speaks, preferring to get her point across with the precise word, she finds her hands now floating about her face in a fluid dance, fingers extending and balling into fists as she outlines her plans.

"First off, I'm heading back to Colorado at the end of August for a reunion with high school friends. It's been over forty years, and I can't wait to be back with the Girls and the fresh air of the Rockies. Then I'm off to Europe. I've spent time there with parents and on business, but I want to ... you know, experience it." Her outstretched fingers emphasize the word and her eyes close to envision the scene. "Gliding down the Avon with Shakespeare. Walking along the Seine with Gertrude Stein. Getting up close and personal with DaVinci and Michelangelo. Sipping a proper high tea or lingering at a sidewalk café with crepes or gelato."

"Can I come with you?" Dr. Hall laughs. "Seeing this sparkle in your eyes, hearing your enthusiasm. I'm so happy for you, Margaret. What will you do with your house? Rent it, sell it?"

"No, I'll keep it. It's been in my family a long time. I know, there are bad memories there, but some good ones as well. Right now Denise is there with me. She'll watch my cat while I'm gallivanting around. With all that space maybe I should create a commune for crones," she says, a self-satisfied smile at her spontaneous proposal.

"Seriously though, Denise and I have talked about how important the company of women is to us, our friends and colleagues. She's my role model for 'an independent woman of a certain age.' She's always lived on her own terms, never crushed under men's thumbs like I was. Once upon a time I believed that all you needed was love and a man. Not anymore."

Margaret shudders, swallowing hard as the sour taste of bile rises in her throat at the thought of her romantic encounters with Jeff. A drunken slob pawing at her genitals, his mix of scotch and Cool Water aftershave making her gag, hoping against hope that he, or at least she, would pass out.

"What I wanted from Jeff wasn't sex, but affection. A tender touch, a hug from the heart, a hand to hold in good times and bad. With him it was get down to business and then roll over."

"Well, I do think women are often more able to express that kind of intimacy. Don't you and Denise display some of those behaviors with each other?"

"Well, yes, but I mean we're not ... gay," she says, the word sticking in her mouth.

"And if one or both of you were? Would that worry you?"

"It certainly worries the Catholic Church and Sacred Heart University. No, we're just good friends. She's like, well, she's like John, my favorite Beatle. An intellectual, witty and irreverent. Doesn't take guff from anyone, stands up for what she believes. We have similar interests, get each other's humor. We often talk for hours like Lewis Carroll's Walrus and Carpenter, of 'shoes and ships and sealing wax, of cabbages and kings' ..."

Oh, my God. She just admitted not wanting anything to do with men and now she's going on and on about Denise as if ... does that mean ... could she be? Is this her first what the hell moment?

IF I NEEDED SOMEONE

CHAPTER 26

The ten o'clock news is over, and Steve is still not home. No calls from him at work or on his cell, Susan's calls going directly to voice mail. She sat on her anxiety all evening, avoided ringing Maureen, Shirley, and the volunteer fire chief because this morning he said he might be late. But this is worst-case scenario late. You've got some 'splainin' to do late.

At midnight Susan feels the bed jostle, rousing her from a fitful sleep. She turns to face Steve as he slips into their bed. An audible exhale makes sure he knows she's awake.

"You could have called," she says.

"I said I'd be late. It's just later than I thought," Steve answers, his voice as cold as his side of the bed. He rolls away from her, pulling the sheet around him.

"Ya think? What in God's name lasts til midnight in this town? I was worried, you know. What were you doing?"

"Nothing. Nothing. I was with the guys from school. All right? We got to talking and lost track of time. Look, I'm tired. Can't we talk in the morning?"

"Sure. Good night." Susan flips back over with an exaggerated bounce. Steve smells of bourbon and cigarettes. And a musky, mesmerizing siren scent. The kind that enchants men into steering onto the rocks.

⌘⌘⌘⌘⌘

Susan washes the dried matter from her eyes and squirts a stinging drop of Visine onto the bloodshot whites, but nothing can conceal the deep purple arcs beneath. It's Saturday, and Steve still sleeps, the stop and start of the freight train in his throat providing cover as she dresses in the closet. She picks up the shirt he wore last night, as always tossed next to the hamper but not in it. Good thing his sport was football and not basketball. She tells herself to just throw it in, but her nose has other plans, and she presses it to her face. Definitely smoke. Hard to get out of a bar without the acrid odor permeating everything. The Jack Daniels is gone ... but not the perfume. It's not a scent that she's ever worn. It rises up from his collar and fills her with nausea. The muddle of her midnight mind automatically locks out the forgivable explanations leaving only the nuclear option. Steve is fooling around.

In the kitchen she pours Bungalow Bill's kibble into his raised dish, adding a bit of water to soften it. As she watches him gulp the mixture with apparent gusto, she forces herself to eat a banana that her stomach clearly does not want. Looking into his cloudy eyes, she gives him a playful tug around his ears, envying his uncomplicated life. Dog and mistress leave the house through the patio door. Bill does his business in the yard and returns to doggie dreams in the dewy grass. Susan heads to her business at the restaurant. Dreams eluded her last night.

Since her health scare in April, she's shed a bushel of burdens and another ten pounds by exercising diligently and watching her diet. Maureen, currently on summer break, is transporting Jenny to doctor appointments and Lamaze classes, though Susan still serves as doula, offering support, advice, and comfort whenever necessary. Jackie took over Linda's care during her chemotherapy treatments, the powerful medication working its magic on the cancer and the cracks in their relationship. Susan's bakery endeavor is now a well-greased process. She prepares and freezes the dough a day ahead, leaving it to thaw out overnight so it's only a rise and shine at daybreak. Her glass is half full and filling, but there are ominous dribbles of good leaking out through this unexpected crack in her marriage.

Bathed in the purples and pinks of the summer sunrise and serenaded by robins and meadow larks, Susan prays that the bike ride to the Homestead will clear her head. She straddles the pale-blue old-fashioned *bicyclette* she's had since her youth. The kind that dips in the middle so her cotton sun dress can drape down, and brakes by pushing back on the pedals, the handlebars free for important things like a musical bell and a basket for baguettes and berries. Susan pumps her legs up and down on the quiet streets of Sullivan, her *petit village*, imagining life as a French woman. Partaking of cream, croissants, and champagne without gaining weight. The effortless sense of style. The composed, confident, captivating attitude. *Cinq à sept*, the time from five to seven p.m. when married men meet up with their mistresses. *Merde*.

She parks her bike at the back of the restaurant and enters through the garden gate, the 'Back Forty' as Rick calls it. The odors of mint, lavender, rosemary, and sage fill her nose. She brushes against a cherry tomato plant, its earthy, sweet smell enticing her to pop one of the ripe red balls in her mouth. Relieved that no one else is here yet, not even Rick, she sinks into the bench and this quiet moment, shared only with a buzzing bee or two.

But her unfinished pastries call to her, and she leaves her Eden, unlocking the door to the building and lighting up the kitchen. She pulls out the bowls of dough from the refrigerators, kneading each ball a final time before pressing them into the flat sheets that she will fill, roll up, and slice. It's a meditative process that keeps her in a balanced present instead of the unpredictable future threatening to knock her ass over teacup.

While the breakfast treats rise, Susan starts the first pot of coffee, adding another layer of aroma to the un-folding feast for the senses. She can't believe there isn't an all Beatles station, but she settles for classic oldies, which now means anything before 1990. Much to her surprise, "For No One" is playing, McCartney's poign-ant tale of a relationship's end not often found in radio rotation. Songs have always marked events in her life, whether through the constant repetition at the time or their relevance to a moment. Perhaps K-GOD, or K-MOM, is compiling a playlist for her this morning.

She hears the side door squeak open, and her heart skips. Rick is here. Time for their *tete-a-tete*. This half hour before the staff arrives has become a coveted inter-lude. A time for brainstorming ideas such as adding sea-sonal desserts, or expanding her paper napkin blueprints into the bakery Susan envisions. Of course they remi-nisce about the good old days and current events, but they have been careful to avoid certain topics. Until to-day.

"Good mornin', Suzie Q," Rick says, reviving his former nickname for her with a broad grin as he peeks around the corner. "What's shakin'?"

"Rolls a-bakin'," Susan replies with her half of their morning ritual though without the usual pep in her voice. "Coffee?"

"Always. Shall we adjourn to the parlor?"

Susan slides the pans of rolls into the oven, sets the timer, then carries the coffee, one black for him, and one with all the frills for her, into the office where the two comrades in arms settle into their designated chairs. They sip in silence, Susan's eyes glued to the hot mocha liquid in her mug though she senses a watchful stare piercing through the rising steam.

"Everything all right, Suze?"

Susan takes a long gulp, her hands curled around her cup, and forces the fluid past the constriction in her throat. John Lennon's "Instant Karma" plays in the background.

"Rick, do you believe in karma?" she asks, finally looking at him. "You know, you reap what you sow?"

"Maybe. They say no good deed goes unpunished," he laughs, "and I've sure had a few things come back to bite me. Why, what have you reaped?"

"We don't talk much about our personal lives, other than my kids ..." Susan hesitates, knowing she's walking along a dangerous cliff. The revelation of past and present secrets, like rocks loosened by a careless step, tend to land with unexpected repercussions.

"We used to," Rick reminds her.

Rick's three words pull her back from the steep ledge, giving her surer footing, a hand to hold as she picks her way into days gone by.

"When you left in '85 ... what ... where ... did you go?" she asks.

"Me and Jeannie went to New York. She had dreams too big for Sullivan apparently. I followed her like a pup for awhile, but I wasn't meant to be leashed. Sittin',

177

rollin' over, playin' dead on her command, so I slipped out of the collar and ran back to these open fields."

Susan sets her empty cup on the desk and lowers her head. Her palms meet at her lips in silent prayer. 'There is a time to plant and a time to uproot what is planted.' Time to reap the harvest of her past.

"We've never talked about that night. Maybe you don't remember."

"Suzy-Q, I remember." Rick shifts from his seat to kneel in front of Susan's chair, laying his hands over hers. "Every time I see you."

Susan draws in a quick, shuddering breath at his touch, as much out of remorse as rapture, and turns her head away. Part of her wished he had forgotten it. An inconsequential one-night stand. Move on, nothing to see here. Then she could bury the memory, and her feelings, in an unmarked grave. But Rick isn't, wasn't that kind of man, and of course the memory bobs to the surface.

"Was it so wrong?" Her shame pulls at the corners of her eyes and mouth, but she faces him and pleads her case to her jury of one. "It was just a moment, a two, maybe three beer moment ..." So easy to blame it on the alcohol, a lapse in judgement, but Susan knows it was more. "Everything had blown up around me. We'd lost our fathers and the farms. The move into town. Steve working days and me evenings. Ships passing. And there you were," her cheeks rising as she eases a hand from his grasp to lift a stray hair out of his eyes, "making me laugh, teasing, or was it flirting? You made me feel like I mattered. And that damn song. "The hands of fate reaching out to both of us."

"Maybe we were star-crossed lovers," Rick says. "Like Romeo and Juliet. Never meant to be."

"I wonder. I mean the very next day Mom had her stroke. I quit, and you left town. Game over. But when my Mom showed up in the Walmart restroom last December ..."

"What? Like Moaning Myrtle in the bathroom?"

Susan jerks back with a bemused look. "You've read *Harry Potter*? Huh, wouldn't have guessed that. Anyway, no, I smelled the perfume she used to wear and suddenly she's leading me by the nose to all these closeted dreams and desires. For instance, back into your life. So now whenever I need to make a decision, or I need a backbone, I wait for her little nudging spritz."

"Oh," he draws out the word. "Did Mom come through last night about us?"

"If only. No, I smelled perfume but not hers. Someone else's, and *it* was all over Steve. I'm probably overreacting, but I'm worried he's seeing someone," she whispers.

"Is that the only reason?" Rick asks.

"No, a few months ago we had a blowup," her fists and breath exploding in unison as she explains. "I blamed him for not supporting my dreams, and he accused me of taking on too much and leaving him behind. Plus, he's been distant ... physically, you know, for a long time. So when he came home way late with eau d'affair on his collar, I'm thinking my karmic debt has come due." Her eyes roll until another possible scenario furrows her brow. "Or ... maybe he's known all along and suspects we're at it again. Playing some kind of cheater's poker, hearts are wild. You know, I'll see your indiscretion and raise you a fling."

Rick chuckles and shakes his head, "Nah, he just doesn't seem the type, whatever that means. Besides one late night and perfume on a collar doesn't necessarily say I'm lookin' for love or lookin' to leave. But like Kenny Rogers says, 'ya gotta know when to hold 'em, know when to fold 'em.' You wanna stay in the game? I mean, do you still love him?"

179

"More or less." God, is that the best she can do after forty years and change? "I mean, we've shared a long life together, kids and grandkids, there's a security in that. But I need more than cold comfort, Rick."

The laughter of the breakfast crew coming through the back door echoes into the office, intruding on their intimate conversation. Rick grunts as he pushes against the chair arms to rise to his feet, and in three long strides crosses to shut the door. When he returns, he bends over and raises Susan out of the chair, wrapping his fingers around hers as he draws her to his chest.

"Suzie-Q," he says, "if you listen to your heart, and your Momma, and you decide to play these cards you've been dealt, then be bold and go all in. As your business partner and your friend, I'll back you all the way. But just know, if the time ever comes when you're ready to cash out, I'll be waitin' for you. 'Cause, darlin', you may very well be the love of my life."

His grip loosens, and his warm palms rise to snuggle her face, the smell of his Brut aftershave seeping into her brain. Her heart feels like it's jumped from a plane, as long denied yearnings hurtle his mouth to hers. And then, Bam. Reality pulls the cord, and lips meet not in passion but in a trembling, tender brush of self-control. As if on cue, the melody of Survivor's "I Can't Hold Back" fills the room. Fate, your timing really sucks.

CHAPTER 27

If they don't drain the fluid, Kathy's father blows up like a beached whale and is in horrible pain. If they poke him to drain the fluid, then he often bleeds from his abdomen, his gums, his nose, and under his skin. When his belly fills with infection, Kathy gives him antibiotics through his IV port, but the doctors now deem that futile. Her father sleeps, or moans, or moans while he sleeps. And Kathy just doesn't sleep at all.

Mary and Lenore have already said their good-byes. Mary over the phone in an awkward five-minute conversation between a father and daughter with nothing to say. Lenore with unhurried strokes of his face and whispered endearments in a lingering adieu of spirits likely to meet again. Brian comes by daily now, but usually in the evening, so he can spend time with Kathy at the end of his shift.

Kathy curls up in the wicker chair she's dragged next to her father's bed, Murphy resting at her feet, and watches his chest go up and down, dreading yet preparing herself for the last rise. Kathy keeps the blinds closed on the expanse of sky and the rise and fall of sun and stars, assuming her father needs quiet and subdued light. But maybe he still senses colors and sounds in his semicomatose state and would welcome the experience. She hears a gentle knock on her door, and calls out, "Come on in, Brian."

"Hey, Kath, how's it going?" Brian pads across the floor in his cushioned shoes, placing his hands on Kathy's shoulders to give them a gentle massage.

"Eh? Been better," Kathy sighs at his touch.

The oxygen tank maintains a steady low hiss, forcing out a sniff of air every few seconds, as her father's labored breaths jump in at random intervals. It has become her white noise to block out the quiet to come, a death watch lullaby that becalms the sea change that awaits.

For now the scene remains steady. The sleeping dog curled head to tail, the compassionate nurse loosening knots in muscles, the devoted daughter in a transient oblivion, the dying father in a moratorium on mortality. She saw a quote online recently. It said, "The butterfly counts not months but moments and still has time enough." She's rejoicing in the moments.

"How will I know when it's time? Will he just ... stop breathing?" Kathy whispers.

"Maybe. Hard to say. Unfortunately, further intervention is not going to be helpful. Making him comfortable is the way to go," Brian suggests.

"And how do I do that?"

"With the morphine. Either orally or through his IV."

Kathy tenses, threatening to undo Brian's hard work.

"Guess it's not like he'll need another twelve step, huh?" Kathy gives a subdued chuckle. "You know, I think the thing I'll miss the most is his laugh. When I was a kid, he'd do something totally inappropriate in public, make a face or put something on his nose. We'd wait for people to look and then bust a gut. We'd giggle watching Red Skelton or Jonathan Winters. Or he'd recite some silly poem or jingle he made up, full of off-color words, of course. Mom would cringe and I'd blush, but inside I thought how cool that Daddy thinks I'm grown up enough for that. We had so much fun together. Too bad he was funniest when he was drinking. Guess the black-berry brandy is having the last laugh."

Kathy and Brian chat over Cokes and a pizza as she learns a little more about her father's angel of mercy. That Brian was born in Colorado, went to school in Boulder, then nursing school in Denver before coming out to California on his own "Magical Mystery Tour."

After sowing his flower powered oats, he settled down to pursue his career. He worked in hospitals, nursing homes, freestanding clinics, even tried his luck as a movie set medic. Along the way, he met his wife and they were together nearly twenty years until she succumbed to cancer, leading him to his current work in hospice care.

"It's a wonder we didn't meet earlier. Guess the timing was off," Kathy says.

"Do you believe in kismet?" Brian asks.

"You mean, in all the houses in all of LA with some-one dying, you walked into mine," she laughs. "I stayed an old maid just waiting for you, eh?"

"Hmm ... maybe ..."

⌘⌘⌘⌘⌘

Brian leaves at ten. He has too much integrity and Kathy still too much skepticism to move the relationship any further. When the professional commitment comes to an end, and the healing process begins, perhaps that will change.

Kathy has been sleeping on a cot in the living room to be nearer to her father, never knowing if he might need something, or wake in a panic, or ... She nods off quickly, but it is a shallow and restless sleep, the thin mattress no match for the comfort of her firm supportive bed.

183

Though the grogginess fights to hold her down, the sound of her name startles her awake. There it is again. Her father calling her. Her feet entangle in the sheets as she attempts to go to him, and she nearly falls to the floor.

"Daddy. Daddy. What is it?"

"Kathy. I believe it's time. I saw her."

"Saw who, Daddy?"

"My mother. She's waiting for me. In the light. Just there. Help me go to her."

Though it's hard to see in the dark, the bright light of the lamp will be too jarring. She opens the shades to let the moonlight wash over the room, bathing her father's face in an eerie, ghost-like blue. This is the first time in days that he has spoken, or even been awake. His voice is clear, steady, coherent. It is both comforting and frightening.

"What are you saying, Daddy? What do you want me to do?"

"Let me go to her. I'm ready. I'm tired of this fight." He reaches out and grabs her hand, bringing it to his wet cheek. "Let me go, Kathy."

Before she can reply, tell him she can't do that, ask him to hang on just a little longer, he closes his eyes and lets out a low, mournful wail. It wakes up Murphy and he too begins to howl. Not sure how to comfort or settle either of them, she leads Murphy to the bedroom and closes the door. Running back to her father, she tries to calm him with soothing words, mops his brow with a wet cloth, rubs his shoulder with gentle strokes. All absolutely futile in alleviating the torturous pain that racks his body.

When Brian was here earlier, he injected some morphine into the IV port to ease her father's restlessness and discomfort. The bottle stares at her from the bedside table, its clear contents tempting her with its liquid mercy, her father's release from suffering.

Why didn't she ask Brian what she should do? Or did he tell her and she's forgotten? How much is the right dose? Is it too soon to give him more? What if I give too much? Kathy picks up the phone seeking Brian's advice, instructions, courage, but before the connection is made, her father cries out again.

"Please, Kathy, please, please, please."

The phone falls to the floor. Daddy, what are you asking me to do? Her brain asks the question but her gut already knows the answers. Kathy grabs the paper-wrapped syringe with both hands, the shaking hampering her efforts to open it. She struggles to attach the needle. Forgetting about wiping off the bottle of morphine with alcohol, she jams the point into the rubber stopper. She pulls back on the plunger and fills the empty space with the medication.

Kathy looks down at her father, the love of her life, her mentor, the wind beneath her wings. Her father has been clear. It's time. She knows what she has to do. She sticks the needle into the port.

"Daddy, I love you. Forgive me," she cries, and pushes the plunger in.

Within seconds her father becomes less frantic. His legs stop moving, then his arms, and at last he lies in peace. His breathing slows, and then he's gone. No longer a sparkle in his fixed blue eyes. His throaty laughter silenced. His dancing feet to glide no more.

Kathy's tears anoint her father as she gathers his lifeless body into her arms, his skin splashed with yellow, purple, and red. The artist even in death. No, butterflies have it wrong. Moments are not enough.

The hiss of the oxygen tank and Murphy's distant whining fill her ears and pry Kathy's resistant eyes open.

She gasps as she realizes where she is. Lying next to her father's cold and rigid body, her hand on his still chest. She eases herself away from the bed, shuts off the useless air, and opens the door for her dog.

"Sorry, Murph. I forgot. I'm so sorry, so sorry. Daddy's gone," her voice cracks as she plops on the floor next to him, arms around his neck, and cries into his fur, "God, please don't hate me. I had to do it."

It's six in the morning now, the sun daring to show its garish face through her patio window. Kathy knows she must call Brian to tell him her father has passed. She knows there will be no autopsy, no blood tests to determine cause of death, no way any one will know exactly how or when he died, or even care for that matter. Yet, in every *CSI* drama she's watched, every police procedural script she's read, the truth is always discovered. How can she face Brian knowing she is the prime suspect, had the only means and motive, possesses the smoking syringe?

Brian arrives, and Kathy takes mental notes of his actions. He listens to Patrick's heart and peers into his eyes, confirming the obvious, and records the time of death on his final report. Three a.m., more or less, per Kathy's recollection. Then he disconnects the tubes from Patrick's body, placing the used medical supplies, except for the morphine bottle, into a red plastic biohazard bag. Why didn't he toss the vial? Does he suspect? He calls his supervisor to report the death and then the funeral home to request their services for the collection of ... her Daddy. Will they put him in a red bag also?

"Kathy, do you want me to stay until the men arrive?"

"No, it's OK. You have other patients. I'll be fine."

Brian reaches out to give her a hug, but Kathy keeps her distance, worried her pounding tell-tale heart will give her away. Unsure if she deserves the warm embrace he's offering.

"I'll call you later," he says. Kathy does not acknowledge him.

Patrick O'Shea is now in postproduction. The backdrops of his life story will be rolled up, location shots recorded in photos and memories, wardrobe and props stored or donated, accounts squared. The divine screenwriter wrote, revised, and tweaked the script many times over the eighty years of the shoot. But Kathy begs to edit that one scene. It won't change the ending, but must her character kill the father?

CHAPTER 28

Margaret's hands are dirty. Actual soil is embedded under her nails. Her knees sink in the soft, moist earth while mud, gloppy brown mud, covers her shoes. OK, it's not shoes, it's her wellies, but still. Father never allowed her to truly experience the outdoors. That was for the common folk. But in high school when she lived on the ranch, Mother exposed her to nature. Cows full of milk and manure. Chickens proclaiming warm brown eggs. Meadow larks heralding the morning. Father's world came boxed with detailed instructions. Life with Mother always unfolded into the unexpected.

Out of the corner of her eye she catches a glimpse of Denise, winding her way down the garden path, waving her arms about. Denise has been staying with her since the Spring term ended. With rent going up once more at her efficiency apartment near the University, Margaret offered her a permanent residence in one of the eight bedrooms on her estate.

Denise wears her standard summer uniform of overall shorts and T-shirt with her sturdy Rockport nautical shoes, her bare face and short hair making each day effortless. Margaret is finding it easier to leave the pearls in the jewelry box while she gardens, but sixty years of etiquette and deportment are hard to put aside.

"Margaret. Margaret," Denise shouts. "Are you ready for this?"

"Am I ready for what?"

Denise lopes the last few yards to the garden patch Margaret is weeding, holding a large manila envelope to her chest. With a loud exhale, she holds out the letter.

"I would have brought it on a silver platter, of which I'm sure you have many, but I didn't know where to look. Not sure if garden shears are the right tool for the job, so I slit it open for you. Here. I'll provide the drum roll."

Margaret hasn't thought about what this yellow envelope most likely contains for several weeks. Her double-edged sword. One side severing the bindings restraining her from her freedom. The other side slashing open the fear of that freedom. Her hands tremble as she reaches in, the papers catching on the clasp. State of Connecticut, Superior Court. She skims through the parties of the first, the wherefores and where art thou's, until she arrives at the final signature page. *Jeffrey Roger King*, or what passes for his mark, near the bottom in bold black ink.

Laying the paperwork on the ground, she slides off her canvas and rubber gloves. On her left hand, fourth finger, sits a remarkably plain band with a one caret diamond. With slow, deep breaths she wiggles the ring until it slides over the first knuckle and slips off, leaving a circumscribed pale indentation.

She clenches this symbol of her marriage in her fist, compressing all the pain it came to represent into a worthless bauble. Winding her shoulder back, she heaves it as far as her thin, flaccid arm can throw. Margaret watches the five and half grams of gold and crystal fly through the air, her body growing lighter with each degree of the arc. When she can no longer see any glint of metal or gem, she tilts her face to the sky, raises her arms, and shouts, "Great God Almighty, I am free at last."

She feels Denise reach down and pull her to standing before lifting her up in a bear hug as they rock back and forth. In a bi-polar moment of laughter and tears, they skip back to the house, arm in arm down the Yellow Brick Road to life after Jeff.

"So how shall we celebrate? Champagne? Lobster? Paris?" Denise asks as they wash up in the mudroom.

"Yes, yes, but Paris might be a bit much."

"How about dinner out? I've been wanting to try this new place downtown. If we can get a table. Do you think Sean would drive us?"

"I'm sure he'd be glad to take us for a spin in the limo. Why don't you call for reservations?"

⌘⌘⌘⌘⌘

The ladies arrive at five thirty and are seated at a table for two at Napa & Company, one of Stamford's hot new venues that features local organic cuisine and an extensive wine list. Luckily for them, the trendy crowd eats later.

While money has never been an issue for Margaret, she has always been conservative with her wealth. But tonight, it's anything goes. She orders a bottle of Veuve Clicquot champagne and escargot to start.

"A toast, dear friend," Denise begins. "Life is not perfect and never will be, but some things come pretty damn close. Your ring finger finally bare, a glass of bubbly, and our friendship. Cheers."

Margaret smiles as their glasses clink.

"You have been a godsend, Denise. There for me so many times over the years. My escort for dinners and concerts. My counselor talking me through my dark nights, and at a much lower rate than my therapist. I'd

191

most likely have become like poor Miss Havisham, living in seclusion, betrayed by my betrothed." Margaret tilts her head back with her hand against her forehead. "I was so naive. Jeff used me as his invitation to the world of the rich and famous, only to throw me in the trash once he made it past the front doors."

"Well, now Mr. A. H. King is out of your life," Denise says.

"Why are you calling him ...? Oh, I get it. Mr. Ass Hole. Ha. You know, speaking of the lower bowel, I think Jeff was my appendix. He served a purpose at some point, but he became useless, too easily inflamed, and threatened to burst open at any moment and kill me. Good riddance."

"Now," Denise pronounces, "no more mention of He Who Must Not Be Named."

The waiter ushers the bottle of eighty-dollar French oaked Vigonier to the table. With great flair he presents the pale-green bottle so Margaret and Denise may examine the label. Removing the cork with swift and practiced moves, he pours a taste for each. Holding the glasses by the stem, they swirl the pale gold liquid, sniff the fruity and smoky vanilla bouquet before sipping the medium-bodied wine. The women 'um' and 'ah' and deem it excellent, pleasing the sommelier.

"This is the perfect wine for stopping to smell the roses," he says. "Enjoy."

"Well, that was an interesting comment," says Margaret, "but he's right. It is time to take the time. There is absolutely no reason for me not to enjoy life. I have an abundance of money, despite giving 'you know who' way more than he deserves. At least for now, without the commitment of a job, my days and nights are my own. The only thing standing in my way is me."

"So when, and not if, mind you, you get out of your way, what do you want to do?"

192

"Apparently eat these delectable entrees," Margaret replies as the waiter interrupts to bring their entrees. Mascarpone ravioli with a butternut squash puree, and pan-seared sea scallops with pea puree, artichokes, and spinach. Oh, and bacon dust, per the menu. Seriously, bacon dust.

"Shall we share?"

Margaret and Denise cut bits of each entree and transfer them to the other's plate before placing a morsel in their mouths. Margaret's future plans are put on hold for several minutes as smells, tastes, and textures mingle on their tongues, the fresh ingredients bold and savory, light and sweet. And, yes, the bacon dust is definitely worth the mention.

"Denise, coming here was such a great idea. Let's do this on a regular basis. A new restaurant every week. But back to your question. What do I want to do? Spend some time in Paris. You must come with me."

"*Bien sur, mon amie,*" Denise replies.

"And I'll be off to Colorado in August. Susan and Kathy were so great back in high school. The other gal, Linda, not so much, but sometimes she'd get off her high horse, hand us the reins, and walk with us. Albeit two steps ahead as befits royalty," she says with a prim and proper accent. "Perhaps she's changed. I've been too lax about staying in touch with them."

The waiter returns to top off the champagne and the Vigonier, making it two or three glasses apiece. But who's counting?

"This is excellent wine, is it not? And you are an excellent friend, dear Denise. My BFF as the kids say," the words falling loosely from her mouth. "You know, to paraphrase a Beatles song, *I* get by with a little help from *you*, my friend. My friend Susan was such a Beatlemaniac. Mad for the Boys. Were you a fan?"

"Oh, of course. I was still in grade school when they burst on the scene, but sure, I got caught up just like everyone. Let me guess, you liked John, right?"

"You know me well. He was a witty wordsmith, but also a rebel. A bad boy. I think I secretly craved that. Maybe that's what I'll do with my freedom. Become a rebel with a cause. Like you, Denise."

"Well, then here's to breaking a few rules. What say you to that, Bestie?"

"Oh, hell, yeah!" Margaret tries to stand to pump the air with her fist, but loses her balance and falls back into her chair.

"Perhaps it's time to go," Denise says, reaching across the table to steady Margaret with her hand.

"What about dessert? My new life calls for dessert. Maybe Sean can stop for ice cream on the way back. I'll get the check and you go get him."

Margaret fumbles in her purse for her credit card and gives it to the server. Her lips feel tingly as she takes another sip or two of champagne while she waits. Luckily the gratuity is included since she struggles to see the printed numbers on the bill. She signs her name with a flourish.

"Thank you very much, kind sir. We'll be back. My driver awaits."

"Madam, let me help you to the door." The waiter takes her arm and escorts her toward the exit where Denise is leaning against the door frame.

"Thanks," Denise says, "I guess we smelled a few too many roses tonight. Thank God we have our designated driver."

Sean steers them to the limo and settles the giggling twosome into the back seat before hopping into the driver's seat.

"I see you ladies had quite a time there. About freakin' time, Mrs. King. Where to now?"

"Sean, dear, call me Margaret," she says, "we need something sweet. What do you recommend?"

"I know just the place." He shifts into gear and eases into traffic, but Margaret is not observing her chauffeur's driving skills. Nor does she see his glance in the rearview mirror.

"Whoa ..." he whispers, "well, I'll be."

CHAPTER 29

After her last chemo treatment, Linda scheduled an appointment with her faithful plastic surgeon to camouflage the surgical disfigurement to her left breast. A satellite facility in Aspen gave her the option of combining the repair with a little mother of the bride touch-up and three weeks of R and R in the Rockies. Now back in town, she's meeting Jackie for lunch, a weekly ritual begun during her recovery.

Linda sips a Pinot Grigio on the patio at NoRTH's near a planter of petunias. A soft pashmina covers her shoulders, a floppy straw hat and designer sunglasses hide her face. The refreshing white wine, her first alcohol in three months, washes over her tongue with notes of citrus and honeysuckle. She's missed this. Holding the glass by its narrow stem, the vague aroma of green apples, the sting on her taste buds, the heady feeling she knows will come. But then everything now seems more vivid, and she takes nothing for granted. Especially her time with Jackie.

"Mom, hey there." Jackie leans over the rail to give her mother a double-sided air kiss. "Almost didn't see you with the hat and all."

"Trying to maintain the good doctor's work, but thought you might like to sit outside."

"Great, but I better go in the proper way. I'm sure they'd frown on me jumping over."

"So how was Aspen?" Jackie asks after pulling up a chair beside Linda.

You know, it's really much prettier in the summer. Instead of winter gray, the skies are vivid blue. Instead of skinny stalks of skis and poles, there's multicolored blossoms outside the shops. And I get to wear my new espadrilles," she says, lifting her foot to show off her strappy canvas shoe. "What's new with the wedding?"

"Just last-minute details, basically. This whole bridezilla thing. I don't get it. Way too much drama for me. I'm glad we're all going to enjoy the wedding."

"Yes, yes we will. Oh wait, Antonio, dear," Linda says, waving over the passing waiter to their table, "could you bring us some bruschetta and two Italian farm salads. I'll take another Pinot Grigio, and, iced tea for you?"

"Yes, please. And could you hold the salami on mine? Thanks." Once the swarthy dark-haired man is out of earshot, Jackie adds. "Mom, is it OK for you to drink?"

"It's fine. I'll be careful, I promise," she says making an X across her chest. "Did you finally decide on the food?"

"Yes, we're starting with a selection of cheeses with veggies, fruits, and crackers. Then Mediterranean tapas, an artichoke bruschetta, veggie samosas, a beet and pear salad, and butternut squash ravioli to finish. Mostly finger foods. And of course Susan's amazing cake."

"Sounds yummy."

Linda still isn't sure about this all-vegetarian menu, but she's not about to say anything. She worries the country folk will balk at no meat, but as Marie Antoinette said, 'Let them eat cake.'\

Antonio returns with their food and drinks. Just in time. Linda was ready to eat her napkin with all the talk of appetizers and such. Jackie stabs up a forkful of greens while Linda crunches through a bite of bruschetta.

"By the way," Jackie says, "Matt and I started taking ballroom lessons with Dad and Marlee. We're having a blast. Say what you will, but Marlee's really a good dancer."

"What, even without a pole? Her expiration date must be getting close. Is he bringing her to the wedding?" Linda says, the crunchy bread sticking in her throat.

"Yes. You OK with that, Mom? I mean, Dad seems really happy with her, but if it's going to create an international incident ..."

What can she do? Her ex-husband's choice in women has never been within her purview. And she certainly can't compare with Marlee now. Unless her preposterous double F breasts leak, melt, or explode. She can dream.

"No, if he's happy. But tell me, do you think he's serious about her? I got the impression it's just another one of his flings."

She remembers his words. Marlee was fun, this wasn't serious. Of course, that was six months ago. Before life went to shit.

"I don't know, Mom. I try to stay out of it. In four weeks she might be long gone. Who knows with Dad? Hey, you never told me the results of the genetic testing."

"Sorry, the results were negative, so I guess I spaced it. Even though I don't carry the gene, they said there's a remote possibility you might. Recessive DNA from your grandmother, even male relatives."

She watches Jackie once again reflexively cover her chest with her arms. She should have told her sooner. She knew before chemo started. She could have just gone with everything is fine. She didn't need the fine print explanation. Now she's panicked her, exactly what she didn't want to do.

"What does that mean? What should I do?""

Start doing self breast checks. Get a baseline mammogram with annual follow-ups. Do the basics you should be doing already. Really, I wouldn't worry about anything now. Your wedding should be the only thing on your mind now," she says, hoping she's doused the fire she started.

"So, are you going back to work full time?" Jackie asks, the change of topic apparently signaling crisis averted.

"No, part time until after the wedding. This situation made me reevaluate my life. Cancer does that. My staff can handle the day to day work. I don't need any more stress right now. So, see you next week, same time?"

"Definitely, Mom. And by the way, you look great."

Jackie heads toward the patio door but turns around to give Linda a wave. Yes, she's finally on the right track, at least with her daughter. The ex. That's a crapshoot, always has been. She waits for Antonio to return her card with the bill and checks for messages on her phone since she'd had it on silence during lunch. Work, work, one from Susan, work, work, the 970 number again. She presses the listen button on that last one and chugs the rest of her wine.

"Hello, this is Sandra Henry again trying to reach Linda Wilson. You haven't returned my previous calls, and I really need to talk with you. I think you might be my mother."

A LITTLE HELP
FROM MY FRIENDS

CHAPTER 30

Susan sorts the clothes into piles in the laundry room. Colors and whites. Towels and underwear. She spritzes the smells and scrubs the stains. The pungent, musty summer sweat that darkens the armpits of Steve's bright-green polos, his name embroidered in yellow thread. The yeasty flour and russet cinnamon embedded in the fibers of her cotton bib apron. And the imperceptible caress of fragrance in the pointed collar of the dress she wore back in July.

The true odor has long since washed from the cloth, no longer even lurking in the folds of her nose, but it lingers in her primitive brain where scent memories form. Where Evening in Paris brings back her mother, and gardenias call up school dances. And Brut never fails to flip the calendar back to August 1984, or to last month's dizzying disclosure from Rick. Those sweet and tender moments, picked at their perfection, remain canned and stored in her brain cellar. But her marriage, the business partnership, and the applecart must not be upset by the scent of a man.

The Homestead now has multiple dozens of rolls in the restaurant freezer for staff to thaw and serve, her involvement on hold for the next few days. With one less ball to juggle, her focus can be on keeping the reunion aloft without dropping Steve on his head. Susan spies the note she left for him on the island, unmoved from where she placed it this morning. Unsure if he read it, she punches in his cell number.

"Hey, are you busy?"

"No, what do you need?"

"Did you see the reminder about the reunion? Kathy and Margaret arrive today."

"Yes, and I know. That's all you've talked about for the last two weeks."

She glances at the calendar, August 24th, the square circled with details bolded in red ink.

"Linda gets here at one, Kath about two, and then we'll all go pick Margaret up at DIA at four. We'll eat dinner at The Homestead. There's leftovers in the fridge for you, or do you wanna join us?"

"You're joking, right? Be the Fifth Beatle? I'll pass. Is that all?"

"Yeah, that's it. See you tonight," impulsively adding, "Love you, Steve."

The dial tone echoes in her ear. She's trying to go all in.

Susan studies the John Deere calendar again. The Red Rocks concert is in two days, then the wedding on September fourth. Her birthday is the thirtieth. A while back Steve announced he was planning a Caribbean cruise for her sixtieth birthday. He even put down a deposit to hold a spot though little has been said about it since. She hopes it's still on the books. After the reunion and wedding, once Jenny has the baby, when everything dies down, a romantic holiday could be just the ticket.

She tends to last-minute details as she finishes up the laundry and puts out fresh towels, deadheads spent blooms on the porches and picks bouquets for tables, and does a final sweep of the kitchen floor. All is set, and she heads upstairs to reinspect the newly decorated guest room.

Taking cues from women's magazines and Linda's professionally designed apartment, she created a welcoming space on a budget. The sage-green walls feel tranquil, inviting, and so much more grown-up than the previous princess theme wallpaper. The two single beds, holdovers from her daughters' teen years, have been refitted with new deeper mattresses, and should provide a good night's sleep for her guests. The closet is clear of its past life and simple, artfully positioned accessories top the repainted dresser and bedside tables. She smooths a wrinkle from one of the earth-toned comforters and rearranges the mix and match of patterned and solid pillows. The welcome mat is out.

Ready for a midday pause before everyone arrives, Susan fills a glass with water and sinks into her recliner, feet up and legs outstretched. The chime of the doorbell startles her. Barely noon, it's not likely perpetually tardy Linda. Even if traffic was light, or road construction minimal, it's too early for Kathy. Plus, she's still in her sweats. After days of tinkering with her woefully fashion-challenged wardrobe, the uninspiring winner is laid out on the bed. The bell rings again.

"Hey, Gramma. You busy?" Jenny asks when the door opens.

"Not for you, Baby Girl." Susan ushers in her pregnant granddaughter, her growing belly hampering the usual full contact hug. She's glad to see twinkling eyes instead of the puffy lids that showed up at the last surprise visit.

"Just finished my last Lamaze class." Jenny reaches her hand up to connect with Susan's for a high five.

"Good for you. So, what'd ya learn?"

"More than I wanted to know."

"How was your Mom? Quizzing the instructor on every detail?" Susan knows role reversals can be tricky. Parent aging to a child, nurse forced to be a patient. But a teacher, especially one like Maureen, in the role of student? Good luck, professor.

"No, she was actually pretty cool. There was another mother and daughter in class so we kinda hung out. Anyway, they served really good cookies so that rocked. I still wish it had been you with me. Woulda been way more fun."

"Yeah, I would have liked that," Susan says, brushing a strand of hair behind Jenny's ear, "but it was better you shared this experience with your Mom." She closes her eyes for a moment, her breathing slow and deliberate, and puts forth the question she's been asking since March. The answer is a no-brainer in her humble opinion. "And the plans for the baby?"

"Well, we talked with some adoption agencies. Everyone says it'll be better for her, give me more opportunities. But ..." Jenny frowns as she cradles her belly, "she's been moving around like crazy. I don't know, Gramma. What do I do?"

Susan caresses Jenny's abdomen and the child inside, intuitively connecting the three generations. Seems like Jenny references the baby with feminine pronouns, but she's heard no names of either gender. At least Maureen's moved on from "it."

"So Justin's totally bailed? What is wrong with his parents? How can they condone such irresponsibility?"

"Yeah, major suckiness. His whole family's leaving town as soon as he goes off to college. We were just a baby bump on the road outta town. I don't need that."

"No, you don't." Susan feels her face flush with a deep desire to kick some teenage, and adult, butt. "Remember, you still have a say in this. Don't forget about online classes and day care. By the way, I know a very loving older woman with tons of experience with children."

"Really? Who's that? Oh," she gives Susan's shoulder a playful shove, "that's you isn't it, Gramma?"

"Yeah, just sayin'. Oh, my gosh, look at the time. Aunt Linda and my friend Kathy will be here in less than an hour and look at me. Think you could give me a five minute makeover and find me something better to wear?"

Jenny nixes most of the 'old crone collection,' but they settle on black polyester slacks, a red and black striped three-quarter sleeve top, and the red crystal earrings she bought at Jackie's boutique. A little class, a lot of coverage, and a selfish prayer that the rigors of jet lag and a long road trip will give her some advantage over her friends.

Susan and Jenny sway on the front porch swing, having a Mayberry moment with some homemade lemonade, and await the arrival of the Beatle Girls. A dark-blue Subaru with California plates drives slowly past the house before backing up and pulling in the driveway. Out floats Kathy in a gauzy white cotton sun dress that highlights her tanned and toned body, her blonde hair tucked under a straw fedora. She sprints across the lawn to Susan, their anticipation overflowing into teenybopper squeals and wobbly bouncing before falling into each other arms.

"Oh, my God, it's so good to see you," they say in unison. They push in and out of their embrace, laughing at the changes time has made but finding comfort in the familiar.

"Kathy, you still look the same. Not fair. Anyway, this is my granddaughter Jenny. Jenny, this is Kathy."

"You're the actress, right? Cool." Jenny gives a blasé shrug as if meeting a celebrity is commonplace. "What were you in?"

207

"A year of *Solid Gold* in the Eighties." Jenny gives no sign of recognition, so Kathy adds, "The last scene in *Grease*?"

Still nothing.

"Maybe you've heard my voice in some animated features. *Pocahontas ... Little Mermaid ...*?"

"Really? I loved Ariel." Jenny replaces her aloofness with enthusiasm now that Kathy is 'part of her world.'

As Kathy shares behind the scenes stories with Jenny, Susan glimpses a flash of red pulling in next to the Subaru. Linda's wedge sandals peek out first from below the driver's side door of the Lexus, followed by the hometown girl turned big city woman. She's dressed in linen shorts and a cotton tee with discreet diamond earrings piercing her ears and gold bangles encircling her wrists. Her makeup is understated, and her hair, once long and straight in high school, curls around her ears and tickles the nape of her neck.

"Well, hello girls," Linda beams, strolling over to the group.

"Linda?" Kathy's eyebrows rise along with her voice. "I almost didn't recognize you. Your hair is so ... different, but really cute."

Linda gives an uneasy smile and pats the back of her head and quickly moves in for warm embraces, letting the conversation turn to things other than her current hairdo. Susan is proud of her for ditching the wig, letting the truth win out over vanity.

"Sorry to break this up, guys, but we better get going or Margaret will think we've stood her up. Let's get your luggage inside, Kathy. I need to feed my dog and then we can take off."

"Gramma, I can stay here and take care of Bungalow Bill 'til Grampa gets home."

"Oh, my God. You named your dog Bungalow Bill," Kathy laughs. "Of course you did."

With luggage stowed away, bathroom breaks taken, and Jenny in charge of Bill, Susan backs out her Taurus and Linda and Kathy pile in for the trip to the airport. Susan plugs in the iPod and sets it on random play. "It Won't Be Long" kicks off the afternoon with real John singing lead while 'Ringo,' 'George,' and 'Paul' perform backup vocals. Off-key notes and forgotten lyrics aside, they're back in the groove.

"So what's Steve doing while we're doin' our thang?" Kathy asks when the song finishes. "I don't remember him being a big Beatles fan."

"Nah, not back in the day, but he's learned the error of his ways," she says with a wag of her finger. "I imagine he'll go to our daughter's or hang with his friends. After all, this is girl time."

As tunes spill out, including "We Can Work It Out," "Getting Better," "Come Together" and "All You Need Is Love," it's obvious some spiritual DJ is in charge of the playlist this afternoon. Susan gives a silent shout out to the Universe and rocks and bobs her head as she sings with gusto.

Arriving at DIA, Susan parks in the short-term lot, and the trio amble into the terminal's waiting area waving day glo poster board signs plastered with pictures of the Beatles, the signal to Margaret that these old broads are actually her high school friends. Most passengers walk by without a glance, suitcases rolling behind them as jet-lagged minds focus on where they've been or where they're going. Several, however, give a thumbs up or flash a peace sign, and a few holler 'Far out.' Fellow flower children all grown up.

Susan is the first to spot the thin silver-haired woman in a black knit suit, her silk top draped with a single strand of pearls, carrying a large purse embellished with the interconnected brass letters of the Chanel logo. The face is recognizable as the girl they knew at Sullivan

209

High, but the jaunty pixie cut with bangs framing her green eyes gives her an edginess that is soooo not the Margaret from 1964.

"Margaret. Hello, hello. Over here," Susan, Linda, and Kathy shout, waving their signs and their arms. They move past the crowd to an open area for a proper welcome, reconnecting their friendship circle, cracked but not broken some forty years ago. They retrieve Margaret's two large suitcases from baggage claim, roll them out to the lot, and load them in the trunk. Then it's off to a shared past when their only worries had been Friday's algebra test, making sure they were home for *Shindig* on Wednesday nights, and having six dollars to buy the next Beatles album.

CHAPTER 31

"I see they painted the water tower," Kathy remarks as they near the exit ramp into Sullivan, the eighty-foot structure looming in the distance. "I always loved that neon orange. This white is so ... blah."

"There was so much graffiti they had to cover it up a few years ago. Steve was bummed," Susan says. "He climbed and beautified that stupid thing every year."

She smiles at the thought of his testosterone-fueled midnight adventures, when he was daring and dashing, and full of life. She eases down the hill and applies the brakes as she comes to the intersection with Main Street, the two-lane divider in the town.

"And, ta da," she proclaims with a flourish, "Our first traffic light. We're a doggone metropolis now."

Before they built the interstate in the mid-sixties, this two-mile stretch of road was part of a central thorough-fare that extended from the west side of Denver to the Kansas border. Now it's just a byway between the neighboring villages. Businesses flank either side—on the north is the U.S. post office, an eight-lane bowling alley, medical offices and a veterinary clinic while the south side hosts a gas station, the bank formerly run by Linda's family, and the John Deere outlet where Steve works.

"Nothing changes, huh?" Kathy sighs as they take a right onto Main. "Wait a minute, where's the Tastee-Freez and the grocery store? And that little café?"

"Gone or turned into something else," Susan says. "Two thousand people live here now, four times what it was when you guys were here. Housing developments five miles in any direction. It's like progress fell on the town and squished it out. You up for a drive down what's left of memory lane?"

First stop, their old high school. It's now administrative offices, replaced by a new facility to meet the growing needs of the community. The historic grade school that Susan and Linda attended was razed long ago, and they literally put up a parking lot.

"Do you think we can peek in?" Margaret asks as the trio walks up to the tan one-story brick building.

"Maureen's car is here. Let me call her," Susan says. "Hey, my friends and I are out by the admin building. Could you let us in to have a look around? ... Just to walk through ... Thanks. Lucky for us the old school's connected to the new."

When Maureen opens the double doors, Susan makes quick introductions before her daughter hurries back to set up her room for the coming academic year. The secretaries have gone for the day, so the only illumination inside comes from the security lighting. The army-green metal lockers, their damn combination locks forever the curse of countless dreams, no longer line the halls, however the framed pictures of bygone classes still grace the walls above them though it's too shadowy to make out faces or names. They skulk down the corridor and peek in the rooms.

"That was Mr. D's classroom," Margaret points out. "My home away from home. *Macbeth*'s witches and iambic pentameter. He basically designed an Honors

212

English curriculum for me." She gives a soft laugh. "Remember diagraming sentences by playing football? Gaining yards by correctly identifying pronouns and participles. Only time I ever got picked first for a team."

They inch their way in the dimness to what had been the science lab, the odors of formaldehyde and rotten eggs wafting from memories.

"Periodic tables and dead things in jars. My home," Linda says. "I'll never forget that ginormous grasshopper, and how I had to cut yours up for you, Susan."

They peer into the last room on the right. Civics and History. A somber mood settles over the women as if that day is happening all over.

"Eleven o'clock," Susan says. "Mr. Mason came in. His eyes looked red, and he told us President Kennedy had been shot."

One hand slips into another as they remember, once again devastated by this unimaginable event. How they had wailed and clung to each other, spending the next four days glued to the television. Time stood still and they knew life was over.

Until the Beatles showed up and gave them all a reason to live and believe.

They troop back to the entrance, stopping in front of the door with the opaque window. The dreaded chamber of the principal's office. It was rare that anything good happened in there.

"Remember when we got called in ..." Susan begins.

"For our Beatles buttons," Margaret interrupts, picking up the memory thread.

"Thought for sure we were gonna get the paddle," Susan winces. "But like good girls, we obediently took them off, went to the bathroom, and ..."

"Pinned them to our bras," Kathy laughs.

"Such rebels. Hey, I've got an idea." Linda gathers them together and whispers her plan, just in case the ghost of The Man is haunting the place.

They line up, backsides facing the door, and in unison they give a wiggle and a shout. "Up yours, you stuffy old wanker."

The Red Hat radicals howl and snort with laughter as they scamper through the front entrance. The Beatle Girls have left the building!

The exuberance of their escapade continues as they cruise up and down the streets, the dust from the past now covered over with asphalt. They point out the former homes of classmates and school girl crushes, and the cantankerous old man whose home was egged every single Halloween.

But the mood mellows as they coast by the dilapidated row houses where Kathy had lived with her Mom and Aunt Marie. Tape covers the cracks in the dirty windows and paint peels from the siding; dead front lawns are strewn with broken toys and rusting, wheelless vehicles. They drive further out to the newly constructed suburbs and estate homes on acreage, the lands where family farms once stood, where Susan and Margaret had played as children. They climb out of the car and lean against one of the wooden fences.

Susan grips the split rail as she looks out at the enclosed properties, their bricks and mortar trespassing on her memories. "Our parents are all dead now. You guys, so many moved away. I don't know most of the people living here anymore. They came to raise their children away from the drugs and gangs and violence, and yet somehow it followed them anyway." She kicks at the dirt along the side of the road. "I feel potbound. I need the promise of open wheat fields."

Susan parks the car in the employee area around the back of The Homestead and leads her friends to the front door, letting them chatter behind her. She runs her tongue over her tacky lips in a futile effort at moistening them, and loosens the phlegm collecting in her throat before entering. She and Rick sealed the lid on the romantic pickle jar they were in and shoved it to the back of the cupboard. Still, Susan worries one of them will open it by mistake.

"Hey, Suzie Q, how's it goin'?" Rick's face brightens as he greets her with an arm around her shoulders.

"Trying to stay cool," Susan squeaks, her blushing face at odds with the words coming out of her mouth. She clears her throat one more time and introduces her friends to Rick. "This is Kathy O'Shea, Margaret Martinet, and Linda Charles. You know, Joe's little sister."

"Oh, yeah. Little Linda. I hear you all are havin' a reunion. The Beatle Girls. Now, me, I'm more of an Elvis guy but you ladies go swoon away with your long hairs." He gives Susan a wink and musses her hair.

"Oh, come on, Rick," Susan titters, looking away as she smooths her curls. She turns to the hostess in hopes of bringing the encounter to a close. "Do you have a booth for us?" She follows the hostess, willing herself not to look back.

"He's rather friendly now, isn't he?" Kathy raises an eyebrow as they slide into their seats. "Care to fill in the blanks. Suzie Q?"

"We worked together in the past and now on my bakery business." Her answer is more abrupt than Susan planned, but nuff said. She unfolds her menu and carries on. "Lots of good things to choose from. Hope you're hungry." Do not open that jar.

CHAPTER 32

Susan meanders about the garden with a late morning cup of coffee listening to "And Your Bird Can Sing" with harmony courtesy of a flock of robins. The perennial rotation of blooms is winding down, though the gaps have been closed with colorful annuals. If only she could fill in the bare spots of her life as easily.

When she and her friends got home last night, Steve was watching a pre-season Bronco game, so only light-hearted banter exchanged between guests and host. Steve did press pause long enough to say Jenny invited him and the dog to spend the next two days at Maureen's, so Susan and friends had the place to themselves. Exhausted from their travels, down the road and back in time, the ladies turned in early. It's almost ten a.m. and the city girls have yet to make an entrance.

"Susan," Margaret calls out, peeking through the patio screen, "sorry we slept so late. Altitude and a comfy mattress, I guess."

"I must say," Linda adds, "for two women used to sleeping alone, we did quite well sharing the room."

Susan joins them in the kitchen and tosses a handful of spent blooms into the trash. Kathy raises her arms in a full body stretch as she descends the stairs. Susan had worried about who would sleep where and with whom, but she made a judgment call that Kathy would be the most OK with a night or two on a cot in her craft room. The other ladies got the higher-class digs

"Just like our first sleep over. Course I could have slept on a rock," she says through a yawn.

"You guys must be starving. What's your pleasure? Eggs, pancakes?"

"Coffee," they say in desperate consensus.

"That I can do. And maybe a cinnamon roll to go with?"

Susan grips the handle of the hot glass carafe with a practiced though currently clammy hand. She offers her baked goods every day to total strangers, but now, with her friends as customers, she's got flop sweat. Go figure.

"These are delicious, Susan," Margaret says, along with a chorus of yums from the others. "What are your plans for the future?"

"If money grew like the hairs on my chin," Susan chuckles, rubbing the new one that popped out this morning, "I'd like to have my own bakery." She moves her hand across an imaginary placard. "Bliss - A Little Taste of Heaven. Or something like that. A small dining area but mostly takeout. I think, at times he regrets it, but this was actually Steve's idea."

"Speaking of, I hardly recognized him," Kathy says. "Not the cocky football player I remember."

"Yeah, well," Susan huffs, setting the coffee pot on the table and pulling up a chair, "he walked off the field a long time ago."

"Susan, I'm sorry," Kathy backtracks. "I just meant ..."

"No, you're right, he's not the same. He's content to stay on the sidelines. But I'm tired of sitting on the bench. Steve's attitude about his health, our marriage, life in general is 'if it ain't broke, why fix it.' Mine is 'put me in, Coach.'"

Her friends' eyes connect in brief glances as they pick at the crumbs on their plates.

"Sorry. Way to ruin a mood," Susan says after a few quiet moments. "I do that a lot."

"No, no. I'm glad we can share. Like we used to," Margaret replies.

They spend the rest of the day unpacking, chatting over iced tea on the patio, wandering through Susan's garden before a lunch of salade Niçoise. Just getting a feel for each other's company, trying to resurrect the camaraderie they shared as teenagers, gluing the bonds that have been loosened with time and distance.

"Hey, it's five o'clock somewhere, ladies," Susan announces. "Time to get this party started. Hopefully I've got what you all drink. Who wants to bartend?"

"I'll give it a go," Kathy says. "Didn't I see mint growing out back, Suze? Ever had a mojito? Nothing better on a hot August night," Kathy promises.

"Sure, I'll try one. I'll go cut some for you." Would a mojito have cooled things back then?

"I'll take a martini-vodka, Grey ..." Linda starts, "but Stoli will do. And three olives if you have them."

"I'll stick with white wine. I better ease into this, altitude and all," Margaret says.

Kathy mixes, pours, and passes round the requested drinks, and Susan proposes a toast.

"OK, I worked on this for a while, wanted to make it a good one. So," she pauses, "here's to "Yesterday" and "Things We Said Today" for "Tomorrow Never Knows." Linda, Kathy, Margaret. "From Me to You." Cheers."

Glasses full of muddled mint, shaken vodka, and deeply breathing wine clink together in friendship. With drinks in hand, they shift to the family room. When Susan presses play on the CD player, the four women of a certain age leave sagging bodies and inhibitions behind

219

and head back for a nonstop homage to the Sixties and the boys from Liverpool. As laughter mingles with the background murmurings in the intro to "Sgt. Pepper's Lonely Hearts Club Band," the Beatle Girls reunion is underway.

Thank God the shades are pulled. Susan, Linda, and Margaret bob about as only aging white people can, trying their best to follow Kathy's professional dance moves. Their droopy arms flail as muscles try to remember the Jerk, the Swim, and the Monkey. Corned and bunioned feet Twist gingerly, leave lumps in the Mashed Potato, and rock side to side with Freddie. And as if these tasks aren't difficult enough, they're trying to belt out the words to Beatles songs.

They all close their eyes with the first line of "All My Loving," shake their heads to the yeah yeah yeah's in "She Loves You." The others mumble their way through the later and more obscure compositions, alternating a remembered chorus or hook with la-la's or nah-nah's. But Susan not only knows all the lyrics but recognizes the tune in the first few notes. Her singular talent.

"Whoa, this old girl needs a rest," Susan pants, and plops on the couch, the others landing beside her. She lifts a banker's box marked High School onto the coffee table. "I've been waiting since Christmas to reopen this little time capsule and share it with you guys."

She raises the lid, half expecting moths to fly out, but only specks of dust float through the fading sunlight. On top is a large spiraled sketch book, decorated with colored photos, yellowed newsprint peeking out at the edges.

"My Beatles scrapbook. Take note," Susan says, holding the treasured tome to her chest before opening it for inspection, "I want to be buried with this."

The women crowd around as Susan turns the pages, lingering when interests are piqued.

"The *Hard Day's Night* ticket stub," Kathy whispers. "I watched that with my Dad before he passed."

"I didn't think anyone was as anal as me," Margaret says in amazement. "You saved all these *Sixteen Magazine* clippings."

They leaf through the remnants of their teenage bible, the final authority on all things Beatle-y. 'The Beatles Ask You to Their Homes.' 'Patti Boyd's Beauty Box.' 'Beatles Biggest Blast.'

"Is this the swatch of carpet they supposedly walked on when they landed at Stapleton?" Linda says, rubbing the shaggy red square. "I forgot you actually sent away for that."

"What can I say," Susan shrugs.

In a corner under English essays and report cards, Susan retrieves a pastel striped bottle containing an inch of dark-green liquid. And next to it, a small orange and pink tube.

"Oh. My. God," Kathy gasps, her hands flying to her mouth. "Oh! de London cologne. And City Slicker lip gloss. I can't believe you kept these."

"Yeah, well, stand back. They may vaporize, explode, or render us unconscious." Susan grunts as she twists off the crusted bottle top on the perfume and sniffs. "Oh, dear. More like Oh! de Sewers of London. Here, check it out."

She passes it around for the group to evaluate while she removes the cap from the lipstick and twirls the improbably soft, pale pink wax to the top.

"Anybody wanna try this? I claim no liability if your lips blister and fall off."

Kathy snatches it and smooths it on her bottom lip. "Jean Shrimpton, eat your heart out." She pouts her lips and sucks in her cheeks, triggering similar model poses from the rest of the group.

221

While the rest of the girls play with makeup, Susan searches through the remaining artifacts for anything interesting. Six years of Stallion yearbooks. And several diaries. Best leave those 'til they get really drunk. At the very bottom is a small pink paperback she's never seen, the owner's name written on the inside cover. Mrs. Geraldine Bliss. Susan's eyes widen as she flips through chapters, embarrassed by the thought of her parents' sexual experimentation, yet curious about whether it worked. She'll leave that for later, and *The Sensuous Woman* slinks back into the box. But tucked inside the pages is a black and white photo of four women labeled The Fearsome Foursome 1943.

"Look at this picture," Susan says. "That's my Mom but is that yours, Linda? And who are the others?"

Linda, Kathy, and Margaret study the print. Each points to a glossy woman and shouts, "That's *my* Mom." The Beatle Girls connection runs deep.

CHAPTER 33

A generation ago the mothers of her close friends had themselves been high school pals. She knows her Mom and Linda's developed a relationship when Shirley married Joe, but she doesn't recall any stories about the others. Had The Fearsome Foursome merely drifted apart like The Beatle Girls did, marriage and moves sending them in separate directions? Or had there been a falling out over a dark secret that shattered their sisterhood, their lips forever sealed to its very existence? With everyone gone now, no one will ever know. Sounds like a Nancy Drew mystery. The Clue in the Banker's Box.

"I think that deserves another round and some food," Susan says, and the group follows her into the kitchen, examining the snapshot and the scrapbook as Kathy prepares fresh drinks.

Susan pulls out a tossed salad from the fridge, her only nod to health tonight, and opens the Sixties party favorite, chips and French onion dip. She orders the pizzas from the local Domino's hoping she won't be three sheets to the wind by the time they arrive.

"So, the Fearsome Foursome, huh?" she says after the call. "What did our Mommas do to deserve *that* name?"

"Perhaps they were Rosie the Riveters, pushed by the war into patriotic pluck," Margaret says, her literary skill on display.

"Or just eighteen and full of passion and possibilities," Susan says in her own style. "Like we were once. I saw a quote on Facebook, Thoreau I think. "Don't be afraid your life will end. Be afraid your life will never begin." I wonder, is there time to move past regrets and start over? Any things you guys wish you'd done, or maybe done differently?" Susan asks, before crunching a chip.

"Of course, Susan." Kathy grabs a handful of mint and divides it into two fresh glasses. "Being foot loose and fancy-free has its perks, but ending up an old maid rooming with her dog was not part of the plan. At least it's not a cat. No offense, Margaret."

"None taken," Margaret says, "but surely a woman as beautiful as you must have been in love many times."

"In like, in lust, yeah, but love? Only once." Kathy grinds the mint to a watery pulp, releasing not just the fragrance but perhaps a deep-seated memory as well.

"What happened?" Linda asks.

"In the early Nineties, I did a show in London on the BBC. *Two to Tango*. Only Brits and longtime PBS fans know about it. I played a dance instructor, and each week I'd have a new crop of students and we'd do the quick-step or foxtrot between quips of wry British humor. My favorite role of all time. Anyway, I fell in love with the actor who played my partner at the studio. I was positive I'd found my soul mate. I was even going to stay in England. Put the kettle on the boil and make a proper tea and all." She adds simple syrup and a healthy shot of rum to the mangled herbs and continues.

"Then I got pregnant. At forty. Unbelievable. Ian and I were both ecstatic. We put a down payment on a little thatched roof cottage in the Cotswolds and arranged for a local vicar to marry us. But Ian was an up-and-coming hunk, and when I miscarried, he backed off. It was obvious he'd only been doing 'the right thing.' When the show wrapped, I flew back to LA and my heart belonged to Daddy for the next twenty years." Kathy flips her palms up and shrugs. "What can I say? I have issues."

"Maybe it's time, you know now that he's passed, to take a risk again?" Susan suggests.

"Maybe." She tops off the mojitos with club soda and hands a cocktail to Susan. "I've gotten close to Brian, my Dad's hospice nurse," Kathy says. "There's potential. We shall see ... OK, who's next? Linda?"

"I have a two-drink minimum before I spill my guts." Linda pops the dry docked olives into her mouth and slides the empty glass toward Kathy. "I don't want to seem unkind, Margaret, but you've eaten from a silver spoon since birth. What would you change?"

The doorbell chimes to announce dinner's arrival with the aroma of pepperoni filling the room as Susan pays the delivery boy. The Beatle Girls dish up pizza and salad, grab their next round of drinks, and gather around the nearby kitchen table, ready for the next installment of "Do You Want to Know a Secret?"

"Now back to you, Margaret," Susan says, picking up the discussion where it left off. "You're divorced now, right? Seems like a perfect moment to start over."

"Yes," she says, "but I doubt another relationship is in the cards for me. However, I do agree with you, Linda, that I've been given everything I could possibly want. Except control over my own destiny. So, I'm taking some time away to figure out where my future lies. I'm on leave from the university, and after the wedding, I'll fly to Paris. Maybe next reunion, we meet there."

Linda and Kathy high five each other. Susan chases a cherry tomato around her plate and pierces it with a squish. Just like any dream of her ever going to France.

225

"And I suspect you'll plan it all out in great detail," Linda says. "But haven't you ever wanted to do something wild and crazy, you know, completely out of your comfort zone?"

Apparently, Linda's touched a nerve because Margaret is squirming in her chair like a two-year- old needing to pee. Susan has never known her to do anything that wasn't well thought out.

Margaret clutches her wine glass and exhales through puffed cheeks. "OK, ladies," she says, blowing out one more breath. "Like that Katy Perry song says, 'I kissed a girl.' And I think I liked it."

The straight-laced professor drains her wine glass, along with the color in her friends' faces. Susan's remaining tomato takes a header off the table.

"Whoa, did not see that one coming," Kathy says, her brows raised ever so slightly. "So, was this in college? You know, the freshman experiment?"

"No, a month ago with my friend Denise." She fingers the beads dangling from her neck as if Holy Mother of Pearl might offer direction or redemption. "We both seem to be feigning amnesia, too embarrassed or afraid to bring it up. I'm blaming an alcohol-induced lapse in judgment."

"So who kissed first?" Linda asks, looking up momentarily from her martini. "You or her?"

"I honestly don't remember. Does that mean one or both of us is gay? Maybe that's why I had little interest in boys and my marriage failed? But right now I'm most concerned that the one relationship that matters the most has been irretrievably damaged."

Susan longs to reach out to her friend, take her hand and soothe her like she would anyone who's upset. So why is she hesitating? Is she a closet homophobe, scared Margaret will kiss her? But Kathy isn't freaking out, and

Linda seems pretty blasé. Of course Linda is more sexually enlightened. Maybe she's switched teams a time or two. Finally Kathy breaks the silence.

"Margaret, you must talk with her. Don't wait, hoping time will work this out," she says, giving Margaret's hand a reassuring shake. "You love who you love, and we make ourselves crazy denying our hearts. In the end, it's love that finds us ... when we're ready."

As the women absorb Margaret's confession and Kathy's conviction, the crunch of lettuce, snap of carrots, and tearing of pizza crust fill the air. Susan thinks she's probably right. Steve wasn't ready for her in junior high, and the timing for her and Rick has been off from the beginning. Maybe, like Linda, a bit more booze will nudge her to tell her tale. Perhaps Linda's ready to talk now about the cancer or her relationships. In a preemptive move to postpone her turn and get the conversation going once again, Susan clears her throat and offers the floor to her.

"Linda, like all of us, you've dealt with life changes. What do you wish had been different?"

"What, what?" Linda mumbles, shaking her head, caught daydreaming in class. "Margaret, you talked about lacking control in your life. I can relate to that. My mother made a decision for me that changed my future." Linda's hand reaches out for Susan's, and Susan knows she better grip it like a bull rider holding on for the eight second count. "Senior year, I got pregnant."

"Only Susan and my Mom knew, at least I hope so. Naturally Mom figured the best thing was to give the baby away, so we did. Locked that door and never looked back. Well, somebody found the key. A woman claiming to be my daughter called me a few weeks ago. My first thought was I'm being scammed, but I googled her, and this could be legit. I haven't called her back yet."

"And why the hell not?" Susan throws her hands in the air, surrendering the burden of the confidence and the constraints on her opinions about the whole situation. "This could be your daughter for God's sake. Aren't you curious about her? Beyond a superficial internet search? You want to take back control of your life? Own up to this."

"But how do I explain what I did? It would be easier to talk on the phone."

"Sure, for you. What if Jackie wants to meet her sister. What about that?" Kathy asks.

"And shouldn't she know about the breast cancer," Susan adds, regretting her words when Linda scowls at her.

"Oh, Linda, I'm so sorry. When? Are you doing OK?" Kathy asks, her eyes narrowed with concern.

"Yes, we caught it early and I had a round of chemo," she says pointing to her shortened hair, "so a good prognosis. Luckily, I don't carry the gene, but, you're right, she deserves to know her medical history."

"What about the father?" Margaret asks. "I'm assuming this wasn't a virgin birth." All eyes lock on the professor and her first comments since her own soul baring. "I mean, this was before in vitro fertilization is all I'm saying."

"Well, yes, but some secrets need to remain just that. He was never in the picture and is probably dead for all I know. There's DNA testing, maybe that will help." She ruffles her hair and exhales. "Mom was always my fixer, took care of my messes, but you're right, I need to call. After the wedding though."

"And you know we'll support you when you're ready," Kathy reassures her. "So, Miss Suzy-Q? What's the story with Rick?"

After two mojitos, her lips are loose. Probably more a liability than an asset. She vowed to keep her relationship with Rick hidden, but everyone else has crawled deep into their chamber of secrets. Besides this is the only one she has, and if she can't trust her friends? She pushes away from the table, creating a fire wall against the impending bombshell.

"All righty then." Susan lowers her voice and clutches her chest. "Remember, Sullivan gossip spreads like fire on a windy day. This stays with us. Deal?"

"Deal," her friends agree, locking their lips with imaginary keys.

"I first met him when I was waitressing at the diner in the early eighties, when Steve and I were going through a rough financial patch ..."

Susan pauses, still unsure if her secret shouldn't remain undisturbed, snug in the folds of a two-party memory.

"Aaaaaaand," Kathy pokes at her shoulder.

"He was like an older brother. He was a teaser, made me laugh but I could talk with him about anything. In hindsight, I guess we had chemistry, but it felt more like the pulling pigtails kind. So anyway we're closing up on one of those hot, humid summer nights when everything's sweating, and instead of our usual coffee we opt for cold beers ..." She closes her eyes and the fuzzy memory comes back into crisp focus. "We decide to share the last piece of Palisade peach pie. So we're picking at it with our forks, chugging down Coors, listening to the radio. Wham and Phil Collins, even John's son Julian had a couple of hits. But when "I Can't Hold Back" by Survivor comes on, it's like the words are meant for us. There's a line about trembling when we touch ..." she pauses and swallows," and that's all it took. Between all the musky sweat, his Brut aftershave, and the sweet spicy

229

peach juice on his lips ..." She inhales sharply before releasing a long, quivering breath. "Let's say we didn't hold back. I swear to God. Best sex I ever had. Sooooo ..."

All is quiet. Except for Susan's heart clanging against her ribs. There's no taking it back now. She prays the Beatle Girls keep their lips together better than she did her legs.

CHAPTER 34

Susan wakes with a start, her heart flopping like a just caught catfish in her Daddy's row boat. The sun bursts through the curtains and her eyes tighten like fists. She squints to see the alarm clock. Damn, she's overslept, and the dog is no doubt peeing willy-nilly on the carpet. And where's Steve? She throws off the covers and swings her legs out. Bam. A rhythmic throbbing hammers the back of her head. Crap, it's a hangover. Her first. And she prays, her last.

She forces herself up and into the bathroom, splashing water onto her face and into her mouth. She remembers that Steve and Bungalow Bill are at Maureen's so no need to worry about either them or the carpet. Grabbing her robe, she tiptoes past the guest rooms. The doors are open. She steadies herself with the rail as she heads down to the sounds of laughter coming from the patio.

"Hello, sleepy head," Kathy says. "Need some coffee?"

"Need a shotgun," Susan moans. "How dare you all look so chipper."

Susan rests her head in her hands awaiting the coffee, and two Tylenol, courtesy of Linda.

"I should have told you to take these last night. Sorry."

"You should have told me not to drink that last mojito," Susan says, plopping the pills in her mouth.

"Or read from your diary," Linda says.

"We now know what's on your bucket list," Kathy says. "To have a romantic liaison with a man with an accent, write a book of desperate poetry, and run off with Ringo on a madcap holiday."

Susan shakes her head in slow motion. "Was that all?"

"Of the interesting stuff. We didn't really care what you had for breakfast on Tuesday, November 18. Anyway, we want to go into town and have a Girls Spa Day before the concert," Linda announces. "I wrangled us appointments at my salon for early afternoon. Facials, massages, hair, makeup, the works."

"You were so apologetic after you spilled the beans about Rick," Kathy says with finger over lips, "telling us how that's in the past and you're set on spicing things up with Steve. So we thought you might like a makeover."

"We're even taking you clothes shopping for tonight and the wedding. Our treat," Margaret adds.

"Guys, that's so nice, but seriously, I can pay."

"No, dear, believe me, let us pay. We're going five-star, Miss Suzy Q. Plus we'll stay at my place after the concert," Linda says.

"I better let Steve know."

"Sure, tell him you'll be home in the morning, and then surprise him with your new look. If he don't jump your bones, Girl, he don't deserve you," Kathy says with a wink.

The Tylenol hasn't quite kicked in and Susan is having serious misgivings about her expose. And her vow of fidelity. Her feelings for Steve still blow like a willow in the wind. If he's in a good mood, then the sun shines and she's over the moon for him, ready to keep on keepin' on. If he wakes up grouchy, complaining, or ignoring her, then she's inventorying their possessions and looking for lawyers. Maybe a change in her appearance is the spark she needs to set her marriage ablaze.

The Beatle Girls pack overnight bags and head into Denver, ready for a day of womanly pampering and an evening of teenage fantasy. Over lunch, they review the pros and cons of the change.

"What if I can't make it look the same at home? I remember all those frizzy perms and the promises it would look different after I washed it. It never did."

"No perms, OK. A layered bob is absolutely perfect for your fine wavy hair. Paulo's fabulous cuts just fall into place. If he can make chemo hair look fabulous, just imagine what he can do for you," Linda reassures.

"What about the makeup? I don't want to look like a hussy."

"Sweetie," says Kathy, "the best makeup is subtle. It'll highlight your best features, your eyes, and cover up the not so good parts like the uneven skin tones. This isn't rocket science. You can do it, believe me."

"You do know I shop in the Big Girls section. I haven't been in single digits since high school." Susan puts down her French fry. Maybe not the best choice for a day of improving her image.

"Well-made clothes make everyone look great," Margaret says. "And we can have it tailored if need be.

"OK, I'm putting my trust in you, but you'll tell me if I look hideous. Right?"

⌘⌘⌘⌘⌘

"Oh, My God, Susan! You look absolutely fabulous!" the women exclaim as the finishing touches are completed.

Susan barely recognizes the woman staring at her in the mirror. The graying nondescript mop is gone and in its stead are caramel highlights woven into shiny chestnut-brown hair. Feathery bangs and wispy side pieces frame her face and hazel eyes. Her skin is all one soft-

233

ivory color, her long lashes are visible, her lips glisten in a rosy pink shade. The *What Not to Wear* team must be around the corner.

"So, whadya think?" Kathy asks.

Susan holds the mirror away from her grinning face and then closer, turning her head left then right, swiveling around in the chair to see how the hair lays in back. She hovers her hand over her head and face as if surrounded by a bubble and with one stray touch, all will be lost.

"Thank you, guys. Thank you. Oh, crap, I'm gonna cry and ruin it all."

It's off to Nieman-Marcus to find the perfect outfit for the concert and the wedding. Susan expects a rom-com soundtrack any minute as she wiggles into jeans, slithers into dresses, steps into slacks, and pokes her arms into tops, prancing about the dressing room while her friends shake their heads or give thumbs up. At last final decisions are made.

The emerald-green Diane von Furstenberg wrap dress accentuates her hourglass figure, and even though her measurements haven't changed, she appears ten pounds lighter. Her dark wash jeans fit snugly without squishing anything out and over. The graphic tee in soft rose flows below her hips, making her butt seem smaller for a change. Yes, she does look younger. And dare she admit it, sexy. Yes, she is "absolutely fabulous."

A quick stop at Linda's to freshen up, change clothes, and nosh on lite bites and they're off to Red Rocks and the concert. While they'll spend time with each other at the wedding, tonight is the last official Beatle Girls event. They unearthed the good old days, updated their current status, and laid out blueprints for the future. And like they had in high school, they trusted each other enough to lay bare their dark and sometimes dirty secrets.

CHAPTER 35

The Beatle Girls make their way up the steep stony inclines leading to the Red Rocks amphitheater, Denver's world renown outdoor venue near Morrison, where the Beatles actually played on August 26, 1964. Tonight the tribute band, 1964, will be playing in their stead. Linda rented a limo to transport them to and from the concert, eliminating the need for a designated driver.

"I'm dying here," Susan gasps, already straining to get her words out and only halfway up the path. Linda and Margaret are using the rail to pull themselves along, and even Kathy looks a bit flushed. "Nobody thought there might be old farts at this concert? Can we ... just ... stop for a minute?"

At last they reach the entrance to the amphitheater and catch their breath while park security scans their tickets and searches their bags for contraband. Black market statins and Viagra, Susan figures. Kiosks line the walkway selling Beatles merchandise and souvenirs, with other vendors offering snacks and drinks, including alcohol.

"Anyone interested in something with a kick?" Linda asks.

"Not for me," Susan says. "One hangover a week is my limit. Besides, I'll need my wits to get back down."

Linda seems to have taken up the drink again. Surely that can't be a good thing after chemotherapy, but she's the nurse after all. Margaret declines as well, but Kathy and Linda opt for plastic cups of wine.

"Oh. My. God. This is absolutely incredible. It really does take your breath away," Kathy says when the Girls enter the sacred space.

The red sandstone rock formations rise hundreds of feet, creating a natural acoustic masterpiece for the performer and audience. The stage is at the bottom and seating extends all the way to the top, so there's a great view from almost anywhere. The rain that poured down on their way over has moved out, and the clearing skies promise a fantastic evening. And for the Beatle Girls, one that's been on hold for forty-six years.

"Kathy, maybe your Mom was right with her warnings," Susan says with tongue in cheek. "This *is* a dangerous place. Look at all the rowdies and bottles flying."

They float amid a sea of graying and expanding sixty somethings in a variety of Beatles tees and improvised Sgt. Pepper costumes, climbing the steps with titanium knees. The only rowdiness has been in the line for the women's bathroom. And the only thing flying about is occasional gas.

"And seriously," Kathy adds holding up her red Solo cup, "I'm drinking out of plastic. I haven't quite forgiven her for not letting us go to the concert, but back then it would have been all adolescent hormones and screaming. Tonight we might actually hear the band."

"*We* knew these guys would last forever, though most said they were a flash in the pan," Susan recalls. "Hell, even the Beatles figured they'd be done by the time they turned thirty. Geez, I guess since they broke up in 1970, that sorta came true, huh."

"Still, I wish we coulda seen the real deal," Kathy sighs, "been as close as we are tonight, seen the sweat dripping off their faces. But, you know, we'd have been so consumed by our mania, we wouldn't have appreciated how special it was. So tonight, if these guys are as good as their press, let's pretend we're teenagers again. Sixty going on thirteen."

Under a cloudless sky and a nearly full moon, the Beatles tribute band, 1964, begins the concert with "I Want to Hold Your Hand." They go on to perform the same play list the Beatles did on that long-ago August night along with other songs released during the short time they toured. The band has the Fab Four personas down - their voices, the witty banter, the incredible musicianship. Add in stovepipe pants, pointy boots, mop top haircuts, some liberal stage makeup, and a bit of imagination, and it's all there. Susan hears every word, every chord, and not a squeal all night. The only sounds from the audience on this warm summer evening are voices singing along to every song, hands clapping in and out of time, and enthusiastic applause at the end.

"That was extraordinary. An absolutely marvelous idea, Susan," Margaret says, as the women navigate the much easier descent to their waiting town car. No one seems anxious to talk. Perhaps the evening needs time to weave itself into remembrance, tying off the loose end of their teenage years.

Flutes of champagne, poured just before their return, sit on the small middle table. Like freakin' rock stars. Susan's ready to flash a peace sign at the passing pedestrians or hide her face from the paparazzi. As the chauffeur winds down the road out of the park and back to Linda's condo, the Beatle Girls clink their glasses to celebrate the music, the memories, the moment.

They change into comfy nightclothes and gather in Linda's large boudoir. Just like after the *Ed Sullivan Show*. Margaret in a chair, curled to one side, with Kathy

237

cross legged on the floor nearby. Linda stretches out on her bed.

"Anyone want a cup of tea before we get all snuggly?" Susan asks. Three nods send her off to Linda's kitchen to nuke water and drop bags in four cups. So much for the lifestyles of the rich and famous. No all-night after show parties for them. Just tea and jammies.

"So, did anyone actually see the Beatles, or even a single Beatle, in person?" Susan asks, passing around the steaming brew. "You know, a close encounter of the 3rd rock star." Susan grabs her mug and leans against the headboard, her knees pulled toward her chest, though only about half the distance as forty-six years ago.

"Once I was in New York City near the Dakota and thought I saw John walking with Sean toward Central Park," Margaret says. "Seemed so happy."

"I was dancing in a couple of clubs in LA in the late seventies to make ends meet, and I'm pretty sure Ringo came in with an entourage," Kathy says. "Some pretty wasted dudes. Not a good time to ask for an autograph."

"How about you, Linda? Any degrees of separation?" Susan asks.

"Rob and I got tickets to see Paul up in Boulder in '93. Part of his New World Tour. Two hundred bucks a pop but it was worth it. Linda was still alive and in the band."

"Oh," Susan says, her voice as low as her head. "I wanted to go but too pricey for me."

"God, I didn't even think about asking you. I should have. My bad."

Everyone of the Girls had a Beatles sighting except her. Yet she was, and still is, the biggest fan. Hardly seems fair. They drink their beverages in silence, sipping a blend of guilt, pity, and regret, until Susan fills the awkward silence.

"And, now there's only two," she says, her eyes misting despite the passage of time. "I was home on the farm, watching TV with Steve, when I heard about John. So unexpected and senseless. I cried like a baby, the kids trying to comfort me. By the time George passed I was a grandmother. Still numb after 9/11. I'd heard rumors of cancer, but still it hit me hard. Both times I felt a part of me die as well."

Susan retreats inward, her gaze unfocused, the lyrics to "Imagine" and "While my Guitar Gently Weeps" running through her mind. They played them over and over on those dark days back in December 1980 and November 2001. The words so profound, then, and always.

"The break-up was hard enough, but this?" she continues. "How could they be gone? I know they talk about creating a New Beatles with Paul and Ringo, plus John and George's children or even holograms. But it's like a beloved pet. You can't just substitute one for the other. It's not the same."

"I know, and how easy it is to forget we're only given so much time," Kathy says. "All the more reason to search our hearts, minds, and diaries for unfulfilled aspirations." She winks at Susan. "Dust them off, rework them. Spirit never puts expiration dates on dreams."

The women raise a silent toast to Kathy's words. These past days have been full of memories and laughter, but also talk of regrets and unmet promise. "Revolution" has become her battle cry for the here and now, but what will be her hymn for the hereafter?

"OK then ladies, here's another question for you," Susan says. "What Beatles song best describes your life? The one you want carved on your tombstone."

"Oh, that's a no-brainer," Kathy says without a pause, raising her arms overhead and then spreading them wide with graceful hands. "'I'm Happy Just to

Dance with You.' And you're all welcome to dance on my grave."

Linda takes a sip of tea before she answers. "Technically it isn't by the Beatles since it's on McCartney's first solo album, but "Lovely Linda." I used to rationalize this was about me. Not that other Linda. But if I have to pick a true Beatles song? Hmm, I'm not sure this is how I want to be remembered, but ... there'd be no mistaking it was me. Let's go with the Narcissist's Song," Linda says, "George's 'I, Me, Mine.'"

"Linda, I'm impressed with your insight. It took years of therapy to admit my fatal flaws," Margaret says, with a brief smile.

"Let's face it, I've spent my entire life looking out for number one," Linda says. "But with the whole sixtieth birthday thing and the breast cancer, I'm realizing there's more to life than work and money. So how about you, Margaret? Maybe 'Paperback Writer'?"

"That's on my bucket list so we'll see. But my undoing has been expecting perfect on the outside to lead to perfect on the inside. I've hidden behind 'a wall of illusion' as George wrote in "Within You Without You." With my career, my marriage, maybe my sexuality. But he also says, 'no one else can make you change." Margaret cradles her cup with both hands before taking a long sip and a deep breath. "Unless it's a cosmic two by four. The reason I finally divorced Jeff ..." She sips again. "New Year's Eve ... he assaulted me."

"Oh, my God," Susan gasps, touching her friend without hesitation this time. "What happened?"

"He flew into a rage and choked me. If not for my chauffeur ... you'd be chiseling my song for real. But, he's out of my life now and I'm ready to make changes."

Susan rubs Margaret's arm trying to smooth away the pain of her ordeal. In comparison, her own life has been so blessed. Yes, she's lost parents and a way of life, but

240

never babies. She's never dealt with life-threatening situations inflicted from within or without. Yet why does she cling to her image as a loser? Nothing but album filler. Not good enough for the A side. Maybe she needs a cosmic whomp upside her head to knock in some gratitude.

"So, I guess I'm the last one for the stone cutter," Susan says. "I ran through a whole list of possibilities while you all were revealing your choices, and different times called up different tunes. The Beatles music will always reflect our lives, but the song I want as my legacy is "All You Need Is Love," because there's 'nowhere you can be that isn't where you're meant to be.'"

AND I LOVE HER

CHAPTER 36

Sweat trickles down Susan's back as she lounges in the shade of her front porch on this Friday before the last weekend of August. Harvest is winding down, school is starting up, and leaves will soon murmur and mesmerize with their colorful swan song. Summer, however, is not quite ready to pack up and turn over the keys to Autumn. Lawn mowers continue to whir and spit out dark-green blades of barefoot grass. Charcoaled meat still sizzles and saturates the air with mesquite smoke. Splashes of mischievous laughter rise and echo from backyard wading pools. The cycles of nature will roll on as expected, but Susan hopes her summer of love and liberation will be endless.

Kathy and Margaret just left on a scenic tour of the Colorado foothills and mountainsides, assured of clear roads though too soon for the gold rush of quaking, tumbling fall colors. They'll travel as far as Aspen, the upscale and downslope capital of the Rocky Mountains, taking in whatever natural and cultural gems sluice out of the pan. Then they'll wind their way back to Boulder for the wedding the following Saturday.

While the flurry of the past few days with her friends has revived her yearning for making changes and taking chances, Susan craves the rhythm of familiar routine and the opportunity to organize her life before the next event of the season. Tomorrow she'll be up at dawn once again and off to the bakery.

Back with Rick. Both sets of lips have been sealed regarding the "kiss" ever since that July morning. But now that the original sin has been revealed, even if only to trusted friends, Susan feels the need to tread cautiously. Let all assume any feelings are long buried. Never mind that the dirt around the grave has been disturbed.

Today she flies the flag of Team Steve, cleaning his castle top to bottom, and fixing him a home-cooked feast to confirm her fealty to her princely partner. He was already at work when the three women returned to Sullivan, so she calls his cell to update her current location and plans.

"Hey, stranger. Got home a couple of hours ago. The Girls are gone 'til the wedding. Thought I'd make a nice dinner and we could talk."

"Figured you'd be all talked out. And yet, there's more."

"Come on, this is about us. Without yelling or insults."

"That'd be nice."

"I just want us to ... 'get back, get back to where we once belonged," she sings. "Sorry, I've OD'd on the Beatles."

"Well, tell me all about the concert and whatever else is on your mind later."

"See you by six?"

"Sure, Hon."

Susan feels her heart beating faster, with that little lump in her stomach that signals good things, or bad things. Hard to tell sometimes. He's stingy with his words still, but one of them had been 'Hon.' Always a good omen.

She pulls three petite filets out of the freezer, the ones she gets at Costco with bacon wrapped around them. There's a roast, but it will take too long to thaw, and besides the filets feel more romantic. She pulls out a chocolate cake mix and stirs the ingredients together, begging the kitchen gods not to rat her out for not starting from scratch. With that in the oven, she begins the task of setting her house to rights. Dusting and sweeping away the remains of the reunion. Gathering up the flotsam and jetsam covering tables, rerouting misplaced items to their lawful places. Unblocking the negative chi that has taken over her home. She plans to wear her new jeans and the wrap top patiently waiting since December to strut its stuff. She'll try her hand at applying the makeup to see if the glamour and confidence of two days ago can be replicated. It's four o'clock and she's loading her right eyelashes with mascara when the phone rings.

"Gramma, you busy?" asks Jenny.

"Well, I've got a minute or two. What's up, Sweetie?" Susan wonders if her name has been changed to 'U Busy.'

"I think I might be in labor."

"What?" Susan's heart plummets. Thirty-four weeks is too early. Panic tugs at her but she knows the voice of calm is what's needed. "Why?" she drawls. "Are you having contractions? How far apart?"

"They kinda come and go. They hurt but not real bad. Should I go to the hospital?"

"Where's your Mom?"

"Where do you think? Tonight's Back to School night. Grandpa being here set her back, she says, so I've been warned not to bother her."

Honestly, where are your priorities, daughter? Bulletin board or baby. Not a hard choice.

"Well, we just might have to interrupt her day," she says with a tad of snark. "It could just be those Braxton

Hicks contractions. Let's talk to Renee and see what she thinks."

"Could you come over, be with me when I call?"

"OK. Just give me a minute. See you soon."

What else can she do? She and Steve need this evening, but if Jenny's in labor someone should be with her. Thank God, Gramma knows what's important. She sticks the thawed filets in the fridge. She can frost the cake and toss a salad later. Do the left eye and call it good. Wait to call Steve when she knows something.

⌘⌘⌘⌘⌘

Susan and Jenny sit side by side, cradling hands, with the phone on speaker.

"Hello, this is Jenny Lawson. Is Renee available?" Jenny asks.

"Jenny, what's up?" Renee asks. "Still coming in tomorrow?"

"Well ... maybe sooner. I might be in labor."

Renee runs down a list of questions for Jenny, a prenatal algorithm requiring only yes or no answers, her voice calm with experience. Confirming that it's most likely the tightening of pre-labor, she offers Jenny some strategies to relieve the discomfort and promises everything will be checked at tomorrow's appointment.

"Good job, Jenny Girl. Do what Renee said, and tell your Mom about this. OK?" Susan kisses her forehead and pulls her in close. "You know, it feels like ages since we talked. Hey, you wanna come over next Thursday and help me bake the real wedding cake?"

"Yeah, that'd be fun." Jenny hunches her shoulders and gives a mischievous grin. "We could talk about baby names."

"What? Does that mean ...?"

"Yeah, I'm keeping the baby."

Susan's smile cannot be contained on her face, and the joy spreads to every nook and cranny of her being. How could anyone in their right mind ever give away their flesh and blood? She rocks the mother of her first great-grandchild and then backs away to take Jenny's face in her hands.

"I don't think this day can get any better."

"I'm so glad I have you, Gramma." Jenny narrows her eyes, "Hey, you did something with your hair, didn't you?"

"Yes, my friends did a whole *What Not to Wear* makeover. Do you like it?" Susan asks turning her head from side to side.

"Yeah, you look younger than Mom."

"I better get Old Bill and scoot on home. Grandpa and I are having a romantic dinner tonight."

Jenny scrunches her nose just enough to let Susan know the news of her grandparents' intimate plans is way too much information.

⌘⌘⌘⌘⌘

Susan called Steve when she returned at four-thirty to update him about Jenny and remind him that dinner was still on for six. It's now six-fifteen. The medium rare filets and moist baked potatoes wait in the warm oven along with the bright green beans. The cake is frosted, and the salad is in the fridge alongside ice-cold beers for her and Steve. Flowers from the yard grace the center of the arranged table and tall candles are aflame. All she needs is Steve. The store closes at five, and nothing in Sullivan is more than ten minutes away. So where is he? Surely he wouldn't forget about this, blow her off because he's afraid of the 'talking.' No, maybe a late customer.

249

Seven-fifteen. The potato jackets will need ironing and the meat is well done shoe leather. The beans. Don't ask. She blew the candles out an hour ago. Damn it. She presses the line for Steve on her phone and hears it ring. If he knows what's good for him, he better be in a ditch somewhere. Two rings, four rings and then she hears the front door knob jiggle.

"Hey, can you let me in?"

"Steve?"

"My hands are full and my phone's ringing."

She opens the door to see her husband, down on one knee looking up at her, his head lowered and hands behind his back. Oh, crap, maybe he was in a ditch.

"Where have you been? You're an hour late."

He sticks out his lower lip and extends a bouquet of red roses. "Sorry," he says, his voice soft and babyish. "These are for you."

She pulls him to standing and into the house, his breath reeking of Jack Daniels. This time, however, the only feminine fragrance drifts from the flowers she lays on the table.

"Steven, why on earth did you go drinking? How can we talk now?"

He leans into her, putting his arms around her neck. Susan longs to mirror his embrace but her crossed arms stay glued to her chest in a tight braid that isn't coming undone without a good explanation on his part.

"You know how hard it is for me to talk ... about feelings. I went with the guys for a shot of courage. And one drink led to one more."

"You must be very brave right now," Susan says, her glare tempered by his honesty. "Listen, all I want is to clear the air. We've been ships passing in the night for months. I'm not gonna psychoanalyze you, for God's sakes. I just need to know we're good. Is that so scary?"

"No, I'm sorry. I'm sorry. Wait, I gotta sit."

Susan pulls out a chair for him. She fills two glasses with water and slides next to him at the table.

"I was feeling forgotten," he starts. "You had all this stuff goin' on. The baking, your friends, the wedding stuff, even Jenny. No time for me. I was just an image in your rearview mirror."

Susan unwinds her arms and lays them in her lap. She looks into his All-American eyes, blue on a field of white and red thanks to the booze, and listens.

"Life is passing me by. I get up, go to a job I don't like but can't afford to leave, then come home and watch TV. If you're not here, what have I got? I need you, Suze."

Suddenly this husky, leather-skinned man begins blubbering like a nine year old boy whose dog just died. Susan eases herself onto his lap and swaddles his jerking shoulders, waiting for this unexpected rush of tender emotion to settle. She strokes his thinning hair as his sobs soak into her bosom. When a heavy sigh signals that the moment has played out, she holds his stubbled cheeks in her hands.

"And I need you too," she says wiping the moisture from his cheeks with her thumbs. "It's just, once upon a time we had a connection. Lately I feel like a live-in maid. I need to be more than that. I know I'm not sexy like the gals at the bar, but see, I'm trying." She leans back to show off her new look and waits. Steve gives her a once-over, but Susan knows he's clueless as to what he supposed to notice. What would be so obvious to a woman eludes the man.

"Wait, your hair is different, right? Yeah, it's nice."

Bingo. "And I'm wearing makeup and have new clothes," she says, pointing out the details like Vanna White. "Hey, that trip you mentioned? The cruise. Is it still on?"

"Yeah, end of September. That's it," he clears his throat and sniffs, "that's what we need. Just me and my good-lookin' wife. I love you, Suze."

"*Je t'aime, mon amour.*"

She kisses him fully on the lips, long and hard with eyes closed. And he reciprocates. Her body tingles as blood pulsates in places long-deemed lifeless. Until she opens her eyes. What the hell? What is Rick's moustache doing on Steve's face?

CHAPTER 37

During college, Kathy had risen at dawn a few times to strap on her skies and schuss down the slopes. Back then, before the interstate was expanded to four lanes, the twists and turns and steep drop-offs had been harrowing, especially in winter. Even when she was only a passenger. Now, the present passage through the mountains allows for moments to soak in the rocky spires, roadside wild flowers, and rushing waterfalls along the way.

"I thought we could stop in Georgetown, ride the Loop Railroad, followed by a cuppa at this charming tea room, dear heart," Margaret says, folding the map to highlight the route. "Then once we pass through the Eisenhower Tunnels, we have two options to reach Aspen. A Rocky Mountain nail-biting high or a rugged but scenic canyon with a dip in the hot springs. Either way we'll be among the rich and famous by evening."

Kathy's 2000 Subaru is used to the stop and go of constantly congested freeways, merging and weaving in and out to avoid tie-ups, getting out of the way of road rage and police chases. Steep grades, falling rock signs, and runaway truck ramps are not a part of the LA driver's manual. And while she's pretty sure the car has enough gas, the thin air at ten thousand feet may leave her lungs sputtering.

"If it's all the same to you, Margaret, I'll take breathing over breathtaking."

"Glenwood Canyon it is then."

⌘⌘⌘⌘⌘

The elegant Dusty Rose Tea Room in Georgetown is housed in an 1875 building transformed from store to hotel and now back to a shop again.

"Oh, my, Kathy, this is just exquisite," Margaret says as they wander through rooms decorated with flowery wallpaper and portraits hung by ribbons, carved furniture covered with velvet, and antique knickknacks on display throughout. "I really think I was born too late. Bring on the corsets and bustles and lace handkerchiefs."

"Yeah, it's beautiful, but a bit too constricting and froufrou for me. Anyway, good thing I'm not wearing a corset 'cause I'm starving," and Kathy scrolls through the menu choices.

After dining on the Petit Tea - a spinach tart, a cucumber sandwich, a scone with Devonshire cream and lemon curd, and a chocolate rum cup - they linger over porcelain cups of Rocky Mountain Morning, a blend of organic black tea, raspberries, and a touch of cream.

"Sitting here in the epitome of Victorian decorum, it's a little ironic that a day or so ago we were discussing societal improprieties that women of these times couldn't have imagined. Well, at least wouldn't have talked about," Margaret adds.

"Right. Affairs, lesbian lovers, extreme spinsterhood. I do believe I might swoon," Kathy laughs, waving her napkin in front of her face. "I bet a lot more went on under those crinoline skirts than we realize."

"No doubt from what I've read. But take heart on the old maid issue. Jane Austen and the Bronte Sisters would have been nothing without the unmarried governess."

"Oh, Hooray for us. Strong willed, opinionated heroines did seem to do all right by the last chapter, didn't they? Maybe Brian is my Mr. Darcy. After he got his comeuppance, of course. Thoughtful, sincere, steady with a purpose."

"Earnest is what he would have been called," Margaret explains.

"And how important to be just that. I think I'll give him a call later. Our truth or dare moments have inspired me, and I want to share something with him. See if he'll come out for the wedding. He's a Colorado native, you know. Maybe he'd enjoy getting back to his roots. I'll get the check this time," Kathy offers.

⌘ ⌘ ⌘ ⌘ ⌘

Three hours later, they're checked into The Hotel Jerome, on Linda's recommendation, and finishing up a quick dinner at the on-site restaurant.

"Whew, either the altitude or the drive is doing a number on me," Kathy moans. "Think I'll call it a night."

"Yeah, I'll be right behind you. I want to check with the concierge about activities for the week first. The brochure mentioned classical music concerts up on Aspen Mountain. And yoga during the week for you. Plus I kind of want to walk around the hotel. Embrace the history and all. Sorry, Kathy, I'll always be the professor," Margaret says with a self-conscious grin.

Kathy counts out money for her share of dinner and tip, and makes a beeline for the paneled lobby elevator. While she'd normally take the stairs, there'll be hikes and walking and who knows what other physical activities later. The only exercise she's up for now is eyelid raises until she can drift into the sweet surrender of slumber.

A quick shower to rinse off the travel sweat, and Kathy is cloaked in the soft cool sheets of her queen-sized bed. A cup of green tea from the amenities selection rests on her bedside table as she scrolls for Brian's name on her cell phone.

"Hey, Brian. Greetings from eight thousand feet."

"Hey, Kath. Where are you?"

"Aspen. Livin' large. A little side trip with my friend. What's up seaside?"

"Only the tide. Somebody wants to say Hi."

Kathy hears Murphy barking in the background, each woof growing higher in pitch as she squeals out good boy praise. She misses her furry BFF. So if Brian is with Murphy then he must be at Max's.

"So, Boy's Night, huh? How's Mad Max?"

"He just raised a beer bottle to you. What about the reunion? Have a good walk down memory lane?"

"Oh, it was fabulous. Drank too much. You know how that goes. It always amazes me that despite the passage of time and experiences we don't really change. Just get grayer around the edges. I did learn a few things about everyone that kinda blew me away," adding ominously, "deep dark secrets ..."

"Care to share?"

"Nah, pinky swears and all. But there is something I need to talk about with you. If I could."

"Wait, let me go somewhere more secure. OK, I'm all ears."

Kathy sips her tea and closes her eyes. Maybe this isn't the right time for this call, but with confessions popping up and out the last few days, her gnawing guilt about her father has resurfaced. She worries her ethically challenged behavior could end up poisoning her future with Brian. If she is to pursue this relationship, she needs to know she can trust him. With everything.

"Brian," she begins, her chest tightening as the guards around her heart close ranks, "I lay awake at night wondering ... if ... if I did the right thing by my Dad. If I tell you something, will it be confidential? Are you like a priest or a lawyer, sworn to secrecy?"

"Not sure I'm that powerful but I hope you see me as a good friend. I don't want to presume, but I've heard most of the stories about regrets from loved ones. Lay it on me. No judgement."

Though she no longer buys into a vengeful God, it feels like punishing hands are squeezing the air out of her lungs and contorting her intestines. Brian's offer of absolution has removed the lid from her pot of sin, and the simmering remorse bubbles to the surface.

"I gave him morphine, Brian. I filled the syringe and shoved it all in."

Kathy drops her confession, glad to be rid of the weight she has carried since her father's death. But like prolonged muscle exertion, the strain of holding on to her shame leaves her conscience trembling. She buckles in a flurry of rationalization.

"He begged me, Brian. Please he said. I said I can't. But I did. I ... I ... killed my Daddy." Her voice disintegrates into unintelligible babble and sobs.

There is no reply from Brian's end, not that Kathy could have heard him anyway, lost in her distress. After several minutes, she composes herself with a watery sniff. She dabs her eyes and nose on the sheet. The eight hundred thread count Egyptian cotton sheet.

"Kathy. Listen to me," his voice matter-of-fact. "You did not kill your father. Chronic alcoholism killed him. He was going to die no matter what you, or I, or any medical person, or even God did. Morphine merely eased his pain, reduced the anxiety, allowed for a more peaceful transition. And he gave you permission. You were

257

doing what your Dad requested. He trusted you, Kathy. Now trust yourself. You did the right thing."

The phone quivers in Kathy's hand as her ears latch on to the words of vindication. She had permission. She did right. He says it's OK. But now that she's told him, why doesn't she feel better about it? She should have done this in person, not over the phone. She could use a Brian hug right now.

"Did you know what I'd done?"

"Yes, as soon as I picked up the vial. It's a narcotic so I had to account for it. But no one really cares much about the amount you gave. I believed you had used it appropriately. Bottom line, the final outcome was already determined. All you did was influence its timing."

Kathy lets the verdict sink in. Not guilty. Not even an insanity qualifier. Just not guilty. She relaxes her shoulders and nudges her heart out into the open.

"Thank you, Brian. I should have said something before I left for Colorado. Speaking of which, think you might make it to the wedding? Next Saturday. On the fourth. I'd love to introduce you to my friends."

There is a silence, and Kathy checks her phone for bars, wondering if she's lost the signal or the battery died.

"Brian, are you there? Can you hear me?"

"Yes, I'm here. Just thinking." Another pause. "I've got some irons in the fire out here."

"What's up?" she asks, scooting back up against the headboard.

"I'll be sixty-five in November. I'm signed up for Medicare and Social Security and I have decent money in my IRA. I'm thinking of retiring."

The topic hasn't come up before in their talks, but it makes sense. "Sounds like a good idea. What would you do?"

"I want to leave California. Go somewhere less crowded and stressful. I've only stayed because of my job. I have an itch to travel, see what else is out there."

She'd been counting on Brian to anchor her ever drifting heart. But in LA. And now he wants to raise the sails and head out to sea. Once again, she didn't see the boom, and she's flailing in the deep.

"So ...," she hesitates.

"Kath, I know this is kinda outta the blue, but why don't you come with me? Or if that doesn't work for you, we could meet up wherever, whenever."

"One of those long-distance relationships? Yeah, those always work so well. I've had on location romances. I'd rather have a long-running weekly series in town. I don't know, Brian," she says with a huff, "I need a nest, and it sounds like you want to spread your wings and fly. Anyway, it's been a long day and I'm exhausted. Why don't you figure it out, and I'll call you when I get back. Later."

"Good night, Ka..."

She ends the call, not wanting to hear any more. She only has enough energy for one breakdown per day. She turns out the light and punches her pillow, as much to knock some sense into it as to mold it to her head. What is it about her and men? Is she too guarded? Too gullible? Or does she just make poor choices? Not see the facts, only the fantasy? Well, as the song says, no, no, no, "Not a Second Time." More like the third, or tenth, or hundredth time.

259

CHAPTER 38

Margaret sits by the window, tea in hand, and watches Mother Sun unwrap the rose and lilac blanket from her newborn day, gently stirring Morning from its slumber. Kathy is still in bed. She heard her thrashing about during the night. Perhaps the elevation and tension from the day- long drive interrupted her sleep, so she will leave a note and head down for breakfast after a quick shower. She feels rested and full of energy after downing some ibuprofen and several glasses of water upon arriving yesterday, hoping to stave off altitude sickness. Some fluffy buttermilk pancakes should help as well.

Her breakfast has just been served when she sees Kathy at the entrance to the Prospect Restaurant and waves her over.

"Sorry, Margaret," Kathy says, her eyes shielded by her sunglasses as she pulls out a chair. "I have such a headache. Like a hangover."

"The altitude. Here. Take these." Margaret reaches in her purse for the Advil. "And drink lots of water. Sounds like we should take it easy today. Give your body time to adjust."

"Yeah, but didn't you want to go to the concert on the mountain? Why don't you go? I can just hang out.

Get my mountain lungs, or whatever they call sea legs at 8000 feet."

Margaret has heard the classics at Tanglewood and Symphony Hall in Boston, Carnegie and the Lincoln Center in New York, even the Royal Albert Hall in London. But she's never heard the masters on top of the world. And this concert combines Bach with the Beatles. The old Margaret would have chalked it up to bad timing and resigned herself to missing it. Not the new Margaret.

"If you're sure you won't mind. I really am excited to hear this. Let's get you something to eat now. I've read that carb-loading helps. Thus the hotcakes."

"Not really hungry. But I suppose some toast, maybe fruit."

The additional food ordered, Margaret pours the blueberry compote over her plate and slices through the rounds. The airy flapjack melts in her mouth, recalling breakfasts on the ranch as a child. It's been ages since she thought about that. Being back in Sullivan is no doubt triggering memories.

"Mother used to make these," Margaret says, her eyes closed.

"Yeah, your Mom seemed cool. Not like mine. Always so negative. But I suppose life dealt her some difficult hands."

"Yes, for mine as well. In hindsight, I wish I had spent more time with my mother. Maybe I wouldn't have been so uptight. I think there's a lot more of her in me than I realized, but Father made damn sure it never got out."

"Our parents, and men, sure can do a number on us, right? Wish they would have taught me more about building bridges instead of walls."

"How true, my friend, how true."

Margaret walks with Kathy to the concierge desk after breakfast and alerts the middle-aged, balding man about Kathy's condition. He promises to keep an eye on her, and Margaret feels certain her blonde, tan, long-legged friend will be watched over closely. Grabbing a light sweater, she heads out for the Silver Queen Gondola and the spectacular view that awaits her.

After ascending another 2000 feet, she reaches the top. The view of Mount Hayden takes her breath away. Literally. She's glad she came early so she can leisurely make her way to the concert site and get a bite to eat along with more water. She takes advantage of the build a picnic option at the Sundeck Restaurant and finds a spot on the grass. There are metal tables available that would be more comfortable, and easier to get up from, but to sit amid the scattered wild flowers, enjoying the splendor of the grass, is worth the extra effort it will require at the end. And hopefully, some kind soul will give her a hand.

As the chamber ensemble adjust the strings on their instruments prior to beginning, Margaret gathers her plastic utensils and containers and stashes them back in the paper sack. Since there's ample room, she stretches out on the green carpet and stares up at the clouds. Has she ever done this? Imagined the white cumulus and nimbus collection of water droplets to be some creature or creation, like a cat, a carriage, a castle, or a dragon? As the notes of Bach's "Jesu, Joy of Man's Desiring" rise overhead, she closes her eyes and shuts out the rest of the world.

She sits up, though a bit ungainly, when the quartet leaps from the 1700's to the 1960's with the Beatles "Eleanor Rigby," the somber story of a lonely woman with its staccato strings and harmony. The song, one of the first that steered the Fab Four from pop ballads into uncharted, experimental rock territory, has always been one of Margaret's favorites. The words echo her own life and fears of being inconsequential in the end.

Drifting seamlessly between the centuries, the concert highlights other compositions utilizing the classical structure and instrumentation that George Martin, the group's producer, scored and engineered. He truly was the unsung fifth Beatle. What a great addition this was to her Beatle Girl reunion experience. Too bad the others weren't able to experience it.

Longing to continue her Rocky Mountain high, Margaret wanders about the area, taking in the panoramic views of fourteeners, forests, and flora. She'd like to stay longer, but her energy is flagging, and she heads for the gondola and the ride down. Shuffling back to the hotel, she notices people walking their dogs, necks festooned with everything from blinged-out collars to tattered handkerchiefs. Overindulgent fashion statements or clan totems? The bond between canine and man is strong in this town.

She's been so busy since her arrival that her little Maya has become an afterthought, but surrounded by other pets, she realizes how much she misses her own fur baby. Plus Kathy's counsel to work things out with Denise has been on her mind. Perhaps it's time to reconnect.

But first she must stop at the front desk to confirm that Kathy is doing fine. Maybe she should go up and let her know she's back. No, the clerk said she'd been sleeping. Leave her be. Margaret stops in the ladies room to freshen up before making her way to a quiet, intimate space near the main bar. Though her nerves could use a little bolstering, she's hesitant to sip anything stronger until she's rested a bit. She finds a small table in a corner that will allow some privacy for her *tête-à-tête* and orders Earl Grey tea from the young waiter.

She tears open the paper wrap and plunges the bag in the pot, before adding a teaspoon of sugar and a dollop of milk to her cup. She twiddles her fingers waiting for the leaves to steep, lost in what she remembers of the event that turned her friendship upside down, much like the current state of her stomach. For God's sake, Margaret, just make the call.

"Martinet-King residence. May I ask who's calling?"

"Ms. Martinet-King, thank you very much," Margaret laughs, too high and too long.

"Oh, Margaret. I didn't recognize your cell number."

"I'm in Aspen playing tourist with one of my friends and wanted to check on my little Maya. Nobody has cats among my group so I'm desperate to hear a meow or a purr."

"Here, let me hold the phone up to her. She's been a good girl. Eating, using the box, no hairballs. OK, ready."

Margaret can just make out a soft mew before Maya voices her true opinion about being disrupted from her catnap, and the interspecies chat comes to a close. She hopes the intraspecies dialogue is more productive. She pours out a cup of her tea, gives it a stir, and carries on.

"I guess she takes after me, preferring actual face time over technology. Sooo," she draws out the word, "how are things at the house?"

"Wonderful. Sean has been hovering like a Jewish mother. Helping with the yard, picking up takeout, conveying me hither and yon. If you ever don't want him, I get dibs."

Yes, Sean is a good man. Maybe he's sweet on Denise, though given what transpired between the two of them, the whole man thing might be a problem. Perhaps this is her segue.

"Sorry, I think I'll hang on to him for a while, unless of course, you and he are ... you know ... interested in each other ..."

"Well, he's hardly my type, if you know what I mean."

Unfortunately, Margaret fears she knows too well what she means. But maybe it's just she prefers blondes instead of redheads. Or that he doesn't have a college degree. Could be anything really. She checks the minutes on her phone. Stop pussyfooting around and come out with it.

"Denise ... I need to ask you something."

"Fire away."

Margaret looks around the room. Only two couples on the far side. There's soft music in the background providing a bit of ambient noise to cover her conversation. Nevertheless, she turns her back to the room, covers her mouth with her hand, and speaks softly.

"That night in the taxi when we, um ... are ... are you ... gay?"

"So here's the thing." Denise speaks bluntly, with no hesitation. "I struggled with my sexual identity for a long time, kept it hidden from family, employers, even you it would seem. But, yes, Margaret, I am gay. And I don't think you're ready for that."

She was prepared for her confession, yet her breath still catches in her throat and her hands tighten around the phone to keep from dropping it. Was she that naive not to see the clues, or has she conveniently closed her eyes and mind to the truth, ignoring reality like she always does?

"You, even I don't know that, Denise," she argues. "Maybe we're both gay. I mean, how ... when did you realize that, you know ..."

"Probably in high school. Donny Osmond did nothing for me, but Marie, oh, yeah," the thrill still lingering in the rise and fall of her voice. "But I still went out with boys to placate the family. The one and done, you know. Look, I grew up Catholic just like you. Who was I going to talk to about my feelings? My parents, the gym teacher, the Sisters of Perpetual Shame. So, I said nothing. And did nothing."

"So why not come out now? People are more accepting, aren't they?"

"Sure, if you're Ellen or Rosie O'Donnell. And who knows? Maybe the hallowed closets and cupboards of Sacred Heart are stuffed full of lesbians. But last I checked, our employer still follows church doctrine. I can't afford to open the door. I need my job." Denise sounds bitter and resigned. "In any event, we both need time to figure things out. Maybe it's best if we go our separate ways for a while."

The words leave Margaret breathless. Her imagined fear now manifest. One night of celebration and spontaneous affection has destroyed all that gives her reason to be joyful in the first place. When the flow of air returns to her lungs, it comes in rapid waves, and she tilts the phone away from her mouth, directing her panic out of Denise's earshot.

"Margaret, are you all right?" Denise asks.

"No," is all that squeaks out after several minutes. Just like New Year's Eve. Back then the future held no interest for her, but now she has grand plans, and they all include Denise. Realizing she's wadded the top of her shirt into a wrinkled ball as she listened, she releases it along with a prolonged exhale.

"No, Denise, I'm not all right with taking a break. I enjoy your company more than anything in the world, and I refuse to put our friendship on hold because of, um, our differences." She bites her lip at using the euphemism, alarmed she sounds prejudiced, not proprietous. "I agree some reflection will be valuable. If you're willing to stay at the house and care for Maya, then we can talk when I return from Paris. Maybe you won't have to hide your love away."

CHAPTER 39

Impressions have always been important to Linda.
The first, the good, the lasting. Back in high school she
bought her clothes at May D & F, not J. C. Penney, securing her status as Sullivan's fashion icon. She dated
the jocks, handsome muscle-bound bumpkins going nowhere but out for long passes, instead of the shy but chivalrous science nerds whose acned faces disguised profitable futures. She was crowned Queen of Everything,
even though her throne was often the backseat of a Ford
Fairlane. Linda's mother did whatever it took to steer her
daughter down the path to success. A little sweet-talk, a
bit of whitewash, or a discreet connection could dispatch
any roadblocks along the way. Whether a bad grade, a
battle with booze. or an untimely baby.

Reminiscing with the Beatle Girls about unmet
dreams and second chances has revived her plan to win
back Rob. If Liz Taylor and Natalie Wood can remarry
their first husbands, why can't she? The right impression
is more important than ever tonight when they meet at
the Club for a pre-wedding gathering with the families.
She may be no match for Marlee's outsized glitz and
glamour, but she's studied manipulation under *Mommie
Dearest*, and knows a thing or two about the man up for
grabs. Plus, she's counting on Jackie's help.

She spent the day at the salon up to her eyebrows and down to her hoo-ha in mud, wax, and emollients. The new highlights in her hair frame the magnificent work of her plastic surgeon and various aestheticians, while her bedroom eyes and sensuous mouth promise to lure Rob back to the chambers of both her bed and heart. She hopes her self-confidence stays as firm and smooth as her retouched face and body.

Linda is the last to arrive and she sashays to the table in a formfitting plum sheath with a scooped neckline, demurely draped with a delicate flower print cashmere shawl that conceals her décolletage ... and her ulterior motives.

"Well, hello, everyone," she says, her smile radiating just the right mix of sincerity and warmth. "I hope I haven't kept you waiting long." The men stand as she nears.

She greets the groom's parents and brother, extending a manicured hand to each in turn, then sandwiches theirs between hers. Making her way around the table, she compliments the maid of honor, Jackie's friend and business partner, on her beautiful original design jacket before delivering a firm but brief embrace to her son-in-law to be. She feels Matt reflexively stiffen, obviously not expecting the new improved Linda. Too bad she's not trying to win over these hearts.

"Jackie, my baby girl." Linda completely enfolds her daughter in her arms, feeling her respond in kind and melt into her for perhaps the first time in years. It's all she can do to break away and get on with the evening, and her mission to complete the family circle.

"Not sure I'm ready for this. How about you?" she asks Rob, stroking the lapels of his jacket before pulling in close to his chest and looking up at him.

"It's been thirty years. Probably about time," he jokes, the space between them widening as he leans back.

With introductions made and the stage set, chair legs scrape on the floor as everyone takes their seats. Two bottles of champagne, Dom Perignon of course, have been waiting on ice. The sommelier unwinds the wire and eases the cork out with a soft pop. A good one never fires it across the room, and he proceeds to pour into the empty glasses.

"Oh, wait," Linda says, waving a hand at the waiter. "Sorry, dear, I should have told you. We need sparkling water for my daughter and her fiancé. Everyone else OK with bubbly?"

There are murmurings of 'just a little' or 'just this once' and soon bubbles of some sort fill each flute. Linda raises her drink and looks to Rob to begin a toast.

"Whoa, didn't know I needed something for tonight. OK, then, let me paraphrase Mr. Spock. May you love long and prosper. Jackie and Matt, to you."

"Thank you, Daddy." Jackie kisses him on the cheek. "You always know what to say."

She watches their interaction. The easy grin, the playful touch. It all looks so natural. Will she ever have that with either of them? No planning, maneuvering. Just being.

"So anyway, let's get the business portion of the evening out of the way. Here's your instructions for to-morrow. Number one. Show up," she laughs, though Linda senses a bit of nervousness embedded in there, mostly directed at her family no doubt. "Second, walk down the aisle. Rhiannon and Mike, you'll go first, fol-lowed by Andrew and Lois with Matt, and then Mom and Dad with me. When the celebrant begins her thing, the parents can sit down. Your jobs are done. It's all very low-key."

"That does sound easy," Linda says, nodding at her daughter. "Jackie finally convinced me that lots of money and hoopla doesn't insure a happy union. However, I do think the fact that our children are older and established in their careers will make a difference down the road. Would you agree, Lois?"

The gray-haired lady in the matronly navy suit nods her head. "Oh, yes, our Matt has a secure nest all prepared for Jackie," she beams at her son. "Now Andrew and I can look forward to dusting off our own wings in retirement."

"Get in a little fun before the grandchildren come along, right?" Linda says slipping in her ace in the hole. "I suppose I'll hang up the old stirrups and speculum before too long myself. You can expect a lot of spoiler alerts from this Grandma." The card is in play.

At least two forks clatter on the china plates, and both Rob and Jackie cough and reach for a glass of water. OK, that was to be expected but she continues her conversation nevertheless.

"You'd think spending so much time around pregnant women and babies, I'd have had enough. But it will be different with my own. I want to do it right this time. And when that time comes," she pauses with her hands in front of her face, "and I'm not pushing here kids by any stretch, but who better to guide those little ones into the world than Rob and I?" She tilts her head at him and interlaces her fingers. "Am I right?"

"Of course, Mom," Jackie jumps in when no one else answers, "all of you are going to be amazing grandparents but, contrary to popular culture, Matt and I would like marriage to come way before the baby carriage. Speaking of which, can you be at the venue by noon? To help with all the last-minute details?"

272

"Of course. Maybe your Dad and I can come together. Show a united front for your big day. How about it, Rob?"

"I'll have to see, Linda. Not sure carpooling is on the must-do list, you know."

No sense in overplaying her hand so Linda backs off the Good Mother track and the conversation flows to other topics of interest to her tablemates. They'll be time when she and Rob are alone.

It's eight thirty when Jackie signals it's time to call it a night.

"Matt and I need to head out. Kind of a busy day coming up, right? Since I made you all promise to be there, we better not oversleep. Are you coming, Rhi?"

"For sure. Bye, see you all in Boulder."

"We'll be on our way as well. So nice to meet you all. We're very excited to welcome Jackie into our family. Here, let me get the tab," Andrew offers and reaches for the bill.

"No," Linda says," blocking his access, "it's already taken care of. See you tomorrow."

Rob stands to shake hands with the new in-laws and prepares to leave as well. Alone at last, Linda clutches his arm and eases him back to his chair.

"How about a nightcap before you go? I have something to run by you." Sensing an urgency on Rob's part to get outta Dodge, she removes her shawl and the firm swell of her breasts is revealed as she leans over. "Just a quick one, OK?"

Grey Goose martinis in hand, Linda scoots closer to Rob and clinks his glass. "I was serious about the whole retiring thing, you know, when and if the kids have children. But for now, I'm thinking about getting back to my roots. You know, midwifery. Running the clinic, dealing with the financing is overrated. I'd rather do what I know best."

273

"But won't that be more physical? Long hours, on your feet or bent over, taking call. You're not a spring chicken anymore, Linda, and the chemo fatigue could linger for a while."

Tell her something she doesn't know. At least they're having a dialogue, and he doesn't have one leg extending toward the exit.

"Yeah, I know, but I won't be doing it alone. I'm hoping my staff will come in with me. Maybe we can take over a suite of rooms and turn it into a Birthing Center. What do you think?"

"Fine by me, but you'll need to run it by the other docs. The money comes in from the other specialties anyway. Infertility, Plastics, so as long as there's cash flow."

She takes a long sip, her half-closed eyes peering seductively over the rim. "My little brush with death has made me revisit my priorities." She skims the base of her glass down and over her breasts, watching as his eyes follow her movements. "I'm still very much attracted to you, Rob," she whispers. She slides her free hand up his thigh which Rob snatches and sets firmly on the table.

"Linda, I was going to wait until after the wedding, but I need to nip this, whatever you're trying to pull, in the bud. Marlee and I are engaged." He knocks back his martini before continuing. "I need to move on with my life. And so do you."

Linda flies back in her chair, Rob's announcement like a punch to her gut. She focuses on his brown eyes, the only thing keeping her from throwing up. She's not sure which hurts worse. That he lied to her or that she believed him. Again. What's the little bitch holding over him?

"Oh, for fuck's sake. Of course. She's pregnant, isn't she?"

"Christ, give me some credit, Linda. I know how babies are made. I'm just ready to settle down."

"Really, it took you sixty-five fucking years to do that. You're a piece of work, Rob," she grumbles and shakes her head slowly. "So now you're off with your little Twinkie and your daughter, who's way older may I point out, gets left in the dust. I thought we could be there for her, together this time."

"Seriously, Linda? I've been there for her from the get go. And now you rush in at the last minute and wanna be Mother of the Year." Rob pushes away from the table and pulls a twenty out of his wallet. "You do what you need to do. I hope things do get better between you and her. But take me out of the equation. I'll always have her back. I don't have to be in your life to do that." He pivots and strides toward the door without looking back.

She tries to rise up to chase after him, but someone's glued her legs to the leather. The sounds of distant conversations and clinking silverware echo in her head. The little bitch has won. Good. She can deal with his irresponsible two-timing ass. Maybe she should cry, but she's damned if she'll waste a single drop on him. Ah, she knows what will fix this. Delete him and his betrayal from her files. She reaches for her martini, nearly spilling it as her hand trembles, and chugs it down. She waves to the waiter and points to her glass.

"Another one. And keep them coming."

CHAPTER 40

It's Saturday morning, September fourth, and the Wedding of the Summer begins at two in the afternoon. After all the fussing and fretting, baking the final three tiered wedding cake was child's play. Susan even bragged she and Jenny could have done it in an Easy Bake Oven. With their masterpiece loaded in Maureen's van, the two of them wend their way to the festivities in Boulder, the rest of the family to join them later. Last night Kathy and Margaret registered at St. Julien's Hotel and Spa where Linda booked a suite for herself and the bridal party. And apparently Rob is bringing his girl-friend Marlee. Things could get interesting.

"Good plan to put the layers in boxes, instead of hav-ing it already assembled, Gramma," Jenny says while en-tering the destination into the van's GPS. "I thought I'd have to sit in the back with my arms wrapped around it." She places her hands on her swollen belly and pats it. "Don't think I could reach."

"The old girl still has one or two good thoughts rat-tling around up here," Susan says, tapping on her temple. "Speaking of plans, where are things with the online cul-inary program?"

"I can sign up whenever I'm ready. Thought I'd wait 'til after the baby comes and things get into a routine."

"Sweetie," Susan shakes her head, "might as well remove that word from your vocabulary. Routine and parenthood are mutually exclusive terms."

"So, how was your date with Grampa?"

"Very nice. Very nice indeed. We seem to be happy campers once again. I'm upping my game today with a new dress and makeup. You can come with me when Kathy puts me together."

The bakers arrive at Gatherings at 11:30, and already it's buzzing with activity. Jackie told Susan she picked the place for its farmers' market meets backyard ambience. Paths lead from the ceremony site so guests can ramble and rest amid arbors and alcoves. Rows of chairs fill an open grassed area that faces a pergola bedecked with site-grown flowers and acres of fall harvest ripening in distant fields. The kitchen staff is prepping appetizers and entrees for the buffet to be served under a tent lit with a mix of twinkling LED lights and battery-operated candles. Susan spots someone who looks official and introduces herself.

"Hi, I'm Susan Anderson and I have the wedding cake. Do you have a cart we can use to bring it in?"

"Sure, follow me. Is it ready to go?"

"No, we need to put it together. We came quite a distance and didn't want our tower of love to topple over," Susan says with a wry smile.

"Yeah, I've seen my share of disasters over the years, so good idea. Wheel it back to the kitchen and we'll store it in our refrigerated space until the reception."

They drape the cart with a tablecloth and stack the pre-frosted layers onto a circular tray, dabbing extra icing over smudges where needed. After artistically poking pink and white rose buds here and there, their romantic vision is almost ready. Susan pulls little plastic figurines out of her purse.

"Are those the bride and groom?" Jenny asks.

"Sort of. Remember when Jackie and Matt announced their engagement on New Year's Day and Linda was worried it was gonna be some enchanted pagan ritual?" Susan stands a unicorn in the center and surrounds it with several wee fairies. "You can't hold back the magic."

Jenny giggles. "This wedding is gonna be so much fun."

⌘⌘⌘⌘⌘

It's now one o'clock and Susan's transformation from frump to femme fatale is complete. Jenny gives her Gramma her highest praise. The exploding fist bump. After a few more ooh's and aah's and some additional primping in the mirror, Susan and company are ready to head back to Gatherings and the main event. As they stroll toward the elevator, chattering about this and that, angry voices push their way into the hallway outside Linda's room.

"What is wrong with you today?" Jackie is saying. "Look, I'm wearing your Mom's pearls and I've got on new powder-blue underwear. Old, new, borrowed, blue. Tradition covered. God, Mom, you're making me crazy. Have you heard from Dad?"

"That fucking bastard," Linda scoffs. "I could care less if he shows up."

"But I care," Jackie says, her voice quivering. "It's my day and I need him."

Nobody, especially the bride, needs this kind of quarrel on her big day, so Susan raps on the door and peeks in, followed by the rest of her entourage.

"Oh, Auntie Suze, everybody," Jackie gives a half-hearted smile and rolls her eyes. "So glad you're here"

"So, how's it going? The usual jitters, I suppose," Susan asks with as much innocence as possible to conceal the accidental eavesdropping.

Turning her back on Linda, Jackie folds her hands in prayer and mouths 'Save me.'

"Hey, Jenny," Susan suggests, seeing the bride's plea for help, "why don't you give Jackie and Rhiannon a hand here and we can take the mother of the bride over to the venue."

"That would be super. I'm almost ready anyway. And would you check on Dad?"

"All right, let's go find the SOB," Linda growls, "and see if the bar is open." She storms out of the room, the rest following at a safe distance.

It was a tense ride over. They forced Linda to sit in the back seat, afraid if she called shotgun she might actually have one. Now the Beatle Girls make their way toward the collection of chairs. Kathy and Margaret veer off to settle into a row, waving at Susan after claiming their primo spot. Linda dashes off to down a much-needed first drink of the day or some equally necessary hair of the dog after a rough last night. Neither one seems like a good idea. No sign of Rob, but Susan spies her family mingling with the other guests near a small gazebo and saunters over to join them. When Steve does a double take and whistles, she tugs at her new jewel toned wrap dress, checking to make sure it's not gaping in the front or riding up in the back, stuck in her pantyhose.

"Well, hello there, good lookin'," Steve says with a wink. "I don't believe we've met."

"It's too much, isn't it?" she winces, covering her face with her hands. "Kathy's used to stage lighting. I'll go wash it off."

"Don't you dare. I like it." Clasping her shoulders, he leans in and plants a kiss on her cheek. "So this is what you and your friends have been up to. Playing dress-up."

"Pretty much." As he rubs her shoulders, a little shiver inches down her back. Linda can find her own ex-husband.

Then as if on cue, Dr. Robert Charles files in with Miss Marlee Jacobs. She's bound in a hot-pink wardrobe malfunction waiting to happen, teetering on "do me" stilettos, her long platinum hair fluffed like meringue. She obviously missed the memo about letting the bride take center stage. Susan huddles near Steve as Linda sizzles toward 'Barbie and Ken,' her lit fuse quickly disappearing behind her. The crowd cowers in collective terror, bracing for the explosion when bitch meets bombshell.

"What the hell, Marlee, ever hear of a dress code?" Linda stands with feet wide, hands on her hips, her words blasting the underdressed plus one. "We're not putting on a burlesque show here. For Christ's sake, Rob, find her a jacket or a blanket ... or something. Our daughter is waiting. Plop your little whore in a chair and let's go. Un-fucking-believable." She pivots and stomps away, parting the flock like Moses, leaving the masses to climb over the rubble.

Everyone finally settles into their seats following the pre-wedding entertainment, gearing up for the next act in what hopefully won't become a three-ring circus. A string quartet plays a selection of romantic ballads to soothe the jangled nerves of the gathered guests.

In lieu of a minister or judge, Jackie and Matt chose a celebrant, a spiritual guide in the form of a soft-eyed, smiling, middle-aged woman who waits in the area designated as the altar. She will serve as the conductor, keeping things in tempo, directing the score she's been given. And if the earlier outburst is any indication, Susan worries she may do double duty as a referee.

The prelude to the ceremony begins as the singer/guitarist joins the quartet for Pachelbel's "Canon in D," predictable perhaps, but a favorite of the bride. The groom's brother and the bride's best friend amble to the altar, he in a dark suit while she wears a deep-rose sheath and carries a bouquet of wild flowers. Matt and his parents follow close behind.

At last, Jacqueline Charles, a white satin buffer between the blatant animosity of her mother and father, begins the journey from single lady to married woman. Susan instinctively takes Steve's hand in hers as the bride passes by, and feels an unexpected squeeze. This day just keeps getting better.

"Welcome to family and friends," the celebrant begins. "Jackie and Matt are honored that you are here to affirm their love and celebrate with them as they begin life as husband and wife. They are grateful to their parents for giving them life, for nurturing them with love and abundance, and for enabling them to step into their future."

Jackie and Matt give their mothers and fathers kisses on the cheeks before directing them to their chairs in the first row. Hand in hand the couple returns to face the celebrant.

"I'd now like to read from *The Prophet* by Kahlil Gibran. "Let there be spaces in your togetherness ..."

There is no talk of either/or dualities, no obeying, or worshiping nor letting death call the shots, but of maintaining their individuality in marriage. When the words are finished, the guitarist plays "I Will" by the Beatles, a simple song of love and promise, while Jackie and Matt place rings on each other's fingers. They overlap their hands, now bound by bands of gold, and recite their heartfelt vows. Susan's makeup is definitely going to need a touch up.

"I marry you because I choose to" Jackie begins. "This is a conscious, considered, collaborative choice. Right here, right now, with you is where I am to be for as long as we love and learn."

"I marry you because we share a journey," Matt continues. "Though we may run, ramble, and rest along divergent roads, we travel to the same destination, and on the way we will make a joyful difference."

"I marry you," Jackie goes on, "because you inspire me to weave creativity, compassion, and connection into every day, to believe my glass not merely half full but overflowing, to achieve balance in body, mind, and spirit."

"I marry you because we love each other. We touch, talk, trust, and treat one another as true friends, respecting our authentic selves," Matt ends.

And in unison they say, "Our love is a blessing in our lives from our hearts to our souls. I love you."

As Jackie and Matt share a kiss, Susan searches for a tissue to dab at her mascara-covered eyelashes, one set of fingers still interlaced with Steve's.

The celebrant presses her palms together at her heart, her lips touching fingertips, before spreading her arms and announcing, "By the authority invested in me by the State of Colorado and through the power of Spirit, I present to you, Matthew Stevens and Jacqueline Charles-Stevens."

Amid aahs and applause, the bride and groom lock hands in the air, and shout, "Woo Hoo!"

CHAPTER 41

As the DJ spins "Celebration" by Kool and the Gang, the newlyweds dance down the aisle with the bridal party, urging the guests to join them in a matrimonial conga line. Susan's palm is sweaty and warm after fifteen minutes of holding on to Steve, but she's reluctant to let go, afraid the newly generated spark will fizzle out. But maybe two hands on a hip is worth one in a fist, so she follows behind him as the crowd snakes into the tented reception area.

"Wasn't that absolutely beautiful?" she sighs, pressing against her chest to hold in the sentiment. "I know it wasn't traditional but ..."

"That's for darn sure," Steve butts in. "No church, no minister, no mention of religion at all. When did weddings become just an excuse for a good time?"

"Come on, it's not only about God. What about love? Isn't that more important?"

"I suppose, but when the honeymoon's over, what's to keep you together?"

If not love, dear husband, then what? A vow to God? A piece of paper? Habit? Squatter's rights? She longs for that martini marriage, intoxicating and full of twists. Steve still lusts for a glass of warm milk. Time to put a little pow in the cow.

"Well, it was still a special ceremony. Why don't you find us a place to sit while I visit the ladies room."

Imagine, rushing off to fix her makeup. The last time that happened was at her own wedding. Is that why her fairy tale slipped into humdrum ever after? Of course not, but her new appearance seems to have opened Steve's eyes, and his heart is peeking out. Her face back to its pristine pre-wedding condition, Susan hurries over to greet her family.

Every time she sees her son Josh, and it's not often enough, he's looking more and more like his Dad, his hairline inching back and the once solid build softening. He gives her a sideways squeeze and a kiss on the head before regaling her with his latest assignments at the *Post*, until his sisters, Maureen and Caroline, snag him away with stories of children and their own careers. With the men expounding on the upcoming Broncos' season, and the older grandkids fixated on cell phones and video games, Susan takes the opportunity to scout the crowd, but not before doling out that timeless maternal mantra to eat.

She spies Margaret and Kathy sitting with Matt's parents. Exuberant voices and sweeping gestures must mean they're discussing one of those topics frowned on at friendly gatherings. Politics, religion, economics, and who should have won the Oscar this year.

"Hey, sorry to interrupt, guys. Just wanted to say hi. By the way, I'm Susan ..." she says extending her hand in greeting.

"The cake baker we hear," Matt's mother chimes in with a corresponding firm grip. "Can't wait to taste it."

"You're not sitting up front with the bride and groom?"

"No, it's a little, um, how shall I say, tense over there," Matt's father replies with a glance in the direction of the referenced group. "Much more pleasant with your friends here."

"I'm sure. Anyway, I'm over there with Steve and everyone. I'll check back later."

A quick scan finds Jackie and Matt busy working the room, bursts of laughter sprinkling animated exchanges between the couple and their comrades. In the background the string quartet and guitarist continue their playlist of subdued classics as circles of people enjoy good food and interesting conversation. Except for the table reserved for the family of the bride.

Linda sits on the right flanked by a few of her midwives, empty glass soldiers already marshaled in front of her. Rob is hunkered on the left, his arm shielding Marlee as he discusses strategy with some of the clinic doctors. It doesn't appear that the two sides are speaking to each other, the probably amiable colleagues forced to declare their allegiance in this family feud. In fact, even visual contact seems minimal, perhaps fearing an inadvertent gaze might spark a conflagration of nuclear proportions. A junior high standoff.

Susan, like Jackie, had been optimistic that the parent-child bond would be stronger than the chains of loss and loathing left over from the divorce. After her surgery, when Linda mentioned her plans to take back her man, Susan had supported her. After all, both of them were trying to salvage marriages that had lost their way. But her Steve was still her husband, and there was no blonde bimbo with ginormous boobs blocking the way. Obviously, the hoped-for detente with Rob has not panned out.

Susan finds her way to the smorgasbord and looks over the selection. An alphabetical cornucopia of fruits and vegetables from apples to zucchini, including produce familiar and totally foreign. She fills her plate and heads back to Steve.

287

"Hey, where you been?" he asks as she slides into a chair beside him.

"On recon. I'd wear Kevlar to Linda and Rob's table. And nothing flammable. That thing could go up any minute. Couldn't they let it go for Jackie's big day? So, how's the food?"

"Not bad if you're a rabbit. Got any Tums in your purse?

Susan rummages in her handbag for one of the white tablets as the harsh feedback from a microphone alerts the crowd to the next event.

"Ladies and Gentlemen, may I have your attention," the DJ announces in a booming voice. "The bride and groom and their parents are ready to kick off the dancing.

Jackie and her father, fresh from the field of battle, and Matt and his mother, elbows locked together, make their way to the dance floor as "I Hope You Dance," Lee-Ann Womack's beautiful waltz about a parent's hopes for a child, begins to play. Midway through the twirls and swirls, Rob kisses his daughter's hand and seamlessly leads her into the arms of her new father-in-law. Matt kisses his mother's cheek and leaves her to secure a wobbly Linda who lists heavily against him. With a visible exhale, the groom rejoins his bride for the last chorus. Though Rob offers his hand, Linda brushes him away and wends her way back to her chair using backs of chairs and shoulders to maintain her balance.

When the couple segues into their first dance as husband and wife, "My Life Would Suck Without You" by Kelly Clarkson, Steve looks upward with a shake of his head as once again traditional expectations are rejected.

"Hey, my life would suck without you, too," Susan says decorating his nose with her red lips and gently wiping it off with her napkin. She taps her feet, bobbing her head and shoulders in time to the music as she watches the under forties wave and press the air with their hands, some partnered but most moving in a group choreography. Steve picks at the label on his second beer. They both react with a start when Matt and Jackie appear at their table.

"How about a dance, Auntie Suze?" Matt asks. "Gotta make the most of my lessons."

"Uncle Steve," Jackie smiles, "the bride requests the honor of your feet, please."

"Come on, Sweetie," Susan says, tugging at his jacket, "just this one, OK?"

It takes Susan a moment to find the rhythm, but soon she's following Matt's lead with pushes, pulls, and spins, enjoying the bouncy swing steps. Steve shuffles his feet like a shy eight-year-old, teetering from side to side. Always his best move. When the song ends, Susan reaches for her husband's hand.

"Dance with me. It's a slow one." She leans into him, pulling him as close as tummies will allow, draping her arms around his neck. He wraps his around her waist, letting his hands dangle dangerously low down her back. Just like in high school when form and footwork didn't matter, only closeness counted. "We haven't done this in so long," she whispers, resting her cheek on his lapel, his shirt moist with sweat. She can feel their hearts thumping, though the rhythm seems out of sync. His is slow and uneven like a seductive bolero while hers flops and flutters against her ribs in a frantic samba. If she faints, at least this time Steve is here to catch her. She half expects her mother's perfume to envelop them, but only the faint flowery scent of her new cologne meets her nose. Estee Lauder's Beautiful, the Beatle Girls' unanimous selection.

"Sorry, Suze," Steve groans. "My heartburn's back, better call it a day." Steve pulls away and rubs the center of his chest. "Can I get another one of those Tums?"

"Sure. Maybe some 7-up?" she offers as they walk back to the table. She unrolls the wrapper and pops out a second tablet.

"Nah, this should work. Must be this vegetarian food."

Jenny sneaks up behind her and pokes her on the shoulder. "Jackie says it's time for the cake cutting, and she wants you up there with them."

"Are you OK, Steve?" Susan says, her eyes narrowing as she cups his jaw and examines his wan face. Maybe this indigestion needs something stronger than over the counter remedies. She'll get him an appointment on Monday.

"Go ahead. I'm good," he smiles weakly. "This is your big moment. Enjoy it."

Susan waits to the side as the newlyweds stand behind the cake holding flutes of sparkling cider, the guests' glasses filled with champagne. Rob raises his goblet to the couple.

"Marriage isn't easy. It takes work." His eyes briefly travel in Linda's direction. "It takes two people invested in each other, and a multitude invested in you. Here's a toast to love and laughter, and happily ever after."

The clink of crystal on crystal echoes in the room.

"Thank you all for being here. And a special thanks," Matt says, pointing toward the beaming baker, "to Jackie's Aunt Susan who made our lovely cake."

Together Jackie and Matt slice a small sliver from the top layer of Susan's confection, eating the piece with impeccable manners, no faces smashed with frosting.

"This. Is. Amazing," Matt gushes. "OK, as the French lady said, let them eat cake."

As platefuls of Susan's creation pass around the tent, appreciation of her culinary skill is acknowledged with raised forks, winks, and verbal thank you's. Yes, the stars are aligned today, for everything has gone as planned. Earlier dust-up aside. Indeed, this has been a good day to get married, and a good day to be Susan Anderson.

As the celebration winds down, the bride and groom do a farewell tour around the tent before leaving with most of their friends for further celebrations elsewhere. The clinic staff make a hasty exit, no doubt off to formalize a request for hazard pay. Rob, along with Linda's nemesis, already snuck out right after the cake was served. That leaves the bride's extended family and the Beatle Girls to turn out the lights.

"Steve, let me touch base with Kathy and Margaret before we go, and thank Linda."

"Yeah. I'll be in the bathroom."

The round table where her friends and Matt's parents are sitting is still abuzz with conversation and laughter.

"Looks like you've found kindred spirits," Susan says.

"I've missed spirited dialogues with fellow academics," Margaret says, her face aglow with the thrill of mental exercise.

"Yeah, thanks, I've enjoyed this as well," Kathy says to her tablemates. "We'll be heading back to the hotel. You guys are welcome to join us if you'd like."

"Sounds like fun, but I think we'll go on home. It's been a long day," Matt's father says. "But we'll have to keep in touch."

"You guys are coming back to Sullivan before you leave for home, aren't you?" Susan asks her friends, not ready to say good-bye just yet.

"Uh, duh? Of course the Beatle Girls need one more night. Think Linda will be able to join us?" Kathy asks.

"I'm steering over to the war zone right now. I'll ask. Can I borrow that white napkin to hold up?"

Linda is resting her head on the table next to her row of wine glasses. Susan isn't sure if she's sleeping or passed out.

"Linda, you OK?" she asks from a prudent distance before jiggling a slumped shoulder.

"What?" Linda mumbles as her head grazes the table when she turns to face the voice. "Oh, it's you. This was a fucking disaster. What happened to our quiet, happy affair? That stupid bitch is what happened."

"Well, that was unfortunate, but really I don't think people noticed all that much," Susan says, her voice loaded with calm and positivity. She sits down next to Linda and rubs her back. "Jackie was beautiful, and everyone seemed to have a good time." Her words no doubt ring hollow to Linda, but it was true. She in fact had a marvelous afternoon. "I know you may not feel up to it right now, but Kathy and Margaret want to spend another night out in Sullivan before they leave. Any chance you can join us?"

"Fuck, might as well," she says raising her bedraggled head. "Seems like as good a place as any to hide."

"So, call me tomorrow or just come out whenever. Everyone's leaving. Are you OK to get back to the hotel? I'm sure Kathy can drive you."

"Nah, I'll catch a cab. I need to tie up the loose ends."

Susan sees her kin loitering near the entrance, but Steve is not with them. Assuming he must still be in the restroom, she strides down the hallway and knocks on the men's door.

"Steve, you still in there? We're ready to go. Steve?"

She slowly pulls the door open and peeks inside. Sprawled on the floor, his face ashen gray, is her husband. Not moving. And for an instant neither is she. Suddenly her hands fly to her head, clutching at her hair. Her chest feels weighted, her scream crushed. All that escapes is a feeble squeak as she collapses next to his body.

She touches him gently at first, but then she frantically shakes him, willing him to wake up so she can stare into his steel-blue eyes. She kneels over him, her arms wrapped around her chest as she rocks herself. Get up, get help. Get up, get help, she repeats in her head, until finally sanity overcomes panic and she rushes out the door.

"Linda, Linda, Linda, Linda!" Her screams reverberate in the hall. "Help me. It's Steve."

"What's the matter," Linda asks, struggling to run in her heels to meet Susan.

"He's in here. On the floor. He's not responding."

"Shit," Linda shouts at the man lying on the tile floor. "Call 911. See if there's an AED."

Susan's paralysis returns as she watches Linda listen at Steve's mouth and press on his neck. When she begins pushing on his torso, her knees nearly buckle. No, no, this can't be happening.

"Susan ... two and three ... Susan ... six and seven ... for Christ's sake ... Go NOW ... and ... fuck ... and ..."

HARD DAY'S NIGHT

CHAPTER 42

"Sixty-year-old male in asystole. Unwitnessed collapse with bystander CPR for 8 minutes. Non-shockable rhythm on arrival. Intubated in the field, line in with 2 rounds of epi."

As an EMT reels off the details of his actions to the attending doctors wheeling her husband into the Boulder Valley Emergency Room, Susan floats behind like a party balloon tethered only to her son's arm. The words drift past her ears, meaningless medical jargon. A uniformed man straddles her husband, pushing on his chest, while grim faces bob in and out of her field of vision. Is she in some kind of shared near-death experience? Hovering in space, observing the action while Steve glides along above, watching her watching him? As the gurney slips out of view into the bustle of activity within the curtained space, Susan's hand slides away from her mouth and reaches out in Steve's direction, offering him a lifeline, a way back home. It's not time yet.

"Mom. Mom." She hears her son's voice and suddenly reality smacks her in the face. "Mom, let's go into the waiting area. Everyone is on their way."

Josh leads her to the relative quiet of a room lined with vinyl-covered chairs, outdated magazines, and empty packets of vending machine snacks scattered on tables and seats, the dregs of bitter coffee evaporating in the glass pot, other families claiming a corner to await news of the fate of a loved one.

"How could this happen, Josh? He was fine. He was, wasn't he?" She doesn't really expect a reply. Surely this is a mistake. The attendant at the Pearly Gates read the numbers wrong or gave Steve someone else's ticket. It doesn't make any sense. Susan replays the day in her head, searching for clues, sorting through pieces of a puzzle that looks nothing like the picture on the box. Her inquest is interrupted by the arrival of family and a flurry of gentle touches and comforting embraces, and soon the space is filled with the chatter of uncertainty and condolence.

Susan stares into the distance, twisting and rubbing her palms with a pause every so often to press them together in a plea for God's help, her lips resting on her wedding ring.

"Honey, I'm so sorry," her sister Shirley says, sitting down beside her and stilling the agitated fingers. "He's in good hands now. Let's all say a prayer."

"He's not dead. He's not *dead*," Susan says pulling away in protest.

"I know, I know, I meant the doctors. But a little help from above can't hurt."

The group joins hands and bows heads for Shirley's brief prayer for Steve's recovery. As the heads raise and the circle breaks, a lone doctor plods through the door of the family room and over to the family. The closer he gets, the colder Susan feels, as warmth drains from her body and hope from her soul. This man in blue scrubs holds the fate of husband, father, grandfather in his report, and he kneels in front of Susan.

"Mrs. Anderson. I'm Dr. Lewis. We did all we could, but the heart damage was massive. Your husband never regained consciousness. He's gone. I'm so sorry for your loss."

Susan inhales sharply and closes her eyes, unable to look at the physician. Her lungs refuse to let the air back out and soon her head begins to swirl. She rocks back and forth, the ends of her fingers reddening under the pressure of tightened fists. Eventually her body forces her to breathe out, and she lets loose a long, piercing shriek followed by staccato sobs. As her grief overtakes her, she slumps forward until elbows rest on knees, her head buoyed by her own hands above the rising sea of despair. When the initial wave recedes, she feels someone gripping her shoulder and a deep voice calling her name.

"Mrs. Anderson, do you want to see him?" the doctor asks.

Susan nods her head, desperate to be with Steve in the hope his spirit still lingers. With a child on either side, lifting under her armpits, and a third close behind to steady her, she enters the sheltered space where her love now lies.

In the dimmed light, she steps on discarded plastic and paper packages, remnants of the frantic struggle to save his life. Tubes that once delivered hope lay draped over trays or dangle from half-empty bags of fluids hanging from metal poles. Machines that recorded his last breath, his last heartbeat are silent. The eerie aura of death blankets the room like the clean white sheet that covers his still warm body.

Susan shuffles over to him, thankful for her children's support when her knees threaten to buckle. She cradles his face again, just like she had only an hour before, and in a tactile mind meld she's immersed in a montage of recent sense memories, projecting from behind her closed eyes. Sitting on his lap as he cried and told her he loved her last week. The passion unleashed with a long overdue kiss. His whistle when he saw her today.

Wrapped in his arms as they danced. Their last dance. Her tears puddle and plop onto the cotton cover.

She watches as his daughters take their father's hands in theirs, rubbing the calloused palms and the smattering of hair on the top side. His son stands guard at the foot of the bed, the succession of defender and protector of the family proceeding in a quiet unquestioned manner. And then she falls across his body, a last attempt to thwart his soul's escape from this earthly form. Susan lays there stroking his thinning hair, reminding him how much she loves him. Thanking God for today's beautiful moments.

"Mom, we need to go now," her daughter Maureen says. "They need the room and we've got so much to do."

Susan rises up and whispers, "I love you, Steve. Forever," and she kisses her one true love on his cooling lips.

"We need to get his things. His clothes, his wallet, his watch. Shall we take his ring off?"

"Yes," Susan says softly, knowing it is her connection to him, the circle that makes her whole. And with her daughters' help, Susan slides the plain gold band from her husband's fourth finger, placed there forty-two years ago. 'Til death do us part, they had promised. 'Til death.

⌘⌘⌘⌘⌘

Linda stands over the toilet in the ladies room of The Gathering, her body still retching though nothing but spit comes up. How had this day gone so wrong? This day when she was to star as the quintessential mother of the bride. When her nuclear family was to reunite in a celebration of love. When the world would praise the more balanced, less driven Linda Charles.

She unrolls several sheets of toilet paper and wipes her mouth. She dabs at the vomit dotting the front of her lacy royal blue, off-the-shoulder dress, the exquisite designer gown that showed off her curves with class and elegance. Not like the cling wrap tube stupid, fucking Marlee painted on her brick shithouse of a body. Surely Rob could see how inappropriately she was dressed. But, no, he paraded her around like a show bitch, thinking with his dick as usual.

Her whole body aches from performing CPR on Steve, compressing his non-functioning heart between his sternum and spine. But, despite being tipsy, she had done her due diligence. Who knows how long he'd been down, and with no AED on site, the likelihood of a good outcome is minimal. Even one of the responders had given a subtle head shake as they carted him away.

Her heels click on the wooden floor on her way to the reception area to close out the bill. The guests are long gone, only the staff remain to clear away the leftover food, collect the dirty plates and utensils, and fold up the empty chairs waiting by the trellised altar. Thank God Jackie and Matt left before all hell broke loose. Who knows where Bobby and the Bimbo are, but it's definitely not here to write the check. She corners one of the clean up crew.

"So who do I give the final payment to?"

"The manager's in the office, just inside the front entrance. He can take it."

Linda kicks off her Jimmy Choos. Her feet are sore and swollen and besides, who's left to impress? She gives the man her money, puts her shoes back on, and calls for a cab to return her to the hotel. The only thing that sounds good at this moment is a shower and a soft bed. And maybe something to wash the taste of puke out of her mouth, and take the edge off, helping to redeem this awful, horrible, very bad day.

Linda wishes Jackie had chosen The St. Julien for the reception. Classy, incredible accommodations and amenities, a central location with access to modern conveniences. Like emergency care.

The T-Zero Lounge at the hotel is crowded. After all, it's Saturday night with live music, and the fall term is just underway at CU, so plenty of parents are still around drowning their sorrows or thanking their lucky stars that the nest is emptier.

"Linda. Hey. Over here."

Not really in the mood for conversation, she realizes she should have gone straight to her room and raided the minibar. However, when she homes in on the voice, she's relieved to see Kathy and Margaret.

"Hello there, MOB. I guess you got her married off without a hitch," Kathy says with her usual lighthearted tone. "I mean, more or less."

"Believe me, ladies, Marlee's entrance was the least disastrous thing," Linda groans. "I need to sit. Grey Goose Martini, shaken, three olives, please," she signals to a passing server.

With half the drink in her stomach and the other half close behind, Linda reveals the details of Steve's unexpected and unfortunate cardiac arrest in her best clinical demeanor. Kathy and Margaret stare at her, paradoxical laughter and the celebratory clink of glasses echoing in the background.

"Everyone left for the hospital. I'm afraid it doesn't look good," Linda concludes.

"Have you spoken with Susan since then?" Kathy and Margaret ask simultaneously, and almost immediately Kathy's phone rings.

"Hi, Maureen ... yes, Linda just told us. We're so sorry. How's he doing? ... No. Oh, my God. How's your Mom? ... Does she need us to come out tonight? ... We'll be out first thing. Give her our love. And all the family."

"Steve died," she pronounces, her voice wavering. "Apparently it was a massive heart attack. No way he could have survived. Susan's on her way home now, with her kids."

Even though Linda expected this, it still comes as a shock. Sure, she's lost patients before. Preeclampsia or postpartum bleeding. But Susan is a friend, and so was Steve. Was. Past tense.

"I'm going upstairs," Margaret says softly as she tucks her purse to her chest and slips out of the chair.

"Right behind you," Kathy says, turning to Linda as she rises. "I'm not sure what our plans are now, but I know Susan will need our support." She opens her arms and embraces her. "Linda, I know this was a hard day for you too, but can you come out to Sullivan tomorrow to be with her?"

"I'll try," Linda says, returning Kathy's offer of comfort. "I just need some time. Some sleep, you know. I'll call, OK?"

Linda sips her second martini, looking through the glass expressly designed for this magical filmy mixture of vodka, vermouth, and olives. Strong and intoxicating. Like her. She's always been able to handle her liquor. Hell, she aced many tests in college after a night of drinking. But what if she hadn't got wasted last night, hadn't downed so much wine today? Did the alcohol cloud her judgement, make her fail Steve's final exam? No, she knew he was dead when she walked in that bathroom. It's not her fault. And Linda orders another.

⌘⌘⌘⌘⌘

Susan gathers her children around her kitchen table to consider what happened and what comes next. They sip soothing cups of tea instead of the usual go-to caffeinated beverage. Sleep will be hard enough to come by

303

tonight. No need to make it any harder. The numbness is gradually wearing off and Susan seems able to put words together into sentences, and not merely one-word answers. But answers are what they all need right now.

"Mom, I didn't know Daddy had heart problems," Josh says.

"Neither did I. He only took blood pressure and cholesterol medicine. But he wasn't one for pills and it's not like I could force them down his throat. But I never heard him complain about chest pains, at least not to me. Maybe some indigestion ... like he did today." Susan feels her own chest tighten at the realization that maybe there had been warning signs. And she'd been too busy to notice. She pulls at this loose thread of blame dangling in her mind, and the argument for her whole revolutionary dream begins to unravel.

"If only I'd paid more attention to him," she says, sliding her palms up and down her chin and throat. "And not all this other crap. I could have taken him to the doctor. All this wedding, the reunion ... and this stupid, stupid, stupid business," her voice cracks as she pounds the table with her fists. "We hardly saw each other for months. And now ... I'll never see him again." She can't hold it together any longer, and she upends her chair as she pushes away from the table. She bolts up the stairs and collapses on the bed, her body curled away from the door.

"Mom," Caroline whispers. Susan feels the bed give as her daughter perches on the edge and rubs her shuddering back. Just like she had done to all of them when their days went south. "This is not your fault. You took good care of Daddy. Of all of us. And you deserve time for yourself and your dreams."

Slowly Susan's breathing eases and she sniffs to hold back the trickling snot. Caroline passes her a tissue and she dabs her eyes before blowing her nose.

"Mom, let's get you into your PJ's. We'll stay here with you tonight."

With her face washed of the remaining traces of makeup and her party dress hung in the closet, Susan slips under the sheets of her now enormous king size bed. She lays on the left side as usual, but she's drawn to the empty space next to her. There were very few times they hadn't shared this bed since they married. After the children were born. The night after her father died and her mother needed her. Like she needed her daughters now. And the recent nights when he came home so late or she left so early that it was like they hadn't been together at all. All those lonely nights had been on her.

Though no form radiates body heat, Steve's presence lingers. His pillow exudes the faint clean smell of his shampoo. The low rumble from his throat, the stop and start of his breathing when he snored, echoes in the dark room. His spirit settles in the hollows where his shoulders and hips pressed into the mattress. There's the promise that she'll wake to his unshaven face in the morning. That they'll share a cup of coffee and laugh about Marlee's outfit. So Susan scoots across, to Steve's side, and cradles the soft cushion where he lay his head, escaping into his essence while she still can.

CHAPTER 43

Susan and her children sort through the albums of family pictures scattered in front of them on the kitchen table. They slide memories from the plastic sleeves, checking the back for the date so meticulously noted by the archivist. The curly red hair as a toddler and the buck teeth from fourth grade. His adolescent swagger as he brandishes his guns, both the muscular biceps kind and the double-barreled kind. The father and grandfather cuddling newborns, or helping unsteady bodies balance bikes, or standing alongside a budding teacher, nurse, and writer to honor their achievements, pride oozing from a smile unimpeded by the aforementioned teeth. They pass them back and forth, trying to decide which best exemplifies the man who will grow no older.

"I couldn't have done this without you," Susan says, caressing the hands of the offspring nearest to her. "You kids made the arrangements, contacted people, handled all the details."

Susan hears Old Bill stretch and whine on his bed in the corner, awake from one of his long naps, and she eases out of her chair to meet him as he limps toward the door.

"I know you miss him so much," she says looking into his cloudy, soulful eyes. "I'm so sorry, Boy." Her chin trembles as she bends down to put her arms around his neck, moistening his graying fur with her sadness, always lying in wait just below the surface.

The doorbell rings as Susan closes the patio door, followed by the voices of Kathy and Margaret greeting her children and offer their condolences.

"How's she doing?" Kathy asks.

"As well as you'd expect. We're all in shock, trying to wrap our heads around it. I'm so glad you guys are still here for her," Maureen says.

"Hey, guys ..." Susan's voice breaks as she rounds the corner, the band-aid once again ripped off her grief.

"Oh, Honey, we're so sorry," Margaret says, and the women fall together, propping up each other in body and spirit as only friends can do.

As the distress subsides, Susan sniffs and reaches into her sleeve to retrieve a Kleenex, one of many placed there. She blows her nose, digs out a fresh tissue to dry her eyes, and addresses her friends.

"God, I've messed things up royally, haven't I? If I'd just been grateful for what I had. A comfortable life with a loving husband. Not some pie in the sky dream ..."

"Susan, don't you dare go there," Kathy admonishes her. "How can you possibly think this was your fault? Steve might have had a heart attack two years ago, or twenty years from now. It just happened. It just happens ... and you go on."

Susan can see the heartache in her friend's eyes, and remembers she too is still in mourning. She takes a deep breath and reaches out her hand to her.

"Have you talked with Linda?" Susan asks. "I wanted to thank her for ... trying to save him."

"We saw her last night and she said she'd try to come out," Kathy tells her. "She looked pretty ragged. I get the feeling she doesn't do well when things aren't in her control."

"So what can we do to help? I canceled my flight for now and Kathy says she's in no rush to get back," Margaret says, receiving a confirming nod from her. "Our furry children are in good hands, so we can stay with you if you need us. Help with expenses, whatever. You let us know."

⌘⌘⌘⌘⌘

It's nearly a week since the day everything changed for her. Susan watches from an alcove as a diverse crowd walks down the aisles of the Presbyterian Church on this second Thursday morning in September. Balding men in baseball caps with weathered wrinkled faces. Women with salt-and-pepper hair in polyester slacks. Thirty-somethings, busy lives on hold as parental mortality calls a surprise meeting. Teens in low-slung jeans, cell phones silenced, forced to interact with live people. Hushed conversations pervade the chapel, but every so often a peal of laughter rings out. Steve's jokes are still making the rounds. The mourners carry pamphlets with a recent picture of the deceased on the front and the particulars of his life inside. Susan has requested a subdued, less fiery discourse for Steve's transition to the afterlife. Josh, the sons-in-law, and high school pals will bear the body from the church to the town cemetery where he will rest next to his parents.

The Anderson nuclear family files into the front pew, extended family and close friends in the rows nearby. The man of the hour lies in the handcrafted, rosewood finished casket. He wears overalls and a chambray shirt. Susan knows Steve would want to meet his maker as his true self, not in a monkey suit with a silk knot at his throat. A video of his life cycles across a screen backed by the Beatles song "In My Life." The selected Kodak moments elicit laughter, especially the early ones, but

309

most serve as quiet evidence of a life, neither grand nor memorable, except to those also present in the photographs.

Susan's eyes remain closed during the video montage. She's previewed the DVD, seen the pictures, had taken many of them, and the moments they capture are preserved in her mind and heart forever. Besides, she has vowed to stay strong for her children, to maintain some dignity in front of the people who have come to mourn her husband. Seeing his face in a continual loop will plow through her resolve as surely as the tractors Steve is riding. The presentation ends and the minister approaches the pulpit. And in that lull, the wooden church door creaks open, followed by the reverberation as it slams shut. The congregation turn their heads to see who dares arrive so late to this sacred gathering. Linda quickly finds an empty space in a back pew.

The minister delivers his sermon, thankfully respecting her wishes for a more personal and less proselytizing speech. His brief remarks are followed by the song "Daddy's Hands" sung by Holly Dunn. As it ends, Josh pulls a folded paper from his suit pocket, stops before the open coffin to press his father's chest, and climbs the steps to the podium to give the eulogy for his father.

"Steven Joshua Anderson was born May 11, 1948 and grew up here in Sullivan. He held a lot in his hands over the years. After unclenching his newborn fist, he began reaching out. For his mother's hair, for bits of food, and for his favorite toy, a little John Deere tractor. As soon as he was able, he grabbed hold of the steering wheel of a real tractor, the Big Gweenie he called it, and began plowing the fields, planting the seeds, doing whatever was needed as he learned the ways of farming. Then he learned how to hold a football and he began taking hand-offs, catching short passes, becoming one of the best running backs the Wildcats had ever seen."

Josh continues with the story of his parents' marriage and the ensuing children and grandchildren, touching on the triumphs and the tragedies as he finishes.

"He told me he had only two regrets in his life. Losing his college scholarship as a result of that career-ending knee injury. And losing the family farm in the Eighties. But, what kept him going, what made life worth living was his family. Susan and the children. He said, 'A lot can slip through even the strongest of hands. But you hold on to love, no matter what.' And my Dad did. And we will. Love you, Daddy."

Josh gives Susan a kiss on her head before sitting down as the last song the family has selected, "If Tomorrow Never Comes" by Garth Brooks, sounds over the speakers. Steve was a longtime fan of Mr. Brooks and this was a favorite, but today his words knife through Susan's heart and resolution. A wail bursts forth from her throat, a keening of unfiltered emotion. She rocks back and forth in an attempt to self-soothe while her children cradle her, rub her back, stroke her hair, anything to calm her suffering. But Susan is channeling one of those Arabic women shown on TV after a suicide bombing kills her child, her pain so visceral, so overwhelming that nothing can contain it.

Through the fog of bleary eyes and numbing sorrow she receives the words and gestures of solace from the stream of townfolk, responding with a listless smile, a brief nod, or a murmured thank you. But all she wants is a few more minutes to be alone with Steve.

She waits as one by one her family say their goodbyes. Some stand at a respectful distance with hands folded at the waist, while others gently touch a sleeve or a brow. A few leave mementos inside the casket. A small orange and blue Broncos football, a gold cross, a green toy tractor. Burial trinkets to accompany him to his next life.

Then it's her turn. Susan leans over her husband, staring at his wooden features artificially colored with makeup. Why do they say a dead person looks like himself? He doesn't. She clasps his ring, dangling near her heart from a chain around her neck, and touches it to his lips and then to hers.

"I wrote you a poem, my love," she whispers, stroking his waxy face, smoothing down a stray hair that escaped from the thick gel. "It's about finding love. The promise, the passion, the pain. And the power of a life well loved. I'll only read the last lines. The rest you can read in heaven."

She opens the paper and blinks to focus the blurry words. Her voice chokes but this is the part he must hear, the last thing she will say to his face. She wipes her nose with a wrinkled tissue and takes a breath. "Because together, my love, is where we belong. Our names are engraved on each other's soul. Ever after."

She refolds her love letter, seals it with the faint pink imprint of her mouth, and places it inside his chest pocket. Her words now with him forever. She takes his face in her hands, warm nose to cold.

"I love you, Steve. My Sweet Man. Always have, always will." Her tears splatter on his cheeks, eroding through the heavy foundation, as she brushes her lips on his. "Your name is engraved on my soul." A final lingering touch and she turns away to rejoin her children.

"Mom," Josh says, "the car is waiting for Dad. Go with the girls and I'll see you at the cemetery."

Maureen and Caroline escort her to the side door of the chapel where Kathy and Margaret are waiting along with Linda.

"Girls, go ahead, I'll just be a minute." Susan welcomes the quiet hugs of condolence from the Beatle Girls, but she pauses before accepting Linda's. "I know I should have called earlier," she says, her head bowed,

312

"but I wanted to thank you in person for being there ... for doing all you did."

Linda draws her in closely but loses her balance and braces against her to shore herself up. "I wish it had gone differently," she mumbles, the stench of alcohol flooding Susan's nose and making her pull away. Away from the same overpowering smell from that night, covered up and forgotten in the chaos of the week. And now, face to face, Susan can see the bloodshot eyes and the dark circles under them, the pasty face devoid of its always artfully applied makeup and realizes her friend is intoxicated and probably has been for quite a while.

"Linda, have you been drinking?" she asks, stepping back with crossed arms.

"Maybe, just a little." Linda gives an impish grin and pinches her thumb and index finger together.

"What about that night? Were you drunk then, too?" Susan already knows the answer. She's just giving Linda the chance to confess or lie or at least prove her wrong.

"Hey, give me a break already," she protests, flipping her hands in front of her face, her tone taking a decidedly nasty turn. "Rob just told me he was marrying his little whore so when she sashays in and sleazes up the joint, how else was I supposed to deal with it? Throw my arms around her and let her catch the bouquet?"

"But when you did CPR? How, how could you do that if you were drunk? He might be alive if you'd had your wits about you." Susan doesn't want to blame her friend, but could that have made a difference?

"Listen, it's not rocket science. Besides, honey, he was already dead. Jesus Christ could have laid hands on him and it wouldn't have changed the outcome. I'm sorry we couldn't save him, Susan, but he'd have been a vegetable. Is that what you wanted?"

"Of course not. God, you can be so heartless some-times. It's just that ... we were at such a good place again. And, he was the only man I ever loved."

"Oh, really?" Linda mocks. "Is that why you fucked the fry cook? I may not be a saint but I never cheated on my husband. Stop pretending you're Miss Goody Two Shoes. You're nothing but an adulterous hypocrite."

Susan's legs buckle, and she falls against the offer-tory table, Linda's accusation blasting her like a shotgun. Her already broken heart and battered self-image now blown away, the gaping hole concealed by a big red A.

Having served her indictment, Linda teeters toward the sanctuary exit, her Italian leather heels tapping out 'shame on you' in stylish Morse Code.

"Hey," Kathy calls out and rushes over to Linda. "You don't mean any of that. Let's sort this out. And so-ber you up. Margaret, go with Susan and I'll meet you back at the house. I'm not letting her drive."

As Linda steadies herself against the wooden door, she glares at her friends. "I'll sober up when I'm damn well ready, so fuck off," she says waving them away. She pushes on the heavy door and upchucks on the hallowed threshold.

"And here I go again," Kathy groans.

CHAPTER 44

Bless the church ladies who responded to the commotion and graciously offered to clean up the precipitous puke problem. The bigger quandary sits in the front seat of Kathy's Subaru, grousing about the spatter on her Jimmy Choo's.

Once at Susan's home, Kathy guides Linda to the bathroom to clean up and slip out of her defiled clothing. A large glass of water and two Tylenol is all she can offer, but hopefully sleep will soon minister its healing properties, and Linda will awake only under the sheets and no longer three sheets to the wind.

While Kathy is grateful she can help her friend, her days of tending to tipplers were supposed to be behind her. However, as a card-carrying Al-Anon member, it's quite obvious to her that Linda's drinking has crossed the line from social to chronic, and it's time to take the next step. She finds Linda's phone in her handbag and scans for Jackie's number.

"Jackie, this is Kathy, your Mom's friend. Do you have time to talk?"

"This doesn't sound good," Jackie replies. "What's up?"

Kathy describes today's little episode and the events surrounding the wedding reception that may have contributed to it, including Steve's sudden death and her mother's efforts to save him.

"I'm so sorry you had to deal with that. Matt and I will be home Saturday, and I'll get her into a meeting. I know I should have seen this coming. I've walked in those shoes. Nearly ten years sober," Jackie says with the hint of pride of the once addicted. "But we hadn't been close for a long time, and she seemed to be doing well."

"Don't worry, this isn't my first rodeo, and believe me, I've done my share of looking the other way. We'll keep her here at Susan's until you can pick her up."

Kathy pours herself a glass of iced tea and wanders out to the backyard. Bungalow Bill is sunning himself and raises his head when she walks by. It's been nearly two weeks since she's seen Murphy, and she could use a little doggie time.

"How's it goin', Bill," she says, her voice tender and childlike as she bends to stroke his head. "Need a little love?" She snuggles next to him, tugging at his ears, scratching under his chin, and rubbing his belly until finally joining him on the warm grass for a nap of her own.

"Kathy, we're here," Margaret calls from the patio door.

Kathy stretches and yawns and gives the dog one more pet before rolling over and up to reconnect with her friends, sharing tea at the kitchen table.

"Where's Linda?" Susan's chin rests on her fist, muffling her words as she stares at the steam rising up.

Kathy hesitates for a second, not sure if she should reveal her location, but the goal is to clear the air. Best to be honest from the start. "Upstairs asleep. Jackie's back in town on Saturday and she'll be out to get her, so in the meantime, we're babysitting. And, how are you, Susan?"

She gives a noncommittal grunt. "I think I'd just like to go to bed. Could you feed Bill for me?"

While Margaret tends to the dog, Kathy readies Susan for sleep, unzipping her black mourning frock and slipping off her low-heeled pumps. She pulls her limp arms through the sleeves of her nightgown and, using a cool wet wash cloth, removes what's left of the carefully applied mascara and the salty stains from Susan's slack cheeks. She's spent the better part of this year doing the same for her father, minus the makeup of course. Mothering and ministering, the essence of her character's long-running role, as she takes her direction from the bottle and from death.

"Did you eat anything at the church?" Susan shakes her head. "How about another cup of tea and a slice of toast before you rest?"

"There is no rest for the wicked," Susan drones and crawls under the comforter, pulling the bedding up to her chin.

"I can sit with you 'til you fall asleep if you'd like."

There is no response from Susan, only her eyelids drawing down, closing the curtain on what must seem like a final act. But it's only an intermission in her friend's life, and Kathy knows the show will go on, but not tonight. Tonight the lights will dim in memoriam.

Kathy darkens the room but leaves the door ajar. She eases down the stairs to join Margaret, who waits at the patio door for Old Bill to finish his business.

"Are you hungry?" Kathy asks. "I'm starving. Wonder what she's got in the fridge?"

The shelves are loaded with entrees, side dishes, and desserts delivered over the last few days by generous members of the church. She pulls out macaroni and cheese and a vegetable salad and scoops out two portions of the casserole onto plates and dishes up the rainbow of produce into bowls. The smell of toasted Cheez-Whiz

317

triggers pleasant childhood memories as the whir of the microwave competes with her gurgling stomach.

"How's she doing?" Margaret asks after seeing that the dog has settled. "I've got my anxiety meds with me if she needs something to help her rest."

"Let's wait and see. Hopefully, both of them will feel better in the morning but, damn, that got intense today, didn't it? We can't let that break up the Beatle Girls."

"No, but they'll need to rebuild their trust in each other."

"Trust," Kathy scoffs. "What does that word even mean? Seems to me, the only person you can depend on is yourself, and that's iffy at times."

The microwave dings and Kathy carries the dishes to the table. She and Margaret eat their creamy comfort food in silence. Mac and cheese is always reliable. But now foodies mess it up with some trendy addition, so you can't even count on that. The two of them talk as they wash and dry the dinnerware, returning the pieces to Susan's organized cupboards and drawers.

"Tell me if I'm out of line," Margaret says, "but you reacted fairly strongly to my trust comment. Anything to do with Brian? You never mentioned how the call went."

"It was kinda like therapy. I spilled my guts, he listened in silence, and then he said our time is up. Apparently he wants to move or go on the road, I'm not sure, but where that leaves me in the grand scheme of things is up in the air."

"So why don't you go with him? What's keeping you in LA now that your father ... is gone? I mean, look at Susan. Can any of us afford to wait?"

Kathy wipes down the counters and folds the towel over the oven door handle, her friend's kitchen returned to its original condition. Of course Margaret is right. Her work has always been intermittent, and if something pops up, she could fly back. She's not getting any younger, and Brian has been the best thing to come along, ever. Maybe it's time to be a free spirit once again. Time for the two of them to explore the road that stretches out ahead.

"But speaking of Susan, I'm worried about her," Kathy says. "I mean, her baking business was just getting started. Do you think she can still work with Rick? She called herself wicked tonight."

"Shakespeare said, "They whose guilt within their bosom lies, imagine every eye beholds their blame." Knowing her, I'm afraid she might put her dreams aside once again if just to avoid the appearance of impropriety. Hole up in her home wearing black for a year. She could even slip into a depression. Been there, done that. But her family loves her and will give her support when we leave."

"I know, but we must keep in touch as well. So how about you and Denise? Where did you guys leave things?"

"She confirmed she's gay but is hesitant to go public, not wanting to ruin either of our careers. She thought we should lay low, but I took your advice and told her I wanted to have a serious discussion when I get back. Perhaps you need to walk a little of your talk with Brian."

⌘⌘⌘⌘⌘

Susan has been drifting in and out of sleep since waking in a panic around midnight, par for the course since last Saturday. Tonight her brain runs amok with thoughts about Rick. He shouldn't even be on her radar, the dirt barely shoveled over Steve's grave. Was Rick at the funeral today? She hadn't seen him, but then she hadn't seen much of anything. Perhaps he stayed in the background, not wanting to intrude. How can she possibly live on Steve's social security and a few dozen cinnamon

319

rolls? It's been two weeks since she baked at the Homestead. What if she can't face Rick? What happens to their business relationship? Just as she sinks into slumber, the phone rings. She pops up from the bed, her heart thumping in her chest, momentarily unable to place where she is. On Steve's side of the bed. She fumbles in the dark for the receiver which thuds on the carpet. When she finally pushes the green button, there are already voices speaking.

"... but she's asleep. What's up?"

"Jenny's in labor and needs to go to the hospital."

"What? Maureen, it's Mom. God, what time is it?"

"Two-thirty, I think. I'm sorry, Mom," her daughter says, "I told her we shouldn't bother you, but she insists you need to be there. Can you come?"

"Of course I can, but I don't think I can drive."

"We'll pick you up in ten."

Susan rests on the edge of the bed, rubbing her eyes and cheeks before stretching her arms overhead and breathing deeply. She pulls on sweats and sneakers and staggers into the adjoining bathroom to splash water on her face and run a brush through her hair. Could this be another false labor? Jenny isn't due until next month. As she opens the door, she gives a little yelp as Kathy is there to greet her.

"Susan, are you OK to go?" Kathy asks. "I heard the conversation."

"I'll be fine. Jenny needs me. And I think I need her too."

"Call us when you know something."

"I will. And sorry, but welcome to whack-a-mole world."

LET IT BE

CHAPTER 45

It's 3:15 a.m. when Maureen, Jenny, and Susan enter the Medical Center of Aurora and the soon-to-be mother is whisked away to Labor and Delivery in a wheelchair. Grandmother and Mother slog through the reams of paperwork before making a beeline to the L & D waiting area and the first of many stale but serviceable cups of coffee. Jenny's water broke at home, so Susan knows this is the real deal but there's a long road ahead. At last a nurse in burgundy scrubs appears through the secured double doors and greets them with her name and a smile.

"She's all settled in. She's a wee bit early at thirty-six weeks, but we don't foresee a problem. She's only slightly dilated, contractions about eight minutes apart, so it'll be awhile. Always takes longer with first pregnancies but right now she's comfortable. Wanna go on back?"

"You bet," Susan pipes up. "My first great-grandchild. Wouldn't miss this for the world."

Susan and Maureen rush to keep up with the young energetic woman striding down the hall to the space where Jenny will labor, deliver, and recover. In the cozy hospital room Jenny rests in a comfy bed easily belonging in any bedroom, except that the bottom third folds down and sock- covered metal stirrups stick up from the sides. A wicker basinet for the newborn would fit the low-key vibe but instead the babe will take center stage on a glass-sided, waist-high table with overhead lights and wires. Down home meets high tech.

"Guess this is happening, huh?" Jenny's face is radiant, her eyes twinkling as she explains the bells and whistles to them. "See, there's her heartbeat," she says, pointing to the stream of short continuous spikes on the machine wired to Jenny's abdomen, "and that line shows when I have a contraction. Just light ones so far. Easy peasy."

"Yeah, well this won't last long." Maureen presses her lips together and shakes her head, her negativity settling over the group. "By the end, you'll feel like you've been hit with a ton of bricks. And then the real suffering begins. Up all night with crying, feeding, diapering, colic. No sleep for nights on end. No time for yourself. Oh, the joys of being a mother."

"Maureen," Susan scowls, resisting the urge to slap her and sliding her arm around Jenny instead. "For God's sake, there's an amazing event unfolding here. Can't you enjoy the moment?"

"Sorry, it's just that I've missed the whole first week of school due to Dad's death, and now I'm up in the middle of the night with this. Cut me some slack, OK?"

"We're all dealing with a lot," Susan replies through gritted teeth. "Why don't you go home, catch up on your work. I'll stay with Jenny. My friends are staying at the house, and they can come get me if need be. I'll keep you posted on her progress."

"That'd be great. She's probably in better hands with you anyway. Hang in there, Jen."

Maureen gives her daughter a perfunctory kiss on her head and scurries out of the room, her sigh of relief clearly audible.

"Gramma, is it really going to be that bad?"

"I'm not gonna lie, Sweetie, it's gonna hurt," Susan replies, brushing Jenny's long hair away from her eyes and adjusting the sheet that covers her. "But all the breathing you learned in Lamaze will help, and they'll give you something for the pain when you need it. And when it's all over, you'll have a beautiful baby." She picks up the remote and presses the on button. "Shall we check out late night TV? Maybe we'll find some incredible new product to make our lives A. Maze. Ing." The two women separated by a generation but connected by the arrival of the next.

⌘⌘⌘⌘⌘

"Gramma, it hurts so bad! It hurts. It hurts," Jenny moans, her face contorted and beaded with sweat.

"I know, Sweetie. Remember your breathing. Pant and blow it out. Focus on your spot. I'm right here. You can do this." Susan's calm voice hypnotizes as she eases her through the pain. She's grasped the rhythm of the tracings on the monitor and can predict the wax and wane of the contraction. "OK, it's winding down now. See, keep breathing."

Susan and Jenny have been at this all day now, making steady progress but no baby yet. The nurses sweep in and out, monitoring the dilation and thinning of Jenny's cervix and the vital signs of mother and baby. They help her walk to progress the labor, suggest more comfortable positions to ease the pain, and support her efforts to cope with the ever-increasing intensity and frequency of the uterine spasms. Susan is glued to her granddaughter's side, wiping the sweat from her brow, offering ice chips, rubbing her back, and allowing her hand to be squeezed into a red misshapen pulp. She sleeps when Jenny sleeps but neither have had more than thirty winks at a time. She did step out a couple of times to update the Beatle

325

Girls, and see how things are going with Linda. And fortunately, all is well on that front.

But when not thinking about eight uninterrupted hours in her own bed, she thinks about how Jenny and her parents are going to survive this situation. Susan's calls to Maureen and Dave go to voice mail. Maureen no longer denies she's going to be a grandmother, but her heart has never been in it. Even now, with the baby nearly here, her career takes precedence. So between catnaps and contractions, Susan makes an offer to Jenny that just might help them both.

⌘⌘⌘⌘⌘

"Gramma, get the nurse, get the nurse!" Jenny writhes in panic and pain.

"Take a breath," Susan says with guarded calm as she presses the call light. She studies the screen with its jagged irregular spikes and low dips and bites her lip to contain her own scream.

As the RN analyzes the printout from the monitor, presses on Jenny's abdomen and, once the contraction subsides, takes a look inside, Susan prays. Everything's all right, everything's OK.

"What's wrong? Is it my baby?" Jenny cries.

"Jenny, we're getting close," she says in a soothing yet firm voice. "Sometimes those long, hard contractions take the baby's breath away just like it does for you, and the heart slows down a bit. But now, see, it's all back to normal," and she points to the steady tracings of normal fetal cardiac activity. "Your doctor's here and should be in shortly."

Susan and Jenny have only seen Dr. Lewis a few times as the nurse practitioner provided most of the care, but now the matronly obstetrician enters the room and washes her hands.

"So, how are you doing, Jenny?" she says, carrying on the conversation as she peeks, palpates, and probes. "It's been about fourteen hours now. I know that must seem like forever, but that's pretty normal for a first-time Mom."

"So, Dr. Lewis, how much longer do you think it might be?" Susan asks.

"She's nine centimeters dilated and 100% effaced, so there's light at the end of this little one's tunnel, but it's best to let things unfold on Baby Time. Is your Mom here, Jenny?"

"She's on her way, isn't she, Gramma?"

"Yes," Susan replies. Or she damn well better be.

⌘⌘⌘⌘⌘

"Push, Jenny, push, push, push," Dr. Lewis commands. "Wait. Breathe. I can see the head. Next contraction, you give me the biggest push you can. We're almost there."

Maureen and Dave arrived with only minutes to spare before the culmination of their daughter's months-long enterprise. While glad they're here to welcome their first grandchild, Susan resents that they get to bask in the glory by virtue of their titles, not their contributions.

"Ready. Give it all you've got, Jenny. Push. Push. There's the head. Stop. Don't push. Let me suction her. Wait. Wait. OK. Now, Jenny, now. Here we are. Time of birth. Twenty O Five. It's a girl," the doctor announces as she holds up the tiny infant covered in what looks like frosting before handing her off to the nurse.

"It's a girl, Jenny, your girl. Oh, my Gosh. It's your girl," Susan exclaims.

Susan wraps her arms around her Jenny's head and shoulders, tears and sweat streaming down both of their faces. But where's the bawling roar she's heard from her

327

other children and grandchildren as they made their entrance into the world?

"She's not crying, Gramma. What's wrong?"

Susan watches the nurses vigorously rub the baby's bluish back and give her oxygen from a mask near her face as she lies on the padded warming table. And she prays. Please, God, please let this baby be all right. After an excruciating minute, a very strong pair of lungs makes it known that enough is enough and it's time to meet her Mom.

"Here she is, Jenny. Just needed a little pinking up. She weighs 6 pounds 3 ounces and is 20 inches long. Congratulations," the nurse says as she presents the now screeching bundle to the young bedraggled mother.

"She's so beautiful. Oh, my God. She's looking right at me. Like she knows me. And look at her little fingers. Oh, my God, Gramma. I know what I'm going to name her."

"What, Sweetie?" Susan's voice is distant, lost in the moment as she strokes the baby's soft cheek with her finger.

"Stefanie Bliss Lawson. For Grampa and for you, Gramma. Bliss isn't just a name. It means great happiness and joy. You give me that, and I want my baby to have that too. I'm so glad we're gonna live with you."

"You're *what*?" Maureen's eyes widen, and she steps back from the bed. "Who came up with that harebrained idea?"

"Maureen, *I* suggested it," Susan says, lifting her head, eyes riveted on her daughter. "With your Dad gone my house is going to be very empty. Jenny will need help with the baby. It's a win-win for both of us." She slips her arm around her granddaughter as she presents her rationale, the bond between them strengthening with each word. "I always thought your father would be at my side, and I'm pretty sure motherhood wasn't at the top of

Jenny's to-do list. Right now, Jenny and I are standing on the threshold of new lives. Call it fate or God's will, but doors have opened. And we're walking through them."

Susan beams at Jenny and reaches for her hand. As they interlace their fingers and raise them in the air, Baby Stefanie pokes her tiny pink arm out of the blanket that swaddles her, and shakes it defiantly. *Vive la revolution.*

CHAPTER 46

Susan slips out and leaves baby, mother, and grandparents to continue their meet and greet. She joins a room full of fathers and grandparents relaying newborn particulars to family and friends, their tired eyes brightened by the sparkle of celebration. Amid the babel of measurements and middle names, she makes her own calls to announce the arrival of Stefanie Bliss. She only wishes she was sharing the news with the baby's namesake.

On the advice of the nursing staff, it's decided that everyone needs a bit of rest so Susan returns to Sullivan with Maureen and Dave. Most likely Jenny and the baby will be discharged tomorrow evening, all she needs to know about the care of an infant somehow magically imparted in her twenty-four-hour stay. Good thing she'll have a live-in tutor at home. It's well after ten when Susan unlocks the front door of her home, only the night lights guiding her to the serenity of a soft mattress.

She awakes from a brief but refreshing sleep, ready to start her new adventure. But first, it's time for some coffee. Good coffee. One by one her current guests wander down the stairs, following the aroma of freshly-ground hazelnut beans.

"You're up early," Kathy says, her arms stretching high over her head. "I didn't hear you come in."

"I tried to be stealthy. I'm practicing for my new arrival." Susan's eyes crinkle, her smile all teeth as she jiggles her fists. "Jenny and the baby are coming to live with me."

Kathy takes a long sip of coffee before speaking. "That's great. It'll be so much easier to spoil her rotten that way. But, and I'm saying this as your friend," her fingers pointing with a cautionary wag, "I can see you losing yourself in this setup."

Susan's hands ward off Kathy's misgivings as she defends her decision. "I know, my track record isn't the best, but I'm riding a new horse this time. Any advice you've got will be most appreciated. Anyway, lots to do to get ready. So, what about your plans? I expect you're both anxious to get home and away from all this drama."

"And back to my own, no doubt. This has been such fun, I mean aside from ... you know, but yeah, we're way past the fish slash guest expiration date. Margaret has a flight early tomorrow morning so I'm going to drop her off at the airport before I head out. And Jackie and Matt will take Linda home today. Then it will be just two women and a baby."

A creak on the stairs announces Margaret, with Linda sheepishly following behind, apparently using her as a shield in case Susan waits with a bat. Luckily for her, the joy of new life leaves little room for the sting of anger.

"Good morning, Margaret," Susan says and offers her a cup. She slides a third mug and a warm and hopeful smile toward Linda who focuses on the floor, arms dangling at her sides, unable or unwilling to make a move. Susan has neither the time nor inclination to prolong the awkward moment, and she rushes over to wrap her arms around her in a show of forgiveness. The protrusion of shoulder blades and the waif-like lightness surprises her. The extent of her friend's downfall made tangible. There will be time to broach the subject of her drinking later, and she chooses to sidestep instead of smacking into the elephant in the room.

"We were both stressed out, Sweetie. As far as I'm concerned, it's in the past. Besides, I'm too happy to dwell on it. How about some breakfast? And then we need to babyproof this house."

Susan calls Maureen to ask if Dave can bring over the basinet, changing table, baby clothes and diapers, plus a week's worth of clothes for Jenny. The rest of her things can be dropped by later. Stephanie Bliss's aunties make short work of the transformation from guest room to nursery, and by noon all is put together and put away, ready for her new roommates to check in.

"I know teenagers have ravenous appetites, but I think you'll need to freeze some of this stuff, Susan," Margaret says, her voice muffled as she rearranges plastic containers in the refrigerator in the search for lunch options. "I forgot how generous countryfolk can be."

"I know. Remember all the clothes you guys gave me when I pulled into town with only my California Girl duds? Flip-flops do not do well in the snow," Kathy laughs, pointing at her currently exposed feet. "My dancing career might never have happened if I'd frostbitten my toes."

"That reminds me. Trivia question. When was the day we first got together?" Susan asks, and four hands reach for imaginary buzzers, shouting out the answer in unison. "February 9, 1964!"

"Surprisingly, it was my mother who was the catalyst," Margaret says. "So worried I'd never make any friends, she convinced your mothers to let you come over to watch Ed Sullivan. Instead of my usual evening with my nose in a book, she was forcing me to watch a variety show on television, for heaven's sake. I can't believe how strait-laced and reserved I was back then." She pauses and sighs, "Thanks for making that first crack in my shell."

"For me, the build-up to that day was almost unbearable." Susan closes her eyes and shivers, the pull in the center of her chest returning as it always does when she thinks of the memory. "It was after church," she says to Linda, "and you were taking forever to pick an outfit. Back and forth between the Bobby Brooks slacks and the blue jeans. You looked just like Colleen Corby on the cover of *Seventeen* with your hair flipped up and your pouty lips. I mean, what difference did it make? It's just girls, I said, and you'll look gorgeous no matter what, so make a choice already."

"It was your room, Margaret, that blew me away. All the books and paintings. I could tell you loved the arts and it made me think of my Dad. And when I mentioned ballet, you stepped into fifth position with an amazing turnout. I thought maybe this place will be OK. Course I had to teach you all the other dances," Kathy says with a good-natured nudge on her friend's shoulder.

Linda has been unusually quiet all morning, a week's worth of alcohol still coursing through her blood. Though Kathy has been plying her with Tylenol and B vitamins and pushing water and other fluids to counteract the dehydration, Susan wonders if she'll need to go into rehab to completely dry out. She sits with her elbows resting on the table, her head braced against her hands as she massages her temples. Susan is surprised when she speaks.

"I think that's the day it all began, you know," Linda says.

"What's that?" Kathy asks. "Our life long Beatles obsession?"

"No, the drinking." She lifts her gaze out to the window, her voice a whisper. "I assumed since you guys were from big cities on the coasts, you'd be cool with having a drink. My parents had cocktails every night, and I read that the Beatles drank scotch and Coke, so I brought the flask. I reveled in the risk. I did a lot of that it turns out. With unintended consequences."

Susan hasn't heard any more about Linda's first child. She hopes they will connect, but now is not the best time for sure. One thing, and one day at a time is what they say.

"Linda, we all cope in our own ways. I think I'm hooked on unavailable men," Kathy says with one of those quick, insightful laughs.

"Maybe we were addicted to the Beatles," Susan blurts out with a shrug of her shoulders. "I mean, during that first *Ed Sullivan Show* I felt like I was in a drug-induced stupor. I knew you guys were in the room, screaming along with the girls on TV, but I was lost in my own little world, crying into a pillow. Just me and the Fab Four." She wraps her arms around herself, squeezing that imaginary cushion. "Those early days were such an incredible high."

"If only we could have bottled that enthusiasm like your Oh! de London," Margaret comments. "Dab a little on when our lives need a pick-me-up."

"Mark me down for a gallon." Kathy rests her chin on her folded hands. "This has definitely been a hard day's year. But I've come to believe that life is like watermelon. You savor the sweetness and spit out the seeds."

"You're right, Kathy. We most definitely have to stay in touch. No more of this waiting for forty years to find out what's going on. I, for one, couldn't have survived without your support over this past week," Susan says reaching out for the others' hands. "I say we get together at least once a year. Deal?"

With a bit of encouragement, Linda slides from her chair and they all lock hands in a circle.

"On three," Susan shouts and their arms raise on the count with a resounding "Beatles and Beatle Girls Forever!" with a "Hell, yeah!" to top it off.

The doorbell rings, interrupting the high fives. Susan opens the door to Maureen, Dave, and Jenny holding Baby Stefanie. A flurry of aahs and oohs fly out, and each of the Beatle Girls examines the tiny pink face, her eyes closed and totally oblivious to all the commotion she is generating. Having little experience with small human bundles, Kathy and Margaret pass on the chance to cuddle and coo on a more intimate basis, but Linda accepts the baby with open arms, secure and steady despite her present condition. Susan watches as Linda gazes at the newborn and wonders who those eyes see. The hundreds of babies she helped bring into the world. Her own daughter, now a newlywed and poised to have a child of her own someday. Or the one that got away. The one she gave up to another family but who now beckons her to come back into her life. Linda's eyes squeeze tight as she returns the baby to Jenny, and a quick pass of the back of her hand blots away the moisture that was forming.

"You know," Linda sniffs, "it's probably best not to expose her to too many people just yet, Jenny. Maybe you should settle her down in her crib."

"Yes, that's a good idea. Dave and I really need to get home to our other children," Maureen says, "so we'll say our good-byes and give you a call later, Mom."

Susan heads upstairs with Jenny to show off the nursery and where she's stored all the supplies. Jenny places the baby in the small wicker crib that will be her home for the next month or so, and they slip out of the room on tiptoe. And of course, the doorbell rings. So much for letting sleeping babies lie. Stefanie is back in her mother's arms as Susan helps put baby to breast. With the sounds of suckling in full swing, Susan returns to see who was at the door.

"Hi, Auntie Suze," Jackie says, "we were just saying we'd love to chat about the honeymoon, which was fabulous by the way, but Matt and I are dead tired and I want to get Mom home, so we'll come out later and give you the details. Do you mind?"

"No, of course not, Sweetie. I think we all need some good sleep, so let me get Linda's things and you can be on your way."

Susan pulls Jackie into the kitchen. "I'm worried about her. She's had so much thrown at her recently. Do you think she needs rehab or something?"

"I don't know. I'll stay with her tonight, and tomorrow I'll call my contacts and go from there. I've been down this road, Auntie Suze, and I know it's not easy. I want everything to be all right, but she has to want that as well. That's the first step. And the hardest."

The Beatle Girls gather for one last embrace. It's been a long and winding road since that February night in 1964. Their bond once so strong and close nearly disappeared at times as life had its way with them. Susan knows they were different people back then just as they are different people now. And she knows they will change with the future. She can now admit that change can be a good thing. And the Beatle Girls will be better for it.

Kathy and Margaret are packed for their early morning departure and asleep in Susan's master bedroom. She figured they deserved one night on a decent mattress before setting out on their trips back home. She'll sleep in the new nursery next to Jenny and the baby. But as the house eases into slumber, she stands over the basinet one more time.

"My little Steffy," she whispers, "I have so much to tell you about your Granpapa."

CHAPTER 47

Linda slumps in the passenger seat of Jackie's Ford Fusion Hybrid, its utilitarian, environmental friendliness adorned only with Obama/Biden and Coexist bumper stickers and various talismans swinging from her rear-view mirror. Her good luck charms have always been made of green paper with pictures of dead presidents. After the events of this year, she wonders if she should place her faith elsewhere.

The nausea and headache have finally subsided following her peri-nuptial binge, thanks to Kathy's careful attention, but she still feels rode hard and put away wet. And she's not sure where she might have ridden to in her inebriated state. She's been lazing about all weekend, drinking copious amounts of caffeine, and yet it's all she can do to put one foot in front of the other. Her thinking is scattered, her mood volatile. Keeping her mouth shut seems the best way to avoid disaster. As she listens to Jackie's honeymoon highlights, thankfully minus the intimate details, she keeps one ear open and both eyes closed.

"The cruise was so much fun. You and your friends should do that, Mom. Gourmet food, pampering, tropical beaches. There were lots of Boomers, not just really old people. What do you think? Mom?"

Let's see, surrounded by multiple bars hawking island drinks and no land to escape to for miles. Falling off the wagon or over the rails with 10,000 feet of water under her doesn't sound like a lot of fun. "Yeah, we'll see. Maybe next year."

"I wish I could have seen Jenny's baby," she sighs. "Did you know her Mom almost made her give it up. How horrible."

You don't know the half of it, Jackie. Her memories of the day she gave birth to Sandra are fuzzy, but there's one that's crystal clear. She pleaded with the staff and her mother for just a peek, just a minute to hold her. No it's better if you don't, they kept saying. Let her go. But one kind nurse relented and snuck the baby to her. And for a few moments she counted toes and fingers, caressed her soft skin, looked into the dark gray eyes and kissed her forehead before they snatched her out of her arms, and out of her life. What if she had ...? Her breathing stutters and she turns to face the window. To face her regret. She startles at the touch of Jackie's hand on her arm and quickly stifles her emotion.

"Mom, are you all right?"

"I'm fine. Just need some sleep. Can we talk later?"

They pull into the parking garage at the condo, and Matt, who has been following in Linda's Lexus, guides the car into her designated spot. He opens the trunk of the Ford and takes out Jackie's suitcase, and the three make their way to the elevator and up to Linda's place.

"Mom, I'm going to stay with you for a few days. Make sure you're OK and get you some help," Jackie says, pulling her close.

Linda pushes back in protest, but she's too tired to give it much effort. The newlyweds share a long kiss, and Matt is on his way. Now, she's in the hands of a sober alcoholic. Jackie's walked this path. The teacher may have come but is the student ready?

Her first assignment? A nice long bubble bath. Linda's schedule doesn't often allow for anything but a quick morning shower, so it's been a while since she luxuriated in a tub smothered in lavender foam. The warmth of the water seeps into her muscles, softening the knots in her shoulders, pulling the ache out through her pores. Soft new-age music floats around her, no words, just flowing notes. Her body is well on its way to nighty-night, but her head is still jumping on the bed. She should have dunked it in the sudsy waters. She reluctantly climbs out and towels off. Wrapped in her plush robe, she joins her daughter in the kitchen.

"I'll fix real meals tomorrow, but how about a light snack for now? Remember that mug you bought me a long time ago? The one with teddy bears that said, 'Bread and water can so easily be tea and toast.' I always found that comforting. That something so basic can transform into this loving, nurturing ritual."

"I bought you that?" Linda shakes her head. "I don't remember. Seems a little too motherly for me. Are you sure it wasn't Susan? Or your father?" She rolls her eyes and blows air through her closed lips. No, don't go there she reminds herself. You'll only get upset.

"No, it was definitely you. That's why I kept it. Let's go sit in the living room instead of standing around out here."

Jackie places the cup and plate on a tray, and they drift toward the couch. Linda has rarely eaten here, crumbs and all on her furniture, but tonight it doesn't matter, and she settles into the leather cushions with her tea. Jackie leaves the buttered bread on the coffee table and stands behind her mother, massaging her head and neck. Linda melts at the touch. Maybe this will tame her beastly thoughts.

"You know," Jackie continues as she strokes and kneads, "in hindsight, you were a better parent than you give yourself credit for. I mean, you weren't all snuggle up and let's bake cookies, but you taught me a lot about being a businesswoman. Your drive and confidence in your career inspired me to take risks and believe in myself. Eventually."

"And I suppose driving you to drink was a bonus? I pushed you just like my mother pushed me. I'm sorry, Jackie."

"Don't be. I'm happy now. You and Daddy got me into treatment, and all I want is to return the favor. I don't know if you need rehab, maybe only counseling, support from AA. You need to figure out your drinking triggers. I'll bet stress is a biggie."

"That certainly pushed me over the edge this time. My diagnosis with cancer, your father getting remarried, Steve's death despite my efforts, and ..." She hesitates, not sure if this is the right time to repeat her confession. Or the right person. The Beatle Girls hadn't seemed all that surprised. Would Jackie be as understanding? Her daughter's soothing hands are relaxing her muscles and her resistance. She lets her secret trickle out.

"I know there are twelve steps and all and one of them is making amends to people we've wronged. I need to deal with one of those now."

"Mom, it's best to go in order because they build on each other. That step is a ways down the list. You need to admit you have a problem before you do anything else."

"OK, I have a problem, and Jackie, you have a sister."

Jackie's fingers stop as if the quarter has run out. "I what?"

"I got pregnant in high school and gave my baby away. I never knew anything about her, who adopted her, where she went, nothing. Until she called me a few months ago wanting to meet her birth mother."

"Whoa." Jackie comes around to face Linda, sitting beside her. "Who else knows? Daddy? Your friends?"

"My mother and Susan knew at the time, and I told the other girls at our reunion. Seeing Jenny with her baby today nearly broke my heart." Linda covers her chest with her hands, the old wound now a gaping hole and she knows only one way to seal it. "I need to tell her I'm sorry. I need to know my baby is all right. Will you go with me?"

"Of course I will, Mom, but let's get you stable. If stress is what sets you off, then this could be major. But when you're ready, I'll be with you, holding your hand, have your back all the way. Let's just do it one step, one day at a time."

One day at a time. Linda's never done anything one day at a time. Hell, STAT, hospital talk for right now, is her middle name. She's used to being able to solve problems. OK, she realizes she's been pretty good at creating them as well. And now she'll be dealing with the prolonged process of getting sober. And staying that way. Before the wedding, she had plans for creating a Birthing Center, incorporating a more homelike and natural experience into labor and delivery. She'd even talked with her staff, and several expressed interest in coming along. But substance abuse could jeopardize her nursing licenses. And how many of them will be on her side now? How many will travel with her on a new adventure when she's carrying so much baggage?

"Jackie," Linda's voice wavers. "I'm ... scared. I don't know if I can do this. It's so much easier to go flying with my Grey Goose."

"I know, I know," Jackie reassures as she rubs Linda's hand. "You are the strongest woman I know, Mom. If I can do it, of course you can. And I'll be there for you. Your friends will be there for you. You won't have to do this alone. You got through all those years of school. You built a successful business. You got through cancer. You've got so much life left to live. You just need to say the words and the process starts."

Linda closes her eyes, breathing through the raggedness of each respiration. She squeezes her daughter's hands and looks at her squarely.

"Hello, my name is Linda ... and I'm an alcoholic."

CHAPTER 48

The splendor of early fall colors in the Rockies gives way to desolate stretches of uninhabited sandstone mesas as Kathy makes her way back to Venice Beach. The dearth of radio stations forces her to listen to a mix of classic head trash and free-form anxiety broadcast by her monkey mind. Old subliminal tapes about abandonment, trust, commitment. About acquiescing to being alone, yet failing to acknowledge that situations change.

After an overnight in a Vegas motel far from its glitz and glamour, she inches along, bumper-to-bumper with the motley crew returning to La La Land. The lowlifes and high rollers. The first-time brides-to-be, the second chance divorcees. And the sixty year old women enveloped in wheeled cocoons ready to make their transformation and dry their wings in the warmth of love.

Pulling up in the alley behind her duplex, she leaves her suitcase in the car and slips around the side to the front door. She spies Murphy, up on his hind legs peeking out the window, tail wagging, and living in canine time - where yesterday fades, tomorrow is a theory, and now is all that matters. Kathy wishes she could do the same.

"Hey, it's so good to see you, my sweet little man," she coos softly as a flurry of tawny hair and slobber greet her. "Oh, and good to see you, too." She looks up at Max and winks. She rises into a long soul to soul embrace, tempered somewhat by concern for his frailty.

"You must be exhausted," he says. "How about a bite to eat?"

"If you spoon-feed it to me. I'm getting too old for driving straight through. Next trip, I'm stopping to smell roses and look at balls of twine."

With a bowl of chicken noodle soup and a piece of toast in her belly, Kathy leans back in her chair, stretching her legs out in front, and sips the last half of her tea. She rolls her neck and shrugs her shoulders to work out the kinks and knots in muscles chained too long to a steering wheel.

"So, you girls have a groovy time braiding hair and having pillow fights, or whatever you did in the sixties?" Max asks with an impish grin.

"Um, let's just say it was more like *Gidget* meets *Ben Casey*. Remember Dr. Zorba's opening lines?" She grabs a pen from Max's table and writes on her napkin as she speaks in the serious tone of the fuzzy-haired neurosurgeon. "Man. Woman. Birth. Death. Infinity. I'll fill you in on the details later. When both my eyes and brain can focus. Anyway, bless you for taking care of my guy." She yawns and scoots her chair back.

"Speaking of your guy, can you keep your head up just a bit longer? There's something I need to talk to you about."

We need to talk. Four little words that usually precede shit hitting fan. Suddenly she's wide awake and braced for impact.

"Is Murphy OK? Did something happen while I was gone?"

"No, he's fine. It's your other guy. Brian."

Her heart sinks as she recalls their last conversation. Wherein she shoots down his offer of a life together by hanging up on him. Guess she screwed that pooch. No offense, Murph.

"He was over here a lot while you were in Colorado, so I got to know him pretty well. Anyway he told me about his plans for retirement." Max leans in to rest his forearms on the table. "Not sure you knew, Kath, but I didn't just wander into your life. Your Dad sent me. Somehow he found out you bought the place and needed a renter. He was in a bad way, Honey, ashamed he couldn't be there for you, and he begged me to pinch-hit for him. You know, keep an eye on you to make sure things went your way." He reaches across and takes her hands, patting them gently. "I came to think of you as my daughter, and like all fathers, I worried some jerk might hurt my little girl. So sue me if you want, but over the years I've sized up your gentlemen callers, questioning their prospects and intentions. And I think we finally have a winner. This Brian fellow. He's a keeper. Responsible, good heart and a kind soul, and funny as hell. Even Murphy likes him." And on cue, the dog wags his confirmation, with a persuasive head scratch from Max.

Kathy lets out an explosive sigh and raps herself on her head. It's all about timing, and hers has been sucking big time.

"Max, I agree wholeheartedly with your assessment, but I basically told him to take a hike. Which he will probably do as he travels the countryside. Without me. I think we're dead in the water."

"I doubt he'll give up that easy. I think patience is another one of his virtues. But Kath, one of your Dad's last requests of me was to promise that I'd walk you down the aisle and into the arms of this man who led him to the Pearly Gates. So if Brian means anything to you, please, don't let him go. Let things develop. Whether you marry the guy, that's your call."

"But everything I love is here. How could I leave *you*, for God's sake?"

"My Sweet Girl. No matter where you go, no matter where I go," he pauses and touches his index finger to Kathy's forehead, "I'll be right here."

Her eyelids drift closed for a second as the gnarled digit grazes her brow, just like E.T. did with Elliott in the movie. "And, dear, dear Max," she whispers, pointing at her heart, "you will always be right here."

He sniffs and rubs at his nose. "Hey, before I smear the ink all over this, here's a letter your Dad gave me a while back. I guess it fell behind my bookcase and Brian found it when he was over."

"Thank you, Max. For everything." And she gives him a full hug, brittle bones be damned.

Murphy bounds up the stairs while Kathy and her luggage drag behind. She's greeted by a bouquet of roses and a card on the counter. Welcome Home. Brian. She takes a sniff of a red bloom, the first of many she'll be stopping to smell. Her mail is neatly stacked beside it, but the only letter she cares about is the one in her hand. She steps out of her jeans and pulls off her T-shirt, dropping them where she stands. She snuggles into the covers of her bed, Murphy sprawled at the end. Her name is printed boldly across the envelope and she opens it, carefully sliding the notepaper out, and unfolds it.

My Dear Little Girl,
I stopped by today, hoping you would be home. But, alas, you must be dancing. That's good because then I know you're happy. That's all I ever wanted for you. And for Mary. I'm so sorry I wasn't a better Dad. Couldn't keep us together. Anyway, water under the bridge. I'm glad you decided to stay in the old house despite all the bad memories. I don't know where I'll be but, I'll be watching you somehow. I

know someone will come into your life to give you the
love you deserve. Don't give up hope.
Love you. Two and a half and a peanut.
Daddy

Kathy turns the page over, checking for a date on the back. Nothing. It must have been written maybe mid-nineties, after Max had moved in. She reads it again, looking past the words, imagining her father writing it. Maybe in a sober moment. Although her father's voice has been silenced, at least his words remain. Words that remind her he loved her.

Suddenly the bone-weariness of the day settles in, the touching reunion with Max and her father exhausting her spirit. This year of ups and downs has nearly drained the depths of her emotional pool. But she feels one last good cry inside her. One more to wash away the past, and create a fresh landscape. She feels the waters churning in her belly, her heart being tossed about in her chest. Eyes squeeze shut, lips and cheeks tighten as she draws her breath in deeply to her core. All signaling the impending tsunami. Her shoulders shudder and release the surging flood. When the tears finally ebb and her muscles still, she drifts into the Land of Nod.

⌘⌘⌘⌘⌘

Kathy awakens to the smell of garlic, oregano, and basil. It's dark outside and in her room, and her quilted comforter is pulled neatly up over her shoulders. The soft lump of dog is no longer at her feet. A muted trumpet plays soft jazz. Brian is here.

She stretches arms over head, pointing toes to the end of the bed with a satisfied groan before throwing back the covers and swinging her legs over the side. Her mouth is tacky, her breath foul from too much java, and the faint odor of perspiration and road trip munchies infuses her skin. She steps into the shower, letting the warm steam open her pores and her heart, reviving her energy and her faith in this thing called love.

"Smells delicious," she murmurs as she sneaks up behind Brian and wraps her arms around his waist. "And you're not even Italian. Are you?"

"A little, on my mother's side. It's a marinara sauce I mastered in college. Used it to charm all the girls." He turns and ladles out a bit into a spoon, slipping the deep red sauce into Kathy's mouth. "More salt?"

Her tongue rolls the sample around. "Nope, it's perfect," she says licking her lips. She spies the opened bottle of Pinot Noir on the table. "Shall I pour?"

"Definitely. This can simmer," Brian says, giving the pot another stir. "Why don't we have a sit. I'm anxious to hear what your Dad had to tell you."

They take their glasses to the sofa, now back in its central location in view of the trees and night sky. The nearly full moon peeks through the branches and, with the dimmed living room lights, a romantic glow bathes the room. Murphy follows and plops at their feet. The perfect threesome.

Kathy curls her legs under her as she sits beside Brian, taking a quick sip of her red wine before divulging the contents of the letter he found.

"A final repentance, I suppose, in case he didn't get the chance to do it in person. Though we covered most of it before he passed, it will be nice to have something in his handwriting." She takes another drink. "He said he was sure someone would bring love into my life, and apparently made Max promise to give me away on my wedding day," she says, eyeing her father's selection over her glass.

"Hmm."

Kathy takes a healthy gulp from her glass before setting it on the table and sliding off the couch to kneel in front of Brian. With her hands on his knees, she stares into his pale blue eyes, his pupils enlarged in the darkened room. She scoots in between his knees and drapes her arms around his neck, her fingers gently running through the graying curls at the nape.

"Daddy, Max, even Murphy have voted for their "someone" and the results have been tabulated and sealed in a mayonnaise jar. And the award goes to ..." Her fingers tap out a drum roll on his shoulder. "The best man to ever come her way. The man she'd follow anywhere. Mr. Brian McDermott."

"Ah, she likes me, she really, really likes me," he grins, pulling her close, their foreheads and noses pressed together. "Kathleen Rose O'Shea, I love you."

"Ditto," she whispers. Their soft and tender kiss quickly gains urgency as hands and tongues feel their way. But a quickie on the couch doesn't do justice to the moment, nor their aging limbs, and they move as one into her bedroom. Can erotic pottery making be far behind?

CHAPTER 49

Most of the time Margaret doesn't think about her wealth. It's more like putting on a rarely worn coat and discovering a twenty-dollar bill in the pocket. A fortuitous surprise. When she canceled her flight to Paris after Steve's death, she took the penalties in stride. Add in this last-minute booking back to Hartford, Connecticut, and she's out a considerable chunk of change. But she would do it again in a heartbeat. Friends are worth every penny.

She's been thinking a lot about friends. Friends in need. Friends forever. Friends with benefits. She's always said she could count her confidants on one hand and have a pinky left to raise at tea. Hopefully, she won't have one more finger to spare.

Her first-class seat gives her plenty of space and quiet to ponder her relationship with Denise. She opened the door at their last conversation, but she's still debating whether to walk through. Of course Kathy is right when she reminded her that you love who you love. And in an ideal world, everyone would be with their soul mate regardless of age, race, religion, class, or gender. Is she still looking at things with her usual rigidity? As they say, is the Pope Catholic? But just what fortress imprisons her attitudes? Outside institutions or her own inner misconceptions?

With no carry-on to retrieve, Margaret is one of the first to exit, and she threads her way through the terminal to baggage claim. Sean is waiting for her in khakis and a polo shirt instead of his official chauffeur's uniform. Without the trappings of a liveried servant, she sees a boyishly handsome and caring man. And a good friend. Perhaps she'll need that other hand.

"Sean, it's so good to see you."

Fresh from two weeks of an abundance of openly expressed emotions, she reflexively reaches out to touch his arm before yanking her hand back, past protocol checking her spontaneous action. No, if she's learned anything, it's that life is too short. Extending her arms, she moves in awkwardly, heading left then right, to clasp him with building intensity. His arms remain at his sides, and she begins to pull away. Until she feels a reciprocal hug.

"Ma'am. Very good to see you as well."

"Is Denise at home? There's so much I need to tell her ... about the trip and all."

"Probably in bed by now. It's a school day tomorrow."

"Oh, silly me," she smiles weakly, "I'm still on holiday time. Guess I'll have to share later." Margaret rubs her stomach, the sudden onset of cramping making her wince. As she flew over the countryside, she memorized a script for her heart-to-heart with Denise, stoking her courage with positive imagery. And now her recitation is on hold. Much like her digestion right now. Maybe it's for the best. She's never submitted a first draft of anything. So after reuniting with a rather indifferent Maya and opening the suitcases full of unworn clothes to let them air, she performs her bedtime ablutions and crawls into her four poster bed. She's not anticipating a restful first night home.

It's nearly nine before she rises, and of course by now Denise is in class filling young heads with the marvels of the English language. Her midnight mind was hard at work until at least two, and she's mulling over one of her insomnia-fueled ideas involving house cleaning, though not with soap and a scrub brush.

Despite their physical absence, the stifling control that her father and husband wielded over her continues to pervade the hundred-year-old stone manor. If her life and her relationship with Denise is to have a fresh start, there can be no lingering malevolence buried in the overstuffed chairs of the study, no murderous conspiracies incubating in the books in the library, no malice lurking in the recesses of bedroom closets.

As a good Catholic girl, Margaret is quite familiar with the Christian concept of the Devil. She's pretty sure she married him. But the evil she feels in her home is more pagan in nature, and she wonders if a cleansing ritual might help exorcize the demons. Once again twenty-first-century technology lays the answers at her fingertips, and Margaret sends Sean off to purchase the needed supplies.

She whiles away the rest of the morning sorting through her unused Paris collection, draping dresses and jackets back on their padded hangers with shoes and scarfs slipped into designated drawers. She wants to have a nice dinner for Denise this evening. Something simple yet special. The meal they shared that night at Napa and Company, the sea scallops with bacon dust. Perhaps the restaurant might be willing to box something up for takeout. After all it had been a wonderful evening, and this time she will limit her wine intake.

Sean says Denise is usually home by three in the afternoon on Mondays this term. Margaret checks her watch, comparing it to the grandfather clock in the entry and then the digital readout on the microwave. All the same. She checks and double checks the refrigerator to verify that all the little Styrofoam boxes of gourmet food are still sealed, ready to be reheated at the appropriate moment. She paces in the foyer, peering out the side window in case her friend comes in through the front door instead of the back entrance. The rumble of the garage opening startles her, and her heart bounces in her chest. She takes a quick peek in the hallway mirror to exchange her nervous smile for one of nonchalance, and dashes to the kitchen to meet her housemate.

"How are you?" she asks slightly winded as Denise strolls through the back door with briefcase in hand. "Care for tea? I just put the kettle on."

"Yes, that would be lovely. Sorry I missed you last night. I'm stuck with an eight o'clock freshman comp class. Not sure if I should feel insulted that the department dumped this on me or honored that my mastery of our language is empowering the future of every student. I'll wait for the first essays to decide."

Margaret knocks over a cup when the whistle squeals, and she hurries to right it and gather the rest of the teatime accouterments on a tray.

"Why don't we use the sitting room today," she says, and the two of them perch side by side on the damask settee to begin the afternoon ritual. "I'll be mother," she offers, adding spoonfuls of sugar and dollops of milk to the china cups before pouring the rich chestnut-brown brew. With a quick stir and a clank of spoon on saucer, they take their initial sips and return their drinks to the table.

"I was surprised to see you back from Paris so soon. I haven't heard anything about the reunion. How was it?" Denise asks.

"I never made it to France. My friend's husband died at the wedding."

356

"Oh, my goodness," Denise gasps, her jaw hinged open as Margaret details the events of the last two weeks.

"It was most definitely a whirlwind trip," Margaret finishes, "and it is very good to be home. And speaking of that. Everyone back there is on the brink of new beginnings, and I'm thinking this house could use a fresh start. My classmate Kathy mentioned she's used a Native American ritual to clear her place of bad juju. Sean picked up the supplies this morning so how about we chase away some of Satan's minions?"

"I'm in unless we have to get naked or sacrifice something," Denise laughs.

Their first step is to open a window in each of the dozens of rooms in the twenty thousand square foot space to allow the harmful forces to escape. Exhausting on many levels. After lighting the sage and sweet grass and allowing it to smolder, Margaret and Denise each take a bunch and begin waving them about the windows, floorboards, ceiling, and corners of the first room. Margaret goes low, Denise goes high.

"Bless this house and all who enter. Cleanse it of all negative energy. Fill it with positive love and light," they repeat over and over as they enter each chamber. The smoke and affirmations are clearing Margaret's mind as well, and a future for the soon to be purified palace begins to take form.

"Denise, this is a lot ... a hell of a lot of space," she says, salting her speech with the mild expletive as she stops to take a breather halfway through the main level. "If I put it on the market, I could make a small fortune. But," she pauses as the vision crystalizes, "I'd rather change it from this forbidding, repressive monstrosity into a welcoming, expansive retreat."

She breathes in deeply, vacuuming the bits and pieces of her plan, before exhaling with her whole body and dispersing her dream into the newly sanctified air.

"I want to fill it with laughter and learning. And divine feminine energy."

"Are you thinking like a bed and breakfast?" Denise asks.

"Partly. But not a place for honeymooning couples or family hikes in the woods. I'm picturing a place where women can connect. Educationally, socially, spiritually."

They light another bunch of dried grass and move up the stairs to the bedroom level. With each step up, her heart races with the effort and the promise. Maybe this is her purpose. To combine her professional skills and unlimited bankroll, and give her passions free rein while serving the community.

"Yes, this would be perfect," Denise cries out, grabbing Margaret's arm. "You and I could run workshops and discussion groups. Organize conferences, seminars, invite speakers. Create our own literary community and engage in Concord Conversations like the Transcendentalists." She picks up Margaret and twirls her around. "You are brilliant, my dear friend."

"I'm glad you like the idea," she laughs, smoothing down her blouse and patting down her hair. "We'll set our own rules and our own schedule. That way we'll still have time for travel or whatever strikes our fancy."

Still abuzz with ideas and options for the retreat, they regroup in the kitchen to reheat the gourmet takeout. But it's barely touched. Bacon dust is no match for the pixie dust sprinkled over this new adventure. Margaret takes notes as they talk, documenting their brainstorming, not wanting to miss a single creative thought.

"Wait," Denise says, clapping her hands, "I seriously think this calls for champagne. I put some in the fridge to celebrate your homecoming, so I say we pop a cork."

"Yes, yes," Margaret agrees. Is this what they call an adrenaline rush? Her heart beating a mile a minute, everything vivid and clear, her feet floating just off the floor. The last time she felt anything close to this was the last time they celebrated. Tonight, though, she's stone-cold sober. At least for the moment. So before any alcohol passes her lips, that other topic must be addressed. When Denise gives her a glass and motions to offer a toast of some sort, Margaret raises a finger to stall her.

"I need to say something first." She licks her lips and exhales a heavy sigh. "So much has changed for me since the beginning of the year. In many ways it's felt like Old Margaret died New Year's Eve, and a new soul entered my body which you, my friend, brought to life. You have guided and guarded me, given me hope. If, as Lord Byron said, 'Adversity is the first path to truth,' then you have helped me move past impossible to I'm possible." Margaret closes the space between them and slides her hands along Denise's rosy cheeks, the warmth matching the flush of her own.

"I would not wish any companion in the world but you," Denise says, her voice low and breathy. "Our Dear William always says it best, doesn't he?" She inhales slowly as she removes Margaret's hands one at a time to kiss each palm.

Margaret's heart trembles, an emotional quake crumbling the bricks of guilt and restraint mortared around it for so long. The shattering of that wall drowns out the censorious voices in her head, letting her truth resound.

"I don't know if I'm ready for any of this. Or if you are."

"We'll take this slow," Denise whispers. "There is no rush."

The lump in her throat threatens to block Margaret's words, and she swallows hard. "It's just ... I've ... I've

359

never felt this way about another human being. All I know is I love ..."

Denise silences Margaret with an index finger that lingers across her open mouth, her friend's dilated pupils now fixed on her. "No words. Just feel."

Denise's voice is at once hypnotic and arousing as she cradles Margaret's jaw in her hands, caressing the fine lines on her cheeks with her thumbs in slow sensual circles. Margaret's eyes close as soft, supple lips meet hers in tender greeting. Two blushing pilgrims Juliet called them. Tethered only by mouth upon mouth, she floats into a weightless bliss of warm pleasure as it flows through her limbs and veins, and into places long thought dead. When Denise's moist tongue craves entry, the lock on Margaret's heart releases. Just feel.

oB-la-di, oB-la-da

CHAPTER 50

The small polished river rock feels solid and comforting, warming in the heat of Susan's bare hand, rolling and sliding across her palm in a tactile meditation. She touches it to her lips before adding it to the multi-colored collection at the base of the tombstone. In the first weeks after Steve's funeral, she came every day she could, spending nearly an hour kneeling in contrition. Now, she swings by on Fridays for a chatty week in review if time permits. The dirt mounded in front of the grave is receding as is her grief.

"It's New Year's Eve, Sweetie. 2011. Can you believe it? Did we ever make it to midnight?" she laughs as she uses her glove to brush the snow from the stone marker. "Heard from The Girls yesterday. Kathy left to look for America with her boyfriend in the new RV. Says they might swing by Ft. Collins. Heard it was the top place to retire. Now Margaret's in Paris with her girlfriend. Hey," she wags her finger, "I can see you rolling over in there, Mister. They love each other and what could be more romantic than watching fireworks off the Eiffel Tower." She shrugs her shoulders and sighs. That fantasy still eludes her. "Not that you care, I suppose, but Linda's three months sober now. She and her daughters drove out for lunch last weekend. Like a real family."

She pulls up the latest picture of their great-granddaughter, his namesake, on her phone and shows it to the impassive granite face.

"Steffi's growing like a weed. And looking more like you every day. Jenny is finishing her last online class and going out tonight to celebrate. Her first time since becoming a Momma. I'm so proud of her."

She picks the pine needles from the top of the granite marker and organizes the rows of pebbles on the ledge, tidying her husband's home as she's always done. She traces the hollows of the engraved words with her finger, her name staring at her from the other side. Steve has a shaft of wheat to designate his legacy. What will they chisel for her? A rolling pin?

With a final kiss from fingers to stone, it's time to head home for the changing of the guard, and the diapers. Her work day is done, and Jenny's will begin soon. The three generations are so far thriving with grandmother and granddaughter each finding a balance in their relationship, the baby and the diner serving as fulcrums.

Ever since Steve passed, Susan's sensory connection to her mother has disappeared. Perhaps Mom's mission to guide her life is completed, and she's back in Heaven playing canasta once again with the Fearsome Foursome, a.k.a. the Beatle Girls' mothers. Never one to fully trust her own judgment, she now listens to the radio and her iPod for significant musical messages to point her in the right direction. As she turns over the engine, the song playing is "Ob-la-di, Ob-la-da. La, la, how the life goes on." That was the first song on the radio this morning as well. Such a happy song and it puts her in a good mood as she exits the cemetery.

She pulls into the garage still humming the tune. With nap time in progress at this time of day, she tiptoes into the house and hangs up her coat and purse on the nearby hooks. Jenny sits at the kitchen table, headphones

364

on as she attends to her cooking course, and holds up five fingers to signal her ending time. With opposite work schedules, breakfasts and dinners are on their own, but the women touch base at lunch, Jenny's homework guiding the menu. The printed recipes for a New Year's Eve dinner of roasted onion and carrot soup, goat cheese ravioli with winter pesto sauce, and broccoli lay next to the infant carrier on the counter. A deep chocolate gateau waits in the refrigerator beside bottles of breast milk. Gives a whole new meaning to Julia Child, Susan chuckles to herself.

"Yum. Somethin' smells lovin'," Susan murmurs as Jenny joins her at the stove for last-minute preparations.

"Is there too much garlic, Gramma? It's New Year's Eve not Halloween. I don't want to drive everyone away."

Susan dips a spoon into the orange soup and the green sauce, smacking her lips and rolling her tongue around the mixtures. A bit much for her palate but she's trying to be bolder, eating outside the casserole, thanks to her granddaughter's chosen profession. She gives a thumbs up to Jenny's nouvelle cuisine.

"It was nice of Rick to close early tonight so you guys can go party. Will you be coming back here to change?"

"Nah, I'll just take my stuff with me." She tilts her head and frowns. "I feel bad leaving you home by yourself."

Yes, the recent holiday season has been difficult, filled with too many first times without, but the next few months should be easier. She doubts Groundhog Day will be a tear-jerker.

"Sweetie, I'll be just fine. You deserve a night on the town. Steffi's ringing in the New Year with your Mom and Dad. And me, Old Bill, and Ryan Seacrest will be rockin' it from Times Square, Girl." They share exploding fist bumps.

Jenny dishes up her gourmet meal and the foodies take up forks and spoons. Just as the first bites settle on tongues, an urgent wail slices through the air. The Princess is awake. While Jenny finishes her meal so she can leave for work, Susan heads upstairs to tend to Her Majesty. Susan finds her red-faced, arms and legs flailing.

"My goodness, such a fuss," she coos as she scoops the infant to her chest. "Granmama's here. I got you."

The maternal quick-change artist's experienced hands have the three month old dry, smiling, and on her way downstairs in minutes. Waiting for her Momma to finish dressing and serve up Steffi's fast food lunch, the twosome wander about, bouncing and rocking, taking in the scene outside the patio window.

"Look, Sweetie, see out there," Susan points, orienting the indifferent infant to the view. "I'm ordering a brand-new swing set next summer with a slide and teeter-totter. And I'll cut down that old tree and plant a new one and build a sandbox underneath it. We'll have so much fun diggin' holes and makin' sand pies and growin' tomatoes and carrots in the garden."

"Ba-ba-ba." Apparently Stefanie agrees.

Susan kisses the wee head of fine light-brown hair. Thank God for you, little one.

With baby fed and off with Jenny to be dropped off with the grandparents, Susan pours a cup of coffee and plates a slice of cake before firing up her computer in the craft room. The Beatles song about Desmond and Molly is stuck in her head as she looks through her Pinterest account. She's finalizing plans to renovate the restaurant's office slash storeroom into a separate facility, and she's collecting ideas and images for her bakery shop that will fill the space. While Susan builds her business, Jenny's hoping to earn enough waitressing over the next three years to enroll in a full-fledged culinary school. Then the two will join forces and take things to the next level.

Which is not happening with her and Rick. It's been business, and only business as usual with him. They are friendly, but the sizzle ignited back in July has fizzled and neither has made any overtures to relight the flame. Susan is thrilled Kathy and Margaret have found love, and with it coming so late in their lives, it gives her hope for herself. But will her guilt and the fear of town gossip doom her to years in black as one of Miss Rigby's lonely people? Or is she ready to be shaken, not stirred, with some dirty twists?

⌘⌘⌘⌘⌘

It's nine thirty on New Year's Eve 2010. The muted TV glows as momentum builds for the ball drop in New York City. Susan's snuggled in her jammies, all alone except for the dog, and deep into a cozy mystery, sleuthing with the heroine as she searches for clues and culprits. She's living vicariously via the humble yet observant baker who rises to the occasion to solve murders via floury fingerprints. She's nearing the end of a chapter with the amateur detective ready to confront the lead suspect when the doorbell rings. She jumps and the book falls in her lap. She slides on her slippers and wraps a robe around herself. Searching for something to beat off an intruder, she grabs her only weapon. Steffie's rattle. With stealthy footsteps she inches to the door and peeks through the peephole. It's Rick.

She's not exactly dressed for company, especially his. The lights are on so he knows she's there. She opens the door the length of the brass chain.

"Hey. What's up?" she asks, peering through the narrow space.

"I brought New Year's," he says, flashing a green bottle with a gold paper top. "Can I come in? I promise. I bring only good cheer."

Putting her vanity aside, she slides back the lock and welcomes him in.

"Can't be too safe. A defenseless widow lady like me," she swoons in a Southern drawl, and shakes the plastic toy. "Why don't y'all open the bubbly and I'll slip into somethin'... less frumpy."

"Yes, ma'am, but you look fine to me," Rick winks.

Susan makes her way upstairs as quickly as she can, seriously considering never coming back down. She splashes water on her blushing face, applies a coat of mascara and lip gloss, and fluffs up her hair as best she can. Luckily the teeth are freshly brushed, so no bits of green from pesto or broccoli peek out from crevices. Looking in her closet for something festive, and unwrinkled, she settles on her teal jersey top and a pair of jeans. As good as it's going to get, she slips back downstairs to find two juice glasses filled with Moët & Chandon and that damn speckled, irresistible moustache.

"Didn't see any flutes on your counter so figured I'd go with these. First time at your house it didn't feel right to poke around."

"I don't think I have the right stemware anyway. So, no parties for you tonight?"

"Nah, if I wasn't here, I'd be in my PJ's too. I haven't seen the other side of midnight in years. Just felt like toastin' with someone. 2010's been a bit crazy, right? But there were some good moments, Suzie-Q. Maybe there'll be more next year."

"We can hope."

They stand on opposite sides of the kitchen island, the narrow but uncomfortable expanse of Formica between them, counting the bubbles in the champagne to avoid eye contact.

"Suzie-Q."

Rick clears his throat and Susan looks up at the sound. Either he has a cold or he's about to say something. Maybe the something she's been hoping to avoid yet longing to hear. Of course it's too soon. Only three months. It's downright wicked to even think what she's thinking.

"Suzie-Q," Rick says again. "I've been bidin' my time. Givin' you space to work through your grief and all. Now I'm not expectin' anything from this, but remember what I said last summer? I told you I thought you might be the love of my life. And I still mean it. Just don't know if you're ready."

Ready? She knows when a cake springs back, it's ready. When cookies are lightly brown, they're ready. But a heart? Is hers too raw still? Should she let it simmer a bit longer at the risk of drying it out, ending up in the garbage bin of regrets? And if she waits, will she miss another chance? Maybe her last one. Three strikes and you're out. If only she had a sign. Like her fluttering heart, for instance.

"Hey, mind if we sit on the couch? I'm feeling a little woozy. Don't worry, it'll pass."

Unless Steve and God are watching from above, ready to smote her for her unseemly thoughts. Rick grabs the drinks, holding them from the bottom with the experienced hand of a food server, while steadying Susan's arm with the other.

"Didn't mean to set your heart a quiverin'. Except in a good way."

"No, I'm fine," she says as they relax into the sofa. "It's just ... I worry what everyone will say if I, we, change the nature of our relationship. 'He's not even cold in the grave and she's carrying on with another man.' I did love Steve very much. He'll always be in my heart."

369

"Of course he will. I'd be concerned if you felt otherwise. But, Suzie-Q, life goes on."

Three times today she's been told that the world still turns, that her future awaits. She catches a scent and her breathing stops. She sniffs again. No, it's not the Brut floating up from Rick's chest, and driving her crazy. It's the other smell. The mystical fragrance that grounds her, encourages her, gives her strength. The one that started her on this journey, and guided her all year. Her mother's Evening in Paris. Mom's back. And now Susan knows what to do.

The crystal ball high atop Times Square is on its way down. "Ten - nine - eight...three - two - one," the crowd yells as the screen erupts in fireworks, confetti, and unabashed kissing.

"You OK?" Rick asks, looking into her eyes. "Gonna faint?"

"No, Rick," she says, looking back, a warm shiver rising from her stomach, up through her heart, and onto her face. Her eyes are unsure whether to crinkle or tear up as she extends her glass toward Rick's. Her lips spread into a toothy grin as the containers of champagne clink. "I feel fine. As fine as I can be. This is going to be a Happy New Year."

ACKNOWLEDGMENTS

The tried and true advice for aspiring authors is to write what you know. So, I gathered bits of my background and pieces of my personality, and developed characters with lives of their own. When what I didn't know far outweighed what I did, I researched online, read other writers, and relied on a network of family, friends, and literary associates to create this story. You need to know how grateful I am to each and every one of you.

MY PARENTS: Despite hard times, they gave me incredible opportunities, and my first Beatles album.

THE ORIGINAL BEATLE GIRLS (Mary Frances Smith, Susan Clemons, Karen Sanders): Our Fab Four on the Farm shared secrets, dares, and teenage dreams while we danced to our own drummer (Ringo, of course).

MY SISTERS (Dody White, Barb Cooper, Petey Martin) and **CLASSMATES** (Strasburg High Class of '67): Your reflections on past and present life in rural Colorado renewed my sense of place.

THE NORTHERN COLORADO AND PARKER WRITERS GROUPS: Without the classes, conferences, and contacts, I'd still be on page one.

MY CORE CRITIQUE GROUP (Hilary Castine, Patrick Daniels, Christine DeHerrera, Link Miller): You guys made me cry (at first), think, laugh, and finally grow into a real writer.

MY CONSULTANTS AND PROFESSIONALS: Dr. Cindy Haviland, your medical knowledge lent credibility to my characters' health concerns. Vici Ward and Lisa Guilfoyle, your LGBTQ perspective was both enlightening and empowering. Kerri Flanagan (content editing), you killed my darlings with kindness while saving the dog. Marilyn Moody (copy editing), you made sure the pages were ready for prime time. Lisa Neuberger (cover art/design layout), you turned my "velveteen" manuscript into a real book.

MY BETA AND ADVANCED COPY READERS (Hilary Castine, Marcia Curran, Debbie Ryan, Patti Stickler, and Jon): I entrusted you with the Girls; thanks for pointing out the sure fire bits as well as the fatal flaws.

MY CHEERLEADERS (Patti and her daughters, my sisters and their families, my in-laws, and a circle of dear friends): Apparently you knew I could do this even though I had my doubts.

THE WOMEN OF WISDOM, WEALTH, AND WONDER FROM CENTER FOR SPIRITUAL LIVING/PARKER: You listened to and encouraged me on my journey as Spirit inspired, guided, and channeled through me from the beginning to The End.

AND OF COURSE, MY HUSBAND AND IT SUPPORT (Jon): Thanks for giving me my space, and rebooting, reformatting, and reeling me in from the ledge when I thought I'd lost everything. You always said I should write a book.

Author Bio

There is creativity in us all if we allow it to blossom. Diana Curran grew up on a farm quietly playing make-believe under Colorado skies. In 1963, she discovered the Beatles. Over the next six years, she immersed herself in all things Beatle-y. She and her friend even talked of starting their own band. Or maybe she'd become a dancer. However, two left feet and common sense suggested a different path.

She graduated with degrees from CSU and CU and began a career as a nurse. For thirty years, she cared for other people's children in a daycare, a hospital, and an elementary school, even being honored as the 2001 Colorado School Nurse of the Year. But it was when she taught and developed curriculum for health related classes, thinking outside the box, that an unexpected sense of bliss enveloped her. And when she retired in 2005, the door to imagination opened wide.

Her late night muse channeled poetry, and some of her poems appeared in the 2011 Northern Colorado Writers Anthology, *Pooled Ink*. Then in 2013, she was inspired to try her hand at fiction. At 68 years old, she published this book, her debut novel. Imagine that. Yes, it's never too late to create.

When not traveling, her life goes on with her husband of nearly fifty years on her land near Denver. Visit her website at www.DianaCurranAuthor.com.

Book cluB discussion questions

1. Did you have a group of friends, like the Beatle Girls, in high school or college with whom you shared a close relationship? If so, what has kept you in touch or made you drift apart?

2. The Beatle Girls had regrets about the directions their lives took - mostly about losing connection with their authentic selves or with loved ones. What regrets do you have and how have you dealt with them? Are you fearing life may end or never begin?

3. Linda and Margaret were very concerned with their images and having the perfect life. They both covered up issues that detracted from this perfection - Linda's high school pregnancy and breast cancer, and Margaret's abusive marriage and feelings for Denise. How do parental influences, personality traits, and society's morals impact decisions about life choices? How have they affected your choices?

4. Susan and Kathy spent much of their lives caring for others, putting their own desires on hold. They grew up during the beginnings of women's liberation, caught between the limited roles for women in the Fifties and early Sixties, and the potential that blossomed in the decades that followed. How has your life been affected by these changes?

5. The Beatle Girls each had their favorite of the Fab Four, chosen perhaps because of shared traits. Ringo, happy-go-lucky. Paul, cute and charming. George, quiet and sensitive. John, intellectual rebel. Which Beatle best matches your personality? Who was your favorite?

6. The Girls each picked a Beatles song that best de-scribed their lives - at present or in general. What is your song and why?

7. Divorces and deaths led to major life changes for the women. These endings resulted in uncertainty, guilt, shock, relief, and regret. Their new beginnings filled them with some of the same feelings in addition to hope, freedom, renewal, changed relationships, and insights. How have significant life events changed you for worse and for better? Have you savored the sweetness and spit out the seeds?

8. In talking with Boomer women about marriage/rela-tionships, their opinions range from "Men, who needs 'em" to "All I want is to grow old with my partner." The majority seem to be longing for some-thing more, better, different. The Beatle Girls' ro-mantic alliances also ran the gamut - Susan wanted excitement, Linda relished her renewed sexuality, Kathy longed for true love, and Margaret's idea of love was upended. How do you feel about love and marriage as a older woman?

9. The Beatle Girls had to make some hard choices re-garding health (breast cancer treatment, end of life decisions), relationships (letting go of past ones, em-bracing the possibility of new), career moves (start-ing, changing, or ending work situations), and for-giveness (of others and themselves). How have you dealt (or would you deal) with these situations?